MW01126071

from

SMOKE

to

FLAMES

USA Today Bestselling Author

A.M. HARGROVE

This book is dedicated to all recovering addicts and anyone who has ever experienced any sort of domestic abuse. xoxo

"I am not what happened to me, I am what I choose to become." - C.G. Jung

From Smoke To Flames
A West Brothers Novel

Copyright © 2019 A.M. Hargrove

This is a work of fiction. Names, characters, places and incidents are products of the author's imagination or are used factiously and are not to be construed as real. Any resemblance to actual events, locales, organizations, or persons living or dead, is entirely coincidental.

All rights reserved. No part of this book may be used or reproduced in form or any manner whatsoever by any electronic or mechanical means, including information storage and retrieval systems, without written permission, except in the case of brief quotations embodied in critical articles or a book review. Scanning, uploading and distribution of the book via the Internet or via any other means without permission is illegal and punishable by law. Please purchase only authorized electronic editions and do not participate in or encourage piracy of copyrighted materials. Your support for the author's rights is appreciated. For permission requests, write to the author, addressed "Attention: Permissions Coordinator," at annie@amhargrove.com

Cover design by Letitia Hasser @ *RBA Designs | Romantic Book Affairs*

Cover Photo: Wander Aguiar

Cover Model: Kaz Vander Waard

Editing Services by: My Brother's Editor

Prologue

PEARSON

EVERYONE REMEMBERS THE EPIC MOMENT WHERE THEY MEET *that special one* ... that single defining point in their lives. Mine wasn't quite so grand nor did it have a happily ever after. It happened when I least expected it. It didn't take me by surprise, sweep me off my feet, or fill me with hearts and flowers. I wish it had been that easy. My first love happened to be opiates—Oxy, Lortabs—the doctor prescribed for pain. It seemed I fell in love with them—I mean head over heels in love—a little too much.

Weirdly enough, I'd never been a huge partier in college. There wasn't time because I was studying too hard to keep my grades up trying to get into one of the best law schools in the country. I'd never even so much as smoked weed. But the first time I swallowed one of those beauties, there was no turning back. It was love at first high. Only my first love took me to a place filled with darkness and nightmares, a place where I ended up begging to escape from time and again. My love turned out to be a demon who changed me into a man filled with self-loathing. I was once proud of who I'd become ... until I transformed into someone filled with shame, someone I wanted to conceal from everyone. I became an addict, something I never imagined I'd be. I was that person you read about, the one on the streets scoring drugs.

Don't be fooled. By day, I wore expensive suits and ties, and showed up at work. But it was all smoke and mirrors. My high-powered career dangled by a thread.

Each night I came home and told myself that was it—no more drugs. But it was a lie. Withdrawal was a thousand porcupines firing their piercing quills into every inch of my skin, and soon the pain and nausea would be more than I could tolerate. The anxiety associated with it cocooned me in a blanket made of glass shards. By midnight, immense chills and body aches would have me pounding the streets in search of a fix. I'd try anything to make me feel normal again. The word *rehab* echoed through my brain time and again, but I didn't want to carry that brand. I was stronger and better than that. Or so I thought.

Spiraling into my own hell, my work suffered, and it was only a matter of time before my reputation did too. I avoided family and friends. Shame, humiliation, embarrassment, didn't come close to what I felt when I thought about asking for help. Family would come running if only I called, but it would show them how weak I'd become, and that could never happen. Many times I thought about ending it all, but the truth was I didn't have the guts to do it when it came down to it.

In the past, both of my brothers had teased me about being a man whore. They were right. I loved women and couldn't help it. But most days ... I was pretty fucking useless below the waist. If they only knew.

Tonight I sat at a bar and drowned my sorrows. I was high and drunk and couldn't even tell you what day it was. Some chick was sitting next to me, rubbing my leg, trying to suggest going home with me. As if. Some mornings I'd woken up with women who'd almost made me sick. Filthy, covered with weeks' worth of grime, I couldn't imagine being with them. How far had I'd sunk over the past year?

The woman next to me kept leaning over, trying to kiss my neck. "Listen, you ought to move on," I told her. Or tried to anyway. Pretty sure my words were slurred. "Not in the mood." I pulled out my wallet and slapped some cash on the bar. Then I stood to leave. It took a few tries before I stumbled to the door.

The woman was on my heels. Her strong perfume permeated the air. Guess she thought she was gonna get lucky. Too bad for her. I walked out the door and headed down the street. I wasn't sure if she was behind me, nor did I care. About a half a block later, I stumbled, and fell, bruising my knees. Even through the haze of inebriation, pain ripped through me.

"You look like you could use a friend." It was the woman from the bar.

"The only friend I need is…"

"Yeah, I know. I can help." She looped her arm through mine, helped me to my feet, and we walked. We turned a corner and she led me into a side alley. She pulled out something from her purse. "I've got exactly what you need."

My eyes eagerly devoured her as she pulled out a packet of white powder and used a small straw to snort a little. Then she passed the packet to me. I put some on the back of my credit card and snorted it. In moments I was floating on a cushion of air.

She leaned into me and breathed, "You needed that, didn't you?"

"Yeah."

"I have something else you need, too."

She put her hand on my dick and rubbed it. Then she began kissing me. She tasted like bubble gum when I kissed her back. Then things got super weird. My vision blurred but not only that, I saw multiple images of her face. As drunk as I was, I knew this wasn't normal.

I pulled away from her. "What was that shit laced with?"

She smiled but said nothing. I couldn't focus and my tongue felt twice its size. My knees buckled and the lights went out.

Chapter One

PEARSON

BEEP. BEEP. BEEP. BEEP. THE STEADY BACKGROUND NOISE had been faint but was getting louder. Then it was hiss, hiss, thump, thump. Hiss, hiss, thump, thump. Beep, hiss, hiss, thump, thump. I blinked, but couldn't see. As I became more aware, I went to move my arms, only to discover it was impossible. I should be frightened but found myself drifting off.

The next time I awoke, it was to voices and a spasm of coughing.

"He's coming around."

"Sir, take a deep breath for me."

I inhaled to another round of coughing. My throat burned like fire. What the hell was going on? My hand automatically reached for my neck, only it was attached to something.

"He's trying to move his arm," someone said.

"My throat," I wheezed.

"Yes, it'll be sore. It's irritated from being intubated. That will go away in a couple of days," someone answered.

5

"Intubated?" I croaked.

"Yes, sir. Just relax."

Relax? Where was I?

"Your sedation is wearing off and then you might be able to tell us what happened."

"What happened?"

"Uh huh." She fiddled around with something else and I heard footsteps. Then silence.

I scanned the room. All kinds of equipment surrounded me — things that my brother might be familiar with because he was a doctor, but I wasn't. The beeping noise persisted. I glanced up to see it was a machine that monitored my heart. The other noises had stopped.

I'm not sure how much time passed when two doctors, accompanied by a nurse, walked in.

"Hi, I'm Dr. Michael O'Shea and this is Dr. Gabriella Martinelli. I'm the hospitalist who has been in charge of your care since you were admitted and Dr. Martinelli is the psychiatrist we called in to handle your situation for your addiction issues. Oh, and this is Sammie. She's the nurse on duty right now and needs to give you your diazepam and methadone." He said the last part as an afterthought. I thought that was weird because to me it was the most important.

I swallowed the rock in my scratchy throat. "Diazepam and methadone?"

"Yes, to control your withdrawal symptoms. Dr. Martinelli can explain all that in a minute. But first, can you tell us your name?"

"My name?" This was all so confusing.

"You were brought in on a 911, unresponsive due to a heroin overdose. You were also pretty banged up. We've had you in an induced coma, because, quite frankly, we didn't know if you were going to make it or not."

"Coma? You thought I was going to die?"

"That's right, Mr.?"

"Um." I blinked because for a moment I couldn't remember my name.

"It's okay," Dr. O'Shea said. "Head injuries can cause temporary memory loss."

"Head injuries?"

"Yes, you had a severe concussion on top of everything else."

My hands tried to reach for my head, but they were tied down. My name suddenly popped into my head, so I blurted, "West. Pearson West is my name."

"Very good, Mr. West."

"What about my wallet?" I asked.

"You had nothing on you. No wallet, no phone."

"What day is it?"

"Friday."

"How long have I been here?"

"Since Saturday night ... well Sunday morning around three a.m.," Dr. O'Shea answered. "Sorry about the restraints. Withdrawal can make patients do all sorts of things, including, extubate themselves."

"Extubate?"

A gentle hand touched my shoulder. "He means pull the ventilator tube out of your throat. Mr. West, do you remember anything that happened on Saturday night?" Dr. Martinelli asked.

"I was drinking. In a bar. There was this woman. She followed me out. And then nothing. It's a huge blank." What hole have I fallen into and how deep is it?

"Okay, that's not uncommon. How long have you been using?" she asked.

I swallowed, grimacing. "Um, a year and a half, maybe two."

"Has it been heroin the whole time?"

"No! It, shit." All I wanted to do was rub my fucking face and I couldn't because my hands were glued to the goddam bed.

Dr. O'Shea said, "You're a lucky man, Mr. West. Most

7

people don't make that 911 call for someone in the street like you were."

"Mike." Dr. Martinelli gave him a look that shut him up.

"Mr. West, Dr. O'Shea is right. You are a lucky man. Can I ask how you started using?"

I laughed, ruefully. "A torn rotator cuff. I had surgery to repair it. They gave me pain meds. Before I knew it, I couldn't get off them."

"Any other history of drug abuse before that?" she asked.

"No. I drank a little, but nothing excessive."

"Well, it won't come as a surprise to you that I'm going to recommend thirty days of inpatient rehab and then I think you should go do a minimum of another month somewhere. I don't have to tell you what a monster heroin is to kick. Then you will live with NA for the rest of your life."

"Yeah."

Her voice took on a whole new level when she said, "There is no yeah about it. If you don't, you will die, Mr. West. Am I clear?"

"Very."

"Is there anyone you'd like to call? Family?" she asked.

"My law firm. And my family."

"I don't believe you need an attorney."

"I *am* an attorney, but I'm pretty damn sure I'll need a new job after this. And I need to call my brothers. Can you please release my arms?"

"I think we can arrange that." She undid the Velcro that had my wrists restrained and the first thing I did was rub the hell out of my face.

Then she spoke to Sammie, the nurse, who I'd forgotten about. "If he experiences any hallucinations, these go back on."

"Yes, Doctor."

"I'm going to hallucinate?"

"Mr. West. You are withdrawing from a potent opiate. We are giving you methadone to control that. On top of it, you are also withdrawing from alcohol. This is a critical time for you. We will manage these symptoms as best we can for the next few days and then transfer you to rehab, where you will see me every day. Unless, of course, you want to live your remaining years as an addict, which I don't recommend."

"Oh, God." What have I done to myself?

"Mr. West," the psychiatrist said in a softer tone. "This isn't the end of the world. You're going to feel like it is for the next few weeks, but the fact that you're here, alive, and going to receive help, are the steps in the direction you need to take. I promise there is hope. Trust me."

Our eyes connected and I saw something there that made me believe her.

"Okay. I tried not to use, I really did."

"I believe you. Most, not all, but most addicts don't want to be where they are. But you must stick with this program I'm going to recommend, or you'll end up back where you were. And I can promise you the end result isn't good."

"I understand."

"Good."

"Is it possible to take a shower?"

She glanced at Dr. O'Shea. "While I admire your tenacity, you've been in a coma for a few days. I think it best if we wait another day. So tomorrow, and then you'll need assistance because you have IVs and a catheter."

It's pretty fucking bad when you don't even know you have a catheter jammed up your dick. Thirty-five years old and I felt like I was ninety.

Dr. Martinelli handed me the phone. "We'll give you some privacy for the calls." She offered me a kind smile and a pat on the shoulder. I was going to need a lot more than that with the news I was about to share.

When my brother, Hudson, answered, I could barely speak. My childhood flashed before me and I broke down and cried.

"Just tell me you're okay. I don't give a damn about anything else. Just tell me you're okay."

I swallowed around the rawness in my throat and said, "I'll make it."

"Where are you?"

I scanned the room to see which hospital I was in, because dumbass me forgot to ask, and then told him. "Do me a favor. Can you come alone or with Grey? I want to tell you first before Mom and Dad."

"I'm on the way."

Next, I called one of my law partners and sprung the great news on him. I thought it would be less emotional, but it wasn't. When I got to the part where I said, "I'm a drug addict," a huge weight was lifted from me.

"I almost died. Someone found me and called 911."

He told me how they filed a missing person's report.

"The hospital didn't know who I was as I had no ID on me."

Then he informed me my job would be waiting for me when I completed rehab. The firm had no choice because of FMLA. But I'm sure I'd face hell when I got back. I'd be practicing sober again and when I was sober, I was the best, so at least there was that.

Sammie knocked and when she came in, she changed out one of my IV bags. Before she was finished, Hudson busted through the door.

"Jesus, what the hell happened?" he asked. Sammie scurried out of the little cubicle.

"Sit."

He glanced around at all the equipment in the room. I was still in the ICU. Dr. O'Shea had said they would transfer me out today.

"I overdosed."

He didn't say anything at first, but the pain in his ice blue eyes was difficult to hide. And then there were the silent tears, as they slowly slid down his cheeks. Hudson had always been my hero, and here I was, a huge disappointment to him.

He grabbed my hand and said, "I need the whole story, Pearson."

And I gave it to him, beginning with the shoulder surgery and ending with this moment.

"Why didn't you say something?" Soft, compassionate eyes stared at me, but guilt nearly choked me.

"I thought I would kick it. I honestly did. I thought I was strong enough. But I lied to you, Mom, Dad, Grey. I was neck deep and covered it up."

"But, Pearson, heroin?" The way he said that ugly word made me cringe, as though I hadn't done enough of that already.

I sighed. "When I couldn't get prescriptions for Lortab, or other pain meds, I went to street drugs. And heroin is so easy to get."

"But …"

"Just say it. I want everything out in the open between us."

"I never thought –"

I let out a remorseful laugh. "You and me both. The first time was supposed to be the only time. But it's obvious how that went."

He slid his chair even closer to the bed and grabbed my entire arm. "You have to beat this. I mean it, Pearson. You could've died."

Shame like I'd never felt before washed over me. "I know. I will. I swear I will." My stomach tightened into a tight ball as I watched his eyes constrict with grief. Doubt lurked in their depths and how could I blame him for that? I had a lot to prove to him and the others.

"What are we going to tell the rest of the family?"

"There is no *we* in this. Only me. It's my burden, Hudson, and I'm going to tell them the truth. My name is Pearson West and I am a drug addict and an alcoholic."

Chapter Two

SAMMIE CAME BACK IN AFTER HUDSON AND I WERE TALKING for about an hour. "I don't mean to interrupt, but we're getting ready for a shift change and I thought I'd check to see if you needed anything before I left."

"Thank you, but I'm fine." She waved as she left. My hands trembled as I slid to the edge of the bed. I turned to Hudson and said, "I have a favor to ask. Will you call Mom and Dad and ask them to come over? I would, but I won't be able to get the words out without breaking down."

"Sure. You want me to do it now?"

"Yeah. The sooner, the better."

Dr. Martinelli walked in right then. "How's it going?"

"As good as it can be, considering. This is my brother, Hudson." I made the introductions.

"Let me explain a few more things. As I told you earlier, we have you on diazepam and methadone. Over the next two days, we're going to taper the diazepam down. The methadone will stay until you go to rehab. That's where you'll slowly get off of that. The good news is you'll have intense supervision there. The bad news is that's where you'll experience the heroin withdrawal. I'm not into sugarcoating. You've already been through a little of that. When you knew you needed another dose? Times that by ten thousand or more. You understand?"

I was already trembling. The methadone was working, but not at a hundred percent. I didn't want to think about what I faced ahead. "Yeah, I do. But I don't have a choice."

"I'm glad you see it that way."

My brother said, "You'll have your family supporting you, Pearson."

"I hope so."

"You doubt it?"

"Right now, I'm not sure about anything."

Dr. Martinelli said, "That's common and you and I are going to have some intensive talks about how to deal with things. You won't be going through this alone. The main thing is not to hold anything back."

"Pearson, Mom and Dad would do anything in the world for you. Never doubt that. Did you call the firm?"

"Yeah. I have twelve weeks leave."

"Mr. West, let's take this one step at a time."

"I'm already shaking. I can't imagine what I'll be doing a week from now."

"You'll be sick. But they won't cold turkey the methadone. They taper it so nothing is extreme. The worst part is the psychological withdrawal. And that's where I come in. I'm available whenever you need me."

A cold sense of apprehension whipped through me. I knew what she was talking about. I had experienced the psychological dependency. It lingered in my mind every day, was anchored in my soul. It was why I hadn't already given up the drug ... why I hadn't voluntarily gone to rehab. Heroin acted like your best friend at first. *Come to me, taste me. I'll take away all your problems.*

You'll have no worries or pain anymore. Just a little bit, you'll see. And you didn't. It was disguised as a white angel. But it wasn't. It was the darkest demon. At first, it was a light puffy cloud you floated on, comforting you, cushioning any blow or pain you may feel. Until you came down and each high lasted a shorter period of time, making you need more and more of the shit. If you didn't get it, you'd sweat, vomit, shake, act crazy as fuck, until you did. And so the cycle went and that was the life of an addict. I wanted that peace. I wanted that cloud. I wanted that comfort. Even if it was only for a few minutes. Because once you attained it, there was nothing to compare it to.

"Mr. West? Are you with us?"

"Sorry. Yeah."

"Pearson, you okay?" Hudson asked.

"Not exactly."

"What is it?" Dr. Martinelli asked.

"Everything."

"You'd better talk now," Hudson said.

"Just anxious over what I'm about to face."

"You won't be alone," he reminded me.

And then I let it fly. "Hudson, you don't get it. You can't possibly understand. You've never done any drug in your life."

He stared at me like the crazy fuck that I was.

Dr. Martinelli said, "He's right. He needs your support, but an addict is in a difficult position. Drugs are very compelling. But Mr. West, your family must love you very much."

"I don't feel very well. I'm sorry, Hudson. But you don't understand what heroin is like."

"No, clearly I don't."

"Can you please call Mom and Dad, and Grey too? I need to get this off my chest."

"Sure."

He left the room.

I looked at Dr. Martinelli. "What are my odds?"

"I don't believe in odds."

"Come on, doc. You've been doing this for how long?"

"Four years."

"Then you must have some kind of knowledge of how many people actually beat it."

"As I said, I don't believe in that. But I have a couple of people I think you should talk to. They might help you out."

"Former addicts?" I asked.

"There is no such thing. We call them recovering addicts."

"Semantics."

"I can give you their names and numbers if you're interested. One of them sustained an injury and ended up on pain meds, which took him down a path similar to yours."

"I'll think about it."

"When you're ready. He's also an NA counselor."

Hudson walked in and announced everyone was on their way.

Dr. Martinelli left and said she'd be back later that afternoon.

Mom and Dad arrived with Grey about an hour and a half later. Grey canceled out the rest of the day and drove them in. Mom immediately ran to me and hugged me.

"What happened?" she asked.

"I need to tell you all something that's not going to be easy to hear. But, I might as well get to the point. I'm a drug addict and an alcoholic."

They all stared at me and didn't say a word.

Mom was the first one to speak. "Pearson, you can't be a drug addict."

"Yes, Mom, I am. I'm addicted to opiates, but the worst part of it is I'm a heroin addict."

She refused to believe it.

"It's true, Mom. Right now they're giving me methadone. Someone found me and called 911. I nearly died."

Her hands covered her face. Disgrace, dishonor, there were too many words to describe the awful emotions that filled me as I watched my family stare at me in horror. I went on to tell the whole story, as I did with Hudson.

Grey asked, "Why didn't you come to me? I could've helped."

Of course he could have. He's a physician and would have connected me with someone.

"I really thought I could control it or beat it. I never thought I'd end up like this."

"Oh, Pearson," Mom cried.

"I know, Mom. I'm going to rehab for God knows how long. I'll do an intensive thirty days and then after that, I'll go somewhere else. The psychiatrist has recommended another thirty days."

"Of course you must go," Mom said.

Dad said nothing. I'm sure his son had destroyed his heart. A bigger disappointment he'd never faced. "Dad, I realize I've disappointed you."

"Disappointed me? Pearson, my God, son, I'm just thankful we're having this conversation and not ..." when his voice cracked, that was when I lost it.

I sobbed out the words, "I'm so sorry. I'm sorry for lying to you. I'm sorry for making you worry. But I swear I'm going to kick this."

Ten days later I would be wondering whether or not I could keep that promise.

Chapter Three

ROSE

"No, I can't pick her up at four. I'm working until five and can't possibly get there until six, as our arrangement states."

"Then I'll just have to take her with us, and you'll miss out on your visitation this time."

"You can't do that," I yelled.

"Then what do you propose? We are leaving at four." I imagined his smug grin.

"Why didn't you give me any notice?" I ground my molars. He did this every time it was my turn for visitation. He was such an asshole. He loved to undermine everything.

"This opportunity just came up."

"I'm sure it did. Can we switch weekends?"

"No, sorry."

"Let me call you back." I hung up the phone, cursing him, his fucking attorney who somehow got him custody of our daughter, and everyone else he knew.

I called my mom, maybe she could pick her up, although she

had as much interest in her grandchild as she did moldy bread. "Mom, can you pick up Montana for me at four? Greg is being his usual mean-spirited self and won't wait for me to get there until six."

"Sorry, honey, but I'm leaving at noon for an out of town weekend with the girls."

"Okay. Thanks."

Shit, fuck, damn. What was I going to do? I had to see Montana. I only got her every other weekend as it was.

My office door swung open and it was one of my co-workers and friends, Sylvie West. "Oooh, that's angry face if I've ever seen one."

"Fucking Greg again."

"Now what?"

"He's leaving today at four and wants me to pick up Montana then. I don't finish until five and can't get there until six. Asshole. He knows this. He waits until the last minute on purpose to keep me from her."

"The great manipulator. Why don't you go back to court?"

"I can't afford it with child support and all."

"Wait, you're paying him child support?"

"Yeah, because he's the custodial parent and even though his earnings far surpass mine, he demanded I pay. Honestly, I don't mind paying, as long as I know the money goes to Montana. But it pisses me off when he pulls this crap, which is all the time."

"Can't you get someone to pick her up?"

"My mom is going out of town, so she can't. And there is no one else."

Sylvie sighed. "There must be someone." She clicked her fingers. "I know. My neighbor. She probably can do it. And drive her here."

"How do you know?"

"Because she's a mom and is an empty nester. She's always telling me how much she misses her kids and wishes they'd have kids except none of them are married or have a significant other yet."

"Are you sure?" Skepticism ruled right now.

"We won't know if we don't call."

Sylvie made the call and her friend, Rita, was thrilled to do it. My hopes soared, but then I realized she'd need a booster seat. Montana was four and couldn't ride without one.

"Greg won't let her borrow one?"

"Are you serious? He does everything he can to make it impossible for me."

Sylvie went to make a call.

"What are you doing?"

"I'm calling Rita back. She can find a car seat."

"They're expensive."

Sylvie waved her hand. "She has plenty of friends who have grandkids. One of them is bound to have one."

Sure enough, Sylvie was right. Rita took care of it and saved the day by picking up Montana for me. Greg wasn't too happy about it, but too bad. I doubted he had plans anyway. He was just trying to prevent me from seeing my daughter.

Right before I left, I grabbed the charts for the cases that would be coming in over the weekend so I could familiarize myself with the new patients. I crammed them into my bag, along with my laptop, and hurried out of there. I was beyond excited to see my daughter. I'd planned to meet Rita in between here and home to save her from driving the extra twenty minutes, so I had to get a move on.

Traffic wasn't too bad, it could've been worse. I didn't care. Just the thought of hugging Montana brought a smile to my face.

I pulled into the Quickie Shop and there was the car Rita had described.

A middle-aged woman hopped out with a warm smile as she greeted me.

"Rose?"

"Rita?"

"Yes," she said.

"I honestly don't know how to thank you." I reached out to hug her. "You're a lifesaver."

"Little Montana's father wasn't very happy to relinquish her to me, so thank God you thought to email that letter."

"I figured as much. He's not a very nice person." That was putting it mildly.

"No, he's not. Anyway, someone is waiting for you."

I opened the back door and there she sat, her black ringlets bouncing as she clapped her hands.

"Mommy." She stretched her arms out and I almost burst into tears.

"My little Pop Tart! How is my girl?" I unbuckled the safety harness and pulled her out of the seat. Then I hugged the living daylights out of her. "Ohhhh, how I missed you, my sweet girl!" I spun around in a circle until a stream of giggles poured out of her.

"I missed you toooo."

"Good and we have tons to catch up on, don't we?"

"Yeah. What's a ton?"

"A whole lot. But first, we need to thank Miss Rita."

"Thank you, Miss Rita."

"Why, you're very welcome. Anytime you need a ride, you just call me."

I pressed a twenty dollar bill into her palm. "Thank you."

Her brow furrowed. "I can't possibly take this."

"I want to … for your trouble."

"It was no trouble."

"Mommy calls me little trouble sometimes."

Rita tickled Montana's cheek. "I bet she does." Then she handed me the money back. "Someday, I may need a favor in return."

"What's a favor, Mommy?"

"It's when someone does something nice for you, like how Rita picked you up today."

We watched Rita drive off and then I put Montana into her own car seat, and we headed home.

"I have a surprise for you," I said as we walked inside.

"You do?"

"Yep." When we got in the house, I said, "Close your eyes." I had made some chocolate chip cookies for her. She loved them and I knew she never got them at her dad's. "Hold out your hand." I put a cookie in it and when she opened her eyes, I was awarded with the biggest grin ever.

"Cookies!"

"Yep. Your favorite. Want a glass of milk?"

Her smile disappeared. "Will I spoil my dinner?"

"Maybe. But it's Friday, so we can let it go this one time."

"Daddy might not like it. I'll just save it for dessert, if that's okay." She set it on the table and went into the small den.

She took a seat on the couch like a prim little princess. This made me worry about what went on over there. Did he ever let her play?

I sat next to her and pulled her onto my lap. "Do you play a lot at your dad's?"

"Sometimes."

"What else do you do?"

"Um, sit in my room." She stared at the floor as she spoke.

"What do you do in your room?"

"Nothing."

"Do you draw pictures?"

"Sometimes."

This was disturbing. She was usually talkative, but she was being oddly quiet today.

"Do you color?" I asked.

She lifted a shoulder. "Can I watch a movie?"

Evasion tactics. I was a psychologist but didn't know how to counsel my own kid. I hugged her to my chest and said, "Sure thing, jelly bean. What do you wanna watch?" I tried to be as jovial as possible, but my heart was breaking.

I was going to have to come up with something to figure out what was happening to her. If it was nothing, then fine. But I needed to have more time with my daughter. Two weekends a month was not enough. I needed at least fifty percent.

We ate dinner, which was a pizza, followed by cookies, and when she started to fall asleep, I put her to bed.

I sipped a glass of wine as I went through the new cases I'd be seeing on Monday. There would be three. The first two were alcohol related. They would be in for thirty days. When I got to the last, I almost cracked the wineglass I was holding. The name Pearson West in bold letters showed up on the file.

"I can't believe this."

Reading through the file, my anger mounted until I lost it. I threw the file across the room until it slammed against the wall. I completely lost my Zen, so I took some deep, calming breaths. Too bad they didn't help. Deep down, I knew there wasn't anything on earth that would help calm my nerves unless someone shot me up with a horse tranquilizer.

How in the hell was I supposed to be objective and give this man the best care? He was in for a minimum of thirty days. Alcohol, opiates, specifically heroin addiction. Oh, how the mighty do fall. It took a long, long time before I could tear my eyes off that.

How could I possibly pull this off? How was I going to be empathetic and counsel the one who was responsible for taking my daughter away from me? He was the bastard who represented my ex-husband in our nasty divorce.

Chapter Four

PEARSON

"YOU'VE GOT TO BE KIDDING ME?" I GROANED FROM THE passenger seat as Hudson drove up the winding road to my new home for the next thirty or so days.

"Everything we read said it was the best," Grey said from the back seat. "And I had several lengthy discussions with Sylvie."

"Sylvie. I haven't seen her since she was eight." What the hell does she know?

"Don't be so harsh on her, Pearson. She came highly recommended by Dr. Martinelli," Hudson said. "And just because you haven't seen her doesn't mean she's not good at what she does."

He had a point. I was just being an asshole. That's what detoxing off alcohol and heroin will do to you.

"True, but look at this place. Have we been hurled through a time machine and dumped out in Haight-Ashbury in the late 60s? Flower Power Serenity Pavilion? The only thing missing is the VW van with the peace symbols painted on it." I spoke too soon. We rounded another curve and there it sat, painted with flowers and peace symbols. "Oh shit." Hudson started laughing. Wooden flower signs and old hippie art dotted the drive all the way to the building. When we arrived, the welcome sign was done in letters reminiscent of that era.

Grey chuckled. "You do have a point. Maybe it's to put you at ease."

"Wasn't that the culture that brought drug use to the forefront? It seems a bit counterintuitive." I wiped the sweat from my brow. This was getting old. The counselors at the other rehab center said I'd experience periods of profuse sweating for weeks to come.

"Reserve judgment. They haven't earned a stellar reputation for nothing," Hudson said.

I kept quiet. I didn't need to keep adding any more snarky comments. They'd had enough of them during the hour drive up here. Flower Power Serenity Pavilion was located on the river away from the city, fairly close to where my parents and Grey lived. There wasn't one bad review to be found on the place. My brothers had done intensive research on it. And my cousin who worked here had also given her side of the story. We'd soon see.

Hudson pulled up to the entryway and immediately someone appeared to assist us. Her name was Starr.

"You must be Mr. West."

How did she know that? "Yes, I'm Pearson West."

"Welcome." And she stuffed a large potted plant of lavender into my hands. "This lavender is to soothe you and help you sleep. Put some under your pillowcase each night."

My brows lifted. "Er, thank you."

Hudson grabbed my bag out of the back, and we all followed Starr inside. We went into the office where we filled out some paperwork. I sat there like an idiot with that pot in my lap as she asked me questions.

Starr told my brothers, "You are allowed to visit on Sundays from twelve to four. Mr. West will be allowed to send emails once a week, but any other phone correspondence must be done through the main office. We strongly encourage letters, but we don't allow any packages of any kind."

When we were finished, my brothers said goodbye. I wanted to beg them to stay. I felt like the reluctant kid getting dumped off at camp for the first time.

We hugged and they left. This was the second time we'd been through this, although this time I wasn't going through severe physical withdrawals, other than the periodic profuse sweating and cravings. The psychological part was still an issue though.

Starr showed me to my room and then gave me a tour of the facility. Meditation music was piped throughout the place and there were hanging beads in every open doorway in the building. Even Starr was dressed in the hippie fashion. She wore a halo of flowers around her head and a bohemian gown. As far as I could tell, she was barefoot.

"Our goal is to have you as relaxed as you can possibly be. We know that coming off of substance abuse is very stressful which is why we strive to create a peaceful environment here." She walked me outside where there was a courtyard and then a huge garden area. "We encourage our patients to take part in gardening. It can be very therapeutic."

"Uh, I see." There were several people out there digging around in the dirt, but I noticed one man in particular who seemed to be excavating a rather large area. I wondered if he was trying to dig a tunnel somewhere—maybe to a different rehab center that wasn't so flowery.

"Do you by any chance have a gym?" I asked.

"Oh, yes. Follow me."

That was where I'd rather be expending my extra energy rather than digging giant holes in the earth. I was pleasantly surprised to see the workout facility.

"We have everything you might need here," Starr said.

"Yes, this is very nice. Is it open any time?"

"Not between ten thirty and five in the morning. We require

our patients to be in their rooms then. Sleep is an important part of your recovery."

"Right." Except sometimes, sleep was an impossibility because all you were thinking about was using.

"Do you have any other questions?"

"Yes. When do I meet with my counselor?"

"Oh, right. You're scheduled for tomorrow at ten with Rose. Breakfast is at seven thirty. You'll go to your first group session at eight thirty."

"Thanks."

That afternoon I met a few other people in the main room, but then settled into my room. It was small, with a twin bed and bathroom. There was a built-in desk, a small closet, and some shelves. It was perfectly compact, but it suited the purpose well. The bathroom was well outfitted with nice fluffy towels, unlike the other place. The walk-in shower was spacious, and the sink had plenty of counter space to store your items on. I was surprised I didn't have a roommate, like I did at the other place. But I certainly appreciated the privacy here.

Dinner was at six, which was surprisingly tasty. It consisted of baked chicken, some potato concoction and vegetables with a salad and dessert. At around eight, I went to work out. I needed to exhaust myself in order to sleep. After an hour on the treadmill, I lifted weights. Working out had been my salvation in the last rehab center I was in. I could barely walk when I got there, but my determination had pushed me and now I was up to an hour of running. Not like I used to, but I was running nevertheless. My body was thinner than it had been, but my muscles stood out more, because there was less fat that covered them.

By the time I got back to the room, I was dripping with sweat and weary as hell. I guzzled some water and after a cool down, I took a shower. It was ten thirty on the nose when I crawled into bed. If sleep came, it would last for about six hours at the most.

At five thirty, I was back in the gym, doing the same workout. This was what I did every day. Except I worked out different body parts with the weights.

Breakfast was excellent. I scarfed down eggs, toast, oatmeal, bacon, fruit, and juice. It was a buffet, thank God. I had extra helpings of everything.

My first session was awful. I hated standing in front of everyone as the newbie, but I'd better get used to it.

"My name is Pearson West and I'm a drug addict and an alcoholic." Everyone listened to my story and clapped when I was done. I never could figure out why they clapped. It was an awful thing. But they say it's because I had the strength to come forward. It wasn't strength, it was weakness, in my book. It was a brush with death. If it hadn't been for that, I would still be using.

Ten o'clock came and I waited for Rose. I sat outside her office until she called me in. She was a much more attractive than I would've liked. Tall with long black wavy hair, she was dressed like a hippie. She had on wide-legged pants and it was hard to tell if it was a skirt or not. Her top was one of those long flowy gauzy things that hid everything. She had one of those flower wreaths on her head.

"Hi, I'm Rose Wilson, and I'll be your counselor for the next thirty days." She scowled.

"Yes, you probably know my cousin."

"Cousin?"

"Sylvie."

"Sylvie is your cousin?"

"Yes. I'm surprised she didn't say anything." Her scowl deepened to the point I was worried it would be permanent.

"So am I. Well, shall we proceed?" she asked brusquely.

Her attitude took me aback. I expected a warmer greeting than that.

"I've had a chance to review your records and you're a lucky man, Mr. West." She flipped through papers in a folder as she spoke.

"Pearson."

"Excuse me?" she asked, looking up.

"My name. It's Pearson."

"Very well," she clipped.

I imagined this place to be less formal than this. Evidently, I was off base.

"I realize that, which is why I'm here."

"Realize what?"

Jesus. Was she that ignorant? "That I'm a lucky man. Didn't you just tell me that?" My tone conveyed my annoyance.

Her eyes lasered into mine as her lips pursed with suppressed fury. What the hell had I done to this woman to piss her off so much? "Yes. So how did you find your first thirty days?" Her tone was now icy.

Now it was my turn to frown. "Seriously?" She should know this, I would've thought.

"Yes, I am very serious," she huffed.

"It was awful. Coming off of alcohol and heroin was no picnic."

She scribbled something down. "And what about now?"

"Are you asking if I still have cravings?"

"Yes," she huffed again. She acted as though I was putting her out being here. Wasn't it her job to be my counselor?

"Of course I do. I'm only thirty-one days out." I was getting angry now. What kind of counselor was she?

She glared at me. "Look, Mr. West ..."

"Pearson."

"Pearson, I'm trying to get a feel of where you are."

I gritted my teeth. "Then let me fill you in. I just went through hell. I'm still craving drugs and alcohol. I'd probably chew off my arm if I could for a hit. How's that? Do you have a feel now?" I fumed.

"You don't have to be rude," she sputtered. Her eyes grew stormy, and I thought again, why the hell is *she* angry. I'm the one who should be pissed.

"Neither do you. I'm the one who's here for help," I growled.

"Maybe you shouldn't have done drugs in the first place," she snapped back.

I narrowed my eyes at her. What the fuck! "Maybe you shouldn't have gone into counseling either." Now we were glaring at each other.

She leaned back in her chair and sighed. "I'm sorry. You're right. I've had a difficult morning. Maybe we should begin again?"

I released the breath I'd been holding and stared at her for a second. I finally said, "That sounds like a good idea."

"Tell me about how you're feeling."

What little wind I'd had in my sails was gone. I was totally dejected by that interchange. My tone was glum as I answered, "I have to work out twice a day. It helps the urges. The nighttime work out helps with sleep otherwise I lie there and have intense cravings."

"I see from your chart that Dr. Martinelli suggested an anti-depressant, but you refused."

"I don't want a band-aid." Adding another drug seemed to only defeat the purpose in my book.

She scribbled something down on her pad of paper. "They can be very helpful in getting you across this bridge."

"That's what she said, but I don't believe any drug is the answer." I went to rehab to get clean and I want off all drugs. Period.

"Then we'll begin by working on coping mechanisms, things to occupy your mind, to fill the void that the drugs created. But I do strongly suggest the antidepressants. They help calm your brain down by binding with the receptor sites there. And they're not addictive like opiates or alcohol are."

"That's exactly what Dr. Martinelli said. You must work with her a lot."

She finally smiled. "We talk some. But that's a common issue with abusers. They find that drugs fill a void. We need to uncover the void your using filled too."

"Okay."

"Are you married?"

"No, never have been."

"In a relationship?"

"Never been in one of those either."

"Now that's significant considering your age. Care to explain that?"

"I'm an attorney. I've seen my share of divorce cases and I don't think I ever want to walk down that messy road."

She bristled when I answered. It made me wonder if she was divorced. I didn't dare ask her.

"I see. Not all marriages end up that way."

"I'm well aware of that," I said. Now it was me who was bristling.

"Your childhood. Tell me about it."

"It was idyllic. My parents are the most loving couple I've ever seen. I was raised not wanting a thing. I'm the youngest and was spoiled."

"Maybe that's the issue."

I shrugged. "Dr. Martinelli mentioned the same."

"Siblings?" she asked.

"Two brothers and yes, we all get along extremely well."

"Did you growing up?"

"Yes, I idolized them both."

"Can you explain?"

"They were both really smart and great athletes."

"Better than you?"

"I wouldn't say so. They were older so we never truly competed, except for fun." She was writing constantly as I spoke. I'm not sure how she listened and wrote at the same time.

She paused for a moment and tapped her pen on the pad. "Were you ever abused?"

"Never."

"Molested? By an older uncle or family friend?"

"No! Isn't that in my chart? I asked. Dr. Martinelli and I had been through all of this too. I guess she hadn't taken the time to look over my background. "I had a very pristine upbringing. The drugs happened because of the shoulder surgery. I got hooked on Lortab and when I couldn't get off of it, I moved to street drugs. I'm sure this is a scenario you've heard before. Did you bother to read my chart?"

"As a matter of fact, I did. And unfortunately, you are among many who find themselves in this situation. I'm only trying to uncover things, something that maybe precipitated all of this. This is my information gathering session with you. I'm sorry if it seems repetitive, but it really is necessary."

"As my chart should state, I thought I could stop, take control of it. I'd tell myself all the time—this is my last one. And then the first time I did heroin, I thought, just this once. That didn't turn out so well. But the thing is, I never would actually take that final step and admit I was addicted. Not until I woke up in that hospital and they told me I almost died."

Her abrupt response had me wondering about whether she enjoyed her job. "You're not the first and won't be the last. Here's the question you have to ask yourself. In here, you're in a controlled environment and you can't use. There are no drugs or alcohol. What about when you get out? How will you handle that?"

"I don't know. Right now, I couldn't handle it."

"Then we have our work cut out for us."

"That's why I'm here. To get that kind of help," I admitted.

"And that's why I'm digging into your life. I'm not going to lie. This won't be easy. But nothing worth fighting for ever is."

Chapter Five

ROSE

DROPPING MONTANA OFF WAS BRUTAL. THOSE TINY ARMS clung to me as I took her out of the car seat. Her dipshit father stood with a smug smile that I'd come to despise.

"She can walk, you know." His voice was like fingernails on a blackboard. I held back a shudder.

"I do know, but I enjoy her hugs. I'm wondering if you do."

His smugness was replaced by a stormy expression. "What the hell does that mean?"

"Do I really need to explain it?"

"Come here, Montana," he barked.

I bit my tongue to keep from calling him an asshole.

Montana wore a forlorn expression as she walked toward him, head down.

"As her mother, I'd like you to furnish me with her play schedule."

"What?"

"Yes. I'm afraid she's not getting enough activity here."

His jaw clenched and a muscle twitched on one side. "Montana, inside now." He snapped his fingers. I wanted to yell, "She's not a damn dog, you ass."

My daughter gave me a quick glance before scurrying inside the expansive home.

"It's come to my attention that Montana spends an awful lot of time in her room," I said.

"Oh, and this comes to you from a four-year-old?"

"Yes. She's a very bright four-year-old and can talk. Or haven't you noticed?"

"I've noticed. I'm with her the majority of the time, or have you forgotten? Can I ask you, what do you propose to do about this situation? Take me back to court?" Then he emitted a nasty chuckle as he eyed me disdainfully. He had a way of making me feel very insignificant.

"I'd imagine so."

"And how are you going to afford it?"

"I'll find a way, Greg."

He lifted one brow. "We'll see. You can pick her up at five in two weeks." He turned and left me standing there. Fucker.

I got into my piece of crap car and wanted to ram into his fancy BMW as I backed out of the driveway. Urrrgh! I needed to calm down as I was on my way into work and had three new patients to check in, one of which I already hated with a passion.

"Deep breath, Rose, deep breath." I pulled air in through my mouth, and released it through my nose, repeating this cycle as I drove. It eventually calmed me, but damn, he was a cruel bastard. The only nice thing he'd ever given me was Montana.

Sweet Montana. Every time I saw her, she seemed to be less bright and cheerful. If I didn't take action soon, I was afraid her brightness would disappear altogether.

Sylvie was the first person I ran into at work.

"Wow, you look terrible." She plunked a flower wreath on top of my head. "This will bring you good vibes." When she noticed my tears, she tugged me by the arm into her office. "Spill."

"It's Greg. I'm worried he's not treating Montana well." And I explained why.

"You know I've never asked, but how did he get full custody in the first place?"

I sagged. "I don't know. He concocted all these stories about how I was never there and was such a neglectful mother. I was going to school full time and did my best to be there, but you know how it is. He had all the money and stripped our accounts. My mom helped where she could, but she works and really doesn't give a damn about her granddaughter or me. It was a nightmare of a time."

"What about your attorney?"

"Let's not go there. He was worthless."

"I may know someone who can help."

"Really?"

"Maybe." She stuck the end of her pen in her mouth and chewed on it. "He's sort of tied up for the moment, but I could ask him later. In the meantime, are you going to be okay to work?"

I thought about my new patients, one in particular, and sighed. "I have to. I can't afford to miss work. I don't have that many paid days off, with the ones I missed when Montana had her tonsils out."

"True. Okay, just let me know if you need anything."

"Thanks, Sylvie."

My first two check-ins went great. They were motivated, ready to begin, and both had issues that stemmed from their childhood. Then I got to *him*.

Large blue-gray eyes with thick lashes homed in on me. I expected him to look a bit pasty like most of the other patients did, but no, this one had golden skin. He wore a short-sleeved T-shirt that hugged the muscles in his arms—muscles that rippled when he moved. He did not fit the usual image of a recovering addict. Not at all. His strong jaw was balanced by high cheek-bones and a chiseled face. Why did he have to be so damned handsome? I remembered him in court as looking perfect in his expensive suit and tie. But here, he was every bit as good look-ing. His golden brown hair was messier, but it made him all the more appealing. When he took the vacant seat across from me, he leaned forward, resting his elbows on his knees.

Watching him so at ease made my annoyance flare. His eyes darkened, which made him even sexier. Sexier? What the hell was I thinking? He was my patient whom I despised.

When I questioned him, it took everything I had to rein in my anger. Weirdly enough, when he told me how he'd gotten addicted, I softened just a tiny bit, even though I didn't want to. People like him had it all. Why couldn't he have handled this in a better way? Heroin of all things? But at least I'd been wrong about him. I wasn't sure if I was happy or angry about it. That didn't make me the very best therapist either. I figured he was the usual guy who dabbled in drugs for fun and took it too far. I hadn't expected it to have been a surgical procedure. I'd read his chart, sure, but when he spoke the words, it hit me harder than I'd expected. I wondered how it must've been for someone as successful as he was to find himself in this situation. At least I could find a smidgen of empathy for him. That was a start.

As he rose to leave, I reminded him about a few things.

"We do follow a rigid schedule here, although your first week is sort of a toe-dipping experience. We'd like to see what you respond to the best. Remember, meditation is a huge part of recovery at Flower Power," I reminded him.

The corner of his mouth curled.

"What? You don't believe in it?" I asked.

"Not particularly."

"Have you ever seriously tried it?"

"No," he chuckled.

"You'll find it's very calming and it is part of the daily requirement here. Next week you'll start each day with a session.

But I'll be seeing you in meditation later today." I looked at his tight jeans and added, "You'll need something a little looser to wear, too."

"Is that right?"

"Afraid so. Unless you want to sit on the floor in the Sukhasana and child's pose in those."

"Seeing as I don't know what either of those are, I'll take your word for it." He got up to leave and a picture caught his eye. "Is that your daughter?"

"Yes," I answered tersely.

"She's a cutie. I have several nieces and nephews. That's something I want to work on. Spending more time with them."

I mumbled, "Wish I could do the same."

"Excuse me?"

"Nothing. I'll see you in meditation."

He stared at me for a second too long. "Have we met before?"

"I don't think so."

With a nod, he was gone. That went a lot better than I'd thought after I'd stopped being such a bitch to him. Only that was session one. I had another month's worth to go. And if things between Greg and I worsened, I'd probably take it out on him. Maybe I should pass his case over to someone else now before I got in too deep. That would be the logical and ethical thing to do. But something was pulling me toward him. I wish I knew what it was, other than the fact that I'd like to strangle him.

Chapter Six

PEARSON

THAT WAS STRANGE. I'M NOT SURE WHAT SHE WAS TRYING TO accomplish—alienation or friendliness. If it was the latter, she was doing a rather shitty job of it. I had the impression these Zen counselors were peace lovers, but she was trying to antagonize me the whole time—or at least that's the impression I got. Maybe she was wearing the wrong kinds of flowers on her head and needed an entire pot of lavender up there.

I was on the way to my next group session when I got hung up in some beads hanging in a doorway. My anger got the best of me and I ripped them off the molding.

"My, someone got up on the wrong side of the bed today." Then she laughed. I checked out her name badge and it was Sylvie, my cousin. She was eight the last time I'd seen her, so I didn't recognize her.

"Sylvie."

"Pearson. You've changed," she said with another laugh.

"So have you. Sorry about these." I handed her the beads.

"Other than the obvious, why the sour mood?"

"No reason, other than the obvious."

"How have your first couple of days been?"

"Dandy." My tone was laced with sarcasm.

"I see. You sound like our usual patient. I swear it'll get better."

"It has to because right now I could chew those beads."

She stopped walking and tapped my hand. I had to force myself not to jerk away from her. I was extremely twitchy today. "Think back to thirty days ago, Pearson. It *is* better, isn't it?"

She had a point. "Yeah, a lot better."

"Are you headed to group?"

"Yeah."

"Come on. I'll walk with you."

"I don't think Rose is very fond of me."

Sylvie gave me a sidelong glance. "What makes you say that?"

"Let's just say I thought this place was supposed to be peaceful and calming. She was more adversarial."

She chewed her lip before answering. "She had a difficult weekend. That may be why. I can talk to her if you'd like."

We got to the room where my group session was held. "No, it's fine. If she's having a rough time, I don't want to make it any worse. Maybe things will straighten out."

She touched my arm this time. Sylvie must be a touchy-feely sort. "There is something I wanted to talk to you about, but it can wait. I'll catch up with you later." Then she left me standing there, wondering what it was. I needed to get moving or I'd be late, so I went into the room for my session, which I was prepared to be painful.

By the end, it wasn't as bad as I thought. Instead of listening and sharing our stories again, the counselor running the session had each of us share how we managed to get through our cravings. This was particularly helpful because some of us were new, some had been here a couple of weeks, and some were getting ready to leave.

Surprisingly, meditation and yoga seemed to be the things that most people found the best.

"What about working out, like running and using weights?" I asked.

"That's a great option too, but sometimes it can actually rev you up, as opposed to relaxing and calming you down. What might be good is a combination of the two. Maybe running and then meditation or yoga afterward," one of the attendees suggested.

Someone else jumped in and added, "Meditation takes practice so don't give up on it too soon. If at first you don't find it helpful, keep at it."

I was still a skeptic, but what did I have to lose? It's not like I had anything else going on. Afterward, I went to lunch and I sat at a table with two other men, Rob and Joe. They started discussing their counselor, who happened to be Rose. My ears immediately perked up.

"She was not in a good mood today," Rob said.

"You noticed that too?" Joe asked.

"Yeah, especially when she practically bit my head off." Rob didn't look so happy about it.

"Oh, she wasn't that bad to me."

"Pearson, who's your counselor?" Joe asked.

"Rose."

Joe looked glum. "And this was your first session with her then?"

"Yeah."

"Don't judge her by it. She's usually great."

I thought about what Sylvie said, but kept it to myself. "Good to know. I did wonder about that."

Rob was sweating and looked a bit gray.

"Hey, you okay, Rob?" Joe asked.

"Not really. I'm not feeling well."

Joe immediately asked, "Did you eat breakfast?"

"No."

He went up to the buffet and grabbed a coke. "Here. Drink. You know how the blood sugar thing works."

Joe looked at me and said, "Rob's sensitive to low blood sugar."

That explained it. No wonder he looked awful. "Should I call someone?"

"Nah, the coke should perk him up."

Rob drank it and several minutes later started feeling better.

"There were so many days I went without food I still struggle with remembering to eat. Breakfast is the worst because in the mornings I don't have an appetite."

"You're lucky you didn't die," Joe said.

"Aren't we all," I added.

They looked at me and Rob asked, "You too?"

"Yep." They weren't in any of my group sessions so I figured I'd share my story. It was getting easier and easier, although I didn't like that it was.

Rob said, "I wish mine had been surgery. I was trying to make my past go away. Abusive father here." He waved his hand in the air.

"Man, I'm sorry." For some odd reason, I wanted to hug the dude. He really did look like he could use one.

Joe didn't add anything and neither did we.

I volunteered, "When I couldn't get my hands on any more Lortabs, I ultimately went to heroin. Alcohol became a problem too."

"Life sucks sometimes, doesn't it?" Rob asked.

"It can, but hopefully we're getting back on track," I said.

"Flower Power," Joe said, raising his water glass.

At first, I thought he was making fun at the place, but he wasn't. He was dead serious. We clinked glasses.

"Do you garden?" I asked.

"I do now. It's very therapeutic," Rob said. Joe agreed. Maybe there was something to this flower shit and digging in the dirt after all. I said goodbye to my lunch buddies and went to change for meditation.

The room was wide open, but everyone was trickling in and grabbing a yoga mat as they did. I followed suit and mimicked what they did, but I laid mine out in the back of the room. Then Rose walked in, dressed in yoga attire. Gone were the hippie clothes replaced by a combination of body-hugging yoga pants and a top that didn't leave much to the imagination. But crazy as it sounds, she looked like an elf. Her leggings were red and white striped, and her top was bright green. I briefly wondered if she had pointed ears. Her black waves were now pulled into a messy twist on top of her head, which only accentuated her long, sexy neck ... a neck that made me want to nuzzle it. What the hell was I thinking? She'd probably bite my head off if I so much as tried.

To my horror, she beelined for me and tapped me on the shoulder. "Up front, so I can give you directions." Then she kept moving. There was a platform she set her mat on and then she put on a headset. I had no choice but to follow her. She indicated where she wanted me. Great. Right in front so I'd be the center of attention.

Music began playing and her voice came through the speaker system loud and clear.

"I hope everyone is having a nice day, but let's make it a lot better. Stretch out, long and lean on your mats. Pretend a band is pulling you from either end. Let your arms rest at your sides, palms facing up. Now take some deep, cleansing breaths, inhaling through the nose, and exhaling through the mouth."

Then she had us move into the three part breath, but I felt her hand on my lower abs as she instructed the class.

"Feel your belly drop. Exhale completely and press here to help expel the air." She applied pressure as she spoke.

Once she had the class into this breathing thing, she told us to start extending our inhalations to a count of three and our exhalations to the same. Concentrating on this was relaxing. I'd forgotten how tense I'd been when I came in.

"Now clear your mind of everything. The focus of this is relaxation. If that's not possible, focus on one idea only."

We continued breathing and for some reason the only thought in my head was Rose. Her voice was extremely soothing.

"If you're having difficulty relaxing, start with your neck, pretend it's fluid melting into your mat. Follow suit with the rest of your muscles."

Her voice, combined with the music, created a hypnotic atmosphere and I found myself drifting. We stayed like that for a while. I wasn't sure how long because I lost track of time.

When she spoke again, it nearly startled me. "I want you to change your focus now. Think of a goal you want to accomplish. Maybe it's just staying sober. Maybe it's tackling your cravings. Maybe it's a relationship your addiction destroyed. Or it could be something entirely different. Whatever the case may be, concentrate on that issue and what you can do to resolve it. Remember, you have the power to do anything you set your mind to."

My goal was staying sober once I left this place, because it scared the shit out of me. I focused every thought on that. I knew I had family support and wondered if I should move into my parents after this. It sounded stupid, but I would need all the help I could get. Before I knew it, she was telling us to move into child's pose, whatever that was.

I unwillingly opened my eyes to see what everyone else was doing and followed instructions. This actually felt pretty damn good. When class was done, and I was rolling up the mat, Rose came up to me and asked, "What did you think?"

"I liked it. You're a great instructor," I told her begrudgingly.

Her cheeks flushed a bit and she smiled. "I'm glad you did. You should start your day with this."

"Yeah, I can see the benefits now." As I looked at her, she seemed oddly familiar to me. "Are you sure we haven't met."

Her smile immediately dissolved into a frown. "No, we haven't." And she walked away. Her abrupt change left me standing there wondering what the hell just happened.

Chapter Seven

ROSE

PEARSON WALKED IN FOR HIS APPOINTMENT LOOKING like hell.

"How was your night? You don't look so good," I said.

"Glad to see your observational skills are keen," he said coldly.

I inhaled and counted to five. Why was he such an ass? "You can't expect miracles," I hit back sharply. "You're only thirty plus days out."

"I am aware." His eyes bore down on mine.

"So tell me about it."

"You're so damn smart, why don't *you* tell *me*."

I pulled my hands into my lap and dug my nails into my palms. The man was downright infuriating. "I'm not a mind reader, Mr. West."

"Pearson."

"If you're going to act like an a … like that, I think I'd prefer to call you Mr. West."

He pushed to his feet and paced. My office was small so there wasn't much room for him to move back and forth.

"Did you by any chance go to meditation today?" I asked,

"No."

"May I ask why?"

He stopped, turned, and practically yelled, "Because I over-slept. I had a rough night."

That's when I moved into therapy mode. I went to his side and said, "Please take a seat. We need to talk this through."

"Talking won't do me much good."

"Okay, how about we take a walk outside?"

His head sliced up and down. I grabbed my coat and asked him if he wanted to get his. "I won't be needing one. Have you looked at me? Really looked?"

Of course I had, but I didn't want him to know I'd been ogling him. Sweat was rolling out of every pore that I could see. "It's cool out there. You may get chilled because you're sweating."

"I would welcome that."

His choice. We headed out the back to a nature trail and walked. "Tell me about your night," I said after we'd been walking for about five minutes.

"Constant cravings. All fucking night."

"What had you been doing prior to them hitting you?"

"I was in bed. They hit about midnight."

"Can you put your finger on any triggers?"

"No, dammit. I've been trying to figure that out and I can't. It doesn't make sense. I'm lying there and bam. All of a sudden it's all I can think about."

Maybe it's your damn guilty conscience that's eating at you.

"You're frustrated I can see."

He threw back his head and laughed. "Well aren't those enlightening words. Is that all they taught you in counseling school?"

"Okay, I've about had it with your insults. I'm supposed to be your sounding board and help you get through the struggles, but don't you dare take out your addiction issues on me."

"Maybe if you'd actually help me, other than suggest we take a walk, I wouldn't. I'm paying an ass load of money to be here and this is all I get?"

"No, but you haven't been here long enough for anything to sink in yet. I'm trying to help you uncover your triggers and if you'd shut your damn mouth, maybe we could both come up with some sort of solution. Can we at least try?"

He stared at me and let out a groan.

"Look, your brain is completely scrambled right now. Being on alcohol and opiates does that. Then, going off of them does it again. I'm going to be honest and I don't know what Dr. Martinelli told you, but it's going to take at least a year for your brain to normalize … to get back to what it was *before* you ever started using. *At least a year,* Pearson. Drugs work in the central nervous system and that's why we suggest an antidepressant. They help with the normalization process. They would make things easier on you, but you have refused that path, so we have to work with that. Your expectations should be one day at a time and if that's too much then make it one hour at a time. Until you can comfortably reach your goal, keep it within that time frame. Does this sound reasonable?"

He blew out a breath and said, "I guess my expectations are higher than that."

"Then lower them. Always set attainable goals. Now more than ever this is so important. It'll be much easier to measure your progress too. For example, if you set hourly goals, you'll be able to say to yourself, hey, I didn't think of using for this entire hour. Keep a journal too. That helps immensely."

He rubbed his arms again, which was common.

"You also have to quit defying me," I said.

"I'm not," he said in a rebellious tone. He reminded me of my daughter when she was about to get disciplined.

"Yes, you are. You think I'm not capable."

"No, I—"

"Pearson, I'm a psychologist. I'm trained to read people and I can figure things out. I can see it in you that you don't have much trust in my abilities."

"It's not that. I don't think you like me."

I almost staggered. No, I didn't like him. I hated the man for how he ruined my life, but I was doing my dead level best to help him. "That's not true."

"Then why did you treat me like shit in my first session?"

"I'd had a rough morning."

"And you took it out on me."

He had me there. "I did and I apologized for that."

"Well, I'm having a rough morning and I'm taking it out on you. I apologize, but I need help." He again sounded childlike.

"I'm trying to give it to you." Damn, the man was frustrating.

He raked his hands through his hair and walked away. "Where are you going?" I called out. He didn't answer but kept walking. I ran to catch up with him.

"Exercise helps so I'm walking fast," he finally said.

Fast wasn't the word. I had to jog to keep up with him and could barely talk. "Do you exercise daily?" I huffed and puffed the words out.

"Yes, and from the sounds of it, you don't."

"I do yoga. I don't run."

"You should. You sound like you need some cardio in your life."

Damn him. He always knew how to poke the bear. I finally gave up because I got the worst stitch in my side that doubled me over. Now I remembered why I hated running. I turned around and backtracked until I got inside. I was still fuming when I ran into Sylvie.

"Hey, your cheeks are bright red."

"They should be. I was just out for a run."

"A run?"

"Oh, never mind." I stomped back to my office where I sat

with a pot of lavender in my lap and inhaled it for a solid ten minutes. That's where I was when Mr. Testy came back by. When he saw me, he laughed. "I'm glad I can amuse you so."

He turned away, and I could hear him laughing all the way down the hall. Asshole.

Our next several sessions were quite the same and I had a devil of a time breaking through his brick wall or the concrete his skull was made out of. I wasn't sure who was more frustrated, him or me. I wanted to kill him. He was devious in the way he answered my questions, always turning the tables on me, exactly like the prick of an attorney he was. That's what he did to me in court as he brought me to tears. This time I didn't cry, I only threw things. At night, I found myself drinking more than the occasional glass of wine and it was then I realized if I didn't do something, I would be a patient myself at Flower Power, right along with that dickhead, Pearson West.

So, a couple of weeks after struggling to be an objective and fair counselor, I decided it was best to pass Pearson along to someone else. When Sylvie came into her office on that following morning, she found me waiting for her.

"Rose, what are you doing here?"

I slapped all of Pearson's files on her desk and said, "I've found that in the best interest of Pearson West, it's not possible for me to be his psychologist." Sylvie's brows nearly met as she frowned.

"What's happened?"

"First off, the man is a total douche. Second, I haven't been completely honest, and I probably should've refused the case from the start, so it's not his fault, but mine. Pearson was Greg's attorney in our divorce, and I find that I'm more than a little resentful toward him. In fact, I hate the asshole."

"Oh, God. I'm sorry. He does have that killer reputation in the courtroom."

"Don't I know it," I said sourly. "He destroyed my life."

"Did Pearson destroy it or did Greg? Pearson was only doing what his client asked of him."

"True, but …"

"You're right to pass him off. I'm not saying that. But I want you to take a look at his side of things. He's good at what he does. He didn't know you from Adam. All he knew was what his client fed him. He did his job."

I moaned. "And I'll be facing huge bills if I go back to court because I have to do something about Montana."

Sylvie thrummed her pen on the desk. "Maybe Pearson can help you."

"Help me? Why would he want to do that when he was Greg's attorney?"

"I don't know, but we can ask."

"We can't ask him until he's through here. I don't want to upset his progress," I said.

"You may be right. Do you want to tell him or shall I?"

"Tell him?"

"That you're not going to be his psychologist anymore."

Shit. I was totally out of it. "Maybe we both should."

"Not a bad idea. When is he scheduled?"

"Ten."

"I'll be there."

I had one client prior to that so I rushed to my office to prepare. It was a very tedious session as my mind was not very focused, but I would make it up on our next visit.

Five minutes before ten, Sylvie arrived. I hadn't been this nervous since I'd faced Greg in court.

"Don't worry. We'll explain everything and he'll be fine."

I didn't have time to respond before there was a knock and he waltzed in like he owned the place. When he saw Sylvie, the surprise was genuine.

"Hi Pearson, have a seat," I said, indicating to one of the empty chairs.

"From the looks of things, I take it this is going to be more than our usual session," he said.

I began by saying, "Actually, we aren't going to have a session at all. I've not exactly been fair to you these last couple of weeks." Then I froze as his compelling eyes latched onto mine. Thank God Sylvie stepped in.

"What Rose is trying to say is there is somewhat of a conflict of interest here."

In a demanding tone, he said, "Clarify, please."

They both turned to me and waited, but the words were locked somewhere between my brain and throat. My mind was completely scattered.

Sylvie continued, "Here's the problem. You were Rose's ex-husband's divorce attorney and it's caused a bit of an issue for her."

"I see."

"It's not as simple as that, Pearson," Sylvie said. "Her ex was awarded custody of their child and now Rose is very worried about her."

I watched for a reaction. He sat there calmly as though Sylvie had said the sky was blue. Anger crawled up my spine and that's when I discovered the use of my tongue.

"Yes, but worried barely touches the way I feel. My daughter's entire demeanor has changed in the last year and my ex makes it very difficult for me to see her on my weekends." I glared at him.

Sylvie stepped in and said, "Rose, back down. Take some deep breaths."

Then he had the nerve to say, "I'm sorry it worked out that way, but you can't blame me for a failed marriage."

"Excuse me?" I wanted to lunge at the bastard and punch his face in. Oh my God, he was creating feelings of intense violence in me. I fisted my hands in my lap.

"Your marriage failed, and I happened to be the attorney your husband hired. If you had hired me, things would've turned out differently. I'm not the one to blame here. I was only doing my job." He said it so matter-of-factly, I wanted to scream.

"Yes, and now my daughter is suffering because of it," I said through clenched teeth.

He steepled his fingers and stared a hole through me. The weight of his gaze set my skin on fire, not to mention my temper. "Let me get this straight. Your ex was awarded custody and now you're blaming me because your daughter's behaving differently. Is that correct?"

"Yes. No! He didn't deserve custody."

"Well, he must have if he got it." His arrogant attitude was my breaking point.

"Why you ass—" I leaped to my feet coming to stand directly in front of him with balled fists.

"Rose! That's enough!" Sylvie said, coming to her feet as well. "I think it's best if I separate you two."

"This is my four-year-old daughter we're discussing," I yelled.

"Rose." Sylvie's voice held more than a note of warning. "Please sit back down." I did as she asked.

Pearson sat there and I did happen to notice two long creases between his brows and a muscle twitching in his jaw. Maybe that counted for something. Who knew?

"Pearson, I had thought of asking you for help here. Rose is really in a bind. I may be speaking out of turn, but I've known her for quite a while, and she is an excellent mother. She didn't deserve to lose custody. Her ex is not a good man. You may have been doing what you were hired to do, but it has cost her dearly. Is there any way you can help?"

This was unexpected and Sylvie took me by surprise. My jaw nearly hit the floor.

"Unfortunately, I can't due to conflict of interest. But I might know someone who can. He's a friend of mine." Pearson glanced at me.

"I don't have much money to pay him. Having to pay child support has really strapped me." I couldn't help the snarky tone.

His thoughtful gaze zeroed in on me. "We can work something out."

I wasn't sure what he meant by that. With his arrogance, it probably included lots of sexual favors. But if he could gain me custody of my daughter, I'd do anything.

"Rose, I know you think the worst of me, so maybe I can redeem myself a little. Or try anyway." His expression was honest and open, which surprised me.

I fidgeted with the hem of my shirt. "I'm not gonna lie. These last couple of years have been the hardest ... I can't begin to explain."

"I wouldn't ask you to. And I can't imagine because I don't have kids."

Silence enveloped the room until Sylvie broke it. "Rose, what do you have to lose?"

"Nothing, I guess."

Pearson asked, "Can you furnish me with a copy of your divorce decree and custody papers?"

"I'll bring them tomorrow."

"Good. I'll take a look at them and give you my first impressions. I also would like to ask you a few questions about your ex-husband afterward."

"Okay."

"We'll still need to assign you to another counselor, Pearson," Sylvie said.

"I understand. I hope we can move forward, though, and not have any hard feelings." He stared pointedly at me.

"I'd like that."

Then he smiled and had I not been sitting, my knees would've buckled. Why did he have to be so damned handsome? Most people who came through here looked like hell, but not him. He managed to look like he stepped out of the pages of a magazine.

When he stood, I managed to thank him. He dipped his head and left.

"Damn," I muttered.

"What?" Sylvie asked.

"He's so ... so good looking."

She chuckled. "Yeah, and you should see the other two."

"Other two?"

"His brothers. But they're married."

"I'm sure when that happened, women all over the universe wept."

"Don't know about that but they are gifted genetically."

"I'll say. But thanks for bringing that up."

"Rose, if anyone can help you, he can."

I shrugged. "You heard him though. He can't actually do it."

"Maybe not, but he can guide his friend. I have a really good feeling about this. Besides, now you don't have to get yourself all worked up over him."

"What do you mean?"

She tapped my arm. "I think there's more to this than just him being your ex's attorney. You're attracted to him."

"I'd have to be dead not to be. He's sinfully hot. My ovaries practically leaped out when I looked at him."

Sylvie stood and gathered his chart and her things. "Well, this means you are free to pursue him." With a wink, she left before I could respond.

"Are you nuts? We can barely tolerate each other. I'm surprised he agreed to help me, but I'm sure it's only because of you." This was so unlike her. Our code of ethics here was not to get involved with the patients. Why on earth would she make such an outlandish comment like that? I didn't have time to ponder it though, because my next patient was due in five minutes, which gave me very little time to prepare. I'd better hustle if I was going to be ready.

Chapter Eight

PEARSON

FOR THE FIRST TIME IN MY LIFE, GUILT SLASHED THROUGH ME for winning a case. When I walked away from Rose's office, I headed straight to my room to change clothes in order to work out. The tension rolled off me in waves. How could I have represented a client such as that? Then I wondered how many people like Rose I'd destroyed over the years, all in the name of a few dollar signs.

All I wanted right now was the blissful release of heroin, or a few drinks at the very least to numb my brain. In the absence of those, I jumped on the treadmill and ran until the demons that chased me were flushed from my mind, and my legs could no longer support me.

I don't know how long I was down there, but I glanced up to see Sylvie staring at me.

"Are you okay?" she asked.

"I'm better now."

"You missed group, meditation, and lunch, so I almost sent out the posse for you."

"What time is it?"

"One forty-five. Wanna explain to me what's going on?"

I scrubbed my face. "It has to do with Rose."

"I see."

"No, Sylvie, I don't think you do. What she told me this morning opened up a huge can of worms you might say. I'd never thought of what I did for a living as wrong, but in the end, I may have hurt a lot of people in the process."

"In doing your job?"

"Yes. Maybe I was too good at what I did."

"Are you open to suggestions?"

"Right now, I'm open to anything."

"You're here for at least another few weeks. Why don't you come up with a plan for what you're going to do when you get out."

"You mean a new career?" I asked.

"Exactly. It sounds like you've become a bit disillusioned by what you used to do. So why not reinvent yourself while you're here? You might think this is crazy but when people go through rehab, many times they realize what they were doing in their previous lives was why they ended up there in the first place."

That was something I hadn't considered before. "I always just thought it was the shoulder surgery that got me hooked."

"Was it really the surgery though?"

"What do you mean?"

She finally sat down across from me, on the floor. "The surgery introduced you to the opiates, right?"

"Yeah."

"And initially, they reduced your pain. But, and be honest here, did you like anything else about them?"

"Mostly it was the high."

"Think back, Pearson."

I forced my mind to go back to the beginning. "I remember

going home at night, totally stressed, and taking one. I guess they had a numbing effect, or maybe more like relaxing."

"And then what?"

"I'd usually fall asleep. And come home the next night and do a repeat."

"How long did this keep up?"

"Months." I remember the shoulder felt fine, but I'd go back to the doctor and complain about how much pain I was in.

"When did your use escalate?"

"Months later. The doctor finally figured out I was abusing the prescription and told me he wouldn't write anymore. He recommended physical therapy, which I never did since it wasn't necessary. That's when I went to street drugs. Soon, I was taking them all day long. It wasn't fun anymore."

"Okay, go back to before, when it wasn't bad yet. You'd come home at night. Your shoulder felt fine, yet you still wanted the pills. Why?"

"I see where you're going here. They made me not care so much about work."

"And why was that so important?" she asked.

"Because I was arguing with my partners all the time about cases they were taking. I was disagreeing with them about things."

"What kinds of things?"

"I don't remember specifically because I was high all the time. Maybe it was that."

"Are you sure about that?"

"I missed court dates because I overslept and some other very important things. So yeah, I'm pretty sure. But I'm pretty fuzzy on a lot of things."

"I can see them getting angry about that. Was there anything else?"

"Before I started using, one of the partners and I would go at it a lot."

"What did you argue about?"

"Ethics mostly. I didn't agree with a lot of the cases he wanted to …" my voice trailed off as I rubbed my arms.

"Bingo." She grinned. "You immersed yourself in drugs to relieve the stress. Think, Pearson."

The light bulb suddenly came on. "Oh, shit. Why didn't I see that?"

"Like I just said. Your brain was clouded. So, how about thinking through the whole process again, starting with work."

"Yeah, I see where this is going. I argued with a couple of my partners, specifically two of them because of the cases they were taking on. I wasn't in agreement with them and didn't concur with their ethics, but they overruled me. It created a huge amount of stress for me, not to mention killed my happy." I remembered the arguments we'd get into time and again.

"Okay, so you'd use opiates to numb yourself in order to handle what was going on at work until you became addicted. You didn't even realize why. The why is because you were unhappy, stressed out, and didn't agree with their ethics. Now that you've figured it out, you can move forward, reinvent yourself, and find your new career path. You already have a name for yourself. All you have to do is start again."

"Sylvie, you make it sound so easy, but it isn't. My firm will make it very difficult. I have a no-compete clause."

"Why do you have to practice in Manhattan? There are other places to set up a law firm."

"Where?"

"Anywhere. Think outside the box. Golly gee whiz, you're brilliant. Use your brain."

"Golly gee whiz?"

"Shut up." She slapped my leg.

Then we both laughed. It felt good too.

"Pearson, have you thought about starting your recovery process with Rose?"

"What do you mean?"

"Okay, hear me out. You said that what you did hurt a lot of people. It's probably not possible to make amends to all of them. But you can with Rose. And it can be a beginning of the healing and recovery process."

She was right. I had time to think about this and make a plan.

"You're exactly right. Helping her can be part of the answer. One thing is certain. If the firm is part of the reason I ended up here, I don't have a desire to go back there."

"You do realize that lawyers are at a high risk of drug and alcohol abuse because of the stress of their profession?"

"No, Sylvie, I didn't. But I do now. Thanks for coming to find me. I really appreciate this conversation."

"Come on. Let's go find some food. You must be starved."

We went to the dining room and she was able to arrange for some lunch for me. I inhaled it as she watched in fascination.

"Out of curiosity, how long did you run?"

"Long enough so I couldn't stand up afterward."

"Jeez. No wonder you were starving. Think you can make it to meditation this afternoon?"

"Sure, I just need to shower first. Oh, do you know who my new counselor is?"

"Yeah, it's Jeremy. He's really good. You two will hit it off."

"Thanks. I'm sorry it didn't work for Rose and me, but I think I can help her. I'll see you later."

Sylvie had given me a lot to think about. And when I did, it opened the door to a whole lot of other things I had kept closed for a long time … things I had never admitted to myself … things that I didn't think mattered. But deep down, they were what had catapulted me to this place I found myself in.

I closed the door to my room and sat on the bed. Turning my arms up, I stared at the now healed needle marks. They were so faint, I had to really search to find them. I was one of the lucky ones. I hadn't been using that long to develop the deep scarring addicts often got. I also was lucky in that I hadn't contracted HIV or some sexually transmitted disease from the countless women I'd had sex with. There were so many, I couldn't even recall their names or what they looked like. Most of the time I'd been so fucked up, I didn't remember bringing them home. It was only when I woke up and they'd been in bed with me, naked, that it came crashing down on me. At the time, I realized it was an escape, but when I'd started to analyze it, I'd swept it under the rug and saved it for another day.

Now I knew why. I wasn't that tough guy I'd always believed I was after all.

Chapter Nine

ROSE

WAS IT POSSIBLE THAT PEARSON WOULD HELP AFTER HOW I'D treated him? I was afraid to think it or to hope for it. Nothing had gone my way and I couldn't bear to be let down again, especially where my daughter was concerned.

My next patient came in and our session went well. She was on her final week and seemed prepared to face the world on her own. Everything pointed in the right direction and she would continue with NA. We had already lined up a sponsor for her, which she would be meeting here before she checked out.

Afterward, Sylvie and I talked and decided Jeremy would be a good fit for Pearson. I set up a time to talk to him so I could fill him in on Pearson's progress. I would meet him this afternoon, right after meditation class.

Then I met Sylvie for lunch.

"Have you seen Pearson since this morning?" she asked.

"No, but I'd have no reason to. Why?"

"He missed group and he's not here. He usually is in here by now."

"Hmm. I don't know."

We ate and then afterward, she said, "I'm going to go look for him."

"Okay. Let me know if I can help." I'm not sure why I offered. I was the last person he probably wanted to see.

I was on my way back to my office, when the director of the facility, Leeanne, stopped me.

"Rose, can I have a few minutes?"

"Sure, what's up?"

"In my office, if you don't mind."

I followed her down the hall and took a seat across from her.

"I don't know how else to say this, so I'll just come right out with it. It seems to me you've lost your Zen."

"What do you mean?"

"I sense a disturbance with your peacefulness. Is there something going on that you'd like to discuss?"

I twisted my fingers. This was a topic I didn't care to discuss with her, but maybe she deserved to know. "I'm having issues with my ex-husband and daughter. He's making it difficult on me and I'm noticing some changes in Montana."

"That explains it." She got up and went to her shelf where a dozen or more small vials were stored. Then she came over to me with one and dabbed a drop beneath my nose. "Breathe in."

I smelled lavender and lime.

"You haven't been using your diffuser, have you? Or wearing your necklace?" she asked.

She was referring to my essential oil diffuser and necklace that held a medallion that contained essential oils.

"No. I keep forgetting."

"This will set you back on track, but you must remember, Rose," she scolded.

"I know." I rubbed my forehead with my palm.

"And don't forget to put it on your pillow at night. I hope you're tending to your potted lavender at home."

I offered up a sheepish look.

"Good Lord, Rose. It's a wonder you're not a patient here." She handed me one of her many pots of lavender, a couple of head wreaths, and said, "Now remember to water this. And talk to it. It will love you back."

"Thank you, Leeanne. I have been so preoccupied lately."

"I'm going to be asking after you every day from now on. We at Flower Power must always be in our Zen."

"Yes, yes, you're exactly right. Thank you for my pot." I scurried out of her office and down to mine. Then I set up my own diffuser and got it running with some lavender and lime oils. It filled the room with its lovely scent in no time at all.

Later that afternoon, I saw Pearson as he was leaving late afternoon group and I remembered the extra head wreath in my office. "Pearson, hang on a second." I ran to my office and grabbed the wreath.

He was waiting for me when I came back. "Sylvie told me you missed meditation today, so I wanted you to have this to wear. It's great for calming and soothing."

His eyes bugged out more than just a little. "Um, Rose, I appreciate it, but I'm not sure about this."

I pushed it down on his head before he had much more of a chance to object. He probably thought it wasn't manly enough for him to wear, but to hell with that. When you were fighting addiction issues, you should be open to anything and I told him as much.

"You really believe all this stuff?"

I stuck my hip out as I gave him the eye. "Of course I do. Do you honestly think I'd give you one if I didn't?"

"Maybe as payback, yes."

"I'm not that kind of a person. Ultimately, I'm here to help you. It will put you in your Zen."

He looked around and then nodded. "I'll give it a go. Can't hurt, can it?"

"Not at all. Let me know what you think." Then I went back to my office. It was time to wrap up the day. I needed to speak briefly with Sylvie before I left.

As I was walking to her office, a text popped up. It was from Greg.

Can you keep Montana this weekend? Something came up and we have to go out of town.

Of course, I'd keep her so I answered him quickly so I wouldn't lose my chance. It would be like him to hire someone instead.

Yes, I can do it.

I saw the three dots indicating he was texting me back.

We'll drop her off at the center as it's on our way. We'll be there at five.

I replied back that it was great.

Then I told Sylvie about it when I got to her office.

"Oh, you might mention that to Pearson. He may want you to do something."

"Like what?"

She shrugged. "It may be worth mentioning though."

After giving it some thought, I decided she was right. I gave her the information I needed to share and then left in search of Pearson. I found him in the activity room, where I shared what was happening with him.

"Have you been keeping a file of everything on him?"

"If you mean all the shenanigans he's pulled, then yes."

"Excellent. Continue to do that on everything he does. Even if you think it's something small, write it down."

I nodded, saying, "I've also asked for a schedule of her play-time because she tells me she has to sit in her room a lot."

"That's stretching it a little since she's … how old?"

"Four."

"Yeah, a four-year-old can have a muddled perception of things."

"She acts frightened of him, though."

"Now that's a completely different story. And you've kept notes of this as well?"

"Yes."

"Good. Make sure you bring me your divorce decree and custody papers tomorrow so I'll have time to review them by Friday."

"I will. And, Pearson? I honestly don't know how to thank you."

"Don't mention it."

I turned to walk away but then said with a grin. "No head wreath, huh?"

A sheepish look came over him. "Er, well, I wore it for a while, but then decided to wear it in my room."

"I see. Not very manly, is it?"

"To be honest, no. But I'm going to give it a try. I promise."

"Just remember, staying calm, however you do it, is worth it and much better than using drugs any day."

"Truer words were never spoken. Thanks." He smiled and I swore my pulse raced.

Chapter Ten

PEARSON

I SAT ON THE EDGE OF THE BED AND STARED AT THAT DAMN wreath in my hands. Normally, the thing would already have been in the trash, but every time I went to throw it in there, guilt blanketed me. That was the last thing I needed. I was carrying around so much of it already, adding to it was about to break my back. With a groan, I crammed the thing on my head.

Don't do it, man, don't do it. You'll regret it.

I should've listened to myself, but I wasn't that smart. I checked myself out in the mirror and it about did me in. "So this is what it's come to?" I looked like I belonged in fairyland. "Good thing Hudson and Grey can't see me. I'd never live this shit down."

Sitting back down on the bed, I waited for the calm to descend. The only thing I felt was ridiculous. I decided to give it thirty minutes. Wearing that special crown of foolishness was wearing down my patience. Time sure did crawl when you wanted it to fly. Twenty minutes later I gave up. The thing was making my head itch. A few minutes later my face started itching too, and it wouldn't stop. I looked in the mirror again. My face was bright red and I had a rash. Did she put poison ivy in that thing?

Maybe a shower would wash whatever was in that thing off. I jumped in and shampooed my hair and face, hoping for the best. Evidently, the best wasn't good enough. It only worsened.

An hour later, I went to the front desk, inquiring about how to see a doctor, since the infirmary was closed.

"Wow! You're really red. What happened?"

I explained and it was determined I needed to see a doctor.

"Can you call my cousin Sylvie?"

"Sure."

When she got on the phone, I had to explain it all over again, but this time she laughed.

"It's not funny. I look like a walking tomato."

"Not to worry. I'm on the way."

Ten minutes later she pulled up in front and we drove to the urgent care that Flower Power contracted with.

Sylvie said, "Glad to see you brought the wreath."

"Yeah, and it's the last time I'll wear one of these."

"I'm impressed you put it on."

"I did it in my room. What's in this? Poison ivy?"

She snorted out a laugh. "I can't wait to tell Rose about this."

"I'm so thrilled you find this funny." I scratched my head.

"Stop that. You're only making it worse."

"I feel like I have a million ants biting me."

"Jeez, you must be really allergic to whatever is in there."

I huffed, "Really?"

"Okay. I know you're miserable."

"That's an understatement. But It can't be the lavender because I've been putting some under my pillowcase every night."

"There's eucalyptus and lemon verbena in there. I'll have to call her to see what else."

The urgent care clinic wasn't busy when we arrived. After taking down my information, they called me back. I asked if Sylvie could join us since she was more knowledgeable about these plants. She had already spoken to Rose and had a list of what was in the wreath.

I got the feeling the nurse and doctor both were holding back a laugh when I told them I'd worn the damn thing on my head.

"It's the lemon verbena," the doctor said immediately. "It has the reputation of causing dermatitis and unfortunately, Mr. West, you've developed a severe case of it. I'm going to give you a steroid shot and I want you to follow up with this dose pack starting tomorrow morning. That should straighten you out. You can also add an over-the-counter antihistamine if you'd like, but I don't think you'll need one."

"Doctor, how long before my face stops looking like an award-winning tomato."

The nurse snickered.

"You'll see some improvement by tomorrow."

"Thanks," I said.

As I was leaving, he said, "Stay away from those head wreaths."

If Rose was here, I'd probably choke her. Sylvie left the room so the nurse could give me the shot in my ass. This had turned out to be quite a day.

On the way back to Flower Power, Sylvie ran me by a pharmacy to get my prescription filled. Afterward, we drove back to the center.

"Rose feels terrible."

"She'd feel a lot worse if she were here."

"What do you mean?"

"My snarky disposition would be letting her know."

Sylvie frowned. "Pearson, she was only trying to help."

"I know, but you should've seen how ridiculous I looked in that thing. Do the male patients actually wear them?"

"Nah. We try but it's a hard sell."

"I felt guilty about not wearing it, so I crammed it on my head and look where it got me."

Sylvie cackled. "I'm sorry. I can't help it. We've never had anyone react like that before. And I really wish I had seen you. You probably looked like Caesar."

"More like Caesar salad. And if you ever breathe a word of this to either of my brothers, you're dead to me."

She snorted again.

"Jeez, do you do that a lot?"

"Yeah, I can't help it. My sister says it's super annoying."

"I wouldn't say that." I glanced over at her as she drove. "Hey, why don't our families get together more often. You're a lot of fun. Or at least you seem to be, especially when you snort. I asked my dad and he was real closed-mouth about it."

"Yeah, about that. I think my stupid mom insulted yours at a holiday get together. My dad wouldn't say what she did, but it didn't go over too well. Dad really likes Aunt Paige, but after that, all invitations were declined. Mom was so hardheaded about it, things just fell through the cracks and never got fixed. The truth is, I think our dads still secretly see each other though."

I stared at the road ahead and thought about it. Life was too damn short not to be close to family. "Maybe we should do something about that. After I get out, that is."

"That's not a bad idea. I'd love to see all the babies before they graduate from college."

"Um, I think you have a little time."

We were pulling into the Flower Power entrance and she said, "Pearson, how are you doing here. Really?"

"I'm doing. I have good moments and bad. It's worse when I'm alone. That's when the H monster shouts at me the loudest." Sometimes I wanted to shout right back at it.

"Would you like a roommate?"

Swiveling in the seat so I could look at her, I said, "No. This is real life and what I need. If I can't cope with being alone, I'm going to have a huge problem when I leave."

"Rose really hated having to send you to Jeremy."

"I thought she hated me." I fiddled with a loose string on the seam of my jeans. "She was so antagonistic, I didn't get it."

"It's none of my business, but she really needs your help. Her ex is a major douche. He pulls the worst kind of crap on her. I'm not blaming you in any way. I'm just making you aware."

My chest cramped in a weird way. I wished this guilt about winning that case would leave me. "I'm going to help her. Maybe we can turn this thing around for her."

"Oh, Pearson, I hope so. Montana is everything to her."

"Montana?"

"That's Rose's daughter."

We sat in silence for a moment. "Let me get out of your hair. It's getting late and you have to be back here soon. Thanks for saving me from the doom of tomato face."

She grinned. "I would never let you suffer, Pearson."

We hugged and I got out of the car. She drove off as I waved.

Montana. The name fit. I bet her daughter was a mini-Rose too.

Chapter Eleven

ROSE

THE NEXT MORNING, SYLVIE SNUCK INTO MY OFFICE AND SHUT the door. "Don't be upset, but I have something to tell you." Then she explained what happened to Pearson. Before she could stop me, I was racing out of my office to find him. He was in his first group session and when I opened the door, I was in time to hear one of the members ask, "Who's that sitting in Pearson's chair?" Then everyone snickered.

Pearson answered, "Go ahead and call me Tomato Face."

"What happened?" someone else asked.

"I had a reaction to lemon verbena." That's when he noticed me standing there. "Will you all excuse me for a moment?"

We walked into the hall and I said, "I am so sorry. You look awful."

"You should've seen me last night. At least the itching is better."

I reached a hand up but then drew it back. I was about to take liberties I shouldn't be. "I had no idea you'd react so badly."

"You sure about that?" he asked as the corner of his mouth turned up.

I frowned and bit my lip. Sure, I was angry over the custody thing, but I wasn't the type of person to intentionally harm someone. "I would never hurt anyone like that. Well, other than my ex."

"I was joking. I know you didn't do it on purpose, but last night I probably wouldn't have been so gracious. My face burned like fire. I thought you put poison ivy in that thing."

I inhaled sharply. The idea of doing that made my insides clench. "Oh, I couldn't possibly—"

"Rose, I know you couldn't. I was only kidding."

It was strange to think about him kidding about this. "Okay," I said hesitantly. "But I hope your face gets better."

"You and me both. Sylvie took me to the urgent care center, and I've taken some medication so I should be fine by tomorrow." He aimed his thumb over his shoulder. "I probably should get back to group."

"Right. I'll see you later. And Pearson, I really am sorry."

"Duly noted."

He went back into the room, and I just stood there like a dork. Why did he have such a strange effect on me? I shook myself out of my Pearson trance and slowly walked back to my office. On the way, I passed Sylvie.

"You okay?" she asked.

"I think so. His face looks awful."

"I haven't seen him yet today, but it was bad last night. Was he pissed at you?"

"Not at all, which is surprising."

Sylvie grinned.

"What?"

"Nothing. I have to go. Busy day."

Her behavior was also perplexing. She acted like she had some kind of secret. I pushed those thoughts aside and focused

71

on work. I had several patients this morning, one being new, so my head needed to be straight.

By the time noon rolled around, I was more than ready for a break. The morning had been tough. That new patient was really struggling, and so were the other two I'd seen. They'd all but drained me. I was just getting ready to leave my office and head for the cafeteria when Pearson dropped by. "Can we talk?" he asked.

"Sure. Are you going to lunch now?"

"I was after we talked."

"Let's go. I'm starved." After we filled our plates and took our seats, he wanted to know what time Greg was dropping off Montana on Friday.

"He said around five."

I watched him place a forkful of lasagna into his mouth and chew. He made eating a sensual experience. His mouth was ... wow. I needed to get my head out of the gutter. Fanning myself would look inappropriate, but it had suddenly gotten very hot in here.

"I'd like to be close enough to listen to your exchange with him. Is that possible?"

"Yeah, you can sit on my lap." What the hell did I just say?

"Excuse me?" He eyed me with a smirk.

I quickly blurted, "The front office. Behind the glass partition. You can sit there."

"Will he be able to see me, because if he does, he'll recognize me."

I thought about this and said, "No, the partition will hide you. He won't pay attention to that."

"Good. I also want you to let him know you want to stay on schedule with your weekends. In other words, this is not a switch weekend."

"He's not going to like that." I could only imagine his reaction.

"It doesn't matter. He initiated this change, not you. I'm

going to record what his response is. I want you to be cordial and just say you want to keep with the schedule and will pick her up at the regular time the following Friday. When he reacts, remain calm and remind him that he requested this, not you."

"What if he gets angry?" Greg didn't just get mad, he became explosive and sometimes violent.

"That's exactly what I'm hoping for. I want him to react negatively."

The thought of Greg getting angry and how he would exact his revenge worried me. Anxiety clawed at my stomach, making it nothing but a twisting jumble. "What if he takes it out on my daughter?"

"Do you think he'd do that?"

"I'm not sure. He's really vindictive."

"After he leaves on Friday, would you mind if I asked your daughter a few questions?"

"As long as it doesn't upset her."

"They'll be questions about games and TV shows, things she does at both houses."

"That's fine, but if you see her getting upset, will you stop?"

"Rose, you're going to be there too, so if you don't like what I'm asking, just interrupt me, but I promise, they'll be very generic."

"Okay." My hands were clenched, but I didn't realize it until he grabbed them and unfolded them.

"It'll be fine. I do have one more favor. I need to use a computer. It's against the rules and I don't have access."

"I don't think—"

"Hear me out. I want to contact my friend to ask him about taking this case. That's all."

I was between a rock and a hard place. He must've noticed my hesitation because he said, "Let me talk to Sylvie. She may be able to help. This way I won't put you in a bad position."

"Thank you. I can't believe you want to help me. I mean after everything ..." My voice trailed off.

73

He flashed me a brilliant smile. "You mean after you turned me into Tomato Face?"

My face heated and I must've matched his in color. "That, but after our beginning, I guess. I really lost my Zen and went crazy for a while, which is totally unlike me. But I'm back in my groove now and I promise not to act like that anymore." I patted the wreath on my head for reassurance.

He grimaced. "Everyone goes through difficult times. Look what I'm facing ahead and we've both apologized, so how about we move forward on this? The way I've treated people because of my addiction ... it's hard for me to even think about right now."

"This may not be any consolation yet, but number nine in the twelve steps will help you deal with that when the time comes."

"I hope I have the guts to face them all. I've injured my family, told lies. And hurt some of the people I worked with. I missed court dates. I hurt clients. There's a lot to own up to."

I tapped his arm. "You're in the company of all recovering addicts I've worked with. You'll get through it. If you follow everything you learn here and then through NA, I promise it will work. It seems like a mountainous task right now, and it is. But you do it one step at a time."

He drank his water, and then his blue-grays homed in on mine. "Can I ask you something?"

"Sure."

"How'd you get into this? I mean, it has to be draining dealing with these types of people."

"To the contrary. I find it to be very uplifting. When I see how I've helped someone and they succeed, it's very rewarding. But I also grew up with a drug abuser and alcoholic who died and never got help. That's what pushed me to doing this." It was shocking that I'd disclosed this to him. This was one of my darkest secrets.

"That must've have been difficult."

Suddenly, my lap is very interesting. This discussion has

become quite uncomfortable. "Yeah, something like that," I mumbled.

"Hey, I'm sorry. I don't mean to pry."

I puff out a breath. "It's not something I usually discuss."

"Understood. I need to get going anyway. I have my appointment with Jeremy soon."

"I hope you are getting along with him."

"He's fine. Let's talk again on Friday morning and you can let me know when to meet you in the afternoon."

"Sounds great and thank you again." I remained seated as he left and wondered why I revealed to him about my home life. That's information even some of my closest friends didn't know. Not only that, he was a patient here and it seemed excessively chummy. I needed to check my behavior with him before I was in too deep.

Chapter Twelve

Pearson

When Friday rolled around, I was fully prepared. It had been quite a while since I'd worn my attorney hat and the excitement had built over the week. I hadn't realized how much I'd missed my work, but I certainly didn't miss the pressure of the firm. Every time I thought about going back, my body reacted in a way that made me want to use. That was certainly telling.

Around 4:45, I went to meet Rose. She was waiting in her office and we walked up front together.

"Gosh, I really hope this works."

"Look Rose, the worst that can happen is he exhibits no reaction at all. But from what you've told me, I doubt he'll do that."

She stopped for a moment. "I just don't want Montana to be upset."

"And we'll do everything we can to prevent that. If he starts to act up, can you send her into the office away from him?"

"I will, but she clings to me when he's like that, especially when she's away from his house."

"Then try to minimize his reaction. Yes, we want him to be the asshole, but we also don't want her harmed in the process."

She reached into her bag and pulled out some toys. "I brought these. I'll put them in the office so she can play with them. If he gets too out of line, I'll tell her these are in there and maybe she'll go and play with them."

"Will she be afraid of me?"

"You'll be outside where she'll be, so I don't think so. Just act busy, like maybe you're doing paperwork or something."

"Got it."

She set me up behind the partitioned glass, as planned, and then put Montana's toys inside one of the administrative offices. Then we waited. At five sharp, he entered the facility with Montana. I heard the girl yell, "Mommy."

Then Rose said, "How's my little Pop Tart doing?"

I imagined them hugging and kissing, and then Rose said, "I sure have missed you."

Greg interrupted the exchange. "I'm in a hurry."

"Oh, one thing. Since this was your request, I'll pick her up next Friday at the usual time."

"Like hell you will," he roared. "You are to have her every other weekend and that's it."

"I'm sorry, Greg, but you initiated this switch. This will throw us off schedule and my weekends are planned way ahead of time."

"Fine, then don't get her the following week."

"I'm not going to do that. That would mean me not seeing her for three weeks and that's not happening. I'll just pick her up next weekend like I'm supposed to."

"Not if we're not there, you won't."

"What does that mean?"

"Mommy," Montana whined. "I want to be with you next weekend too."

"Honey, why don't you go into that door over there. Some of your favorite toys are inside so you can play."

Greg sneered, "You indulge her too much."

"How is that even possible? I'm only with her four days a month."

"Exactly. Because you're an unfit mother."

"And can you explain how I'm an unfit mother?"

"You don't do anything for her."

"So, I don't do anything for her. Did I get it?"

"Yes."

"Is there more?"

"Hell yeah, there's more. We have to do it all."

"Greg, I would gladly do more, but it's not possible in four days a month."

"You don't deserve even that."

"And why is that?"

"Because you're a terrible mother."

"You keep saying that but don't back it up."

As I sat and listened, the desire to see his body language was overwhelming. His tone was hostile, but was he making threatening gestures? I didn't dare stand up, although I wanted to with everything inside of me.

"I don't have to back it up goddammit. I'm the custodial parent and you obviously can't get that through that stupid head of yours."

"Greg, please. You don't have to insult me."

"I wasn't insulting you. I was telling you the fucking truth," he said in a blistering tone. This guy clearly had anger problems. She had not provoked him in any way.

"Watch your language, please."

"I'm a grown man. I can say whatever the hell I want to. You're nothing but a conniving bitch. Let me tell you something. If you think you can manipulate our visitation agreement, you have another thing coming. I will take you back to court and strip you of all visitation. I will get Montana to lie about how you're treating her."

Rose gasped. "Why would you do such a thing? She's my daughter!"

"Because I can and because I would derive great pleasure from it."

"But I don't understand why."

"I know. You never understand anything. I'll pick her up on Sunday. Enjoy the weekend. It just might be your last."

I heard the door open and close. Rose walked back and tears were flowing down her cheeks.

"You heard?"

"I have it all on here." I held up my recorder. "He has problems and I'm very sorry. But I'm going to help you. I promise. Now I think there's someone who's anxious to see you."

"I'm sure, but I need a minute."

"Do you mind if I talk to her now? I'll record everything."

"Go ahead. Nothing could possibly be as bad as what she goes through every day with that father of hers."

"Hopefully, he treats her okay, but that's what I plan on finding out." I hoped she'd be open enough to talk about it to a stranger.

Opening the door, the curly-headed girl looked up at me from her book she was flipping through.

"Who are you?"

I expected her to shy away from me, but she didn't.

"My name is Pearson. What's yours?"

"I'm not 'sposed to talk to strangers. You're a stranger." She folded her tiny arms and stared at me. I wanted to chuckle but didn't.

"I'm not really a stranger. I'm a friend of your mommy's."

"Nope. I never seen you before." She pointed a finger at me. "I know all mommy's friends."

"Would you believe me if I told you I lived here?"

Her tiny brows scrunched together, and she reminded me of my niece, Kinsley. She did that a lot.

"Mister, whatcha gotta live here for?"

"It's only for a while, but I'm here for help. You know how your mommy helps people? I'm one of those people."

"Oh. Can I see your room? Does it have flowers on the walls. You got your own TV?"

"Maybe you can see it later. And I don't have my own TV. But what's your favorite TV show?"

She hugged the book to her chest. "Don't have one."

"You don't? Why not?"

She pulled her little shoulders almost up to her ears. "I don't watch TV much."

"Aw, you don't like it?"

"I do. But my daddy won't let me."

"Some daddies don't let their kids watch it. Does he let you watch movies?"

"No. I got to watch a movie on my birthday. And got popcorn too." She doesn't sound very enthusiastic.

"What's your favorite thing to do at home?"

She puts a finger on her cheek and says, "Um, I play with dolls in my room. I stay there mostly."

"Do you play games in there?" I asked.

"What kind of games?"

"Oh, I don't know. Does your daddy come in and play with you?"

"No. He says he's too busy and not to bother him."

"What about his wife?"

She started swinging her legs back and forth. "She doesn't like games."

"Montana, are you ever scared there?" Her lip started quivering and this was worse than I thought. "Hey, come here." I opened my arms. She hopped off the chair and ran right into them.

"Don't tell my daddy, okay? He said never to tell."

"It's okay." I rubbed her small back and mumbled soothing words to her. "I used to be scared a lot when I was young." But not every fucking day of my life. I picked her up and sat her on my knee. "Are you scared at your mommy's?"

"No, I like it at Mommy's. Daddy yells when I go there."

"I see. Do you play games at your mommy's?"

"Yeah. And Mommy reads me stories."

"What's your favorite?"

"The Secret Garden. I want a garden. With lots of flowers. Do you like flowers?"

As long as it's not lemon verbena. "I love flowers. What kind of flowers are your favorite?"

"Like Mommy has, red ones. And pink ones. I like pink best."

"What's your favorite thing to eat?"

She smiled. "Mommy's chocolate chip cookies. Daddy never lets me have cookies. He says they're not good for me."

"Ever?"

"Nope. Only fruit. I get meat." And she made a funny face. We laughed together.

"I love meat."

"Yucky."

Rose walked in then and smiled at us. "I see you've met my friend."

"He was a stranger but said he was your friend. I said he wasn't cuz I know all your friends."

"Good girl for checking," Rose said. She gestured to me and then said, "Montana, can you wait here for just another minute and then we can leave."

"Okay."

I set her down on the chair and followed Rose out. When we got out of hearing distance, I turned off the voice recorder and said, "I'm not going to lie. Unless she just filled me with a bunch of BS, your girl is basically a prisoner in her room over there. I'll let you listen to this and you can tell me if you think she's telling the truth or not. I'll need it for my notes though. This is compelling evidence of neglect on his part, not to mention the things he said to you before I spoke to her. And I'll say I agree with you. The guy's a major asshole."

Rose looked like she was going to cry again.

"Rose, listen to me. You have to play this off like you don't know. If we're going to catch this guy at his worst, he can't know what you're up to. Go get Montana, take her home and have a fabulous weekend. I'll start working on this, get in touch with my friend through Sylvie, and get the ball rolling. But I need to send this to him. And I'll also need to stay in touch with him because —I'm not trying to pat myself on the back—but I'm a better attorney when it comes to winning these cases."

They left and I went to hunt for Sylvie. She was still in her office, finishing up paperwork.

"Pearson, glad to see your face has returned to normal."

Not waiting to take a seat, I rushed in saying, "Thanks. I need an urgent favor. I need to send an email to a friend—the one who I'm going to ask to represent Rose in her custody battle."

"Whoa, whoa, slow down, buddy. Excited much?"

"Not lately, but this is really important. I just witnessed, well, more like heard, the interaction between Rose and her ex. The guy's a major prick. And her daughter? I asked her some questions and let me just say, I'm all in on this one. But I need to contact my friend, Miles Sinclair. He's the one who I'm going to ask to handle the case. I know I don't have access to a computer for another two weeks, but this can't wait until I get out. If you can send it care of my name, we can get this thing started."

She gave me a hard look. "Are you sure about this? Montana is Rose's world. No false hope here?"

"I'm never one hundred percent sure about winning a case, but I won it for him, and I think I can unwin it." I held up the recorder.

"What's that?"

"It's a handheld recorder. I use it for work but brought it with me. I figured I'd record my thoughts when I was super down or doing really well so I could replay them to help me combat the lows. Anyway, it came in handy today, because I sat behind the glass partition and recorded Greg and Rose's interaction. Then I asked Montana some questions and recorded that too. Miles will need to hear this for the case."

"Are those admissible?"

"The one between Rose and her ex might be but not the one between Montana and me. I want Miles to go for child neglect though. That's why the urgency. And I can't be involved since I'm a patient here anyway."

"Okay. What do you want to send?"

I asked if I could type it out. "You're free to read it. It's just easier for me."

"Sure. Have at it."

I quickly typed out the email, which ended up being fairly long. I had to explain why someone else was sending it. I also told him where I was and why I couldn't take the case. I did tell him I would reimburse him for it too. When I was done, I told Sylvie she could look at it.

"I trust you. Go on and send it."

I did and hoped he didn't ignore it. If I didn't hear back in the next day or so, my next step would be to ask Sylvie if I could send it from my own account. I knew that was completely overstepping my bounds, but I didn't know what else to do.

We parted ways, and I went to my room to formulate a plan. Miles would need information from Rose, as in how many times she had issues with Greg. She said she'd kept records. I was hoping they were meticulous. I was also hoping that her experience as a psychologist would aid us in this. I would ask Miles to have Montana analyzed by a child psychologist and pull all her preschool records—what her interactions with other students were like as well as her teachers. He needed to see if there had been any significant changes in her behavior over the last eighteen months.

My notepad quickly filled up with things for him to do. I hoped he didn't resent me or think I was being bossy, but I wanted no stone unturned. When I read the custodial arrangements, it was easy to see how Greg won custody. He was more stable at the time because Rose was still in school and working while they were separated. I had made the case that she wouldn't have much time to spend with Montana. Currently, the situation was totally different. If worst came to worst, we could push for a fifty-fifty split.

But then I realized something. I didn't want a fifty-fifty split for Rose. I wanted her to be the custodial parent. And this time it wouldn't be because of the money I'd gain in winning the case. This time it wouldn't be because of the recognition I'd get from the partners in the firm. This time it would be because it was the right thing to do.

Chapter Thirteen

ROSE

"Mommy, why does Daddy yell at you all the time?" Montana asked. I knew the questions would come eventually, as they always did.

"I don't know sweetie. But, how about pizza night tonight?"

"Yay! Daddy never lets me have pizza."

We were home by now and I'd gotten her things out of the car. As we walked inside, I asked, "What do you do at Daddy's?"

"Stay in my room." The excitement left her voice when she told me that.

"Does Caroline play with you much?" Caroline was wife number two.

"No, she says not to bother her. And Daddy yells at her a lot too."

Taking her hand in mine, I went and sat on the couch and pulled her onto my lap. Brushing her curls back, I asked, "What do you do after you get home from school?" She went to preschool from morning to noon.

"I eat lunch then go to my room."

"Do you ever have any playdates?"

She stared at her lap as her head swiveled back and forth.

"What do you do in your room?"

"Play with my animals mostly. And my friend, Mazie."

"Mazie?"

"Yeah. Miss Caroline yells at me when I talk to her. She tells me not to do that."

"Why not?"

"Because she's my make-believe friend. I talk to her real quiet so she can't hear me, but she sleeps a lot. And is mean. Her and Daddy fight when he gets home, and he yells at me too."

My hand rubs circles on her back. "Oh my, sweetie. Why haven't you told me this before?"

"Daddy says never to tell you anything."

"Montana, does Daddy ever hit you?"

She bows her head and nods.

"He does?"

"Sometimes. When I don't hear him, but I can't when I'm in my room."

"What do you mean?"

"He calls me and he's in the kitchen, but I can't hear him."

"Why do you stay in your room?"

"The door is locked. I have to."

What the fuck! "The door is locked?"

"Uh huh."

Bile rose to my throat when she told me this. The bastard was locking her in her room. What the hell was going on over there?

"I have an idea. When the pizza gets here, let's have a movie night? How does that sound?"

She clapped her hands and yelled, "Yay! Fun night!"

I got up and brought over a stack of DVDs I'd bought for her so she could pick one out. Then I decided to try to get Pearson on the phone.

"I have to make a phone call, sweets. I'll be right back."

When the center answered, I asked them to page him. He came to the phone and I relayed everything she told me. "Do you want to talk to her again tomorrow?"

"Rose, it's not really necessary. I'm waiting to hear back from my friend and as soon as I do, we'll institute a plan. I'll pass this along to him. My guess is he'll file a lawsuit demanding sole custody and request that Montana undergo a formal psychological evaluation to see if she's been traumatized. Your ex will fight that of course. He'll call my firm and they'll tell him I'm unavailable. Someone else will handle the case. That's good news for you because no one there is as good as I am." He chuckled and the sound caused electricity to race up my spine. I shouldn't be feeling like this while discussing my daughter's wellbeing.

"Pearson, I'm really frightened."

"I can hear it in your voice. I promise to do all I can."

"On Sunday, should I say something to Greg?"

"I wouldn't. He may take it out on Montana for telling you."

My stomach twisted into knots. "I hadn't thought of that. He's always been a jerk to me, but I never thought he'd treat her like this."

"Try to stay calm and enjoy your time with her. And make it a fun time for her. She looks forward to being with you."

"Okay. I gotta go and order pizza. Thanks. You've been a big help."

"See ya Monday. Oh, and Rose. When he picks her up on Sunday, make sure you record him."

"Great idea."

"You can do it on your cell phone."

"Right. Thanks for the tip."

I ordered the pizza and then checked on Montana. She was happily watching TV, because I suspected it was a novelty for her.

"So, doodlebug, what would you like to do tomorrow?"

Her mouth scrunched up as she asked hesitantly, "Can we go see the monkeys?"

"You mean at the zoo?"

"Uh huh."

"Sure! I think that's an awesome idea. I miss seeing them."

She got up and hopped around then suddenly stopped and looked at me. "What's wrong?"

"I'm not supposed to do that."

"Do what?"

"Jump up and down."

"Why ever not?"

"Miss Caroline says it hurts her head."

What's this Miss Caroline crap? "Hmm. Well, guess what?"

"What?"

"It doesn't hurt mine a bit so jump around all you want. In fact, since we are going to the zoo, I think we should pretend we're animals and we have to try and guess what each other is. Want to do that?"

"Yeah!"

"You first."

She put her hands in front of her and started hopping around the room. She resembled a kangaroo, but I said, "You're a bunny rabbit."

"Nope."

"A frog?"

A giggle burst out of her. "I'm not a frog."

"A leaping lemur."

Now she was all out laughing. "What's a leaping lemur?"

"Well, it kind of looks like a monkey but has a long striped tail."

She hopped over to me and laid her head on my lap as she giggled. "I'm not a leaping lemur. I'm a kangaroo."

"A kangaroo? Dang, you got me!" Then I tickled her until she rolled around.

"Your turn, Mommy."

I stood and hung my arms in front of me. I swung them back and forth.

"You're an elephant."

"How'd you get to be so smart?"

She lifted her shoulders up. "I dunno." She had a huge grin on her face and my heart twisted. If I couldn't get her back from the man who was stealing away her happiness, I was pretty damn certain I'd die.

"I do. Because you're my daughter. Get over here right now so I can give you a big fat squishy hug."

She ran straight into my arms and we squeezed each other. "Have I told you how much I love you today?"

"Nope."

"I love you more than pizza and stars."

"I love you more than Mazie."

"I love you more than pancakes and chocolate chip cookies."

"You do?"

Pulling her away so I could see her face, I said, "Montanaroo, you are the most important thing in the world to me. Do you understand what that means?"

"I think so."

"It means I love you more than everything else in the world."

"I love you too, Mommy."

The doorbell rang and she hollered, "Pizza's here."

"It sure is. Let me go and pay for it. You sit right here."

I grabbed the money and made the exchange. Then I got our plates and napkins and put the movie *Coco* in. Thirty minutes in we were happily munching on chocolate chip cookies and an hour later, she was fast asleep. I picked her up and carried her to my bed. I didn't want to spend one minute away from this little treasure. It broke me into pieces every time I thought about her expression when she told me about having to stay in her room. Something was seriously wrong over there and I was going to get to the bottom of it.

I got ready for bed and climbed in with my baby. Then I read a book for a while before falling asleep. The next morning, I decided it was going to be chocolate chip pancakes for breakfast.

Slipping out of bed, I got the coffee brewing and the batter ready. Montana was an early riser, so I expected her to be up any minute. I had one large stack of pancakes warming in the oven when she made it into the kitchen. Her hair was a tangled mass of curls and she looked absolutely adorable.

"Oh, my goodness. Look who's awake! It's the cookie monster." Bubbling laughter tumbled out of her.

"I'm not the cookie monster."

"Yes, you are. But guess what? We have chocolate chip pancakes for breakfast. And whipped cream."

"We do?"

"You bet. Come on and sit. I'll fix up our plates."

Everything was ready, minus the syrup and whipped cream, which I snagged out of the refrigerator. I poured on the syrup for her, then the whipped cream. Admittedly, they looked yummy.

"Cheers." We clinked glasses—my coffee mug and her milk glass. She loved doing that. Then we dug in.

"Mmm. These are good, Mommy."

"I'm glad you like them."

We both polished off our breakfast, then I hopped into the shower while she stayed in the bathroom. After we were dressed, we left for the zoo.

I snapped dozens of pictures of her petting the deer, goats, and llamas, and then we went to see the monkeys. After that, we checked out the bears, elephants, tigers, and lions. During the day, we ate tons of junk food. Every time I went to buy something, she'd ask if it was okay if she ate it. I had to assure her that it was fine. It made me wonder what the poor child was fed over there.

On the way home, she conked out in her booster seat. When we got home, I woke her up, but a huge dose of sadness nailed me. I realized my time with her would be ending soon and I didn't want it to. I wanted to hold her forever and never let anything bad happen to her. But I knew tomorrow would bring darkness into her world. Until then, I would make the rest of her stay as much fun as I could.

We went inside and I let her pick out any TV show she wanted to watch. Then I asked her where she wanted to eat dinner that night.

"You mean we get to go out?"

"Why not?"

"Daddy never takes me out. If he and Miss Caroline go out, they get a babysitter."

"When the babysitter comes, do you play with her?"

"Sometimes."

"When you don't, what do you do?"

"Stay in my room."

It made me wonder whether or not they actually even got a babysitter. Maybe they were leaving her at home alone. I needed to tell Pearson about this.

"Well, you and I are going out to dinner tonight and you get to pick the restaurant."

"I pick McDonald's."

Oh, boy. Lucky me. I was hoping for something nicer, but it was her choice.

"Okie dokie. That's where we'll go."

"Can I get a sundae for dessert?"

"I don't see why not."

She skipped around the room and yelled at the top of her lungs. "I get a sundae tonight."

"But first, I need to brush your hair."

"Do you gotta?"

"Yep. You look like a ragamuffin."

"What's that?"

"It's a messy muffin."

She ran up to me and squeezed my cheeks together. "Muffins can't be messy, silly."

"Oh, yes they can. Watch this." I picked her up and started

tickling her until she screamed. We both laughed like crazy. "See how messy that was?"

She cocked her head to the side, then plowed her hands into my hair and pushed them around making my hair look like a rat's nest. "Now you're a ragamuffin too."

"I'm really gonna get you now."

And the tickling commenced. We laughed until we couldn't laugh anymore.

That night, I dreamed all sorts of horrifying things. Montana was crying in her room for hours and no one came to check on her. She was frightened and all her father did was yell at her to shut up. I woke before the sun rose, shaken and disturbed over having to send her back to him. How could I do this to her? I didn't have much of a choice, other than to ask him if I could keep her for the week. It was at least worth a try.

At eight o'clock, I called him.

"Yeah."

Nice way to answer the phone. "I was wondering if you minded if I kept Montana for the week. I'd bring her back to you next Sunday."

His hostile voice came back to me. "Now why would you ever think I'd do that?"

"Because I'm her mother and I love her."

"You honestly don't get it, do you?"

"Get what?"

His cruel laughter sent cold chills throughout me. "I don't give a flying fuck about your feelings or hers for that matter. I'll do anything I can to keep the two of you apart." And he hung up. How could I send her back there? I ran to the bathroom and threw up. My daughter, my life, was being mistreated and there wasn't a damn thing I could do about it.

Chapter Fourteen

Pearson

THE URGES HIT ME DURING THE NIGHT. THEY WERE WORSE than I'd had in a long time. I ended up waking one of the counselors on staff so they could talk me off the ledge.

"It's stupid because I know I'm safe here."

"It's not stupid," John said. "Heroin does this. Just when you think you're getting away from it, it grips you again. Think about your day. Do you have any idea what could've precipitated this?"

"Yeah. When I was an attorney, I had unscrupulous clients that I represented. Now I'm feeling guilty about it."

"And the drugs would make you forget."

"Not forget exactly. They would make it easier to accept it. My partners were all about the money and I went with it."

John leaned forward and asked, "Pearson, what pushed you into this thought process? Something must've triggered it."

"A friend of mine is going through a custody battle. The problem is, it's my fault she's there right now."

"I'm not sure I get it."

"I represented her ex and gained him custody of their kid."

"Ah, I see now. And the guilt is weighing down on you."

"Yes, dammit, because he's a son of a bitch. She's the good one of the two."

He stood and squeezed my shoulder. "You're doing the right thing. Accepting and acknowledging your wrongdoing and moving forward."

"You don't understand. She's just one."

"What do you mean?"

"She's just one of hundreds I did that to."

He crouched down in front of me and locked eyes with me. "Guilt is a terrible thing to carry. Do you believe in a higher power? It can be God, Buddha, or whatever you choose."

"I do."

"Then you'll have to ask that higher power for forgiveness, because it's probably unlikely that you'll find all the people you've caused harm to over the years to do it individually. In the twelve steps, number eight has you do this whenever possible. It may not be for you. In your case, you'll have to lean on your higher power."

"I can try."

"Yes, you can. But your law firm would have to release those case files to you. Do you think they would?"

He was right and I had no intention of returning there. "No, since I'm not planning on going back."

"Pearson, there are many ways to make amends, but right now, you're jumping ahead. Let's get your urges under control. The great thing about this is you figured out the trigger. When you feel this way, we have to find out how to handle it."

Would I ever get to the point where I could deal with it on my own, and not run for help? I felt like such a big pussy.

"I see those wheels spinning in your head. You're six and a half weeks out. You have made amazing progress. Think about where you were six and a half weeks ago. You nearly died!"

I rubbed my palms together. He was right. I tended to see the negative side of things. "True. I need to start being more positive."

"Exactly. When you have those urges, remind yourself how much less they are now than they used to be. Can I ask you something?"

"Sure."

"When you were using, how often did those urges hit?"

A bitter laugh filled the room.

"I think you just answered me. And now? Every day? Once a day?"

"Not even. Every other day."

Would you consider that progress?" he asked.

"Yeah. But I don't want them at all."

"No one does. I'm going to tell you something. It will never be that way. You are always going to have them."

I hung my head and said, "I know." It was difficult to realize, but I knew I'd live with this for the rest of my life.

"You'll find a way to live with them. You'll have to. That's where NA comes in."

"How do you do it?" I asked.

"With great difficulty, but I've learned so much about myself. And it's earned me a family who loves and supports me, so I won't let them down." John was a recovering heroin addict too.

"And the urges? How often?"

"Not every day, but I still have them."

"How many years?"

"I've been clean for seven years."

"Congratulations."

"I never take a day for granted." He pulled out his chip from NA. "It's with me all the time."

"Thanks. For listening and for helping."

"Anytime, man. You know where to find me. Every day is a discovery."

All the words made sense. Every single one. If I could come

out of this a better man, maybe the addiction was all for a purpose. And if so, I was going to make something of it.

When I crawled back in bed, sleep came easy. John helped with the guilt, but I prayed for God's help. It was the first time I did that in as long as I could remember.

The next morning, Sylvie stopped me and said she had an email from my friend I needed to read and that I should come with her to her office. On the way, we saw Rose. She looked terrible.

"Rose, what's going on?" Sylvie asked. That's all it took for Rose to break down crying. Sylvie put her arm around her, and we all went to Sylvie's office.

When Rose explained what her ex said, and what Montana said, I wanted to smash my fist into the wall.

"Can he do that?" Sylvie asked me.

"Yeah, unfortunately. But let me see Miles' email." I read it and it was good news. He was taking the case and wanted everything we had. I relayed the information to the women.

"That's great," Sylvie said. Rose didn't respond.

"Sylvie, I'll need you to scan Rose's divorce and custody decree and email it to him. And can you mail the audio tape of what we have from Friday. Is that possible?"

"Yes."

"Rose, did you get anything else on audio when he picked up Montana on Sunday?"

"Just a little." She handed me her phone and I listened. On it was him reminding her he would do his best to keep her away from Montana as much as possible.

"This will work. Can I copy this to the tape I'm mailing him?"

Rose was so despondent, she only gave me a slight nod. "Listen, Rose, we're going to get him. It may take a while, but we'll do it."

I took her phone to my room and quickly recorded what Greg said, then went back to Sylvie's office. Sylvie caught my eye and slightly shook her head. I handed Rose her phone and said, "I'm going to help Miles. I promise you, this evidence should help push the judge over to your side. We'll also go for child support. I want to hire a private investigator and look into what they do when they go out. If they're leaving your daughter home alone, locked in her room, that's child abuse by neglect and we can have her removed from the home immediately."

"You think so?" Rose asked, perking up.

"I know so. We'll get this ball rolling today."

"Um, Pearson, we, as in you, Jeremy and I, need to discuss what you're going to do as of next Friday."

"Next Friday?"

"It's your soft release day."

"Really?"

Sylvie laughed. "Don't tell me you've had so much fun here you haven't kept track of time.

"Yes, I mean, no. I'm just caught up in Rose's case I suppose."

"You have the option of extending it week by week if you want. Do you think you can live on your own?"

"No! I mean, last night I had to get John's help, so I'm not ready."

"Understood. What about a group home?" Sylvie asked.

"I'm not sure that's for me either."

"Your parents'?"

I chuckled. "Um, no. I love them to death, but they would drive me crazy."

"I get that too. Do you have any other suggestions?"

"I do," Rose piped in. "I have a room I can rent to you."

Sylvie and I both stared at her, with Sylvie being the first to speak. "Rose? Are you sure about this?" Her tone was laden with skepticism.

"Yes. The extra money would be beneficial."

"But a roommate. And a man?" Sylvie asked.

"Yeah, and what about your privacy?" I added.

"That won't be a problem. I have two bathrooms, one in my bedroom. I have a TV in my room, so if I want my privacy, I can sneak off there."

"But what if you want to bring … like what if you have a date or something?" I asked.

"Then I have a date. But the point is, you'll have an addiction counselor at your beck and call, which will help you get through the next transition. And you'll be attending NA every day. And I'll have some extra cash from your rent."

It did sound plausible and like a pretty good deal. "What about when Montana visits?"

"What about it? She has her own room and sometimes she sleeps with me anyway."

Sounds like she'd thought it through.

"Okay. I'm in if you think you can tolerate me. Sylvie, your thoughts?"

Sylvie eyed the two of us then grinned. "I think it's a smashing idea. I like it because Rose will keep good tabs on you, Pearson. As long as you two don't kill each other."

"I think we've established a solid truce. What do you think, Rose?"

"Seriously? With everything you're doing for Montana and me, I'd be crazy not to have called one."

It's a deal then." I held out my hand and Rose took it. Her skin was soft and smooth, and I had an urge to turn her hand over and press my lips to it. I hoped this was a good idea. It might be a challenge for me in more ways than one.

Chapter Fifteen

ROSE

WHEN I WENT TO PICK UP MONTANA THE FOLLOWING FRIDAY, Greg wasn't there. No one answered the door. I stayed for two hours. Anger, frustration, fear for my daughter's welfare were bubbling inside like a volcano on the verge of erupting. In an act of desperation, I decided to walk around the house in search of Montana's window. I wasn't even certain if her room was on the first floor. But I checked in each of the windows, even though I had to stand on my tiptoes, and when I got to one of the side windows, a light was on. I pressed my face against the window, trying to see between the slats of the blinds. I saw a figure lying on a bed, but it was too large to be Montana. It must be Greg's room. I guess they just didn't want to acknowledge my presence.

Returning to the front door, I rang the bell again and pounded on the door. Greg wouldn't answer his phone either. I decided to call Pearson.

When he came to the phone at the center, I asked, "Should I call the cops?"

"Tell me what's going on first."

I filled him in.

"You could make a case that he's not sticking to the agreement. Do you have it with you?"

"I actually do."

"Call Miles first."

"Okay. Thanks."

When Miles got on the phone, he said, "Call the police, but not the 911 number, since this isn't a true emergency."

"Oh, God, I'm scared. This is really going to piss him off." I looked around the neighborhood. It was getting dark already.

"Rose, did he ever hit you?"

My brain fired into a million different directions. Scenes flashed like lightning in front of my eyes, but I willed them away.

"Rose, you still there?"

"Uh, yeah, I'm here," I said hoarsely.

"He's an abuser, isn't he?"

I cleared the clotted mess out of my throat. "Yeah," I whispered. "I told my divorce attorney, but he didn't do anything about it."

"Stay put. I'm on the way." It was very difficult to stay put when your nerves were raw, and you feared for your child's safety. But Miles pulled up about twenty minutes later.

He parked behind me on the street and flew out of his car at a run. "The police are on the way. Are you okay?"

"No! I want my daughter." I shoved my custody papers into his hands.

"I've already got everything ready to be filed on Monday. If the courts believe she is in danger, then a court date won't take long."

"I want her removed from this prison. If he's abusing her, I don't know what I'll do."

"Rose, have you ever seen any marks or bruises on her?"

"No, but that doesn't mean anything. There are all kinds of abuse that leaves no marks."

A police car pulled into the driveway. Two uniformed men got out and approached us.

"Can you tell us what's going on?" the driver of the car asked.

Miles did the talking and the one officer looked at the papers under his flashlight since it was full on dark by now. He turned to me and asked, "This is your weekend?"

"Yes, sir, but he won't answer the door or his phone. I've been here for over three hours now."

"Step back onto the driveway and let us handle it."

Miles and I did as he asked. They banged on the door, and yelled, "Open up, police." I felt like I was watching a TV show. No one answered. They banged on the door again and rang the doorbell, and hollered, "Open up, Mr. Wilson, police."

The porch light came on and Greg opened the door. He was scowling. "What's going on?"

"Mr. Wilson, your ex-wife is here to pick up her daughter."

"What? It's not her weekend."

"According to this, it is." He held up the paper in his hand.

Greg gave his fake laugh. "Oh, that. We switched weekends."

"No, we didn't Greg. This is my weekend."

Greg's lips pressed into a thin line. "You can't just decide to come and get her. I'm the custodial parent."

Miles stepped forward. "Yes, she can, Mr. Wilson."

"And who are you?" Greg asked.

"I'm her attorney. Now please get your daughter."

Greg's eyes danced between Miles, the police, and me. He must've decided he was in a no-win scenario, so he went back inside and a few minutes later returned with Montana.

"Mommy!" She ran straight into my arms.

"Hey, pumpkin patch. How's my snickerdoodle?"

"Okay." She sounded glum.

"Let's go home so we can play."

I turned to the officers and thanked them.

Greg yelled, "You'd better have her back here on Sunday at five sharp or else."

"Or else what, Mr. Wilson?" Miles asked.

"Or else I'll call my attorney."

"I suggest you do that," Miles said.

We all turned and walked to our cars.

"Mommy, I don't have a bag."

"It's okay. You have enough at our house to get you through the weekend."

"Can I stay with you forever?"

"I'd love nothing more. I'm gonna put you in your car seat and then I have to talk to Mr. Miles for a second, okay?"

After I buckled her in, I shut the door. "He's going to make one of us pay for this."

"Not if I can help it, he won't. I'll call you Monday with a progress report."

"Thanks. I just hope I can bring her back here on Sunday."

"If you think you need an escort, let me know."

"I wasn't talking about that. I fear for Montana's safety."

"Let me see if there's any way I can get her removed from the home over the weekend. I doubt it's possible, but I'll try. If she reveals anything to you, call me."

I nodded and got in the car. It was so difficult acting happy when my heart was cracking wide open for this innocent little girl. She had never done a single thing wrong in her life, other than having an asshole for a father.

Why hadn't I seen this in him? His true colors didn't emerge until after I'd gotten pregnant. But when they did, they exploded with vivid clarity.

Chapter Sixteen

PEARSON

"Have you made any plans for after you're released?" Gray asked. He and Hudson had come to visit.

"Yeah, I have, and Sylvie wholeheartedly approves."

"Don't keep us in suspense," Hudson said.

"I'm going to move in with one of the counselors here." We sat in one of the activity rooms around a table, drinking coffee.

"That's great," Grey said. "That way, you can always go to him for help if you need it. Sort of like built-in therapy."

This is where it got tricky. "Exactly. But it's not a him. It's a her. Her name is Rose. Rose Wilson."

They both wore the same frowns. I knew that look. They assumed I was doing it all for the wrong reasons.

Hudson spoke first. "Pearson, are you sure that's wise?"

"Yeah. That's what I was thinking."

"It's not what you two think. Rose is … well, she has a three bedroom house with plenty of room and it was actually her suggestion. I don't think I'm ready to live on my own. The group homes aren't quite what I want either. This would be more of a one-on-one atmosphere. And she is one of the best counselors at Flower Power."

"I'm just gonna throw this out there," Hudson said. "Your reputation with women is less than stellar."

I held out my hand. "Listen guys, she is so not my type. She's very hippie-ish, all the way down to the flowery skirts. She even wears those flower wreaths in her hair. And get this. She teaches meditation and one day she was dressed like an elf." I was telling myself a big lie, but I couldn't admit to them how attracted to her I'd gotten.

"An elf?" Grey asked.

"Yeah. She had on red and white striped tights and a green top." Grey eyed me curiously but said nothing.

Hudson chuckled. "Definitely not your type."

"When you two meet her, you'll understand. She's always talking about her Zen and shit. But I've figured out that I need someone like that to talk me off the trigger ledge, which is why she'll be good to live with."

Grey touched my arm. "As long as you don't use her as a crutch."

"Don't worry. I'll be going to NA every day. And, Dr. Martinelli said she's going to put me in touch with someone who runs an NA group. He went through sort of what I did. Got hooked after an accident."

Hudson scanned the room and commented on how many people were visiting today.

"Yeah, it's much more crowded than the last time you guys were here. So, how's Mom and Dad? Were they upset I asked them not to come?"

Grey shrugged. "Somewhat, but they understood. They're looking forward to your release. When you're ready, they want to have everyone over for a family dinner."

"That would be great. I'd love to see all the kids," I said. "How are the twins?"

"Mine are great," Hudson said. "Wiley is hilarious. Every day he asks Milly when they're going to walk. He has no concept of a year."

"I bet he's gotten big."

"Yeah, he's getting taller for sure."

"Grey?"

"Oh, mine are belting out a lot of noise when they're hungry and Kinsley already has plans to buy them clicky shoes. She's still bossing everyone around too. All I can say is Marin has control of the house, thank God."

"You totally lucked out in finding her," I said.

"Could not agree with you more."

"You guys want to take a walk out back?"

They both agreed and we went out around the gardens and the rest of the property as they caught me up on the kids, my parents, and the dogs. Those crazy dogs. Hudson was a veterinarian and soft-hearted when it came to animals. He and his wife currently had four and a half dogs. Seriously. His wife owned a Mastiff that my mom fell in love with. She begged Milly to keep it part-time and it soon became a joint custody deal. Every time I thought about it, I cracked up. I even joked about drawing up custody papers for them.

"I'm guessing that Mom and Milly are still sharing Dick?" Dick was the aforementioned dog.

"Yep," Hudson said. "I've asked Mom if she wants one of her own, but nothing doing. You won't believe her with him. She has all kinds of outfits for that dog. And he lets her dress him up."

"Let's not go there today. I don't think my brain can handle it."

Grey laughed. "Yeah, it's started a whole thing with Kinsley. She tries to dress Marshmallow up, but she rips off the clothes as soon as you put them on." Marshmallow was their Golden Doodle. "I told Kinsley if she keeps it up, Marshmallow will run from her and won't let her pet her. Guess what she said."

"What?"

"She said all she really wanted Marshmallow to wear was a pink tutu so she could watch her dance in her clicky shoes."

"Jesus, that kid and those clicky shoes."

"Tell me about it," Grey said. "Poor Aaron. She constantly badgers the kid and he can barely get away from her."

"My sympathies, man. Just keep him in sports," I said.

"That's the plan."

"Wylie runs from her too. I told him to give her some soccer cleats for her birthday."

Grey looked at Hudson like he was batshit crazy. "Marin will kick your ass from here to Texas."

Hudson shrugged. "No, she won't if I'm not there."

We wound our way back inside and took seats again at a table in the dining room this time. I got coffees for everyone. I chuckled. "I'm glad I don't have to deal with kids."

"You might someday."

"Nah. I don't want to bring them into this world with a chance they would follow in the steps of their old man."

"What do you mean?" Hudson asked the question, but both of them stared at me.

"I wouldn't want any child of mine to ever go down this hell-hole I'm in. That's what I mean."

Grey was the first to speak. "And you think because you have an addiction problem, your child would be at risk of having one?"

"One hundred percent yes."

Neither of them said anything. What was there to say? I did the job for them. "I realize it's difficult for the two of you to put yourselves in my shoes, but you can't possibly understand what it's like. And I wouldn't wish this on anyone."

"We don't understand. Not at all and can never. But you don't know your kids would ever do this."

"True, but I don't want to risk the chance. This has been hell. Or worse. And I'm still at the beginning. The truth is I'm scared. Scared to death of what will happen when I leave. That's why the idea of moving in with a counselor is so appealing to me. Nighttime is the worst and she'll be there to help. Like right now, I have zero urge to use. But when darkness hits, it comes on with a vengeance."

"You can always call us, you know."

"You guys have families and careers. It's not like you have a whole lot of extra time to spend on your drug addict brother."

Hudson slammed his hand on the table. "What the hell does that mean? You're our brother and we love you, if you haven't noticed."

"Hudson is right. We'll do anything for you. All you have to do is ask," Grey said.

The tension was building in my shoulders. I hadn't meant to upset them. "I'm sorry, guys. That probably came out wrong. What I meant was you two have your hands full with work and family obligations. I understand how it is. Hell, that's how I ended up here. The stress of my job was a major factor. All I was saying is I didn't want to add to that. But you have to know how much I appreciate everything you've done for me."

Hudson's shoulders slumped. "Hey, didn't mean to overreact on you. Have you thought about when you're going to return to work? I know this is really early, but I thought I'd ask."

I hadn't told them or my parents of my decision and there was no time like the present. "I'm not going back."

"Say what?" Hudson asked. Grey had been particularly quiet.

"You heard me. I can't. The pressure is what landed me here."

"I thought it was the shoulder surgery," Grey said.

"That was only the beginning. Then I liked how numb the meds made me feel. When it came down to it, it was because of my job."

"Oh, man. What will you do?"

"Start a new practice somewhere else. But it won't be in

Manhattan because I signed a no-compete clause. I have to go thirty-five miles out."

"Eh. That's not bad," Grey said. "Look at me. I'm more than happy where I am."

I scraped my teeth over my lower lip. "There's more." I lifted my eyes toward the ceiling, wondering how they'd take this news. "I've decided to do some pro bono work too."

Grey lifted his brows. "Seriously?"

"Yeah."

"Why?" Hudson asked. "You're one of the best attorneys in Manhattan. Your reputation is stellar."

A bitter laugh ripped out of me. "My reputation is stellar when it comes to winning cases, but as I've found sobriety and faced what was going on in my life, I've analyzed the types of cases I've won. I discovered it wasn't always the right thing to do. Now I have regrets. Lots of them. This is a way of paying back for some of those … mistakes I made."

Grey said, "I don't know what to say."

"There really is nothing to say, except tell me you support my decision."

"Of course we do. We only want what's best for you. My shock stems from not knowing this was going on."

"Same here," Hudson adds.

"How could you when I never talked about the bad and only the good?"

Grey offers up a slight smile. "Can I just say I'm glad we're having this discussion? And I'm also glad you're finding your way? Life's too short to be unhappy."

"That's the damn truth," Hudson says.

"You two would know." They both went through some terrible times. Grey lost his wife in a plane crash leaving him a widower with two young kids and Hudson's wife left him for another man when his son was only eighteen months old. Luckily, they're both happily remarried now.

"Listen, Pearson, and I'm fairly confident I speak for Hudson and Mom and Dad here, all we want is for you to stay sober, no matter how you do it. And we want you to be happy. Whether that's practicing law in some huge firm making millions or doing pro bono work, that's up to you. We just want our brother back. We have him now and we want him to stay."

I put my hand out on the table and they both covered it with theirs. "Maybe we need a knife to do the blood bothers tie."

"Nah, we have each other's DNA and that's better than anything," Grey said.

"I love you guys and am so thankful you're my brothers." We all stood and hugged. They were the most important people to me, other than my parents, and I wanted to show them how much.

Chapter Seventeen

ROSE

MILES CALLED ON SUNDAY MORNING. MY HANDS SHOOK AS I picked up the phone.

"Just checking in. How was your weekend?'"

"It was fine until today. I don't know if I can take her back." I whispered so Montana wouldn't hear.

"You have to. I'm going to do everything I can tomorrow. This weekend was a bust. Do you want me to show up there just in case?"

Clenching the lapel of my robe, I muttered, "I don't know. It may anger him more."

"I have an idea. When you get there, call me and keep your phone on. I'll park down the street. I'll be able to hear everything. If anything happens, I can be there in moments."

"Okay. But be there early."

"What time are you going?"

"I have to be there by five on the nose, or else."

"I'll get there ten minutes early and wait. Try not to worry, Rose. This is going to work out."

"I wish I believed you. But right now, I can't." I hung up and the nightmare that had awakened me kept flashing in my mind. It had been so real, so fucking real, I thought Greg had stolen Montana away. I jumped out of bed and ran to her room, only to discover she was still sound asleep in her bed.

The coffee was done so I poured myself a cup, but spilled it all over the counter. I needed to pull myself together. I leaned over, gasping for air.

His fist slammed into my stomach, pain exploding like a million stars in my eyes. I doubled over, trying to drag a breath into my lungs.

"What did you just say?"

My mouth opened, but there was no air to speak. He grabbed a fistful of my hair and jerked my head up. For a brief moment, I thought he was going to snap my neck.

"I asked you a question."

I stared at his eyes and saw something evil move in their depths. No, not evil. It was hatred. He hated me. How had I not noticed this before?

"Answer me, goddammit!" He pinched, then twisted the skin on the underside of my arm. He was always careful and knew exactly where to injure me so the bruises wouldn't show.

"I'm pregnant." The two words wheezed out of me.

"You fucking bitch." He slammed me against the wall, with a force that cracked the sheetrock. My shoulder and then the side of my head were the contact points. Something warm and sticky slid down my cheek. The skin must've split. It's a wonder I was still conscious. "Get rid of it."

"Can't," I mumbled.

"You can't? We'll see about that." I didn't understand what he meant until I saw his foot aimed at me. I curled up, trying to shield myself from the kick, but it wasn't very effective. Blow after blow continued until things turned hazy and then dark. When I woke up, I was in the hospital.

I slowly opened my eyes to see him holding my hand. When I tried to snatch it away, he gripped it so hard, I squealed. The nurse in the room came running.

"Mrs. Wilson, are you in pain?"

Greg's hand eased up and I shook my head. "What happened?"

Greg answered. "I came home to find someone broke into our house and beat you. They stole your jewelry and some cash."

My eyes pinged around the room, because he was lying, but had obviously convinced everyone this was the truth.

"The baby?" I asked.

The nurse smiled. "It's fine."

I smiled and rubbed my belly. Greg looked at me from beneath lowered lids. I knew he had plans, but if I could tell the nurse the truth after he left, maybe someone would believe me.

Only my plans were blown. "Mr. Wilson, they'll be bringing in a recliner for you momentarily. And I'll get you some sheets for tonight."

"You're spending the night?" I asked.

"But of course, darling. I wouldn't dream of leaving your side while you're here."

IT WAS A LIFE I THOUGHT I'D LEFT BEHIND AND HERE IT WAS again, haunting me. Haunting my beautiful innocent daughter. I had to stop him somehow.

Getting Montana in the car wasn't easy. "I don't wanna go there, Mommy."

"Why not?"

"It's not fun."

"Can you tell me more about it?"

"I hate staying in my room all the time. Sometimes I'm scared and no one comes."

I knelt down beside her. "Can you tell me where your room is? Is it upstairs or down?"

"Downstairs. In the back. The scary woods are there where monsters live."

"What kind of monsters?"

"Mean monsters."

I brushed her curly hair back with my fingers. "Have you seen these mean monsters?"

"No, but Daddy said they'll come and get me cuz they live in the forest. And I hear them."

"What do they say?"

"The big mean one says he'll hurt me if I'm not good. And I know he hurts the others. I can hear someone crying."

She talked about them. Was she dreaming this? "Honey, are you having bad dreams?"

"No, Mommy."

"Why didn't you tell me this before?"

"Cuz the mean monster would come and hurt me."

The monster had to be her dad. I knew that monster. He'd hurt me enough over the years. A broken nose, broken ribs, broken arm, wrist, bruises to match. That bastard was brutal. If he ever touched her like that, I would find a way to kill him. I'd bought a gun when we were still together and wouldn't hesitate to use it to protect my daughter.

"Montana, I'll talk to your daddy about this."

"Noooo! He'll get mad at me." Her head shook back and forth almost violently. She clung to me as though she feared for her life.

"Montana, it's okay, sweetheart. I promise not to say anything then."

"I wanna stay here Mommy. With you. You don't got any monsters."

"Can you keep a secret?"

"Yeah."

"Mommy wants you to stay here too. I love you so much and I hate it when you're not here. But Daddy wants you too, so you have to stay there."

"I don't want to."

This was killing me. How could I make his home sound

wonderful when I knew she hated it there? "Maybe I can talk to your daddy to see if you can stay here more. Would you like that?"

Her head bobbed up and down furiously.

"Okay, but you have to promise not to say anything to him. Can you do that for me?"

She made a cross over her heart like I taught her. Then I did the same thing. "Now give me a big squeezy hug." I still noticed the tension in her features, the slight crease between her eyes. She was four fucking years old! It made my head ache and my belly knot up.

We loaded up her things in the car and I wanted to scream in frustration at the unfairness of it all. This child deserved so much better. I had been raised in a house filled with darkness and anger. I did not want that for my precious angel.

When we got close to my ex's, the phone rang. It was Miles.

"Hey."

"I'm about four houses down on the right."

"Okay. I'm about to turn on the street."

"Don't hang up. Slip the phone in your pocket. How are you doing?"

"Not so good."

"Let's see what we can make happen."

I pulled the car to a stop in the driveway behind his fancy car. I wish I could've rammed the thing straight into his garage door. I didn't know why he never parked in there. It was probably to show off his expensive car to his neighbors. He'd always been ostentatious like that.

As soon as I turned the engine off, the front door of the house opened. Then he stalked out to my car.

"You're a minute late," he snarled.

"No, I checked the time when I arrived, and it was five on the dot."

"Where's Montana?"

"She's stuffed in the trunk. Where do you think she is? She's in her car seat for Pete's sake."

His lips pressed into a thin line. "Don't you dare get smart with me."

"Or what? Are you going to beat me like you used to?"

"You always needed a good beating, and you sure could use one now."

"Yeah, I have plenty of healed up broken bones to show for what you did to me."

"And you deserved every one of them."

"Are you hitting Montana? Because if you are …"

He stepped closer to me. "What? What will you do?"

I didn't cower from him, which surprised me. "I'll make sure you never do it again."

"If I'm hitting her, it's because she deserves it like you did."

"You bastard." I raised my arm to slap him, but he grabbed me, picked me up, and threw me down in his driveway. I broke the fall using one of my hands. Pain shot up my arm, which wasn't a good sign.

. "You jerk. You have no right to touch me." I sat there for a minute, rubbing my wrist and collecting my thoughts. I could barely think because of the pain I was in, but never in a million years would I let him know.

"I can do whatever I want. You're on my property threatening me." He leaned over me in an intimidating way.

"You were threatening my daughter."

"That's my right as her father. I can do whatever I want. I'm the custodial parent and it would serve you well to remember that." He marched to the car, opened the back door, and yanked her out of the booster seat. She was crying out to me as he did it.

"Shut up, Montana, or you'll be punished," he said cruelly. Her lower lip quivered, and it was easy to see how frightened she was of him.

"You're scaring her."

"Mommy, don't leave me."

"I said, shut up." And he shook her. Her curls went flying around her face as she cried.

"Stop it, Greg." I ran over to him, but he knocked me down again. Only this time, Miles pulled up in front of the house. It was about time. He jumped out of the car and helped me up.

"Who's that?" Greg asked.

"I'm her attorney, don't you remember? You've just made a huge error, Mr. Wilson. I think it would be in your best interest to hand Montana over to her mother."

"I'll do no such thing."

Then I heard sirens in the distance. They were getting closer and closer.

"It would be in your best interest if you want to continue to have any kind of relationship with your daughter. Domestic violence is not looked upon very kindly in the courts, Mr. Wilson, and from what I overheard, you will have some serious charges against you."

"What do you mean overheard?"

Miles took out his phone and I followed his actions.

"That entire conversation was and still is being recorded."

His features contorted into a mask of hatred. "Why you conniving little bitch."

"No, Greg, not conniving, only concerned for the welfare of Montana."

Then he looked at our daughter and asked, "Did you know about this?"

Her eyes grew wide and she trembled in his arms.

"You can't be serious?" I asked.

He was squeezing her arms so tight she cried out, "Ouch, Daddy. That hurts." Then she sobbed. Miles snapped pictures of the way he held her.

Two police cars pulled up in front of the house and Greg finally put her down. Montana ran straight into my arms, still sobbing her eyes out. I dropped to the ground and pulled her against me.

Miles went to talk to the officers and Greg came up to me. "You think you're so smart. But this isn't over, Rose. You might think you've won, but I can assure you, you'll never win at this. Not until one of us is dead." His eyes were cold, dark, and evil and they sent chills racing down my spine. He never said something unless he meant it.

Chapter Eighteen

WHEN ROSE TOLD ME WHAT HAPPENED, I NEARLY FLIPPED. Turned out, Rose broke her wrist when her ex knocked her down but didn't realize it until later that night. She'd been so upset over the turn of events that it wasn't until she got home, things settled down, and her adrenaline wore off that she found herself in pain again. Miles drove her to the emergency room where they discovered it was fractured.

I sat across from her in her office, listening to this bizarre turn of events. "Jesus Christ. He could've really hurt you or your daughter."

"Miles was smart to have us record him and call the police. When they came, and he played back the recorded conversation, they took him to jail. But now I'm really scared."

"Why? You have your daughter and from what it sounds like, he's not going to get custody. He'll only see her in supervised visits."

"True, but he said something to me that freaked me out."

I scooted closer to her. "What did he say?"

"That this was only the beginning. And that I'd never win at this. One of us would be dead first."

"Idle threats. Did you tell Miles?"

"Yeah, and he said the same." She absently rubbed the cast on her wrist. Then her eyes met mine and I nearly wilted in my seat. "They weren't idle. He meant every word. He'll do something. The man hates me, hates me for getting pregnant, hates me for having Montana. He wanted me to get rid of the pregnancy. When I wouldn't, he uh …" She swallowed, then said, "he beat me so badly I ended up in the hospital. I thought I'd lost my baby."

"He what?"

"Yeah, he beat the crap out of me."

I grabbed her uninjured hand, or I thought it was until she winced. I flipped it over and saw the abrasions. "Jesus, you did this when you fell?"

"Yeah. It's just a scrape."

Anger and disgust rolled through me in waves. How did I ever represent this asshole? How did I not see through him? Oh, yeah. I was probably high and fucked up at the time and didn't give a shit.

"When you landed in the hospital, didn't the doctors suspect anything?"

She chuckled. "He called the police and said he came home and found me like that. Blamed it on someone breaking in and stealing cash. He's a psychopath. He can be very charming yet callous and can manipulate others with charisma and intimidation. He feels no guilt about hurting people either, even his daughter. Guilt or empathy don't exist for him and he's very narcissistic. I was so naïve when we met and when I started school and declared my major, he became even more cruel. I think it was because he knew I'd spot these characteristics of his."

"Why didn't you leave?"

"I did. It took me several tries because the first couple of times he beat me so badly I couldn't leave the house."

Sitting became unbearable so I got to my feet and paced the small room. "I don't know what to say other than I'm sorry you had to live through that."

"You didn't know, but I really hated you for letting him take my daughter from me."

"Rightfully so. I gave him the means. But one thing is good. With me living at your place, you won't have to worry so much."

She eyed me curiously. "Why's that?"

"I'm bigger and stronger than he is. I will beat the shit out of him if he tries anything."

A smile tugged at the corner of her mouth, but I was serious as hell. I may be a recovering addict, but domestic abuse of any kind was intolerable. Just because some dude was bigger than she was did not give him a right to push her around and threaten her. "Pearson, if he tries to do anything to Montana, I'll shoot him."

Rose, peaceful Rose, just shocked the shit out of me. "You own a gun?" I'm pretty fucking sure my brows were glued to the ceiling.

"Yes, and I won't hesitate to use it if I have to."

Her tone actually scared me. "Okay, but let's hope it doesn't come to that. And if you do, don't shoot anyone else in the process and for God's sake, make sure he is inside your house."

She pulled her lower lip between her teeth and clutched the necklace she wore. It was one of those medallions that diffused essential oils to calm the nerves. "I took classes on gun safety."

"Fine, but in the heat of the moment, when passion flares, things can go south when you least expect them to. My concerns are you and Montana."

"I don't care so much about me."

I knelt down in front of her and took a hold of her hand. "Listen to me, Rose. If something happens to you, where will she end up? You don't want her with her father, do you?"

"No!"

"Then have a care with that gun."

She licked her lips and swallowed as I watched her throat work. "I hadn't thought about that."

"People normally don't when things go haywire. I'd rather you let me handle things if he decides to pay you a visit." I had a vision of a shootout at her house with disastrous results. "Where is Montana now?"

"She's here, up front. I'm trying to get her into a preschool nearby. They said maybe tomorrow or the next day."

"Should you even be here today after what you just went through?"

"No, I'm not staying. I needed to stop by and pick up a few things. But ..." She wouldn't look at me.

"What is it, Rose?"

"Miles said he made bail. He should be out later this morning."

I was still kneeling in front of her. "You're afraid to go home, aren't you?"

She nodded, her head moving in a quick jerky fashion. "What if he shows up and takes Montana away?"

"That's abduction. I doubt he'd do that."

"I don't."

She was terrified. "Call Miles and let me talk to him."

When Miles was on the phone, we discussed having Rose stay in a hotel until the weekend when I got out.

"I can't do that," she said.

"Why not?"

"I don't have the money."

"Stay here a minute." I went in search of Sylvie. Once I explained things to her, I was sure she would let Rose and Montana stay with her. I finally located her, but she was in session. Then I checked the time and realized I needed to get moving to my own. Maybe Jeremy would let me meet up with him later when I explained things.

What a crazy morning. It wasn't even ten yet and I was busier than I'd been in weeks. Jeremy eyed me when I practically jogged into his office.

"What's up with you?"

"Hey, I need a favor. Rose is in a bind. Is there any way we can move our session to a different time?"

"Sure. Can you tell me what's going on?"

After I gave him a very brief rundown without going into detail, because it wasn't my story to share, he said, "Let me talk to her. She can stay with me. My wife and Rose get along great and she'd love to have her."

Rose gave me a questioning stare when we entered her office, but I shook my head. Jeremy didn't wait and said, "Pearson told me you needed a place to say for a few days. I know Cindy would love to have you. Why not stay with us?"

"Oh, I ..."

"Really, Rose, we would both love it."

"My daughter would be with me."

"That's great. I didn't know you had her now."

Rose's lower lip trembled, and Jeremy noticed it immediately. "Hey, what's going on? Does this have anything to do with that?" He pointed to her cast.

"Yeah." Big fat tears bubbled out of her eyes as she broke down crying. I was a fish out of water here, so I let Jeremy handle it. He put his arm around her and comforted her and as I watched him, I thought that should be my job. A feeling of jealousy rose over me and I pushed it down because it was a completely alien emotion to me. I'd never been involved with a woman before ... never had the desire or inclination. I'd seen what happened when it didn't work, and Rose was the perfect example. Okay, maybe not, because her ex was a brutal son of a bitch, but still.

As I watched and listened, I took note of how Jeremy comforted her and got her to explain what happened. When she was finished, he said, "You're staying with us until Pearson gets out on Saturday. It's only for a few days and Cindy will love it. I'm not taking no for an answer. We have the room and there's not a reason in the world you can possibly give to get out of this. I'll go home with you to pack your bags and follow you to my house at lunch." His voice was firm, and she finally agreed.

Jeremy drew me out of her office as he left. "Can we meet this afternoon instead?"

"That's fine. Thanks for doing this," I said.

"You were right to come to me. I had no idea her ex was that bad." The frown he wore told me how upset he was.

"Now you might understand how terrible I feel over representing him in their divorce." Even after all this time, my gut still crawled into knots when I thought about what I'd done. It was a vicious cycle that kept repeating itself in my head.

"Yes, but you had no way of knowing. You're going to have to find a way to let that go. Look at what you're doing for her now."

"I'm not doing anything. It's my friend who's doing it all." I raised my voice in protest as I ran my hand through my hair.

"Pearson, calm down. Think about it. If it weren't for your help, Rose wouldn't have gotten Montana out. It's because of you, she had your friend on her side."

That much was true, but it was because of me she'd found herself in this predicament in the first place.

"Right now, I could use a strong hit of something. Anything." I wanted to scratch my skin off.

"Deep breaths. Let it go," Jeremy said. "Your craving is coming from your guilt and you can't change the past. You can't go back. What matters now is you're doing the right thing." It took some doing, but he eventually talked me down. "Meet me in my office, say around two. I'll see you then and we'll hash this out some more. Take a meditation class this morning. Got it?"

"Got it." I went back into Rose's office and saw her huddled in her chair.

"You okay?" I asked.

"I suppose."

"I am so sorry. We're going to fix this."

Her head lifted and hazel orbs targeted mine. It was obvious she'd been crying by the sheen on her cheeks. I went to her side and something overtook me. I didn't mean to do it, but somehow, I pulled her to her feet, and she ended up in my arms. I was suddenly kissing her soft lips. She tasted salty from her tears and stopping wasn't an option. Cupping her cheeks, I brushed my thumbs along her delicate cheekbones, wiping the moisture away. When her arms crept around my neck, I angled her face and went for gold. I knew I should stop. Alarms were going off like crazy, but I couldn't. It was like hitting the jackpot with Rose. Besides, this was only a kiss. But her mouth was heaven and I wanted more. I shouldn't, but I did. When I finally pulled away, I did with an intended apology on my lips.

Instead, I said, "I should say I'm sorry, but I can't. I wouldn't trade that kiss for anything."

She smiled, and it was a lazy one, the kind you have when you wake up in the morning after a great night of sex. "I wouldn't either. I'm not sorry one bit so I'm glad you're not." Then she touched my face. "And to think I hated you."

"What are we going to do?"

She did a funny kind of giggle-laugh. It made me happy because I hadn't heard her laugh ever. "I guess we'll take it one step at a time."

"Is there a twelve-step program for relationships because I really suck at them?" I asked.

Then she let out a big belly laugh. It was contagious and I found myself laughing right along with her.

"That bad, huh?"

"Yeah. Really bad. I blame it on the job."

"I'll admit after my marriage, I'm relationship-phobic too. I guess we're even in that department."

I did something I'd been dying to do for a very long time. I ran my fingers through her hair. "Just as I thought."

"What?"

"I've been wondering what it would feel like to do this. And it's even better than I'd imagined. You have beautiful hair."

She glanced away. Suddenly her feet seemed to be extremely interesting. Tipping her chin up with a finger, I said, "It's something to be proud of, not ashamed."

Her hand wrapped around my wrist. "You don't understand. He used to tell me it was ugly, that I was ugly. He'd use it as a weapon."

I ground my molars at what she said. "What do you mean?"

"He'd grab handfuls of it and yank it so hard, sometimes chunks of it would come out."

"Jesus, I don't know what to say, Rose, other than I'm sorry you had to endure living with him." What I really wanted to say was I'd love to wrap my hands around that bastard's throat and squeeze the life out of him, after I beat him to a pulp.

"That makes two of us. But it's over and done."

"You have to know he said that to be cruel because you're gorgeous." Then a thought hit me. "This is off the subject, but does your house have a security system?"

"Yes, why?"

"I was going to recommend one if it didn't."

"I've had one since I moved in. I've never trusted him."

"I can understand why." I also thought about hiring her a bodyguard. They can be very discreet, but if she thought someone was following her without her knowledge, she'd freak. "What do you think about a bodyguard?"

She laughed. "I don't have that kind of money."

"I do and I know a few guys who are very discreet. I thought about doing it without your knowledge, but if you noticed someone following you, I was afraid it would scare you." I waited for her reaction and she seemed calm about it.

"It sounds like a good idea, but I'm more concerned he'd go for Montana."

"My thoughts were for both of you."

Her hand fiddled with the buttons on her shirt as she asked, "How would it work exactly?"

"However you'd want it to. They work within the client's parameters. For instance, if you wanted them to take and pick up Montana from school, they could do that. Wherever you think she's at the highest risk of being exposed to him. And you too, of course."

"I'll have to think about it. He's really smart and cagey. What are your thoughts?"

My brain fired up and I remembered a few other clients with similar situations, but they lived in the city, so their situations were a bit different. "Why don't we ask the few guys I know and see what they say. A couple of them are ex cops so they understand the criminal mind."

Rose perked up. "I love that idea. You don't mind?"

"If I minded, I wouldn't have suggested it."

She picked up her phone to check the time. "Don't you have somewhere to be?"

"Not as important as here." And it was true.

"How are you doing, by the way."

"I have good days and bad, but many more good than bad now. I see Dr. Martinelli tomorrow for my final visit with her. I'm a little nervous about that."

"Why?"

I shrugged. "What if she tells me I need another thirty days?"

Rose sat up straight and gave me a hard stare. "Do *you* think you need another thirty days?"

"No, I don't."

"What will you do when the urge to use strikes at night?"

"Knock on your bedroom door, what else?" I was totally serious, and she laughed. "What's so funny?"

"I completely forgot you would be living with me." She slapped her knee and actually snorted.

"Oh, God, you sound like Sylvie."

Her hand covered her mouth. "I've never snorted in my life."

"Right. I'm sure that's what you tell everyone."

"No, it's true!" She kept laughing.

"Can we bring this back around to me?" I asked, winking.

"Sure. So, you'll knock on my bedroom door, huh?"

"Well, yeah, for some counseling."

"Counseling, huh?"

"Yeah, what el… oh, you're a naughty girl when I'm trying to be serious." A sly smile stretched across her face as she waggled her brows.

"Did you have an ulterior motive when you asked me to move in?" I asked suspiciously.

"Not at the time."

"And now?"

"Maybe."

"This sounds intriguing. But you have to promise me something first."

"What?"

"If this doesn't work, we both agree to call it quits before either of us hates the other again. I wouldn't want things to end badly."

"Agreed," she said. I held out my hand and she shook it with her uninjured one.

"You don't believe in wasting time, do you?" I hoped I wasn't too much of a blabbermouth and acting like her significant other already.

"Not when you've been through what I have. Not to mention, I, er, haven't been with anyone in a couple of years," she stuttered.

Two years? You're joking.

"No, not joking. Ever since my divorce."

"Wow. I mean, just wow." I didn't know people could go that long without sex.

"Pretty sad, huh?"

"Not sad, just … long." I rubbed my forehead thinking about it. I don't imagine you could die from a backup of sperm, but where did it all go, if you didn't eject it? Then again, women were different and didn't have to ejaculate so maybe it wasn't as bad for them. I'd never asked one, so I didn't really know.

"What are you thinking?"

I slashed a hand through the air. "Nothing important." Blue balls was a killer. Could women get a blue vagina?

I must've had a weird expression on my face because she asked, "Oh, no. With an expression like that, it has to be something."

"Can a woman get ... no never mind. You'll think I'm really strange. Maybe someday when we're closer, I'll ask."

"Wait a minute. We're discussing sleeping together and you can't ask me a simple question? Now I do think you're strange."

"Okay, but don't say I didn't warn you. Can a woman get a blue vagina?"

Her expression contorted into something similar to a pretzel if that's possible. "Blue vagina?" Then she burst out laughing.

"See, I knew you'd think I was weird."

"What in the world is a blue vagina?" Her laugh turned into a cackle.

"You know how men get blue balls?"

"Oh." Then she snort-laughed again but covered her mouth with a hand.

"See, I knew I shouldn't have told you. You think I'm an idiot, don't you?"

"No, but I've never heard it put that way before. We don't exactly get that. We usually take care of things before it gets bad and we don't have, um, stuff in there."

"Stuff?" I smirked. It was cute she didn't want to say cum.

"Yeah, stuff." Her tongue poked the inside of her cheek and seemingly she was trying not to laugh.

"What kind of stuff?"

Her finger popped out toward me as she said, "You know what kind of stuff."

"No. Explain."

"Liquid stuff."

"You mean ejaculate?"

She snapped her fingers. "Yes, exactly. So, we don't get backed up."

"Backed up, huh?" I was totally enjoying this conversation. "Is that what happens?"

"Well, yeah. Doesn't it? Isn't that why they turn blue?"

"So, they don't actually turn blue, they just feel like they do. Some guys say they turn bluish, but mine never have. Oh, and the blue is the result of the blood supply in the balls, not the ejaculate."

"Good to know," she said, putting a finger in the air, grinning. "Now that I'm educated on blue balls, I have to say that women only get frustrated in the same situation. No blue vaginas that I'm aware of. But then again, how would I know because I've never had a way of actually inspecting in there." Then her laugh hit me again. I couldn't help but join in.

"True. This has been an interesting discussion," I said. Then we both cracked up again. Before she stopped, I was kissing her again. If this kiss was any indication of how the rest of her would taste, I may be in serious trouble.

"I need to go. Meditation starts soon, and if I don't leave now, I may be going in with blue balls."

"We wouldn't want that, would we?"

"There's no *we* in it. I'll see you later."

Rose was a twist in my plans, but maybe a twist that my life desperately needed. And maybe that's what had been wrong all along. I had always planned everything out, never letting things flow. It was time to let go of the control freak, because look where that had gotten me—up to my ass in opiates and alcohol.

Chapter Nineteen

ROSE

PEARSON LEFT ME WITH A HUGE SMILE ON MY FACE, something I hadn't worn in quite a while. Then it hit me. I'd hated that man for so long, how in the world did *this* happen? Sylvie burst into the room then and saw me sitting there grinning. She came to a screeching halt and stared at me.

"I heard what happened to you and came as quickly as I could and here I find you looking as happy as I've seen you in ages. What gives?" She popped out her hip and rested a hand on it, waiting for my answer.

I mimicked Pearson as I waved my good hand through the air and said, "Oh, it's nothing."

"Nothing, my ass. For weeks you've been freaked about Montana, worried to death. And now you look like you won the lottery." She snapped her fingers. "Tell it all. You can't fool me."

Damn. What should I say? I didn't want to give Pearson away. What if he didn't want her to know? Although she did mention something about us getting together.

Before I could come up with a single thing, she asked, "Does this have something to do with that hot cousin of mine?"

The heat in my cheeks had to give me away.

"Aha! That's it, isn't it?"

I aimed a finger at her. "Okay, yes. But don't say anything because I don't know how he would feel about you knowing."

She fist pumped the air and said, "It's about damn time the two of you figured it out."

"What's that supposed to mean?"

"Duh. Only that the chemistry between you two was as intense as a lab experiment."

My hand flew out as I said, "Stop. You're making that up." Could that be true and I blocked all those feelings because I kept telling myself I hated him?

"Get real, my friend. You just refused to see it. You have to admit the attraction between you two is off the charts, right?"

I chewed on my lip for a second as I thought about it. "At first, I thought he was hot, and it pissed me off because I hated him so much. I asked myself why couldn't he be ugly? But then, as he began helping me, I forgot I hated him and yeah, the attraction for me was there. I just didn't know it was reciprocated."

By this time, she had plopped down in a chair. "You are a blind woman, my friend."

"Shut up. I've been so worried about Montana, the last thing on my mind was if he thought I was hot."

"It's kinda hard to miss. Damn, he stares at you as if he wants to own you. As for him, even though he's my cousin, it's hard to ignore his looks. That face alone is perfection."

"You're sick," I said with a laugh.

"Yeah, I know. Can you see me as a patient, following him around?" She snickered.

I threw a pen at her and she caught it. "Seriously. What is that called when you think your cousins are hot?"

"It's called you think your cousins are hot. Now shut up."

Then she asked, "So, have you two made plans? He gets out in a few days."

"You don't remember, do you?"

"What?" She frowned.

"He's moving in with me."

Her frown instantly disappeared, and her mouth morphed into a smirk. "No wonder you were grinning like that when I walked in. I imagine you two have been *planning*?"

"That, my friend, is none of your business."

Sylvie suddenly looked like a whipped puppy. "You can't mean that. I would tell you."

"He's your cousin. If he wants you to know, he'll tell you."

"No, he won't. It's a guy thing. They never tell."

She was right. Most men didn't talk like women did. They didn't share things and I could never figure that out. "How about this? I'll give you a thumbs up or a thumbs down, but no details. That's just too intrusive into his life and I can't do that."

"Sure, I can work with that."

"Oh, my God. You're sounding like *my* counselor now."

We stared at each other and then fist bumped. "It's hard to shed that role, isn't it?" Sylvie asked. "How are you going to handle Pearson when he's with you full time?"

"I hope to help him or at least help prevent him from taking a tumble."

"Thank you." She put her hands over her heart. "And I mean that from the bottom of my heart."

"You don't have to thank me."

"Rose, he almost died. My family was so scared of how this would work. The fact that he's leaving here after thirty days is a miracle. Even Dr. Martinelli is amazed at his progress. Jeremy says he's iron-willed. But if you could've seen him in the hospital. He doesn't know I was there. And I don't ever plan on telling him, but his brother, Grey, called me right away when they were looking for places to send him. It was awful. My aunt and uncle were freaking. His family is very close-knit and caring, but to see his parents break down, was heartbreaking for me."

"I knew he nearly died, but I didn't know the rest. Why didn't you tell me?"

Sylvie shrugged and wiped her eyes. "It was so personal, so close to the heart, I suppose. And I didn't know how he'd do. It was one of the reasons why I wanted him with you. I knew you would work really hard to get him on the right track, but I never knew you had a past with him."

I chuckled. "And who knew it would turn out to be the best thing for Montana and me?"

"Right?"

I got out of my chair and went to hug her. "Thank you."

"What for?"

"If it hadn't been for you asking Pearson for his help, this never would've happened. I don't know how I'll ever repay you."

"That's what friends are for, Rose."

"This is something I'll never forget. You gave Montana and me a chance at a new beginning. The best chance ever."

Her expression indicated there was more on her mind she wanted to ask. "What?"

"Montana. How is she?"

"Shaken." The way her little body trembled when I held her yesterday and how she clung to me made my stomach bottom out all over again.

"Have you thought about what's next for her?"

"Sure, counseling. As in intense. I think she has PTSD. Know anyone?"

"Why don't we check with Dr. Martinelli? She's sure to know someone. She's coming out tomorrow."

"Right. Great idea."

"Montana's here, isn't she?"

"Yes. She starts a new preschool tomorrow and we'll be staying with Jeremy and Cindy until Pearson moves in."

Sylvie took my hand, saying, "You have all your bases covered then. Let's go see your little one."

When we got to the front, a surprise awaited us in the form of my ex. "Greg, what are you doing here?" My heart kicked up until I thought it was going to jump out of my chest. It was a wonder no one else saw or heard it.

He snarled at me. "I'm here for my daughter, which I have custody of. Where is she?"

Chapter Twenty

I WAS IN MEDITATION, TRYING NOT TO CHUCKLE, BECAUSE ALL I could think about was my conversation with Rose about blue balls and blue vaginas. My eyes were closed when someone whispered in my ear.

"Pearson, we need you up front. Fast."

I opened my eyes to see Sylvie. Her expression told me it was serious. Leaping to my feet, I quickly hurried after her. When we made it to the hall, I asked what was going on. She explained as we practically ran up the steps and on to the front.

"I need to call Miles." Sylvie handed me her phone and I made the call.

"Miles, Pearson here. Rose's ex is here trying to get Montana from her. He's claiming he's the custodial parent."

"I'm on the way." Click.

Handing Sylvie her phone back, I said, "Miles is coming."

When we arrived at the front, Rose was pacing, and Greg

was yelling. I stepped in. "Mr. Wilson, if you don't calm down, we're going to call the police."

"West, what are you doing here? I've been trying to get in touch with you." Then he took a good look at what I was wearing, glanced around, and smirked. "No wonder you wouldn't answer any of my calls. The mighty Pearson West is in rehab." Then he laughed.

"If I were you, Mr. Wilson, I wouldn't be so concerned about my business. Now it would be for the best if you'd leave."

"Not without my daughter, I won't."

"We can make this easy, or we can make this difficult. You no longer have custodial rights of your daughter. You lost those when you committed acts of domestic violence against her mother and went to jail for them. The state doesn't look kindly on that. As I said earlier, it would be in your best interests if you left now, or we'll call the police."

He stepped forward, into my personal space, and said, "Why you son of a bitch. Who gives you the right to act on that?"

Rose moved closer. "I do, Greg. And my attorney does."

Wilson whipped around to Rose and before I even saw it coming, his fist flew out and he struck her. The bastard hit her in front of everyone present! For a moment I was so stunned, my body froze. But then I went into action. My hand balled into a fist and I treated him to the exact same thing he dished out to Rose. Only I was packing a hell of a lot more muscle than he was. He doubled over and gasped for air. When he dropped to his knees, I grabbed the hair on top of his head and said, "Stand up you motherfucker and take it like a man." He struggled to his feet, but I was stupid and hadn't watched his hands. Then he struck and when he did, a blade slid across the front of my shirt, slicing into the flesh of my abdomen. He flashed a superior grin as he regarded me with contempt.

"It's your turn to take it like a man," he said, his lips curling with disgust.

Oh, I'd take it like a man, all right and he was about to see exactly how much. But as I started to go for him, the doors slid open and several police officers rushed inside.

"Drop the knife and put your hands in the air," one of them said to him.

Greg's eyes momentarily widened in alarm, but then he said, "Thank God, you're here, officers. This man attacked me."

I was helping Rose to her feet and asking if she was okay when Sylvie said, "Are you crazy?" to Greg. Of course, he was one hundred percent on the crazy train, but she wasn't thinking straight.

Once Rose was on her feet, I said, "Officer, I'm Pearson West, and this is Rose Wilson. This man, Greg Wilson, was just released out of custody this morning and he came here and attacked his ex-wife *again*. There are witnesses here who can corroborate this."

Greg yelled, and pointed at me, "He attacked me."

"Of course I did, to get you away from Rose. You were beating her. And then you assaulted me with a knife." I pointed to my blood-covered shirt.

Everyone started talking at once, agreeing with what I'd said. The officer interrupted and said, "One at a time, please." He started with Sylvie and then went through all the other people that were there, of which there were four. About then, Miles ran in. I wanted to laugh. It had become a circus, except we were missing the elephant.

"Where's Montana?" Miles asked.

"In there." Rose pointed to one of the offices. "With an employee."

"Thank God she hadn't seen any of this." Then Miles explained to the officers about Greg getting released on bail this morning. After taking statements from everyone, they cuffed Greg and hauled him back to jail. Before they left, they asked me if I needed to go to the hospital. This was important as it would be admitted as part of the case and help keep Greg in jail.

"I don't think he'll be getting out so fast this time," Miles said.

"He needs anger management," I said.

"He needs psychiatric treatment," Sylvie said.

"He needs both," Rose said. Then she noticed the blood on my shirt. "You need to go to the hospital."

"What about you?" I asked. "He nailed you in the face."

Rose touched her cheek, as though she'd forgotten. "It's fine. Only a bruise. Nothing that a little ice won't cure. I've had much worse from him. Let me see your chest."

I lifted the shirt and realized the cut was fairly deep. Sylvie grabbed my upper arm and said, "Come on. Let's go."

"What about your patients?" I asked.

Her head tilted back, and she looked at the ceiling for a moment and said, "Rose?"

"I have Montana, but she can come along. Let's go."

On the way, Montana drilled me with questions. She wanted to know why I just didn't put a Power Rangers Band-Aid on it.

"Good question. I think it's too big for a Band-Aid."

"But maybe they have real big ones like this." And she held up her hands to demonstrate.

"I'll ask the people at the hospital when we get there."

"Mommy, how come when I get cut, I don't go to the hospital?"

"Because, Pop Tart, only real real bad cuts have to go to the hospital."

"But I had a bad cut that time my pinky finger got caught in the door at Daddy's."

Rose was quiet, but I'm sure she didn't like hearing about that. "Maybe it wasn't that bad."

"Daddy had to wrap it up and put ice on it. It was smashed up and bleeding."

Rose's knuckles turned white as she drove.

"It's all better now, isn't it?"

"Yep, all better now, only the top part is a little crooked. See?" She held it up and it was hard for me to tell, but I nodded to make her feel better. Rose added, "Mommy will kiss it when we get out of the car." That was enough to satisfy her.

We pulled into the emergency room parking lot. It wasn't too crowded when we arrived, and I gave them all my information. Thank God Sylvie had run to my room to get my wallet.

It took them twenty minutes to call me back. Montana wanted to come, but we thought it best she didn't watch them sew me up. She'd been through enough these last couple of days. More trauma wasn't what she needed.

The doctor took one look and had the nurse prep me for stitches. I explained how I'd been assaulted with a knife and the police had been there. I gave them the information so it could be used in court, if necessary.

"A knife?" she asked. Her eyes bulged. "I'm going to call the police station and verify all of this. I hope you're good with that."

"Actually, I'd prefer if you do because this is likely going to court."

"I understand. Let's get you fixed up here first."

Then the nurse asked, "When was your last tetanus shot?"

"Um, I can't remember."

"It's going to be today." She patted my arm and said, "You'll have a sore arm for a few days, not to mention sore abs."

After I was good and numb, the doctor ended up putting in fifteen stitches. I left with instructions and we headed back to the center.

"You okay?" Rose asked.

"I'm fine."

"Did they give you a Power Rangers Band-Aid?" Montana asked.

"No, they didn't have any big enough."

"Can I see?"

"When we get back, I'll show you."

As soon as we got out of the car, she tugged on my shirt. "I'm ready to see your boo-boo."

I lifted up my shirt and she announced, "That's a crummy Band-Aid. They didn't give you no Princesses, or nothing."

Rose covered her mouth to keep from laughing and I shrugged. "Guess I'm just not as important as you."

"Guess not." She shook her head and marched inside as we followed. Over her shoulder, she said, "Next time you tell them they gotta get better Band-Aids."

"Yes, ma'am." I gave her a salute.

Chapter Twenty-One

ROSE

SATURDAY WAS HERE AND MY NERVES WERE ON OVERDRIVE. I had filled my essential oil medallion with enough lavender, bergamot, and frankincense to smell up the room and it still wasn't working. My hands were shaking, and my knees were knocking.

Montana and I went to the center to meet Pearson. He was moving in today, but that's not why I was freaking. It was because his entire family was coming today. Yes, his mom, dad, both brothers, and both sisters-in-law. Talk about a monumental moment. For him, yes, but for me too. Sylvie was coming, not because of the family, but because I threatened her with death if she didn't. I told her I would put arsenic in her coffee every day for the next month if she didn't show up. She knew I was joking but still. A little hand-holding was necessary today. Okay, maybe a lot of hand-holding.

We were on the way to the center when the questions started.

"Mommy, will he eat all my cookies?" Montana asked.

"No, I won't let him, and I'll make plenty so there'll be enough for both of you."

"Promise?"

"I promise."

"Mommy, does he like pizza because if we can't eat pizza no more, he can't stay."

"You know what? If he doesn't like pizza, he can just make what he wants to eat, and you and I will still get pizza. How does that sound?"

"Good. If he likes pizza, will he eat it all?"

I laughed. "I promise, if he likes pizza, I'll order one for him and you and I will split one."

"Okay. Does he like to watch movies cuz boys don't like movies."

"Who told you that?"

"Daddy did."

"Well, maybe Daddy didn't like them, but if Pearson doesn't, he can go to his room and do something else, or we can flop out on my bed and watch one. Is that good?"

"Yeah. Can I still sleep with you sometimes?"

"Now what do you think, Pop Tart?"

"Yay!" She clapped her hands.

"Only if you don't hog the bed."

I parked the car and pulled her out of her booster seat. "I'm not a bed hog, you are."

"You are," and I started making piggy noises. She giggled and imitated me. We walked toward the doors holding hands and laughing.

"I'm happy with you, Mommy." My heart filled with sunshine and pure joy and I dropped to my knees to hug her.

"Aww, give me a big ole squeeze." Her little arms went around me as much as they could and I said, "I'm soooooo happy with you too, my beautiful girl."

We started jabbering back and forth saying, "You're beautiful. No, you're beautiful. No, you're beautiful."

By the time we were in the lobby, I didn't realize we had an audience until Pearson said, "I think you both are beautiful."

Montana clapped and said, "Hey Mister. Mommy said you won't eat all the chocolate chip cookies."

"Mister has a name, Pop Tart. It's Mr. Pearson, remember?"

"Uh huh, but that's a lot to say, so I'm gonna call him Mister for short."

"Honey, that's not how it works. You either call him Mr. Pearson or Mr. West."

"Nah, I like plain old mister."

I was getting ready to launch into an explanation of mister, when an adorable girl of maybe eight years of age came up to us and said, "Hi, I'm Kinsley."

"Hi, Kinsley. "I'm Rose and this is Montana."

"Montana, do you like to dance. I have clicky shoes at home and I could teach you."

Another woman came running up to us and said, "Not now, Kinsley. Maybe later. I'm Marin, Pearson's brother Grey's wife."

"Oh, hi. I didn't realize his family had arrived already."

She leaned in and whispered, "Oh, yeah. It was like holding back a stampede, if you get me. Be prepared." She winked.

"I'm Rose, by the way, and thanks for the heads up." I wasn't sure what she meant by that, but when I looked across the room, a sea of curiosity stared back at me. And then it hit me. Holy shit. Those West Brothers. What the hell! Sylvie was right. What kind of genes had they been gifted with? And where was Sylvie anyway? With trembling knees, I entered the circle of doom.

"Hi everyone, I'm Rose Wilson."

They all stood at once and I was overwhelmed by a dose of … there was no name for it. Pearson was by my side handling all the introductions. He started with the parents, and then Grey. Marin was married to him. God help me, I needed a fan. Then he went to Lilly. No Milly. Milly, Milly, Milly. Milly. Marin. Both M's. I had to remember this. Milly was married to Hudson. Hot as hell Hudson. The parents were Rick and Paige. I gotta be honest here. Rick was handsome too. He was probably in his fifties, but damn. And Paige ... she was positively gorgeous. No wonder the kids had turned out so perfect.

Rick and Paige were the first to approach me with their thanks.

"You have no idea what this means to us for you to open your home to our son. We know he's going to need help but for you to do this. We can't possibly thank you enough. If there's anything you need, please let us know." Then Paige hugged me. All of her warmth enveloped me, and I could tell why this family was so close. It all stemmed from their mother.

"Oh." This completely took me by surprise. My hand covered my heart. "I'm happy to do it and it will help me too with my mortgage payment while he's there."

Then Paige took my good hand and said, "As a mother, I'm sure you can understand how worried I've been."

I thought about Montana when she was with her dad and how scared I was. "I certainly can. I will do everything I can to help him when he needs it. His days are fine. It's the nights he seems to have the most difficulty with and that's where I'll come in. Don't worry, Paige, Pearson is working hard to conquer this. He's so dedicated. And he understands that once an addict, always an addict. This will be his life from now on. Many patients here don't want to accept that, but fortunately, that hasn't been an issue for him."

Relief washed over her features. "This makes me feel so much better to hear you say that."

"If you ever need to talk, please call. I'm around here every day."

"Thank you."

The two brothers approached me next and I wasn't sure my ovaries could handle it. "Hi, I'm Grey."

"It's nice to meet you."

"And I'm Hudson."

"Pearson speaks about you two all the time. It's finally nice to match faces with the names."

"We can't tell you how much we appreciate you doing this."

"No, he's also helping me out too. Pearson has been a blessing to me and my daughter. As I told your mom, he's dedicated to beating this and he understands this will be his life from now on. Oh, and if you ever want to visit him, please do. My home is open. He'll be busy during the day, but in the evenings, feel free to come over. I'm not sure how far away you live, but please come."

Grey said, "I'm not far nor are our parents, but Hudson here is a city dweller."

"Yeah, I have a practice in Manhattan."

"Practice?"

"Veterinary."

"Ah, that's really cool."

Hudson went on, "And big bro here is a cardiologist about fifteen minutes away."

"Nice. You and your family should stop over."

"Yeah, about that. My daughter, Kinsley has this thing about dancing."

I chuckled. "She already tried to recruit my daughter."

Grey huffed. He didn't appear to be the eye-rolling type of guy. "Sorry about that. She's a persistent thing. Anyway, I have a three-year-old son that is in constant motion and then we have twin babies, so it might be hard bringing the entire family."

Suddenly this adorable little boy ran up to Hudson and said "Daddy, do you think she has a big Dick?"

"Wiley, I thought I told you to hold all your Dick questions," Hudson said. Then Hudson turned to me and said, "It's not what you think. We have a one hundred fifty pound English Mastiff named Dick, and sometimes he's called big Dick. Wiley loves him and wants everyone to have one."

My bugged eyes turned back to normal and I laughed. "For a

minute there I wondered what the heck, but the answer would be no. I don't have any dogs."

Wiley looked crushed. "Your baby doesn't have any pets to play with?"

"I'm sorry, no she doesn't."

"You need a dog. Like Chester. He's real good and small. Isn't he Daddy?"

"Yes, he is, son, but not everyone can have dogs."

"Why not?"

"Because they work and don't have anyone to take care of them. Your nanny takes care of ours."

"Oh." Wiley still looked crushed.

"Go play with Kinsley."

"She wants me to dance."

Grey told Wiley, "Tell her your daddy said you didn't have to."

"Okay." And he ran off.

Hudson looked over at me and said, "Sorry about the big Dick comment."

"I confess, it did catch me off guard." Then I chuckled. "Great name by the way."

"Everything in our house will catch you off guard. Poor Milly. When we met, I'm not sure what she thought of us."

"Well, the invitation is open for both of you, kids or no kids. Big Dick, I'm not so sure about."

There was a third man there who I knew didn't carry the West genes. He was extremely handsome, but his features didn't look at all like any of them. Pearson said, "Rose, I'd like you to meet my best friend since we were kids. We grew up together and were college roommates. This is Evan Thomas."

Evan held out a hand and I took it. "It's great to meet you, Rose. Pearson has told me great things about you."

"It's great to meet you too, and I hope he didn't exaggerate too much."

"I'm pretty sure he didn't."

Sylvie rushed in then, looking totally flustered and Evan's attention turned to her. I saw how he looked at her and wondered if there was something between them, but she totally ignored him, so I was probably imagining it. "Hey Aunt Paige, Uncle Rick. Everyone else. Sorry I'm late, but my car wouldn't start. I had to get my neighbor to jump it."

Now I felt guilty about being peeved at her. "Are you okay?"

"Sure, other than being angry at my car. After this, I'm going to get a new battery."

She dragged me off to the side and said, "How is everything?"

"Couldn't be better. And for the record, I won't poison you. But I am pissed off. You didn't get close to describing how good looking your cousins were. And why didn't you tell me about Evan?"

She snickered. "Yeah. I forgot about Evan. What about that?"

Pearson walked up and asked, "What about what?"

"I was telling Sylvie that it sucks she has to get a new battery."

He regarded us skeptically and then said, "I'm going to let this one pass. But I'll get it back somehow."

"What do you mean?" I asked, frowning.

"That's for me to know and for you to find out." He winked and meandered away.

Chapter Twenty-Two

PEARSON

AS WE WALKED OUT TOGETHER, ROSE SAID, "WOW, YOUR family is awesome. What a great support system, not to mention Evan."

"Yeah, I'm a lucky guy." When we reached the parking lot, I said, "I'll follow you."

"What do you mean?"

"Hudson brought my car, so I'll be driving. He's already loaded my bags for me." I scanned the lot and saw where he parked. "I'm right over there."

"That's your car?" She gawked at the black Mercedes AMG. No doubt, it was a beaut. She packed just under six hundred horses and could hit sixty mph in under four seconds. I wanted to laugh at Rose's expression but didn't.

"Uh huh."

"Wow. You must've been really successful."

"Oh, yeah, and see where it got me?" I spread my arms wide

and spun around. "A place at the head of my class at Flower Power."

She pressed her lips together as though she was suppressing a laugh. "I'm sorry. The situation is far from funny, but the way you said it …" Then she broke into a belly laugh.

"The way I see it is you gotta laugh, right? It takes the heaviness away. I've had way too much of that lately," I said, not taking offense at her finding this funny.

"So have I. You know my car. My place isn't far from here, maybe ten minutes."

"See you there." I held my hand in the air and ambled off to my ride. As I slid inside, it was a strange sensation as I hadn't driven in over, what, two months? It felt … good. No, it felt awesome. I inhaled the scent of leather and enjoyed the way the seats wrapped around me. Then I realized these were things I'd taken for granted in my old life. I pushed the ignition and listened to her purr. Rose was waiting so I put the car into drive and off we went.

We pulled into the driveway of a nice little pale gray bungalow with black shutters. Rose slipped out and then got Montana out of her seat. By the time I pulled my two bags out of the trunk, they were on the front porch unlocking the door.

"You need some help, Mister?"

I guess that name was going to stick for a while. "Nope. I've got it, muffin."

"I'm not a muffin." She stuck a hand on her hip.

"Well, I'm not a mister."

"Uh huh. You're Mister Pearson."

Damn if she didn't have me there. "And you're Muffin Montana."

She said, "Am not," then scampered into the house.

Rose said, "She's a mess. Sorry my house isn't very extravagant."

"It's perfect." We entered into a hall that led down to what I thought was a kitchen. To the right was the living room.

"Let me show you your room so you can put your bags down."

I followed her down the hall. The kitchen was ahead on the right and then the bedrooms were at the end. Two were on the right and one was on the left, which was the master. "This is mine." She pointed to one at the end. "That's yours." We walked in and it was small but very tidy. There was a twin bed, a small dresser, mirror, and a small desk. "It's really small."

"No, this is great. I love it." I dropped my bags on the floor and looked around. There were some very nice paintings on the walls. "These are lovely."

"Thank you."

I walked closer and inspected them. They were all scenes of various things—forests, fields of flowers, and a river flowing through the woods. "This artist is very talented, at least in my opinion. I don't really know that much about art, but these are beautiful."

"Um, I did them."

"Really? Rose, they're fantastic. Do you still paint?"

"No, not because I don't want to, but because I don't have the time. I stopped not long after I got married."

"I don't have to guess why."

She fiddled with her cast. "Yeah, he told me my work was shit."

"I suppose he was an expert."

She shrugged. "It didn't matter. When someone who supposedly loves you tells you those things, you believe them. I put my canvas and paints away and stopped. That's when I went to school. He hated me even worse then. He never wanted me to make anything of myself."

"Of course not. You were a threat to him then. He would lose his power over you."

"Ugh, I was so stupid back then. Looking at things now, I can't believe I stayed with him." She tugged on her shirt.

"You have to look at it differently. My brother, Grey, had a really bad first marriage. It ended when his wife was killed, but his life turned out great after he met Marin. However, his first marriage brought him Kinsley and Aaron, his children. If it hadn't been for that, he would've missed out. And so would my brother, Hudson. He had bad luck the first time around, but he got Wiley out of it. You got Montana and look at what you would've missed without her in your life."

"You should've been a psychologist instead of an attorney." Her smile was a bit faltering.

"You would never have said that if you'd met me before rehab. I've changed and I'm hoping it's for the better." My confidence level was so-so. I knew the path I was on was the right one, but there were still miles ahead on my journey. Some days would be more difficult than others, and it was expected.

"Looks like we're both different people now. And that's a good thing."

All of a sudden, a little voice interrupted us. "Hey Mister, you gonna come and look at my room?"

Little chatterbox was back. "Sure thing, Muffin."

"Humph. You always gonna call me that?"

"As long as you call me Mister, I am." She put her tiny hand in mine and pulled me along behind her. She reminded me so much of Kinsley, bossy and chatty as hell. Her room was cute as hell, with pictures of all sorts of animals hanging on the wall. Rose had followed me in, so I looked at her pointedly.

"Yep, I did those too."

Montana ran up to one of a monkey and said, "This one's my favorite. I love monkeys." Her expression morphed into one of pure joy when she asked, "Mommy, can we go to the zoo?"

"I don't see why not."

Then she grabbed my hand and said, "Mister, you gotta come too."

"You know what? I'd love to, but I have a meeting in" —I checked the time— "about a half hour." I was attending my first Narcotics Anonymous meeting today. Dr. Martinelli had set me up to meet my intermediate sponsor and he was driving out from the city to attend with me here. It was a huge favor, so I needed to get going. It was a fifteen-minute drive from here.

"You're meeting Reese, right?" Rose asked.

"Yeah, and he's driving out from the city."

"You'll really like him, and he'll be an awesome sponsor for you."

"He's actually going to introduce me to my main sponsor here but said I could also use him as one if I wanted to attend the NA group in the city."

"Can you come to the zoo after?" Montana asked.

This was my first meeting and I wanted to spend some time with Reese afterward. "I'm not sure how long the meeting will last. Maybe we can go another day." Disappointment coated her features.

Rose came to my rescue. "They'll be plenty more times we can go, honey. Maybe instead of the zoo today, we can go to a movie. How's that?"

She jumped up and down. "Yay, a movie. Can I get candy and popcorn?"

"Maybe candy *or* popcorn," Rose said.

"Lucky muffin, you are. Can you show me the bathroom and then I have to leave."

"Sure."

"I can," Montana yelled. She hopped her way out the door and down to the bathroom. "Here it is. And don't forget to wash your hands after you go. Germs are icky."

"Yes, ma'am." I saluted her and heard her giggle as I closed the door. That child was something. She was a different kid since leaving her dad's home. If that wasn't telling, I didn't know what was.

I left shortly after and made it to the meeting a few minutes early. A tall man with sandy colored hair approached me as I entered. "Are you Pearson West?"

"I am."

"Reese Christianson. It's good to meet you although I wish it were under different circumstances." We shook hands.

"I'm glad to meet you and I'm actually glad to be here. This is saving my life. Oh, and thanks for driving out here. I've heard nothing but great things about you."

He ran his hand through his crop of hair. "Yeah, don't believe everything you hear. I hear you're an attorney."

"Yeah. I, um, I'm not sure where I'll end up after this. I've decided to leave the firm I was with though."

"You've been sober for what, sixty days?"

"Yeah. On the nose."

"If I could make a suggestion? Don't make any life altering decisions for at least another sixty days, minimum. Your brain is still unscrambling itself and will for a while. It's been screwed around with so much for the past however long you used, it's going to take some time for it to normalize. I'm sure Gabby mentioned this."

"Gabby?"

"Sorry. Dr. Martinelli."

"Right, and she did several times. But honestly, the practice I was in was so high pressure, I don't want that anymore."

We walked over to a table where coffee and all the fixings were set up. Then we each made ourselves a cup.

Reese said after he took a long slug of his java, "Now that's a different story altogether. High pressure is not good and that's the last thing you want to subject yourself to after you've been through rehab."

"I'm interested in setting up a practice somewhere up here to help people pro bono and, of course, do other cases as well. But not work for anyone, just myself."

"I get that. I'm an attorney too. I went to law school after I rehabbed. I'll tell you the story after the meeting since it's getting ready to start."

We took our seats, and soon, I was standing up saying, "My name is Pearson West and I'm an opiate addict and an alcoholic."

It had gotten easier over the last month to do this, but these were new people, so it was a bit unsettling. You'd think after sixty days of this, I'd be used to it. Only I wasn't. Shame still filled me each time I said it. I imagined it always would. Admitting one's failures, especially one of this nature wasn't easy. Doing it daily wasn't easy either. But I accepted it, because if I didn't, I would end up down that drug-filled hole and be looking at death square in the eyes. That was not something I would willingly choose to do.

The meeting ended and as we were walking out, Reese said, "After five years, I still get new messages from these meetings. Today I learned that you have to spare some time every day, even if it's just a couple of minutes, to focus on what was broken inside, because if you don't reflect on that, it won't ever get fixed permanently. I know that, but sometimes I forget."

I thought about that for a minute. "I used to think my life was perfect and that the reason I became an addict was only because of shoulder surgery. I didn't think it had anything to do with me or my career. But when I dug down deep, it was all the internal and external pressures that kept me using. Before I knew it, I'd moved to H. I was a fucking mess."

"Hey, you wanna go grab some lunch?" he asked.

"Sure. I don't know what's around here, but there has to be something."

He pulled out his phone and found a place a few blocks away, so we drove over. Once we were seated and ordered our food, he told me this unbelievable story about himself.

"So, Gabby wanted me as your sponsor because I ended up on drugs after a pretty serious beatdown that nearly killed me."

After a short laugh, I said, "My beatdown nearly killed me too, but in the end, it's what saved my life. I don't remember what happened, but I wish I could find the people who did it so I could thank them. Ironic, huh? Tell me what happened to you."

"Are you into ballet?"

I shrugged. "I'd go here and there. My parents would be the ones to ask that."

"So, I was a ballet dancer. I studied at the Royal Ballet in London when I was a kid and then came back here to study contemporary ballet at Joffrey. I was picked up by Metropolitan Ballet Company. I became their principal dancer. My stage name wasn't Reese Christianson. It was Reston Blakely. Anyway, one night after a performance, we all went out to party and when I left the bar, I was mugged and beaten. My leg was broken, and I could no longer dance. That's when I started using."

"It ruined your career." No wonder he went down the hole.

"That's an understatement. It destroyed me. I spiraled. Like you, first it was pills, then it was whatever I could get my hands on. I finally met Gabby and Case."

"Case?"

"My NA sponsor. He saved me from death."

"No wonder Dr. Martinelli wanted us to meet." I thought about his experience and how much more he went through than I did. "How did your family take it?"

He laughed. "My dad and I never got along. He would've chosen a different career path for me. My mom was a dancer until she got pregnant with me and I ruined her career, or so I thought. Turned out she gave up dancing because she couldn't bear to be away from me. Only I didn't know that at the time and I resented both of them. I was pretty much a jerk. Things are great now, but they weren't for a long time. My aunt, actually my mom's aunt, was my champion. She was my biggest supporter growing up."

"I'm sorry, man. I count my blessings. My family is awesome. I remember at the beginning of therapy, everyone kept asking about them, and I reiterated how great they all were. It finally sunk in that it wasn't my upbringing or family. It was me and my current situation."

"In many cases, that's easier to overcome. Not always, and

I'm far from a professional. But in the people I've worked with, that's been my experience."

I put my hands together in the prayer pose. "All I know is I'm on the right track and I plan to keep it that way."

He grinned. "Keep it up, man."

"So, an attorney, huh?"

"Yeah. After my attack, I wanted to protect victims of crime and I figured I could do a better job of it if I went to law school and became a prosecutor. I work in the DA's office now. My long-term goals are to get the laws changed on the perps. I'd like for them to stay in jail longer and for the victim not to have to worry about them being released. Our laws are too easy on the criminals, in my opinion."

"That's great. I love that you have long term goals. That's what I need."

"Whoa, buddy. Your only long-term goal right now should be sobriety." His expression was stern. "I mean it. That's huge, Pearson. If that's not your number one priority for the next at least six months, you need to rethink things. Anyone at NA, or even Gabby will tell you that. Your one-year goal, even two-year goal, should be sobriety. When you get to that point, we can talk long term afterward. One day at a time, my man. One day at a time."

"You're right. I jumped the gun. But I'm psyched for you."

"You can be that, just stay focused and committed on yourself and don't let anyone deter you. Oh, and here's this." He handed me a white card with nothing but a phone number on it. "Anytime, day or night. If you need me, call. I'll always answer this number. You have the list of all the meetings nearby."

"Thanks. You do know I'm renting a room from one of the counselors at Flower Power?"

"I didn't, but that's awesome."

"I didn't exactly feel ready to be on my own yet and living with Mom and Dad … just no. I love them like crazy, but the hovering would've driven me back to using."

He chuckled. "I'm going to like working with you, Pearson. And any time you want to come to a meeting in the city, call. I'm at one every day, but I can meet you out here every Saturday."

"I really appreciate it."

I paid the lunch tab and we left with plans to talk on the phone tomorrow. He was a great guy and I'd have to let Dr. Martinelli know at my appointment this coming week how much I appreciated her arranging for him to be one of my sponsors.

Chapter Twenty-Three

ROSE

MONTANA AND I GOT HOME FROM THE MOVIE AND PEARSON walked in right afterward.

"Hey Mister. You didn't get any popcorn or McDonald's." She held up the toy she'd gotten in her kiddie meal

"Sounds like I really missed out, Muffin." He made a sad face.

A grin spread across her face. "Yep, and I ate all mine, so I don't have none for you."

"Montana, it's I don't have any for you," I said.

"Yep, I don't. Mister's just gonna hafta come with us next time and get some. You can get a toy too. Can't he, Mommy?"

"He probably can," I said, hiding a chuckle.

"I wouldn't want to miss out on that," Pearson said.

"How did it go?" I asked.

We walked to the living room and sat down while Montana skipped to her room.

"It was motivating. You know my sponsor is Reese, and he's impressive, like you said. We ate lunch afterward."

"Aw, nice. I knew you'd like him. He spoke at one of our conferences and his story blew me away."

"It blew me away too. I can't even imagine. He lost everything but built a whole new life for himself."

"Yeah, he did. Reese is special. There are so many special people associated with NA and AA that I've met throughout the years. They always amaze me at how much they give of themselves to others." It was true. Before I started in this business, I never imagined the kind of people I would meet that would inspire me along the way.

Pearson didn't say anything for a while. But then the words gushed out of him. "I now realize how much time my job took up. I didn't even have time to see my family or get to know my nieces and nephews. It was ridiculous how much my job stole from me." He sat there shaking his head as though it filled him with distaste. "I don't want to be that person anymore and at the time, I thought it was what I wanted. My parents would call and invite me out for their weekly Sunday dinners, and I'd make up excuses every week. And that was before I was using. And what good did it do? Fill my bank account? Allow me to drive a fancy car? So what? I was so empty inside."

I listened to the words spill from him. It's funny when you hear this side of successful people's lives. Like they say, money isn't always everything. Yes, it pays the bills, but it won't buy you happiness. Pearson is a hard example of this. A guy who had everything at his fingertips and look where it landed him.

Leaning closer to him, I touched his hand. "Pearson, the greatest thing about this is you understand. It's brought you in touch with what you want and don't want. And it's made you realize how important your family is. We go through life, taking things for granted. You've been given a second chance, a chance to show everyone how much you love and appreciate them. So now all you have to do is take those next steps and do it."

He jumped to his feet, holding his hands in front of him. "Hey, I have to go to my apartment in the city tomorrow to get some things. Would you like to help me? Bring Muffin too?"

"Yeah, we can come."

"Great." And he walked away. I was getting ready to go into the kitchen to see if I needed to go to the store for dinner food, when he came back in. "Would you like to come with me afterward to my parents' for Sunday dinner?"

"Um, dinner at your parents'?"

"Well, that's what we call it, but it's really a lunch. We eat around one thirty or two."

Shit. Would it be awkward? I'd only met his family once.

"The whole family usually goes, unless someone is sick or something. I'd really love it if you and Muffin could come."

"Okay, why not?"

"Great. I'll text Mom." He tapped the message into his phone, then smiled at me. My knees almost caved in. "What's wrong? Do I have something in my teeth?"

"Something ... no, why?"

"You're staring at me."

"Oh." I blinked. I'd have to go into ogle control around this man. I left the room and went into the kitchen to check for dinner items. He followed.

"What are you doing?"

I told him. "Why don't I take the two of you out?"

"You don't want a home cooked meal after eating at the center all month?" I figured after all that cafeteria food, he'd be all over this.

"Wow, I hadn't thought about it. Okay, I'll go with you to the store, but I'm buying all the groceries. By the way, how much is your mortgage?"

"Why?" That was a real personal question.

"Because if I'm going to be paying you rent, I thought I'd ask so I could write you a check."

That made sense so I told him. It was embarrassing because it wasn't huge, but it still strapped me each month.

He nodded and went to his room. When he came back, he handed me a check. The amount on it was far too much. "I can't accept this."

"Why not?"

"It's too much. It's half of my mortgage."

"True, but you have utilities to consider." Then he grinned. "Besides, I'm a lawyer and you'll never win this argument. Just take it. You're doing me a huge favor by letting me stay here. And don't forget, I'll be using your counseling services too."

He did make more than one good argument. "Okay, but I promise to cook."

"That's fine. I'm fair on the grill, but that's about it unless it's a salad or baked potatoes. Getting back to the store, are you ready to go?"

"Let me get the kiddo."

Montana made a fuss, but Pearson bribed her by telling her he'd buy her a surprise.

"What kind of surprise?" she asked.

"If I tell you, then it wouldn't be a surprise."

She crinkled her forehead and then said, "Oh yeah."

"Let's go."

We rode in Pearson's car after putting Montana's car seat in the back. We'd be taking it tomorrow too, so it made sense to do it now.

As we walked through the store, Pearson kept adding things, sweets and snacks. "You're going to make us fat."

"No, I'm not. We'll work it off. I run every day. What about you?"

"Um, I do meditation and yoga."

He roared. His deep laugh was sexy and made me tingle in unmentionable places.

"Wait a minute. That's not funny! Have you ever tried yoga? It's hard."

"True, but how about some cardio?"

I knew that was important, but I couldn't do it all. "I don't have time for that."

"You do now. I can watch Montana while you work out."

Damn. Now I'd have to, and I hated cardio.

"Or we can use the gym at the center," he suggested.

That wasn't a bad idea. "I like that thought."

"I can come right after my meeting every day."

I agreed because it did make sense. Then I spied him tossing in a can of whipped cream. I raised my brows. "You'll see. It's for the little one."

Later he grabbed beef tenderloins. "Will she eat this?" he asked.

"She eats everything."

"Do you have a grill?"

"I do. You cooking?" I asked.

"I am tonight. Do you have potatoes and salad?"

"Yes, I'll handle that if you handle the steaks."

"Done," he said.

When we got to the frozen section, he threw in some popsicles but did it when Montana wasn't looking. I grabbed a carton of vanilla ice cream."

"Hey, what about the chocolate?" he asked.

"I have hot fudge at home."

"That'll work."

"Mommy has sprinkles. Do you like sprinkles?"

"Love the sprinkles," he said.

We checked out and when I went to pay, he slid his credit card in before I had a chance. Then he smirked.

"You weren't supposed to do that."

"We never established grocery shopping rules," he said, winking.

The cashier gave us an odd look as she handed him the receipt. He pushed the loaded cart out and Montana and I followed. When we got home, I unpacked the items, but he wanted to help so he knew where everything was.

"Where's my surprise?" Montana asked.

"Close your eyes," he said. Then he took the paper off of a popsicle and said, "Open your mouth. When she did, he stuck the tip of the popsicle in. "Can you guess what it is?"

"A popsicle!"

"What kind?"

"Cherry!" She opened her eyes and he handed her the popsicle.

"Montana, what do you say?"

"Thank you, Mister."

"You're welcome, Muffin."

She giggled up a storm, then ate her popsicle with gusto. When she was finished, Pearson said, "I have another surprise for you."

"Another surprise?"

"Yep, but you have to lay down on the floor."

"Okay." She did as she was told.

"Now close your eyes real tight."

When her eyes were closed, he went to the refrigerator and grabbed the can of whipped cream. "Are your eyes closed?"

"Yeah."

"Keep them closed and open your mouth real wide."

When she had her mouth open, he shot a stream of whipped cream into it. "Now close." Her cheeks were bulged out and it was hilarious. "You can swallow it."

After she did, she hollered, "Whipped cream!" Her eyes twinkled.

"Did you like it?"

"Yeah, can I have some more?"

"Okay, but keep your mouth open real wide."

"Can I keep my eyes open?"

"Yep." He was about two feet above her when he shot it out of the can and missed her mouth entirely—I'm pretty sure on purpose. He sprayed it on her nose and cheeks as she laughed and laughed. I was cracking up. She was a mess.

"Mommy's turn now."

Pearson turned to me and wiggled the can in front of my face. "Okay, but if I go then so do you."

"Fair enough."

I dropped to the floor next to Montana and opened my mouth. A stream of whipped cream hit my lips and filled my mouth until he shifted to my nose and cheeks. I was a young girl again before things got super shitty at home with my parents, and I laughed and laughed as though I didn't have a care in the world.

"Isn't it good, Mommy?"

"The very best."

"Now it's your turn, Mister."

He handed the can to me and our fingers brushed. An electric shock ran through me from my hand to my toes. What the hell was that? He stared at me as though I'd shot him. At least I hadn't been the only one who'd felt it.

I watched him lie down, and his shirt rode up slightly, so I saw a thin ribbon of skin above the waist of his jeans. I wanted to cover it with the whipped cream and lick it off until it was gone. I clenched the can as my mind raced to more inappropriate thoughts of him.

"Mommy, hurry." I jerked myself away from my fantasy, and back to the can I was holding. Bending down, because I would never trust my aim, I squirted the can and watched him open his mouth. His tongue probed the mess I made on his lips and was it ever hot. So I squirted some more, only this time, I intentionally missed. I circled his mouth several times so he'd have to lick it off. I wanted to lean over him and help him. His eyes were locked onto mine the whole time, never moving at all. If Montana hadn't been there, I'm pretty damn sure, there would've been more whipped cream play, only she said, "Mommy, more."

I leaned back on my heels and then moved over to her so I could give her shot. This had shaken me to the core. I knew I was attracted to him, but this went beyond that. He was more than just an attractive man. There was a lot of substance to Pearson West and I was falling for him. Was I setting myself up for a gigantic heartbreak? It was too soon to tell and right now, I didn't care.

Chapter Twenty-Four

PEARSON

AFTER DINNER, WHICH WAS DELICIOUS, ROSE TUCKED Montana into bed. She yelled from her room, "Hey, Mister, come and give me a goodnight kiss."

She had a voice that could carry for miles. By the time I got there, which took all of twenty seconds, she scolded me. "What took you so long, slowpoke?"

"I'll have you know I can run fast, Muffin. We'll have to race tomorrow so I can prove it."

Her stick-sized arms reached out from under the covers. "Okay, but I gotta sleep first."

I hid a smile as I bent over the bed and hugged her. She smacked a big kiss on my cheek and said, "Good night, sleep tight, and don't let the bugs bite."

I said back to her, "See ya later alligator." Before I could finish, she added, "After while crocodile." We fist bumped and I left so Rose could do the final tuck in. She sure was precocious, and cute as hell.

I was already channel surfing by the time Rose joined me. "She really likes you, Pearson."

"Yeah, it's pretty obvious. She's so damn cute, the feeling is mutual. She sure has come out of her shell since she's been here."

"This is what she's always like around me. That's why I was so worried about her. There is something really bad going on in that house."

Taking her hand in mine, I said, "You don't have to worry about that anymore."

"When do you think my court date will be?"

"I'll call Miles on Monday and check on things. But I'm sure your ex will have a struggle getting out of jail this time. The second offense won't make it easy for him. The private investigator we hired couldn't find anything. I wasn't too pleased with him though, so we released him. With Greg in jail, it doesn't matter now anyway."

"I don't trust the system and he's such a snake, he'll be able to slither his way out of this."

"Even if he does, he won't be able to slither his way back into Montana's life unsupervised."

She studied me and the weight of her gaze was pressing. Then she nodded, saying, "I trust you."

"Good, now pick out a movie for us to watch. I'll even cave in to a chick flick."

After a playful swat, she took the remote and scanned the channels. She put on a murder mystery.

"No chick flick?"

"Nah, I wouldn't do that to you."

"I think I love you."

She chuckled. "Don't say that. One day I'll force you to watch a chick flick marathon."

"I rescind those words then. If you do that, I'll force you to watch a football marathon."

"That's great. I love football." She gave me a saucy wink.

I tugged on the hand I still held and drew her closer to me.

"I'm loving this arrangement, and you, more and more every day. A woman who loves football. I thought I'd never meet one. Tell me who your team is."

"I have a few. I'm a home girl fan. I love the Mammoths and I wish they'd get their crap together. I also love—and don't even ask me why, but I love the Wildcats. There are a couple other teams I follow, but those are my main ones."

"We'll have to go to some games then if you're such a fan."

Her hand covers her chest. "Oh, that would be amazing. I've never been to a pro football game."

I pulled out my phone and ordered up season tickets. "We're definitely going."

Her face brightened like a full moon. "Oh, my God! Now I can't wait for football season."

"You'll have to since it's only the beginning of May."

"Yeah, but it'll be here before we know it."

She squeezed my hand and thanked me over and over.

"Stop. You've done so much for me already, and who knows how much I'll need your help in the coming months. It'll be my pleasure to take you. Now let's watch the movie."

It turned out to be good, but Rose didn't make it through. She fell asleep on my shoulder, and it was the perfect chance for me to admire her lovely face. Smooth skin, beautiful full lips, and hair that tempted me way too much framed her beauty. I wanted to pull her against my body and hold her tightly. I'd never wanted this before. Not physically, but emotionally. I wanted whatever was between us to grow. She was kind, loving and honest. I'd observed her with Montana and love streamed out of her like a river. This was a woman who didn't want anything but the best for her child. She didn't use people, like the women I was used to. Rose was pure. And the best thing about her was she knew me, knew all my dirty secrets, so I could be myself around her.

When the movie ended, I picked her up and put her to bed. She sighed as I tucked her in, but barely woke. As I crawled between the sheets of my own bed, I fell asleep for the first time, content, and not craving the drugs that usually haunted me every night.

I was in the place that was neither sleep nor awake, where you're floating in the comfort of your bed, when something stabbed the tip of my nose. I swatted it, thinking it might be a bug.

Dozing off again, the damn thing came back. I was lying on my side so I opened one eye and Montana was only inches from my nose. Her finger was extended, homing in for another attack. I intercepted it before she had a chance. She let out a squeal of surprise, then bubbles of laughter spilled out.

"Why are you poking my nose?"

"I was wondering when you were gonna wake up. Mommy's making pancakes and you don't wanna miss 'em."

"Is that so?"

"Uh huh." Her head bobbed with her answer. "Hey Mister, whatcha got those for?" She pointed to the tattoos on my chest. Then her tiny fingers outlined the large rose over my pec.

"Because I like them." I made a move to get up, but then I remembered that I was naked beneath the covers.

"I like the flower. You like flowers too?"

Before I could answer, Rose tapped on the door and asked, "Is trouble in here?"

"Not trouble. But I did hear pancakes were in the works."

"Yes, there are, but did she wake you up?" There was a bit of a warning in her tone.

"You might want to ask Muffin that."

"Montana, did you wake him?"

"I didn't want him to miss out, Mommy."

Rose crossed her arms and wasn't happy. "What did I tell you?"

A sad Montana answered, "I'm not supposed to ever come in here unless I'm invited."

"That's right. And did Pearson invite you?"

"No." She sure looked pitiful with that lower lip poked out.

"Then no whipped cream on your pancakes." Now she was absolutely crushed.

I started to say something, but Rose's hand flew up, so my mouth slammed shut. "If you'll excuse us, we'll allow you to get up, Pearson. Come on, Montana."

She dutifully followed her mother out the door, allowing me to throw on some clothes. When I reached the kitchen, the aroma of pancakes was like heaven to my nose.

"Ah, it smells delicious."

"Mommy makes the best pancakes in the whole wide world."

"I don't know about that, but they aren't bad. You ready for coffee?"

"Please." She pointed to the coffee maker and I hurried over and grabbed a cup.

"How'd you sleep?" she asked.

"Great. It was my first night with no cravings."

"Really? That's awesome."

"Yeah, I thought so too. Must be the environment."

I observed her as she finished cooking. There was a huge stack of pancakes in the oven that she pulled out and added the last batch to. The table was already set with all the necessary items.

"Have a seat," she said. "Montana, go wash your hands."

Montana cast a glance at me and said, "Come on Mister, you gotta wash yours too."

Setting my coffee cup down, I started to follow her, but Rose stopped me. "You know you don't have to let her order you around."

"True, but I do need to wash my hands."

She gestured toward the kitchen sink. "You can do it there."

"Nah, I'll go with the Muffin."

Her eyes twinkled with mirth as she nodded. I caught up with Montana as she stood by the sink. "You gotta scrub the germs off before you eat."

"Can you give me a squirt of soap?" She pumped some foam into my hands, and I washed them until they were clean. We both dried off and hustled back into the kitchen. Rose had already served us our stacks, so we sat down to eat.

The first bite melted in my mouth. "Oh, God, these are delicious."

"Told ya," Montana said with her mouth stuffed.

"Montana, you're not supposed to talk with your mouth full."

"Sorry." She chewed, then swallowed. "Mommy's pancakes are the bestest in the whole world."

"I agree," I said, going in for another forkful. I polished off the stack on my plate when Rose asked if I wanted more. "Are there more?"

"Plenty more."

"Then, yes!"

She went to get them, but I beat her to it. "I'm a grown man who can serve himself. Can I get anyone anything?"

"Nope," Montana said.

Rose corrected her by saying, "Pop Tart, you should say, 'No thank you.'"

"No thank you," she mimicked her mom.

Rose didn't want anymore, but I loaded up for round two. I couldn't get enough of these.

After everyone was finished, I started to clean up the kitchen. Rose tried to object, but I said, "You cooked, I clean. It's only fair. After I'm done, I'll shower and then we can go into the city to grab my things. How does that sound?"

She finished off her coffee and said, "Sounds great. I'll jump in the shower now. Montana, I laid out your clothes for today. I want you to get dressed now."

They both left me to clean up, which was a breeze. Then I headed for the shower. By the time I was dressed, they were both waiting on me.

The drive into the city was quick since it was Sunday morning. I pulled into the parking garage and it was strange since it had been so long since I had been here. My apartment was a half block away. I lived in a building with spacious lofts. When we walked up to the door, I said, "Just a warning. I haven't been here in a while, so I have no idea what shape the place is in."

"Hey, don't worry," Rose said.

"Hudson came by a few times, but other than that, it's been empty since, well, you know." I unlocked the door and was met with a sign that said, "Welcome home, bro." I chuckled at it. "My brother." I checked everything out and it was immaculate. "He must've had the place cleaned because I can assure you this is not how I left it."

"I see. But this place is fantastic."

"Have a look around."

Montana took off and ran up the steps to the loft. There was a sitting area up there, but I never really used it. My nephew, Wiley, had some toys up there because he called it his fort. She yelled down to us, "You got toys up here."

"They're my nephew's, but you can play with them."

There was also a TV and some video games. I went back to my bedroom to gather up some clothes. When I went into rehab, Hudson only packed casual things. I needed some suits, dress shirts, and ties, in case I went to court with Miles. I also needed more clothes, so I packed two large suitcases. There were other things I wanted, such as my computer, iPad, chargers, and messenger bag. In my desk drawer, I kept dozens of flash drives from my files at work. I was mostly interested in the one from Rose's divorce. They were labeled by month and year. I took them all so I could look at them later. I packed a few more pairs of shoes too. As I was zipping up the duffle, I heard, "Knock knock."

I looked over my shoulder to see Rose standing there. "Come in. I was just grabbing some extra shoes."

"I love this place. Do you rent?"

"No, I bought it then had it done to my specs."

"It's fantastic. I love the way you designed the kitchen and the open floor plan, but the bedroom areas are so private. And you have so much space. It's amazing."

"Yeah, I enjoyed living here, probably a little too much."

"It's so well thought out, even the closets." The doorbell rang, cutting into our conversation.

"Would you mind answering that? I'll be out in a sec."

She left and as soon as I had everything together, I went out to the front door to see who was there and fuck it all. Standing there was one of my former heroin suppliers.

"Pearson, where in the hell have you been? You owe me money for a shit load of H and Dwayne has been on my ass, threatening me. I've been stopping by for over two months now, but you never answer your fucking door. What the hell is going on?"

Chapter Twenty-Five

ROSE

WHEN I ANSWERED THE DOOR, I SHOULD'VE LOOKED through the peephole first, but I didn't. It never occurred to me that whoever was out there posed a threat. I turned the knob and the door was shoved open, nearly knocking me on my ass. Then a woman, and I use that term loosely, marched through into the room.

"Who are you?" she asked.

"Shouldn't I be the one asking that question?"

She grabbed my shirt with her fists and jerked me up against her. "Shut your fucking mouth. Who are you and where's Pearson?"

She smelled like garbage off the streets, her hair was snarled and filthy, and her clothing didn't look much better. About that time, Pearson came into the room. She let me go and started in on him, wanting to know where he'd been.

"How much do I owe you, Letty?"

"Five, but I need to charge you interest for taking Dwayne's fist too many times." She was so filthy I hadn't noticed the bruises on her face at first. But now as I inspected her more closely, sure enough, they were there. One on her cheek and another on her jaw.

"I'll pay you."

He left the room and came back with a roll of cash. Who the hell keeps that much cash around?

"Here. Count it out."

She did and there were fifty-five hundred dollar bills there. He must've been using a ton of heroin to owe her that much money. She slipped the roll into her bra. "So, where've you been?"

"That's none of your concern. And just so you know, I won't be needing you to stop by anymore."

"What do you mean?"

"I mean I'm out of the market."

"What? You mean you got clean?"

"That's right," he said. His posture was straight and firm.

She let out a bitter laugh. "How many times have I heard that? Don't lose my number, sweet cheeks. You'll be calling me."

"I don't think so. Do me a favor and lose my address."

"You're that sure of yourself?"

"I am."

"And how many times have you tried to quit?"

"My first and only. I won't be going through it again."

She stared at him for a long time. "Well, just in case, you know where to find me."

As she started for the door, I said, "You may want to consider the same thing before it's too late."

"Ha. And who are you to know what I need?"

Before I could stop myself, I mumbled, "I know you need a bath."

She was on me like lightning. Pearson yanked her away and told her never to come back. The door slammed behind her and he said, "I'm so sorry about this." Then he escaped to his bedroom.

I followed because it was nothing to be ashamed of. There would be countless people who would remind him of his old life, and I would help him get through it. He wasn't in his room, but the bathroom door was closed.

"Pearson, can I come in?"

"Give me a minute." It sounded like he was sick, as in throwing up. I heard the toilet flush, and then the water running in the sink. When he emerged, he wore a downtrodden expression.

"I'm sorry. That whole encounter literally made me ill."

"Hey, don't worry about it. Situations like that may happen again. You never know who you'll run into."

He sat on the bed, with steepled fingers, his gaze riveted to the floor. "You don't understand. I ... uh, slept with her. When I was high and drugged out." His tone was smeared with disgust. "I don't remember any of it, only waking up next to her. Thank God I got tested for HIV. Did you look at her, I mean really look at her? She made my skin crawl and the whole idea of being with her ... that's what made me sick." His hands trembled as he spoke. "I'm so fucking humiliated."

"Remember, you weren't in your right mind. People do all sorts of things they regret when they're high on drugs, Pearson."

"But, she was foul. Totally disgusting. How could I have done that? I'm not sure how I'll ever get past that."

I sat next to him and took his hands. "You're going to have to find a way. I was proud of the way you stood up to her. You showed her you had a backbone. A lot of people would've curled up against someone like her. She noticed it too."

It took a few minutes before he braved a glance at me. "You don't condemn me." It wasn't a question.

"You should know this already. Addiction is a disease, not a choice. Of course I don't condemn you." I put my arms around him and hugged him.

"Thank you. It seems I'm always saying those words to you. But I know I really need to attend my meeting today."

His bed was covered with two large suitcases, a messenger bag, a duffle bag, a large garment bag, and a backpack. It was doubtful we'd make this in one trip. "Let's get this stuff down and then you can get the car and we'll load up. How's that?"

"The best idea I've heard. I need to get away from here."

I took the two suitcases, he put the messenger bag and backpack on, and grabbed the garment bag, and pulled the duffle bag, which had wheels. We ended up, by some miracle, making it in one trip. Montana and I waited while he got the car. We were on the way home in no time.

"I liked your playroom," Montana said.

"You did?" he asked.

"Yeah. Can we go back sometime?"

"Maybe."

"Yay," she yelled.

Once home, we put everything in his room, but he had to rush out to make it to the NA meeting. "I'll be back in an hour and a half. Be ready because we'll leave right away for my parents' house."

"Yes, sir." I saluted him and Montana mimicked me. He chuckled and tickled her under the chin.

"See you later, Mister."

"After while, Muffin." She waved as he drove off.

"Mommy, who was that mean lady who came to Mister's house?"

"She was just someone he used to know."

"She was bad, wasn't she?"

"Yes, she was."

"Was she going to hurt you like Daddy did?"

"No, and if she had tried to, Pearson would've stopped her."

"Oh. She scared me so I hid. Miss Caroline scared me like that sometimes." She played with the buttons on her sweater as she spoke.

"What do you mean?"

"Sometimes Miss Caroline would get mean like that lady. And she would smell bad. Daddy would yell at her a lot. She would fall asleep after she took her medicine and I wasn't allowed to wake her up. When she woke up was when she got mean."

Jesus Christ, she sounded like an addict. Is that why they locked Montana in her room? And is that why Greg had gotten so crazy? Was he using too? Come to think of it, I hadn't seen Caroline in months.

"Guess what?"

"What, Mommy?"

"You don't have to be scared anymore or worry about that anymore either. Now come give me a big ole kiss."

She popped off the couch and ran to me. Her arms wrapped around my neck and squeezed. Then she gave me a loud smacking kiss on the cheek. "Boy are you ever getting strong."

"I know. Look." She bent her arm to show me her muscle.

"Who taught you how to do that?"

"Mister did."

"He did?"

"Yeah. He's fun."

"I'm glad you like him."

"Do you like him, Mommy?"

Hell yeah, I liked him. He was hotter than any man I'd ever seen. "Um, of course I like him. He's a very nice man."

"Are you gonna kiss him?"

"Why do you ask that?"

"Because I want you to. He has a nice flower right here." She pointed to her chest. I noticed that lovely rose myself. I wanted to lick the damn thing and if she hadn't been in his room, I probably would've fallen to my knees and praised it.

"He does? Is it pretty?"

"Yeah, and it's real big. You should ask to see it. I want one like that."

"I think you'll have to wait until you're older. You can get one when you're legal."

"What's legal?"

"It means when you're eighteen."

"Oh. How many fingers is that?" She started counting but ran out at ten. "How many more?"

"Eight." I held up mine in order for her to count.

She frowned. "That's a lot, Mommy."

"Yeah, but you'll be eighteen before you know it. In the meantime, we can get you a temporary tattoo."

"What's that?"

"It's one that washes off."

That got her hopping around the room in excitement, so when Pearson got home, she told him.

"Mommy says I can have a flower like yours since I don't have enough fingers."

He looked hot even with a confused expression. "She wants a tattoo like yours, but I told her she has to be eighteen, hence not enough fingers since she only has ten. I'm allowing her to get a temporary one. What kind of flower is it?"

His puzzled look disappeared and was replaced by one of pride. Then he said with a sexy grin, "It's a rose. What else would it be?"

Chapter Twenty-Six

PEARSON

AFTER THE HORRENDOUS MORNING, THE MEETING WAS GREAT —exactly what I needed to expunge the guilt I harbored over Letty. It didn't really expunge it but allowed me to accept it and move on. There were so many things I had remorse over, we discussed ways of dealing with it. One of them was through apology. I did that with Rose this morning. It had been humiliating to face the truth of sleeping with Letty. Rose had been right. I never would've slept with her had I been in my right mind. But I hadn't and now there was nothing to do about it but accept it and move forward.

The group talked about the prayer, "God, grant me the serenity to accept the things I cannot change, the courage to change the things I can, and the wisdom to know the difference." The first part was true with me. There were going to be many times, as Rose had said, that I'd probably run into people from that life. I would need to accept and realize I couldn't change what I'd done. Going forward was the only way.

Montana eagerly waited for me when I arrived back at the house so she could tell me the news about the flower. I closely studied Rose as I told her what flower it was. A lovely pink flush spread from her neck to her cheeks.

"You were expecting something else?" I asked.

"I don't know."

"Would you care to see it?"

"Uh huh."

I unbuttoned my shirt and showed her. She moved forward and ran her fingers lightly across it.

"Kiss him, Mommy."

"Montana, hush," Rose said. Her face turned an even brighter pink. "You shouldn't say those things."

"Why not? I like Mister. He's nice and you should kiss him."

"I agree," I said. Montana clapped.

I stepped even closer to Rose and said, "I can help if you want."

Her large eyes zoomed in on my mouth then my own eyes. I didn't wait for more of an invitation. I took my chance. Her lips were silk and velvet and when mine touched hers, she sighed. I wanted more, so much more, but we had an audience yelling, "Yay." I stepped back and winked. Then I asked Montana, "Was that good enough?"

"More, Mister."

"Maybe later. We have to go."

We paraded out to the car and made the short drive to my parents' where everyone waited on us, including the dogs.

"Listen up. Don't be alarmed. Mom and Milly share custody of a big dog named Dick. He's huge, but he's a gentle giant."

"I like dogs, don't I Mommy?"

"Yes, Pop Tart, you do."

We were getting out of the car when my dad and niece ran out. "Hey, do you wanna dance?" Kinsley asked Montana.

"Kinsley, let her get out of the car first, and it's poor manners not to greet everyone first."

"Oh, sorry. Hi Uncle Pearson and Miss Rose. Can Montana come and dance?"

By that time, I'd gotten her out of her seat. "Can I, Mister?"

"Sure thing." The two girls ran off. Dad came up to Rose and greeted her.

"We're so happy you could join us today."

"Thanks for having us," she said.

We walked inside to mayhem. Dick was barking at Chester, the French Bulldog, as he ran around chasing Aaron. Wylie was yelling at Dick to stop, but he didn't listen.

"Where's Hudson?"

"Out back. Hi Pearson," both Milly and Marin said. "Hi Rose."

Rose walked over to speak to them and see their sets of twins. Mom came inside and hugged me then went over to talk to the girls. I walked out back to hang with the guys. I took the dogs and Wiley with me. Hudson threw the ball and the dogs chased it as we chatted.

"How's it going over there?" Grey asked.

"So far so good, but it's only been one night." I laughed at them.

"True."

"I went to my second meeting today and it was good. I like the group."

"That's encouraging," Dad said.

"I agree. I'm happy with things so far. Rose has been great too."

"What about the daughter?"

"She's a little spitfire. She told me today she likes me. I guess I passed her test, whatever that was."

"That's a good sign," Hudson said.

I shrugged. "I'm a loveable guy. What can I say?"

Hudson play punched me in the gut. "Your lack of humility hasn't changed much."

"Ha ha."

We talked a bit more and then Mom called us in to eat. The dining room table was set and she'd set up a smaller table in there for the four kids. She made her Sunday special chicken, mashed potatoes, gravy, mixed vegetables, salad, and homemade rolls. I patted my stomach in anticipation.

"This looks really great, Mom," I said as my mouth watered.

"Yes, it does. Pearson has bragged about your Sunday dinners," Rose said.

"Gosh, I hope I live up to the expectation," Mom said.

We started eating after the kids were settled and it was delicious. Everyone raved about it and Rose asked for the chicken recipe.

"I don't really have one, but I can give you my best guesstimate."

"That would be awesome. It's addicting."

Everyone stopped eating and looked at me.

"Hey, I don't want to be that gray elephant in the room. You can say the words addict, addicted, addicting or anything to do the drugs. I'm not that sensitive about it. In fact, if you have any questions, I'd prefer you ask them instead of keeping them sealed up inside."

The tension flowed out of the room. "Dang, I didn't know it was that bad."

Rose piped in. "Oftentimes, people are afraid to offend the recovering addict. But it's really best to keep things in the open. That way no one feels like they're stepping on eggshells and it's a much healthier environment all around, but especially for the one recovering. Don't be afraid to ask him about it either. When he goes to his meetings daily, that's what they discuss."

I sent her a grateful smile. "Rose is right. This should be an open forum. I don't want to hide anything. Oh, and Hudson, thanks for cleaning up my place. We went there this morning and it was immaculate."

"That was Milly's idea, actually. And thank our cleaning lady.

She spent a day there. I, uh, took the liberty of destroying all of your drugs and paraphernalia before she got there."

"I appreciate that. I actually wondered where all that stuff was because that was the first thing I intended to do when I got there. Thanks for saving me from having to deal with that."

Grey asked, "Do you think it would've been a temptation?"

"I'm not sure, to be honest. I had Rose there as reinforcement. And if I'd felt the slightest weakness, I would've called to her. Don't get me wrong, I have my moments, too many of them. But they seem to hit at night. That's the main reason I wasn't ready to live on my own."

Mom asked, "What's it like? The heroin I mean?"

I quickly glanced at the kids because I didn't want them to overhear this conversation, but they were immersed in their own conversation with Kinsley leading the group. They weren't paying us the least bit of attention.

"At first, it's like floating on the best cloud you can possibly think of. You're totally aware, but all your worries vanish. And you think, now I get it. This is why people love this so much. When you come down, you immediately want to do it again, but it's not an overriding need. It's just because you felt so awesome. So you wait and then the next time, the feeling isn't quite as great, but it's still pretty damn good. You keep doing it, but you find that every time you do, you need a little more, and that initial high you got has diminished. Soon, you hit a point where you're doing it because you have to, not because you want to. The first time I did it was because I couldn't get my hands on any Oxy or Lortabs. It was only supposed to be a substitute. But it's so easy to get and cheap. I could find it anywhere and have it at my disposal so much easier, so that's why I switched. Each time I bought it, I'd tell myself that would be the last time. You all know how that went. Then I told myself I'd stop. I started drinking heavily to replace it, to replace the withdrawal symptoms, but they'd get so bad, I'd hit the streets to get some anyway."

"When we saw you at the fundraiser, you were high?" Hudson asked.

"As a kite. And Milly, I should apologize for hitting on you. That was unacceptable."

She shrugged and chuckled. "Hudson warned me about you, so don't worry about it."

"My reputation was pretty bad back then and the drugs were partly to blame."

"Partly?" Hudson asked.

"Well, I can't help that I'm attracted to beautiful women." I set my eyes on Rose and her cheeks flushed that pink again. I adored that about her. Mom's brows rose, along with most everyone else's at the table. I grasped her knee under the table and said, "By the way, I'd like to tell you that Rose and I are … well, dating." Rose gaped at me. I guess I should've discussed this with her first, but things felt so right with her.

"Dating?" Mom asked curiously.

"Yeah, but we're being very discreet because of," and I aimed my thumb over my shoulder in the direction of Montana.

Milly and Marin shared a conspiratorial glance.

"What?" I asked them.

"We figured something was going on between you two," Marin answered.

"How so?"

"Call it women's intuition," she said as Milly nodded.

"Okay."

I noticed how quiet Grey and Hudson were. It was normal for Dad to be, but not them.

I asked them, "What's up with you two?"

"Nothing," Grey said, just a little too quick for my liking.

"Um no. Something is up. I'm an attorney and can read people. Spill it."

"Fine. We're worried you're moving too fast. We don't want either of you to get hurt."

Rose and I both spoke at the same time, then chuckled. "You go first," I said.

"First, thank you for caring about that. I am a little shocked that Pearson told you. But I went through a devastating marriage and am probably the most cautious person you'll meet." Hudson and Grey shared a look and then laughed. "Did I say something funny?" Rose asked.

"We're sorry, but we were exactly like you with the devastating marriages, so we understand," Hudson said. "Sorry to interrupt. Please go on."

"What I was saying is I won't be careless because there's someone else to consider in this too." She flicked her head toward Montana.

Grey said, "Oh, we totally get that part as well."

"Right, then you know how it feels then to be guarded. I can assure you I am overly protective of us both."

I jumped in there. "You both know me. I've never been involved with anyone before so for me to take this step, you should know how important this is. And to take this even further, recovering addicts have scrambled brains for a while. It's hard to explain, but we are encouraged not to make any life changing decisions for months out of rehab until things normalize. In other words, Rose and I will be taking things slowly. One step at a time as they say."

Smiles finally appeared on both of their faces. "Our brother has finally grown up it appears," Grey said.

"It may have taken a while, but I think you're right."

Then Mom said, "I wish you all would eat before I have to reheat the food."

Kinsley called out, "Gammie, can we have dessert?"

"See? They're already done, and you have barely touched your food."

"Mom, we had important things to go over," I said.

"I'll get them dessert," Marin said. She left the room before Mom could protest.

We finished our dinner and were treated to one of Mom's famous chocolate pound cakes.

"This is so good," Rose said. "You should sell these."

I laughed. "She'd never do that. She's too busy having fun with all her grandkids."

Dad patted Mom on the shoulder. "That she is. We're running all over the place now because if Paige doesn't get her 'baby fix' I'm in big trouble. She pouts like a four-year-old. You know what they say? Happy wife, happy life."

That was a new one for me, but I acted like I'd heard it before. Hmm. Happy wife, happy life. What about happy husband? Didn't they count for something too? I'd have to ask my brothers about that.

Each of us helped clear the table and the women shooed us out of the kitchen while they cleaned up. I tried to help, but they told me to go hang with the guys. We traipsed out to the back yard where Hudson threw the ball for the dogs to fetch. That's where I decided to ask my question.

"Hey guys, what's this happy wife happy life stuff? What about the husband? Doesn't he deserve to be happy too?"

"Seriously. You did not just ask that, did you?" Grey asked.

"Yeah. It doesn't seem fair to me."

Both my brothers actually guffawed. They laughed their asses off at me. Even Dad was cracking up too.

"What? I don't get it."

"Exactly," Hudson said.

"Huh?"

"Happy wife, happy life. Make her happy and she'll make you happy. Think about it, dude."

I did and it suddenly nailed me in the brain. "Oh, shit." I pointed a finger at them. "See, I told you my brain was scrambled."

"No shit," Hudson said. "I'm assuming you two haven't done the deed yet then?"

"What kind of a question is that?"

"A normal one. Why?"

"It's none of your business, that's why."

"Man, you have changed. You would've dumped all kinds of info on us before," Grey said.

Dad put his arm around me and said, "I for one am more than happy you're a new man. As your father, I was never fond of those conversations, which was why I always walked away. Parents never want to hear about their children's sex lives."

I cringed. "Yeah, and I'm truly sorry about that. I was usually high or drunk when I said those things. While we're on this subject, I might as well do step number eight with you and that's make amends for all my wrongdoings. I know I said I'm sorry for all the pain I've caused you, but I'm also sorry for all the embarrassment, worry, and everything else I put you through. If I could take it back, I would. Since that's not possible, I can only apologize and move forward. I want to thank you again for standing by me and supporting me in the worst time of my life."

We were standing in a circle and ended up in a group hug. "I can't possibly tell you all how much I love you."

"The feeling is returned, son, and I'm happy for you that you've found the right track in life."

"I second that," Grey said.

"As do I," said Hudson.

"I thank God every day for giving me the greatest family in the world." I wiped my face because it was damp with the tears I'd shed. One thing about going through rehab was it made me unashamed to cry.

Chapter Twenty-Seven

ROSE

WHEN I'D MET PEARSON'S FAMILY YESTERDAY, I THOUGHT they were awesome. After today, I knew he surely had been blessed. Comparing them to mine, I wasn't sure he understood quite how fortunate he was to have been born into a family that had so much love to give. It surrounded them in everything they did. It was evident his parents still adored each other by the way they looked at and touched each other. Their tiny gestures were so sweet, I found myself thinking back to my parents and never remembering anything like that. No wonder I had hooked up with Greg. I hadn't known what to look for in a man because I never had a role model.

His brothers were the same way with their wives and their gestures were reciprocated. I could also see it in Pearson. I hadn't noticed it until we were there. Growing up around it, he most likely picked it up by seeing his parents doing it. He often touched my hand or my cheek. He wasn't nearly as intimate as they were, but I could imagine him becoming that way.

Montana chatted all the way home about how much fun she had. "Can I go back there and play with Kinsley? She likes to dance a lot and wants to teach me with her clicky shoes."

"Clicky shoes?"

"Yeah, she has this thing for Irish step dancing," Pearson said. "If you let her, she'll end up teaching you too."

"Really? She's that into it?" I asked.

"Yes. She even makes Aaron and Wiley do it, though from what Hudson tells me, Wiley refuses to these days. I'm pretty sure when Aaron is a year older, he will too. Then she'll move on to both sets of twins. She's convinced she's going to be on TV one day."

I covered my mouth so Montana wouldn't see me chuckle.

"Mommy, she's real good. She kicks her legs up. Can I get some clicky shoes?"

I twisted in my seat to catch her eye. "We'll have to wait and see, okay?"

"Okay."

Pearson immediately offered to buy her some.

"Yay. I'm getting clicky shoes."

"While that's awfully nice of Pearson, I think we should wait. You don't know the first thing about that type of dancing. Maybe you need to find out more about it first." Then I poked him in the side and shook my head. I didn't want him spoiling her with everything she asked for.

"But I know how. Kinsley showed me."

"Then you can show us when we get home."

We were turning onto our street, so she started swinging her legs in anticipation. As soon as the car stopped, she was unbuckling herself.

"Hey there, slow down. One of us has to get you out of the car first," I said.

"Hurrrrrrry!"

Pearson did the deed while I unlocked the front door. She darted past me in a blur and came to a halt in the living room. As we stood there, she began kicking her legs out in strange angles while her arms were stuck like glue to her sides. She looked like a broken marionette.

"See, I know how!"

"Is that how Kinsley did it?" I asked.

"Yep," she said as her legs kept moving in those odd kicks. "I'm real good, huh?"

"Uh, yeah, you are," I said. I looked at Pearson and took a finger to close his lower jaw. He shook his head slightly as though he was clearing the cobwebs.

"She looks exactly like Kinsley. It's amazing."

"You're joking."

"No." He took out his phone and videoed her. She continued on until she tired herself out.

"I'm real good, huh Mommy?"

"Why, that's one way of putting it."

"Can I have my clicky shoes now?"

"Maybe we should think about dancing lessons first. That way you'll really know if you like doing it."

She crossed her arms and pouted. Her lower lip stuck out so far it was a miracle she didn't trip over it. "I already like it. And I don't need no lessons cuz I'm already good."

"But if you took lessons, you could get even better."

Pearson said, "Muffin, I'm pretty sure Kinsley takes lessons."

Her pout magically disappeared. "She does?"

"Tell you what. Why don't I call her daddy and we'll find out."

He leaned over and whispered, "I just sent them that video. I'm sure they're getting a good snicker out of it." Then he made the call.

"Hey Grey, does Kinsley take dance lessons?"

"Uh huh. Okay. Can you text me the information?"

"Cool, thanks." The call ended.

"Here's the deal. She takes lessons on Wednesday after school. He's going to get Marin to text me the information. She loves them, by the way. And they wouldn't get her any clicky shoes unless she took lessons."

I took Montana's hand and we sat down. "Here's the deal, Pop Tart. No lessons, no shoes. Here's why. I want you to learn how to do this the proper way. And I'm not going to spend any money on shoes unless you agree to take the lessons and finish the term. In other words, if I sign you up for twelve lessons, you complete all twelve, even if you don't like them."

"But I know I'm gonna like them."

"Sometimes you think you'll like things and you end up not liking them, but I won't allow you to quit, even if you don't like it. Do you understand?"

"Yes, Mommy." Her head bobbed up and down.

"Okay, I'll call the dance place and get you signed up."

She hopped around the room, saying "I'm taking dance lessons, I'm taking dance lessons." She stopped and asked, "Will I be with Kinsley?"

"Probably not because she's been taking them for a while. You'll be in the new students group."

"Okay."

"When can I get my clicky shoes?"

"After I sign you up and talk to the instructor."

"Yay. Can you call her now?" She was so excited, I hated to burst her bubble.

"Honey, it's Sunday and I doubt they're open today."

Her expression crashed, but then she asked, "Tomorrow?"

"Yes, I'll call tomorrow." She threw her arms around me and said, "Thank you, Mommy. I love you."

"I love you too, Pop Tart. Now go practice in your room so you can be ready for when you start." She scurried off, humming to herself. What a precious child. How did I ever get so lucky?

"That was some kind of dance, wasn't it?" Pearson asked, taking a seat next to me.

"Uh, yeah, and I practically had to scrape your jaw off the floor."

"God, I know, but she's as bad as Kinsley. Those legs."

"I've never seen anything like it."

"You haven't seen Kinsley. I thought maybe she'd be better, but no. I hope her lessons will help. They haven't helped Kinsley."

"Don't tell me that," I said.

We stared at each other, then cracked up. "Can you imagine the recitals? Grey said they were torture. He and Marin would scoot down in their seats because everyone in the audience would be cringing when she'd dance."

I couldn't help but giggle. "Oh, God, that would be awful."

"That might be us."

"We can sit with them and go through the pain together."

Our smiles drifted away and suddenly his hands were in my hair as he tilted my head. His mouth landed on mine and his lips were heaven as our tongues twisted together. This kiss was proprietorial as he took ownership of my mouth. Other than Pearson, I hadn't kissed a man in a very long time. It made me want more with him, so much more. He was igniting things inside of me that I'd forgotten existed. My breath hitched as he deepened the kiss. I slid my hand under the hem of his shirt, touching his warm skin. Things were moving fast and as I thought we needed to stop, he pulled away. Cupping my cheek, his thumb ran along my lower lip.

"I could do that for hours, but I thought we should stop before we get carried away."

"You read my mind. I wouldn't want Montana coming in and catching us."

"You're beautiful."

"So are you," I said.

"No, but I'm glad you think that. And I'm sorry for telling everyone about us at dinner today. I hope it didn't upset you."

"Not upset, but surprised. I wasn't prepared for that."

He scrubbed his face and then his gorgeous eyes homed in on mine. "Oh, God, I'm making a mess of things. It's just that I want this between us to be something. I hope you do too. I know I'm probably the worst partner material, but I swear those days are over. I'm on the straight and narrow now. I had a glimpse of what I'd been today and it," he shuddered. "It not only made me ill but gave me a deep insight into what my life had been. I don't want to be that guy. I want to be this man. I want it to be right for you and for me."

"I'm so glad you said the me part because it won't work if you don't do it for yourself. You have to want it for you."

"I do. I want to be on top again but in a different place. Reese told me not to make any major decisions for a while and I know you'd agree with that. But I'm not going back to the Manhattan law practice. That was part of the problem to begin with and I don't want or need that pressure in my life. I don't need that kind of money. I invested and saved wisely. I have plenty of money. I want to practice somewhere small, maybe up around here. Change my direction. Help the people who need it."

He was blowing me away. I knew he wanted to do something different, but this was awesome. "You're a different person than when I met you."

"I don't think I am. I think you had a different opinion of me. I was a different person when you got divorced. I won't deny that. But I changed the day I woke up in that hospital bed and found out I almost died."

I pulled my knees to my chest, thinking about what he said. "You know what? I've changed too. I like to think I'm not as quick to judge people anymore, as I was with you. I had you all wrong."

"I was an ass to you, which was a part of the old me, but I was in the defense mode, which was the absolute wrong thing to do without hearing your entire story. I can't apologize enough for that."

"I'm sorry too. For striking out at you."

He laughed. "It seems like I'm always apologizing. I suppose

I need to get used to that. I've wronged a lot of people over the last couple of years."

"Look how far you've come, though."

He shrugged. "A day at a time, a famous counselor told me."

"Oh yeah?"

"Uh hum. And she was really pretty too. So pretty that I might have to take a cold shower."

I playfully punched him in the arm. "If Montana were asleep, I might have to sneak into my toy drawer."

His eyes popped open. "You have a toy drawer?"

"Doesn't every woman over the age of eighteen?"

"How would I know?"

"Right. How would you? So now you do."

He waggled his brows. "Care to show me?"

"Hmm. Maybe someday you'll be lucky enough to see it."

Then he got a sneaky look about him. "Maybe someday, I'll add to it."

My eyes danced with mirth. "I hope you don't get me one of those cheap-o ones."

"What kind do you like?"

"Lelo brand."

"And where would one find them?"

"Online. You can google them. L-e-l-o." I figured spelling it out would help.

"Good to know."

Montana rushed into the room saying, "Okay Mommy and Mister. Watch. I've been practicing." She proceeded to perform the second worst dance I'd ever seen. When she finished, I wondered if her legs were injured. I kept a close eye on her as she walked, but she didn't limp at all, so I was sure all was fine.

"How was that one, Mommy? I'm real good now."

"Uh, er, yeah. Yes, you are." Lying was the best option because there wasn't anything in this world that could make me break her heart.

"Mister, did you like it?"

"Yep, liked it a lot," he eeked out.

"Um, honey, can you kick your legs out straight in front of you?"

"Uh huh, but that's not how you do it."

"Oh, I see." That relieved me somewhat. I was worried she was that uncoordinated.

Montana skipped back to her room and when I noticed the expression on Pearson's face, I told him, "I think I'm going to enroll you too and buy you a pair of clicky shoes."

Chapter Twenty-Eight

PEARSON

THAT NIGHT I WENT TO MY ROOM AND PREPARED FOR BED. I was sliding under the sheets when the cravings tore into me like they hadn't in weeks. My skin erupted in bursts of pain, like it used to during withdrawals. The urge to scratch myself was relentless. I paced for a few moments before I found myself in front of Rose's door and didn't remember walking there. Without hesitation, I opened it and found her sitting in bed reading.

She took one look at me and jumped up. "Let's talk."

"I … I can't. I … my skin is crawling. It's that feeling of a thousand pieces of glass tearing into me."

"Sit."

"I can't." I paced. No, it was more like race-walked.

"Pearson, look at me. Focus."

Her voice did it. I stopped and zeroed in on her eyes.

"Deep breaths. Inhale, one, two, three. Exhale, one, two, three. You're allowing the anxiety to control you. It's not withdrawal."

Oxygen filled my lungs as I listened to her soothing voice. I continued with the breathing, almost like a meditative exercise.

"Let your breath fill you, cleanse you of the carbon dioxide." She drew me to her bed where I lay down. "Remember meditation. Let your belly relax and fill it with oxygen." Her hand rested on my abs. "Good, keep going. Relax your muscles. Sink into the mattress and become one with it. Let the negative energy flow out of you." Her hand moved to my head and she ran it through my hair, massaging as she went. "Keep the breathing up. Your body needs the oxygen. It helps get rid of the toxins." As I breathed, her hand worked magic on my muscles and soon the panic and edginess dissipated until it was gone. I opened my eyes and watched her. When her hand reached mine, I turned mine over and clasped ours together.

"I'm better now."

She dropped down and sat next to me. "Let's talk this out."

"Yeah." I explained what happened.

"No trigger? No thoughts?"

"No. It just slammed into me."

"Do you think seeing Letty this morning did it?"

"Ah, shit." I squeezed my eyes shut. "Maybe I'd shoved that to the back of my mind. I suppose that was it."

"Let's get that out in the open. Having it lurking in your mind will only cause issues down the road. I know you're ashamed that you slept with her. Can you tell me more?"

I rubbed my eyes. I didn't even want to look at Rose. She was so damn pure and to think she knew I slept, no fucked, Letty wasn't something I wanted to discuss. It made me sick, so I couldn't imagine how it made her feel.

"You know you can talk to me about anything. Or I should say, there's nothing you can tell me that would shock me. I don't judge, Pearson."

"Rose, I realize that. But here's the thing. It made me physically ill today to recognize I'd slept with someone like Letty and she wasn't the only one. But for *you* to see that, I can't even imagine how it made you feel."

"Would you like to know?"

"Not really, but I want you to tell me anyway." I was waiting to cringe when she would drop her bomb. But it never happened.

"Letty is a mess who needs help, I don't deny that. But the man I'm looking at right now would never sleep with someone like that. You're not the person you were when you slept with her. What you need to come to grips with is that addicts do things they wouldn't normally do if they weren't addicts. When someone is under the influence, be it high or drunk, their actions change. Now, if you told me you'd sleep with her right now, my opinion of you would drastically change. But, and now listen to me Pearson, you are not that person. And there's something else. Addiction is a disease, not a choice. Yes, it's a choice to get help and go into rehab and recovery. But the disease had control over you. You're not accepting that."

I did not deserve to have this woman in my life and those were the next words out of my mouth. "I'm not worthy of you."

"And those thoughts are what set off your anxiety attack, because that's what happened. You *are* worthy of everything. You only have to believe it yourself."

"But—"

Her hand came up to halt my speech. "No buts. One day at a time. Don't forget that. Think back to where you started and where you are now. Your strength is astounding. And the last thing I want to say is I believe in you."

Believe in myself. Maybe that's what's been missing. "You know something. All this time I've believed I could kick it, that I had the strength to do it, but you're the first person who's told me they believed in *me*. Sure, my family's behind me, but they never used those exact words that I can remember."

Her smile lit up the dim room. "That's what you need to succeed. Without that belief, you'll succeed for a while, but not long term. You have so much going for you, so much more than most people."

"What do you mean?"

"Your family for starters. Your intelligence. Your bank account. And don't laugh. Some people have trouble paying for rehab. You are coming out of the starting gate fully prepared to face everything in the way you need to. And ... you're willing to do the hard work. All you need now is to have confidence in yourself. Let the past go. You can't do anything about sleeping with Letty or anyone else. What you *can* do is move forward, *one step at a time*."

"You make me feel strong and it's a strange thing. I've always had a shitload of confidence when it came to the courtroom and my ability as an attorney, but for a lot of other things, I've questioned myself."

"Maybe that's why you never had any relationships." Our hands were still clasped, and I brought hers to my lips and kissed it.

"Not sure about that. I was never one to want to walk down the divorce path."

"You positive about that or was that just something you told yourself?" Her hand brushed through my hair.

"I don't honestly know anymore. I've told myself that for so long it's what I believed."

"And now? We're together according to what you told your family, so you must have changed your mind."

I definitely have changed my mind and it was all because of her. She had me wrapped around her finger. I didn't want to tell her that though. It might scare her off and that was the last thing I wanted, especially since I still didn't think I deserved someone as pure and innocent as her. Not to mention, she'd already been through one terrible relationship and I sure as hell didn't want to put her through another.

I chose my words carefully. "Rose, I'd love to think you and I could make something happen between us. I'm not naïve though and realize how much I have to go through yet. You've been through a rough time in yours. I don't want to hope for too much with you, nor do I want to hurt you. Am I even making the least bit of sense?"

"No. Why do you think you'll hurt me and why do you think you're hoping for too much with me?"

I shrugged. "Because in my eyes you're perfect."

She laughed. "I'm not perfect." Her smile became a frown. "I wish I were. I'm so weak it's ridiculous. It's what got me into this mess with Montana in the first place."

"You're not weak."

Her eyes clouded with pain. "You couldn't be more wrong. I should've left him when I found out I was pregnant and gone to the local women's shelter. But I didn't. I was such a chicken shit. I let him bully me."

"Rose, that's what bullies do. They frighten and trap you into staying until you feel there are no other options."

"Don't I know. I lived that life twice and learned my lessons the hard way."

What is she talking about? "Twice?"

A lungful of air rushed out of her. She repositioned herself on the bed, crossing her legs. "It's not a very pleasant story."

"And my past is?" Her eyes took on a haunted look. I'd never seen her like this except for when she dealt with Greg. "Does this have to do with your ex?"

"No, unfortunately, I was abused by my father."

Holy shit. This puts a new spin on things. No wonder she stayed in her marriage. "Now it all makes sense, why you stayed that is."

"Yeah. I was his perfect victim."

I pulled her into my arms and held her. "Do you want to talk about it?"

"There's not a whole lot to say other than he beat the shit out of me. See, he was an alcoholic, a very mean one. Once he was through beating my mom, he'd come to find me. My mom wasn't a whole lot better, but she finally got clean. And when she did, she kicked him out. There were times I hid in the attic for hours because I was so scared. That was a life I didn't want for Montana, but then I set her up for it by not leaving. That's how weak and stupid I was."

"It's the repetitive cycle."

"That's why I wanted to go into counseling because there's always a way out. My goal was to help others that were in the same situation that I was. Many women don't see it, because fear is such an overriding factor. It blocks everything out so you can't think straight, but if you can get control of it, just like if you can control anxiety, things are so much easier to see."

As I rubbed circles on her back, I asked, "Then how did you end up in drug rehab counseling?"

"I found that's where I excelled and helped people the most. It was because I had experience with living and growing up in an alcoholic household. Now I recognize that they both had a disease. It was hard as a kid because I used to think they did it because they wanted to. I didn't know what they were going through. Sure, my dad was mean as hell, but he wasn't like that when he wasn't drinking. I knew I could help more people and I love working with recovering addicts."

This triggered a thought, something I wasn't feeling very positive about. "I have to ask you something and don't be hurt by this question, but I have to know. You aren't interested in me because I'm a recovering addict are you and because you think you can help me?"

She lifted herself up to lock gazes with me. "Absolutely one hundred percent no. If I had wanted that, there were plenty of guys who've been through the center that I could've kindled relationships with. There was something different about you that … well, that attracted me from the first time I saw you."

"Yeah?"

"Yeah."

"Tell me." I was that puppy begging for a treat.

"Oh, come on. Surely you must know," she said. She had a timid smile.

"Know what?"

"How …" She blinked a few times.

"Yes?"

Then she blew out a breath. "How genetically gifted you are."

"Genetically gifted, huh?"

"Yes!"

"No one's ever told me that," I confessed. I'd had women after me by the dozens, but they'd never actually come out and said what they thought about me.

"You can't be serious."

"I am. But I like that you think it. Genetically gifted. What exactly does that mean." I was playing with her and having fun.

"You know exactly what it means."

I nuzzled her neck with my nose. "No, I don't. Tell me."

"It means that you have a large, bulbous nose, and buck teeth."

I guffawed. "Buck teeth?"

"Uh huh. And I noticed you have large amounts of hair sprouting out of your ears and nose."

"Is that so?"

"Yep."

My fingers zeroed in on her ribs and commenced to tickle the hell out of her. She begged for mercy, but I wouldn't give in until she took it all back.

"Okay, I cry uncle."

When I stopped, she lay panting on the bed and I couldn't stop myself from capturing her mouth. Her leg wrapped around mine and I flipped her over so I was hovering on top.

"Okay, you don't have buck teeth."

"What about the hair in my nose and ears?"

"I made that up. I love your nose. It's perfect."

"Good, because I think yours is perfect too. And now that I'm checking it out more closely, I don't detect a single hair."

She burst out laughing. "Thanks for looking. I'm glad to know I'm trimmed up in there."

"You're welcome. Is there anywhere else you'd like for me to inspect?" I waggled my brows and her cheeks grew pink.

"Ah, no."

"I love it when you blush. Your cheeks turn such a lovely shade. You embarrass so easily."

"That's not embarrassing easily. You were discussing my, er, you know."

"What? I only asked if you wanted me to check other areas out. You were the one who automatically thought that. I was thinking perhaps your legs."

"Uh huh. And you expect me to believe that?" she said, smirking.

"Okay, no. But I am willing to help in that department."

"Are you an esthetician?"

"I don't even know what that is."

"It's someone who does hair removal. I guess that puts you out of the running."

"Hang on a sec. I'm great with a shaver, so it doesn't."

"How about this? You trim your own nose hairs and I'll take care of my own stuff?"

"One day you'll trust me." Then I kissed her again. Her lips set fire to my blood. I wanted her, badly, but I didn't want to push things too fast.

She tugged my shirt up, indicating for me to take it off. Then her fingers traced my ink. She slowed when she got to the rose. It was pure coincidence that the flower was the same as her name, but I took pride in that. Maybe it was prophetic that I chose that particular one. I got into ink when I'd started using. It was a way for me to think of the future. I'm not sure why but somehow it spoke of brighter days.

"You're beautiful," she said as her eyes ranged up and down my body.

"Even with buck teeth?"

"Shut up." Her smile lingered as her pupils dilated.

I was positive she could feel my erection pushing against her. This was the first time in months that I'd been with anyone and I was worried I'd blow any minute.

"Can we do this? Or maybe I should've asked are you ready for this?"

"The correct answer is no, but that's not what I want to say."

"Please tell me it's yes."

Chapter Twenty-Nine

ROSE

DENYING HIM WASN'T POSSIBLE. MY LUST FLARED ... NO, IT raged within me. His magnificence, as he lay above me, was more than a woman could ask for. He was humorous, kind, gentle, caring, honest, and had learned humility. What else could a man offer? The fact that he was a recovering addict should bother me, but it didn't. I dealt with this every day. I knew the signs of those who would fail and those who would succeed. He showed every one of success. And he had the support structure set to do it.

"The answer is yes." I wrapped my arms around his waist and hugged him.

Then he said, "One other thing. When I was admitted to the hospital, I was tested for everything, including HIV and sexually transmitted diseases. I'm clean as a whistle and obviously haven't been with anyone other than this." He held up a hand and wiggled his fingers. My cheeks instantly burned. "The reason I'm telling you this is I was wondering if you're on the pill or any other form of birth control and if so, can we go bare, as long as you're healthy too?"

If my face burned before, it was now on fire from my neck to my hairline. "Um yeah, I'm healthy. Like I told you before, I haven't been with anyone in over two years and I have been tested too. I did it after I got divorced. I'm also on the pill."

"Then you're okay with it?"

If he only knew. "Yes, I am. Now I think we need to get rid of some more clothes, don't you?"

"That's a great idea, but I'd love to be the one to undress you. I've been dreaming of this for so long now, it's almost embarrassing."

"Why?"

"I'm that teenager with wicked thoughts of you naked."

That was the cutest thing he could've said. I wanted to squeal and hug him again. "I'd love to hear those wicked thoughts. I'm all yours to undress."

My eyes lingered on him as he shed his boxers. I was more than impressed as his erection sprang free. But then I noticed the bandage where my ex had sliced him with the knife. "Does it hurt?"

"What?"

"Your injury?"

"Not now. I'm only thinking of one thing."

I had to stop myself from crawling to him and touching him. He came back to the bed and pulled off my top, then slid my bottoms off. Finally, I was left with only my panties, which he hooked his fingers into and tugged off. As I lay there, naked, my nipples pebbled under his gaze. My core instantly tightened as his eyes swept over me. One finger circled a nipple and then the other. A soft moan escaped and before I could inhale, his mouth had latched onto me. He sucked, flicked his tongue, and softly bit one nipple, as he pinched and tugged on the other. My back arched to get closer as I became drenched.

He lifted his mouth and asked, "How wet are you?" But

before I could utter a word, his hand moved between my thighs and found the answer himself. He rubbed my clit between his finger and thumb, and I moaned again. "God, you're so ready for me."

"Ah, yeah."

I thought he was going to go for it, but instead of his cock, he put his mouth over me. Holy mother of tongues. I hadn't had a man go down on me in ages. Greg never did so this was divine. Pearson seemed to know my body as well as I did. It wasn't long before everything in me ignited at once, sending me into an unbelievable climax.

"Jeez, holy crap." I was huffing and puffing. It had been way too long since I'd been with anyone and Greg was like having sex with a rock. The truth was, I'd never orgasmed during sex before so this was unreal for me.

He didn't give me time to recover before my legs were shoved up and he was pushing inside of me. He was large and it had been a while for me. Thankfully, he took it slow, inching his way in. He was finally fully seated, and I was stretched as far as I'd ever been.

Now he was the one breathing hard. "Are you okay?" he asked, cupping my face.

"Yeah. Are you?" I put my fingers lightly on his bandage as I was worried he'd tear his stitches open.

"Never been better." His voice was deep and sexy, sending shivers over my skin.

"Take it slow for now."

"I will. I can't promise I'll last. It's been a while here too and you feel amazing." His mouth brushed over mine, once, twice, and then his tongue pushed through the seam of my lips and I could taste myself on him. He rested on his elbow as one hand held my cheek and the other held my hip. He set up a perfect rhythm, as he rocked his pelvis against mine and as his tongue plunged into my mouth. It wasn't long before his thrusts became more forceful and I wanted more from him. I gripped his ass, my nails biting into him as I did.

He broke off the kiss saying, "I'm sorry, I can't hold back." And I knew when he came by his groan and the heat of him inside me. "I'm so sorry. I tried."

"It's fine. I had an epic orgasm before."

"Well, you gave me one back, so we're even. In fact," he said with a sexy grin. "You may have exploded my balls."

I couldn't hold back the laughter. "Ball exploder. I guess that's better than ball buster."

"A hell of a lot better." He ran his hands through my hair and said, "You are amazing. Have I told you that?"

"I think so."

"And you're beautiful," he added.

"You're not so bad yourself."

"Don't you mean genetically gifted?" he said, his eyes twinkling with mirth.

"Are you making fun of me?"

"Me? Never."

"I love your eyes. Why is it the men get the greatest eyelashes?"

He shrugged. "Yours are gorgeous. What are you talking about? You have the most perfect skin I've ever seen."

"Thank you." It was difficult hearing compliments from him when I was told so many times by my ex how ugly I was.

He took my chin and said, "Hey, don't be shy when I compliment you. You are stunning and should be aware of that. If you could only see yourself through my eyes, you would understand."

My heart thudded so hard beneath my ribs, I was certain it would land on the bed. No one had ever said such wonderful things to me before.

"Your eyes are lighting up the room right now."

"You're the first person to tell me that," I confessed.

"Then everyone one else were blind fools. There isn't a thing about you I'd change, Rose. Your name suits you perfectly because the rose is the most beautiful flower, lovely colors, velvety petals, and a scent that is rivaled by none. You are much the same. Now I guess I should go to my room so we both can get some sleep, though it's the last thing I want to do."

"Stay."

"But what about Montana?"

I frowned. "You're right. It wouldn't be good if she found us together."

"I'll go, but don't think I want to."

"And don't think I want you to either."

"Goodnight, sweet Rose." He kissed me and left. I still felt his lips on me, his hands, and my body still tingled from where he touched me. The delicious ache between my thighs also reminded me of him. Was I falling in love with him? I'd only known him a month and I wanted to take this slow. We just had sex and two people could do that without being in love. But he said all the right things to me, and I believe he meant them. I trusted him anyway. He gave off the right vibes. I hope I wasn't making a mistake and moving too fast. I had Montana to think about.

The smell of coffee brewing woke me. I got in the shower and when I was done, there was a cup sitting on my dresser with a note that said:

GOOD MORNING, GORGEOUS. HOPE YOU SLEPT WELL. P.

Damn, I liked this kind of service. I grabbed the mug and took a long swallow, and then made my way into the kitchen. Pearson and Montana were chatting about the merits of cereal for breakfast.

"But it's good for you cuz it tastes good," she said.

"Uh, that doesn't make it healthy. Why don't you eat eggs instead?"

"I want cereal. Or waffles. Do we got waffles in there?" She pointed to the freezer.

"They're as bad as cereal. You should have one healthy breakfast every other day."

"Why?"

"So you can be healthy."

"I'm healthy. Am I, Mommy?"

"Yes, but if you don't eat properly, you won't always be. Pearson is right. You should have eggs and fruit."

"Is banana fruit?"

"Yes," Pearson said.

"I like bananas in my cereal."

"What about oatmeal today?" I suggested.

"With bananas?"

"We can do that."

"Okay."

Pearson frowned. "Will you eat eggs tomorrow?"

"You won't make those orange kind, will you?" she asked.

"Orange kind?"

"She means ones with runny yolks."

"No, I make scrambled. No orange kind."

"Okay, I'll have those tomorrow. Can I have toast too?"

"Yes, you can have toast," he said.

While I was making her oatmeal, he asked, "What else will she eat for breakfast?"

"She likes yogurt and fruit too. Sometimes I make us smoothies and put extra things in there that she doesn't know about. And some protein powder."

"Good. I'll get onto that too. I was going to make eggs. Would you like some?"

"I'd love some, thank you."

We ate up our breakfasts and it was time for me to take Montana to her new preschool and then go on to work. Before I left, I asked Pearson, "Do you mind if I put your name on the pickup list, just in case of an emergency?"

"Not at all. I'll be willing to help out however I can."

I touched his arm. "Thank you." Then we were out the door.

I'd forgotten we'd left her seat in his car. He helped me make the switch. That didn't take long and then we were off. Montana's new preschool was only five minutes away, which was awesome. I walked her inside and her teacher met us. After we talked, she left with Montana and I stayed to fill out all the paperwork. Then I was off to work.

The day flew by and before I knew it, I was picking up Montana. She ran out to greet me, holding a big picture.

"Look what I drawed today!"

"Oh, my goodness. That's wonderful. Is that you?"

"Yeah. Look at my clicky shoes." Dang it. I was hoping she'd forget about those. But no. She had drawn them as huge things on her feet with some sort of gigantic platforms on the bottoms. I'm not sure what she thought clicky shoes were. "And this is you and Mister." I stared at the drawing because she had Pearson and me kissing. Our lips were bulged out and touching even though our bodies were a foot apart. It was super funny, but I didn't dare laugh. Her teacher just raised her brows and the way her tongue poked the inside of her cheek, it was obvious she was holding a laugh back as well.

"Come on, Mommy. I want to show this to Mister."

"Hang on a minute. Let me speak to your teacher."

"Okay. She headed over to the toys while I talked to her teacher, Cathie. "She's a joy in the classroom, very well behaved. But is his name really Mister?"

"No," I chuckled. "I told her to call him Mister Pearson, but she's decided to only call him Mister."

"I was wondering because she kept referring to him as Mister and I thought it was quite odd. Other than that, we had a great day. She gets along with the other students and plays well with others. You have a fine daughter, Ms. Wilson."

"Please call me Rose, and thank you. I guess we'll see you tomorrow then."

I called to Montana and we left for the house.

"How was it?"

"It was fun. Ms. Cathie's real nice and lets us play games and stuff."

"Good. She said you behaved."

"Yes, Mommy."

"That's a good girl. And the other kids are nice?"

"Uh huh. I like almost everybody 'cept one boy who's mean. But I don't play with him."

"Good job. That's the best thing to do. Just stay away from him."

"We got home, and she ran inside to show Pearson the drawing. "Look Mister. I drawed this."

"He took one look and his body shook, only he didn't make a sound. "Wow. That's something, isn't it?"

"Yep, I'm good, huh?"

"I'll say."

"Mommy, where can we hang it?"

"Er, I don't know. Let me think about it."

"I'm gonna go play. I want to practice my dancing."

"Okay, go on and practice."

When she was out of earshot, Pearson said. "Our lips are a foot wide." Then he doubled over laughing.

"Oh my God, when I looked at it, I could barely keep a straight face and the poor teacher. She wanted to know if your real name was Mister."

We both had a major case of the cackles. Montana came barreling into the room, saying, "Mommy, Mister, watch."

I wasn't sure if we could get through this performance. She started at one end of the room and ended up crashing into the opposite wall. We both jumped up to help her, but she barely noticed.

All she said was, "I'm supposed to turn right there." And she started again. I jumped up and ran into the kitchen with my phone.

Montana hollered, "Where ya goin'?"

"I'm calling the dance studio that Kinsley goes to. I want to see when they have classes." This child needed help. And fast.

After hanging up, I was happy yet sad. I got her into a class, but it didn't start for another month. Would Pearson and I be able to hold out? God, help us. I relayed to the news to both of them. Montana shouted for joy and Pearson almost cried.

"They don't have any openings now?" he asked.

"'Fraid not. The new classes don't start until then."

"I'll be so good by then, Mister. Just wait." She bounded back into her room as we stared open-mouthed.

"If this was the old me, I'd say I need a drink."

"Good thing those days are over," I said, kissing his cheek. "I'm not sure what's worse—the dancing or the picture."

"It's a close call from what I can tell." He picked it up from the coffee table where it sat. "I know one thing. She didn't inherit your artistic gene."

"We don't know that. I didn't get into it until my teens. Before then, my perspective was totally off."

Pearson only stared at the picture. "You mean there's hope? Because our lips look like those balloons they make wiener dogs with."

I checked out the drawing again and cracked up. "Oh my God, they do. I guess she didn't want us too close together. Did you check out her clicky shoes?"

"Is that what they are? I thought she was wearing wooden blocks on her feet."

We dissolved in laughter until our ribs ached. "I'm going to put this up in the kitchen, in a place that's sort of obscure."

"Where, like in the pantry?"

He followed me as I searched for the perfect spot. "It's too big for the refrigerator."

"What about here?" He gestured by the back door. I held up the drawing to see if it would fit and it did. "Where's the tape?" he asked.

We hung it up and then chuckled again. I prayed she wouldn't bring too many of these home. As I opened the refrigerator to get things out for dinner, Pearson said, "I need to talk to you about something." My heart skipped a dozen beats as I stood up straight.

"What is it?" I asked in a rush.

"Don't panic. It's fine. Miles and I spoke today. Greg's arraignment is this Friday. We won't have a court date until that's settled. Miles is certain everything will go in our favor, given the circumstances Greg is currently facing. An account of domestic violence and then the aggravated assault aren't exactly demonstrations of great parenthood."

"Aggravated assault?" This was the first time he'd mentioned this.

"Rose, please sit." He pulled out a chair for me at the table and we both sat down. This was scary stuff. "Greg assaulted me with a knife, and I had to have a lot of stitches. The next day I called the police station to inform them of this. They had already been notified by the hospital. I told them I wanted to press charges. That charge is aggravated assault. They told me he wants to press charges against me for assault, but they said there were too many witnesses stating I was only trying to pull him off of you. Your broken wrist is another piece of evidence we will use against him."

"Gosh, I didn't know you would end up a part of this."

"I don't mind if it will keep him behind bars and prove to the court he's not worthy of having custody of a child. Anyway, you'll have to testify in court."

"Me?"

"Yes, because you're also pressing charges, remember?"

I'm such a dumb ass. I'd cocooned myself into this little nest with Pearson where fear no longer ruled my life. "Right. Out of sight, out of mind."

"I'm glad you're no longer afraid."

"No, not with you living here." Instead of thumping with fear, my heart was now beating with emotion. He leaned closer, wrapped his arms around me and pulled me into the brick wall of his chest.

"I will always keep you safe, Rose. You're my flower, my haven." Then he tilted my chin up and kissed me.

Chapter Thirty

PEARSON

A MONTH HAD PASSED, AND GREG'S ATTORNEY HAD PLAYED the game of dragging his feet. I should've known because I taught him. He'd hired one of my former protégées at the firm, of which I had officially resigned a week ago. They weren't too pleased, but I had informed them that because of the high pressure included with the job, there was no way I could come back any time soon. The best thing for me was to walk away entirely and set up a practice somewhere in Tiny Town, USA.

My former nemesis smirked. "It got you, didn't it? I knew you were never cut out for this, West."

"No, that's not what did it. It was the pressure of dealing with my conscience every night when I went home. But I imagine you can't relate to that, can you, Tom?" His smirk vanished and turned into a scowl.

"I wanted to give all of you the courtesy of my reasons for leaving. Thank you for everything. I appreciate you bringing me in, but I did bring a lot to this firm. I think we can negotiate an agreeable buyout among ourselves. Everyone, except Tom, smiled. One of the two major partners said, "Of course. This firm owes you a lot, and as a junior partner, you will be paid your share.

Tom glowered at me, but I didn't give a shit. He was a junior partner as well and was probably worried I was taking his share, but screw that. I'd started a few years before he did and worked my ass off. He was cutthroat enough to catch up and get his due. By the time I left, we'd negotiated a hefty sum that would be deposited in my investment account by the end of the week. I had enough money to open my own practice or not work for the foreseeable future.

Miles and I had discussed practicing together, which seemed like a nice plan. His goals were aligned with mine, but we needed to dive in a bit deeper into our long-term ideas before I'd commit to anything. The times I'd met with Reese Christianson, he kept pounding this into me so I would adhere to his advice, even though I was eager to move on. Miles had me doing some work for him, along with helping him on Rose's case, and it was a relief to feel useful again.

The highlight of every day was going home in the afternoon and waiting for Rose to get there. Sometimes if she was running behind, I'd pick up Montana to help her out. The first time I did that, her teacher told me, "It's great to finally meet Mister."

We shared a chuckle at that. "Yeah, she refuses to call me anything else. She's something, that kid." Montana must've heard my voice because she came barreling into me, yelling, "Mister, Mister, you're not my sister."

This was a new one, so I needed a quick come back. I swung her high in the air, saying, "Muffin, Muffin, stop that huffin'. Or you I will tickle till you turn into a pickle."

She gurgled with laughter until she said, "I can't turn into a pickle."

"Wanna bet?" I dug one finger into her ribs, and she squiggled around as she giggled.

"Stoppp, Mister. Please stop."

Cathie, the teacher, smiled as she looked on.

"We'd better get going, Muffin. I'm sure your teacher needs to go home too."

"Okay, Mister."

I put her down and she stuck her hand in mine. That feeling of trust she had in me sent a warm glow rushing through me. My brothers told me how it was with kids, how they depended on you, and how much love they had for them. But I never understood the emotions until Montana. I had fallen hook, line, and sinker for this kid. She was adorable and had managed to tie me around her fingers—every one of them —and knot the string in a perfect bow. The thing is, it had happened before I'd even realized it. I'd do anything for her, anything at all.

As we walked to the car, where I now had my own car seat for her, she jabbered on and on about her day. Rose was taking her to counseling, just to ensure she didn't have any post-traumatic effects from her time with her father. The only issues that had developed so far were her hatred of the dark, and she refused to stay in any room with the door closed. Unfortunately, that included the bathroom. We encouraged her to use Rose's bathroom because it was more private, but more often than not, she'd use the one I shared with her and it was what I called an open-door policy for her.

Montana's first dance class was this week. Rose and I couldn't wait for her to go. She seemed to think she'd gotten really good, but she looked the same to us, with those awkward kicks. We worried she'd tear an ACL before she ever learned the moves properly. When her clicky shoes arrived, she was slightly disappointed. Apparently, she had this idea that they would click on their own, without any help from her.

Rose had said, "But honey, you have to make them click. You put your feet on the floor to the music and make the sound."

"Oh."

"When you take the lessons, it will make more sense," I added.

She inspected them from every angle and finally it sunk in. She put them on and went to the kitchen. From then on all we heard were those damn shoes. Rose finally had to restrict her to an hour a day in them.

"Mister, can we stop to get a surprise for Mommy?" she asked from the back seat.

"I think that's a great idea." I looked at her from the mirror. "What did you have in mind?"

"Flowers. She likes pretty flowers."

"That's perfect, Muffin. I know just the place." There was a floral shop right by the grocery store, so I pulled in and we checked out what they had available.

Montana went straight to the roses and said, "Look. It's like your picture." She was referring to my tat.

"Yes, it is. Do you know what those are called?"

"Nope."

"Those are roses." Her tiny mouth formed a circle and her eyes matched it. "Shall we get those?" Her head turned into a flurry of ringlets as she bobbed it up and down.

"Can we?"

"Of course. What color?"

"Red!"

The store owner heard us and came over. "Can I help you?"

"We'll take these. And make it two dozen."

"Very well. Would you like some greenery? I can make up the arrangement in a vase."

"That would be great." I turned to Montana and said, "Let's write her a card to go with them."

The man pointed us in the right direction, and we found them. "What do you want to say?"

"How about you're prettier than these flowers. Love Mister and Muffin."

"I think that's the best." I wrote it exactly as she said only I signed it Muffin and Mister. Then I handed Montana the card. "I want you to give this to her and tell her these are your words."

She grabbed the card, saying, "Okay, I will."

I paid for the flowers and we left. When we got home, I took the flowers and got Montana out of her seat. "Your mommy isn't home yet so we can surprise her with these."

She smiled and then caught me off guard by asking, "Do you love my mommy as much as I do?" I was carrying the heavy vase and nearly stumbled because I'd never quite thought of loving Rose before. Did I? Had I fallen in love? How could I answer that question because the truth was I'd never been in love with a woman in my life. Rose was different than anyone I'd ever been with and if I were honest, I'd ever felt about anyone the way I felt about her.

"Do you Mister? Love my mommy?"

As I opened my mouth to speak, my phone rang. Saved by the bell. "Hello."

"Pearson, it's Miles. They released Greg. He's out on bail. His attorney convinced the judge he wasn't a flight risk because he wants to go to court and fight for custody. Just wanted to give you a heads up."

"Thanks."

"We can talk more tomorrow."

"Right. I'll see you in the morning."

Looking at Montana, I worried now about her safety and Rose's too. "Come on, Muffin, let's go inside." Now I had to explain to Rose that her ex was out again, and I didn't trust the bastard as far as I could throw him.

Chapter Thirty-One

ROSE

WHEN I WALKED INTO THE HOUSE, I WAS GREETED BY Montana's hug as she handed me a small card. Her little grin put one on my face as well. I opened the card and my heart swelled with joy. On the kitchen counter sat an enormous vase filled with red roses. They were beautiful, but the card was a killer. Montana said Mister had written it, but she'd told him what to write and he stood watching, nodding his agreement.

"What would I do without my little blessing here? Come here, my precious little darling."

"But Mister helped. Is he your darling too?"

"Of course he is. You both come here before I cry."

"Why would you cry?" she asked.

"Because I'm happy, that's why."

"But I only cry when I fall down or when I'm sad."

I crouched down and put my hands on her arms. "This may be a little hard to understand. But sometimes grownups cry when they're happy."

She frowned. "Oh. Maybe that's why Miss Caroline cries all the time. Maybe she's really happy and not sad." Pearson and I shared a look. I doubted that was why she cried, but I didn't mention that to Montana.

"Guess what you have tonight?" I asked.

"Dancing. Should I wear my clicky shoes there?"

"I'd take them and change there. We have to leave in a few minutes," I said. "Do you need a snack before you go?"

She asked for an apple, so I cut one up for her and gave her some water. While she ate, Hudson told me about Greg in a hushed voice. He said he'd go into more details while she was at dance.

"Hey, Pop Tart, after dance, we'll go out to eat. Okay?"

"Yay. Where?"

I shot a glance at Pearson. He shrugged and said, "Your call."

"How about Italian?"

They both agreed. When we got to the dance studio, we saw Marin and Kinsley. She had a lesson at the same time but was in a different class.

Pearson asked her, "Are you staying?"

"I can't. I have to run an errand, but I'll be back."

Once she was gone, we took seats and he explained what was going on with Greg.

"How did that happen?" I asked.

"He retained a good attorney. It's one I trained, so he knows what he's doing. Greg's attorney told the judge he doesn't present any risk because he wants custody of Montana. The judge bought it."

My belly churned as I digested this information. "Shit. I have Montana to worry about again."

"No. I've already engaged the services of some bodyguards. We'll have continual coverage on her. I'm not taking any chances. I'd like to set someone up for you too."

"I'm sure I'll be fine. She's the one he wants." My hands

twisted in my lap. Greg was so unpredictable who the hell knew what he'd do?

Pearson touched my arm. "Rose, please listen to me. You get that cast off in a few days but look at what his temper has done to you so far. I care about you far too much to risk anything else happening to you. If you don't allow me to protect you as best I can, I'm going to do it anyway, only you won't know it. I'd rather be out in the open with you, but I don't want to take any risks with your safety. Greg's too much of a loose cannon for my taste."

"I hate this. But when you put it like that, you're right." I took one of his hands and wrapped my fingers around it. "Thank you for caring so much. No one else has ever been so kind and considerate of me before."

He squeezed my hand back. "Montana asked me today if I loved you as much as she did."

"She what?"

"It threw me."

"Oh, my goodness. I'm sorry."

"Why? She loves you and wanted to know. It was a really good question, I thought."

"Maybe but intrusive." Jesus, what the hell!

"How was she to know that? She's just four."

"Almost five."

"Oh, and that makes such a huge difference. Kids are inquisitive. She was just wondering, that's all."

"It's embarrassing."

"It shouldn't be. You had nothing to do with it. Well, not in the sense that it was your fault she asked. But it did make me think. I'll be honest, I didn't know what to say. I'm breaking new ground with you, and I'm happy you're the one I'm doing it with."

"So am I. You're a lot different than her father."

"I agree with you there although I can be a jerk. But you … you make me want to be the best man I can possibly be, which

led me to think about my feelings for you. I don't know the defin-
ition of true love, but I do know I want you in my life."

What was he saying? All of a sudden, my throat clammed up
with a huge knot.

"Uh, Rose, this is the part where you're supposed to say
something back. Or at least I think it is. Did I get something
wrong?"

My head swiveled back and forth, and my eyes targeted his. I
forced whatever it was blocking my throat to go down and said,
"No, you got it a hundred percent right. And I guess you stole
the breath from me."

When he smiled, I felt myself grinning in return. The man
was sin wrapped in flesh and muscle. How could any human be
this gorgeous? "If we weren't in this clicky shoe place, I'd crawl
on your lap and do all kinds of lustful things to you."

"Shit. Why'd you say that?"

"Because it's true." Then I offered up the most innocent smile
I could conjure.

"Don't look so virtuous. I know what lies beneath those
clothes and I know what that mouth of yours can do to me."

"Umm hmm, and you'll have to wait it out. Sorry," I teased.

"No car sex then?" His tone was hopeful.

"Nope, not here."

"We could drive somewhere," he said, eagerly.

"Nah, I don't want to risk getting caught. I'm a chicken."

"I could bang you pretty fast, and I'd be on top."

"Bang me, huh."

"Oh, yeah. Bang, bang, bang, done." He smirked.

He had me almost cackling. "No, way. I want a happy ending
too." I poked his ribs.

"Oh, ye of little faith. Who said anything about no happy
ending for you? You know what they say about assuming?"

"Okay. But no car sex. I'm not quite there yet."

"Oh, babe, just wait until you are."

"You *babe'd* me."

"And why wouldn't I? You're my person. My one and only. My *babe*."

"Aw." I leaned my head on his shoulder. "I like that. Being your person and all."

He tipped my chin toward him. "If you ever doubt that, come to me." Then he took my hand and pressed it over his heart. "You're mine, understand?"

"Yeah. Yours. And don't forget something either. You're mine too. I would be completely lost without you. And Montana... I'm not sure what she'd do without her Mister. You're the best thing that could've happened to us."

"It's a mutual thing then. It seems we were destined to meet. Sometimes God does work in mysterious ways."

Chapter Thirty-Two

It was almost eleven when I snuck into Rose's room. She was just walking out of her bathroom with her robe on. When she saw me, she smiled seductively. The erection that had already begun went into full attention as she untied her robe and slipped it off her shoulders. Why? Because she was naked underneath. I stalked toward her and didn't waste a second before she was in my arms and we were kissing. Lifting her up, her legs wrapped around me as I backed up to the bed. I sat and she straddled me.

"I'd like to have your luscious mouth on me, but there's something I want more right now."

"What's that?" she purred.

"Ride me." Reaching between us, I started to pull my cock out, but her hand stopped me.

"Let me do that." She took over and pumped me a few times until I asked her to stop.

"I need inside you. Now, babe. Not that I'm not enjoying this, but I've had several hours to think of you and I'm not sure how much more I can handle."

She released me and slowly took every bit of me inside of her. When she was fully seated, she put her hands on my shoulders and began rocking to which I joined in, meeting her.

"Damn, you're tight."

She let out a little chuckle. "Only cuz you're big."

"Glad we fit perfectly."

When she moaned, I almost came but held back. I wanted to see her get hers first. I moved one of my hands from her ass so I could play with her clit. I circled it with my thumb and she turned her slow movements into faster ones.

"Ah, yessss."

"Good?" I asked.

"So good."

Then I grabbed her hip to increase the speed even more. I thrust up, hard, and she responded with almost a growl. She met me with her own motion and soon, her tiny muscles were contracting against me, which set me off into my own climax. She collapsed on my chest, snuggling into my neck. Her hair spilled across me like a silken curtain and I ran my fingers through it, enjoying its softness.

"You're so gorgeous when you're making love." I moved to lay us down, taking her with me.

"Making love?"

"Umm hmm. I don't exactly consider this a quick fuck, do you?"

"Not at all," she said, lifting up to look at me.

"Well, if it's more than plain old sex, and it involves deep emotion, which I perceive this did, then what would you call it?"

"I suppose I'd call it making love," she said shyly, then hid her face in the pillow.

"Whoa, whoa. Why are you hiding?"

"I'm not hiding." Her voice was muffled.

"Oh no? Then why is your face jammed in that pillow?"

"It's not."

I almost howled but didn't for fear of waking up Muffin. She felt my body shaking and her hand smacked my shoulder. "Ouch. That stung."

"That's what you get for laughing at me." She finally lifted her head and brushed her hair off her face.

"But really, why the sudden case of shyness?"

"I don't know. It's dumb really. All this talk about making love just felt ... weird."

"Why?"

"Because talking about love is serious stuff."

"I know. But Rose, what would you say if I told you I love you?"

"I'd faint."

"Do you have any smelling salts?"

"Wait—are you serious?"

I rolled to my side and cupped her cheek. "I would never in a million years joke about something like this. And, you don't have to say anything back. But you should know that I do love you and Montana."

Then she did something unexpected that surprised me. She cried. I gathered her in my arms until she stopped. "I didn't mean to bring you to tears."

"No one since that rat bastard and he never meant it, ever told me they loved me except Montana."

"Your parents didn't?"

"No. My dad was an abusive drunk, as I told you before and my mom, even though she eventually recovered, still never told me. I think when she had me, she didn't know how to handle a kid. Her life changed so much after me she never forgave me for it."

"You don't ever have to worry about that because I'm going to shower you with more love than you can imagine—that is if you'll have me."

"Have you? Are you crazy? Of course I'll have you. I love

you too, Pearson. I never thought I'd trust anyone enough to say those word to, though."

"I promise you I will never give you a reason not to trust me. I've waited a long time for the right one and I'm not going to do anything to ruin it. Not only that, you're one of the reasons I now understand the true meaning of love. Yes, I've had the best role models in my parents, the greatest family, and the perfect childhood. But loving you, being in this relationship with you, has given me courage to face this uphill battle I'm fighting, and it's made me believe in myself."

"I know you can win. Remember, I believe in you too." She kissed me, long and slow.

"Rose, I want to spend the rest of my life with you, but only after I prove to you I can stay sober for at least a year. I won't risk anything until then. And, not only that, I want to live on my own first. I want to prove to myself I have the strength to do it." I took a chunk of her hair and twirled it.

Her finger traced the outline of the tattooed rose on my chest. "I think that's an excellent idea. It will allow you time to learn how to cope on your own. And you'll know that I'm always here, with an open door, if you need it."

"I've been here a little over a month now. Maybe another two or three weeks. My meetings are going well. Reese has mentioned that too. He thinks it would be a good idea."

She pushed her hand through my hair. "Do you know how proud I am of you? And before you say anything, let me tell you why. When I first met you, I figured you were some cocky dude who thought he could just waltz into the center and do whatever he wanted. And you kinda did, *but*—and this is a huge but—you listened to everyone who had something important and meaningful to say and took it to heart. After I figured I wasn't a good fit for you and saw how you were changing and developing there, I *knew* you were going to succeed. I'm not saying that because of us. You would've succeeded despite that. You have what it takes, Pearson. A strong will, dedication, and a positive attitude. You also had a strong supportive family, you got involved in activities, were responsible about fulfilling commitments and all those things that ultimately lead to success. I've learned a lot from you, but one of the biggest things is not to be so quick to judge people as I did you."

"Since we're sharing secrets, can I tell you something?"

"Sure."

I half-smiled and said, "I thought you were a hippie."

Her brows shot up. "Me? A hippie?"

"Yeah. All those beads and stuff over there and then I walked into your office and you had one of those head wreaths on. I was like … where the hell have I landed? When my brothers dropped me off and we pulled into the drive, I saw that old hippie van and the Flower Power sign and wanted to turn around because I came from the city. You know, suits and ties. I felt like I'd been beamed over to Haight-Ashbury."

Her hand covered her mouth as she suppressed a loud laugh. "Oh, God, I can just hear the sarcasm rolling off your tongue."

"Oh, I don't think you can. I was definitely a surly ass. Sweat was pouring off me and I was a wreck. And then here I come to the land of hippie-ville. It was a true *what the fuck* moment."

Her laughing slows and she finally asks, "And how do you feel about hippie-ville now?"

"I loooove the place. I mean look who it brought me." I lean over and kiss her.

"Oh, remember that wreath I gave you?"

"Remember? How could I forget? One of the guys in group the next morning wanted to know who was sitting in my seat. It was God awful the way I itched." I chuckle at the memory.

"I felt horrible for it too, but I'd never had anyone react like that."

"My new motto is just say no to heroin, Oxy, and lemon verbena."

She laughed, then said, "Now you're stuck with clicky shoe recitals." She tapped my arm.

"I'll gladly go with you. Maybe she'll improve."

"God, I hope so. She can't get any worse."

"I'll have to ask Marin about Kinsley. I'm not sure if she's improved or not. Speaking of, Marin texted and wanted to know if Montana could spend the night this weekend with Kinsley. I forgot to mention that to you."

"I'll ask her, but I'm sure she'd love it. Poor Marin and Grey with that dancing."

I waved a hand. "They're used to it. Or maybe they have a large supply of earplugs."

She snapped her fingers. "That's a great idea!"

I checked the time and it was close to one. "I'd better be off to bed, babe. The morning will be here soon. I'm getting up early to run."

"And I'm doing Yoga. Goodnight."

Though I hated to leave her, I needed the sleep too. Six would be here way too soon. I'd been getting up every morning to run because it seemed if I waited until after the end of the day, I didn't get it in.

When I got to my room, I grabbed my phone to ensure the alarm was on. That's when I saw the message from Miles.

Greg's arraignment has been moved to tomorrow. Will keep you informed.

How the hell did that happen? I'd call the bodyguards first thing in the morning. If he was released, I dared not take any chances on Rose's or Montana's safety.

Chapter Thirty-Three

ROSE

I STUMBLED INTO THE KITCHEN WITH A YAWN AND HEADED straight for the coffee pot. I smelled the aroma, indicating Pearson had already brewed it. After pouring myself a large mug, and adding a liberal amount of cream, I turned around and nearly jumped out of my skin, stifling a scream. Pearson and some large dude dressed in black sat at the kitchen table, observing me.

When he saw me jump, Pearson was on his feet, rushing to my side. "It's okay. This is Axel. Remember the bodyguards I mentioned? He's one of them."

"Why would we be needing them now?"

"Come on and have a seat. We need to talk," Pearson said, ushering me to a chair.

I extended my hand to Axel as I sat. "Nice to meet you."

He dipped his head slightly. "My pleasure, ma'am." His voice was as I expected—deep. I couldn't read anything in his deep-set brown eyes. They were neither friendly nor unfriendly. He'd be challenging in poker with his expression, or lack of. His hair was cut close to his scalp and the man looked downright scary.

"Miles texted me last night," Pearson began. "Greg's arraignment has been moved to today."

"Today? How did that happen?"

"We don't know, but what matters is your and Montana's safety, which is why Axel is here. His team will be on duty around the clock. I'm going to let him explain."

Montana and I each would have a bodyguard at all times. They would drive the same type of vehicle—a black SUV. Why did this not surprise me? They asked to take Montana to school every day, and then me to work.

"Is that really necessary?"

"Ma'am, we like to do it so we can get a feel of your daily activities. It also allows us to see if anyone is following you, watching your place of employment, home, or your daughter's school."

An ice-cold chill ran up my spine, followed by goosebumps popping out everywhere. What if Greg tried to abduct Montana and take her out of the country? He had enough money to do it, or at least he did when we were together. I'd never get her back then. I didn't give it any more thought before I gave my answer.

"Yes, that sounds like a great idea."

"We'd like to start today. Meeting your daughter, introducing us is the first thing we need to do. We don't want her to be frightened of the circumstances, but we also want her to know that there is a potential for danger and that it involves her father. He was someone she trusted at one point, but now he could be a threat, so we need to explain this to her."

"I have dreaded this moment. Who wants to think of their father like this?"

"Ma'am, we handle a lot of cases such as this. Would you like me to help you?"

Pearson said, "I think all three of us should."

That was a great solution. She loved Pearson and with all

three of us telling her, she would likely be more comfortable than with just Axel and me. "That's a great idea. I'll go wake her up."

Montana was rubbing the sleep out of her eyes when we came back to the kitchen, but the instant she saw Pearson, she ran straight for his lap. "Whatcha doin' Mister?"

"I'm waiting for you, sleepyhead."

"How come you don't got no shoes on?"

"Because I want to be like you." Montana loved to go barefooted.

"Then how come your toenails aren't pink?"

"Because you haven't put pink polish on them." Oh, man, Pearson was in for it.

"Hey Pop Tart, aren't you forgetting your manners?"

"Huh?"

"There's someone else in here, you know."

She turned to see who I was talking about. Pearson said, "Muffin, this is Mr. Axel."

"Hello, Mr. Axel."

"Honey, Pearson, Mr. Axel and I have to talk to you about something."

"What?"

"You remember how your daddy got into trouble when he hit me and knocked me down? That's when I broke my wrist and had to wear that cast for a while?"

"Yeah."

"And then he got into trouble again and had to go back to jail?"

"Uh huh." As I was talking, she was rubbing the fabric on Pearson's shirt sleeve between her fingers and thumb.

"Your daddy is going to be released from jail today and wants to try to get custody of you again. Do you know what that means?"

"No." She frowned.

"It means that you would have to live with him part of the time," I said.

235

Her head swiveled back and forth, almost violently. "I don't wanna, Mommy. Don't make me go back there." Then she looked at Pearson and said, "Mister, don't make me go."

Shit. This reaction was awful.

"Muffin, we're not going to make you go back there," Pearson said, hugging her.

I added, "No, baby, we won't do that. Okay?"

"Okay. I don't like it there."

"I know and we want you here all the time. But Mr. Axel is going to be your friend to make sure nothing happens."

"Like what?"

I was trying to formulate a response, but Axel beat me to it.

"Montana, I'm one of the people who will keep you safe and chase away the bad guys. Is that okay?"

"Are there bad guys chasing me?"

"Not that we know of. But in case your daddy tries to take you away, I'm not going to let that happen. Does that make sense?"

"Uh huh. You won't let my daddy take me somewhere and be mean to me?"

"Never. And when I'm not with you, one of my friends will be. Would you like that?"

"Okay. Who are your friends? Are they nice?"

"Well, there's Samson, Mitch, Leon, and Petey."

"Do they like to dance with clicky shoes?"

Axel looked at both of us. "She means Irish step dancing," I answered."

"Um, I'm not sure if they know how, but maybe you can teach them."

"Yeah, I'm real good, huh, Mommy?"

"Oh, yeah." I glanced at Pearson and he was shaking his head, no, but Montana couldn't see him.

"Montana, Axel is going to take you to school and me to work today. So, let's eat breakfast and get a move on."

Since it was still early, I cooked eggs and bacon for everyone, including Axel. I was pretty sure he held back on how much he ate because he only ate as much as I did. Pearson helped Montana dress as I went to shower. When I came out of my room, everyone was in the living room as Montana gave a demonstration of her clicky shoes dance. Axel wore a horrified expression.

"I think you need to change your shoes, Pop Tart. We need to go."

She scurried off and I said to Axel, "Sorry. She's absolutely dreadful and is taking lessons, so beware and you might want to pass it on."

"Pearson piped in. "Sorry about her outfit too, but she insisted on putting that together and no amount of discussion could change her mind."

I batted a hand. "No problem. I don't worry too much about that." When she came back out, I saw what he was talking about. She had on flowered jeans with a plaid shirt. They weren't even in the same color scheme. She was a sight today. I kissed Pearson goodbye as Montana giggled and we followed Axel out.

Both of us climbed into the back of the black SUV and I noticed her car seat was already there. I buckled her in and off we went. I introduced Axel to her teacher and added him to the list at school, in case he picked her up without me. Not much later, he dropped me off at the center. On the way, he told me a man was going to be placed at the school and he would be there all day. Another one would be at the house.

"You really think that's not overkill? I'm only asking because I don't know."

"No. Who knows how desperate this guy is and what lengths he'd go to?"

"I'll defer to whatever you think. In your experience, how soon after something like this do these people usually act?"

"I can't really say. Your ex has to go to court to see if he gets any kind of custody. He may wait and see what the result of that is. If he gets totally stripped of all parental rights, then that's most likely when he'll act."

"That's what I think too. Thanks for that, though." I waved as I walked toward the door.

He called out to me. "If you need me, just call." Pearson had put his number in my phone. I gave him a thumbs up.

That afternoon, I had just finished with a client when my office line rang. I answered and his voice jolted me into a ramrod position and sent chills racing down my spine.

"Hello, Rose. I wanted to let you know I look forward to getting my daughter back soon."

"That will never happen."

"I beg to differ. It will most certainly happen, one way or another."

"What does that—" but before I could ask anything else, the line went dead. •

Chapter Thirty-Four

PEARSON

ROSE WAS A WRECK WHEN SHE GOT HOME. THAT BASTARD, AS far as I was concerned, didn't have the right to call or upset her. But the words he'd used made me rest easy that I'd hired those bodyguards. The guy definitely had something up his sleeve and I didn't want to wait to find out.

I would be glad when her court date got here. With him out of jail, at least Miles could press for one now.

On the upside, Montana loved having her guy, Petey, who'd been assigned to guard her, hang out with her. Petey was every bit as huge as Axel, only he was younger. His hair was longer, and he had blue eyes. You could tell he liked being around Montana by the way his eyes sparkled when she held his hand. She wanted to bring him to show and tell next week so they could put on a clicky shoes dance show. Petey was appalled. He didn't know what to tell her, so Rose had to break it to her that Petey didn't have any clicky shoes and couldn't afford any.

"But, Mommy, he can just pretend his shoes click and he really doesn't need any. I just want Petey to dance with me."

Poor Petey. "Muffin, even though you absolutely love dancing, and we are so excited that you do, show and tell is for you to bring an object in to show the students. I don't think it's for you to actually dance for them. Does that make sense?"

"Maybe. But what if I ask them first?"

"How about I check with Miss Cathie and see what she says?" Rose asked.

"Okay."

That satisfied her and we could let Cathie know how awful she is so she can use the object excuse too. I suddenly had this image of the huge Petey dancing with Montana with those awkward leg kicks, and I had to run out of the room so I could bust out laughing. I put a pillow over my face so no one could hear me. But Rose followed me, checking to see if I was all right.

When I told her why I ran, she stole my pillow.

"Oh my God. I can just picture it."

We stopped laughing just in time as Montana came hopping into the room.

"What are you doing?"

She hopped next to the bed, so I grabbed her and tickled her. "We're having a tickle party, what else?"

That evening, Montana drew a picture of Petey and her dancing so she could give it to him in the morning. When she did, the guy melted. She had him wrapped around her pinky.

At the end of the week, Miles was notified of Rose's court date. It was set for next week. I had talked about finding a place of my own but decided to wait until the custody battle was over and Rose was safe again.

"Thank you for staying." She hugged me after I told her.

"I want you to understand something. This is going to be a

slam dunk for you. The man is facing two charges—aggravated assault and domestic violence. Those are very serious. When Miles gives the judge his statement, there isn't any way possible he will award him with custody of any kind. He will glaringly point out that it would be child endangerment. I also want you to know we are going to put Montana on the stand. Do you have any issues with that because if you do, we need to hash them out."

We were sitting on the couch and it was after Montana had gone to bed. Rose hugged herself and asked, "Is it necessary?"

Without hesitation, I said, "Yes, and let me explain why. I want her to tell the judge in her own words why she doesn't want to go to her daddy's and why she's afraid. Of course, Miles will have to do the questioning because it's his case. We'll talk to her first and make sure she understands that she's safe. Petey will be there, right up front, so she sees him. Does this make you more comfortable?"

"To a point. I don't want her to feel threatened when she sees Greg."

"We'll take care of that by explaining where he'll be in the room. We'll draw a picture of where she'll be sitting and show her where he'll be. Then we'll emphasize to her not to look at him. I used to do this all the time and demonstrated it with dolls and stuffed animals. It gives kids a better representation. I'll do the same with her."

She rubbed her hands up and down her thighs and stood. She paced, but I didn't interrupt her thought process because this was something she had to work out on her own. The last thing I wanted was for her to be uncomfortable with this. It was a parent's nightmare to pit a child against the other parent. But Greg was not a good man. We both worried what went on in that house and the way Montana was so fearful of going there gave us really bad vibes.

I knew everything was going to work when Rose said, "Fine. You are obviously the expert here and her counselor says she's doing really well. I'd like to discuss this with her though. As much as I hate for her to be up there, I'll do anything to keep her away from him and if this is what it takes, then let's do it."

I stood and pulled her into my arms. "This is going to work. I promise."

"I hope you're right. But I have to tell you I'm impressed by the way you're handling this. With the dolls and stuffed animals, I mean. It sounds like you've had a little bit of psychology in your background."

"The firm I worked with employed a psychologist so I can't take credit for that."

"Very professional. I'm happy you picked that up."

"Same here. Now, will you give me the kiss I've been thinking of all day?"

"All day?"

"Umm hmm." I didn't wait for her but brushed my lips across hers. Then I lifted her up and took what I'd been deprived of all day. Her kiss was soft and demure at first, but I wasn't going for that. I owned this mouth, so I showed her exactly that. My tongue swept past her lips and our tongues collided. Every time it happened, I wanted more. One hand reached under her shirt to feel her warm, smooth skin. She pulled back from the kiss and one word came out of her in a breathy rush.

"Bedroom."

Holding her, I walked us there, closed the door behind us, and we fell onto the bed. The sound of metal clinking as she unbuckled my belt made my already hard cock, even stiffer. She wrapped her hand around it, slid down and put her luscious mouth on me. My breath turned jagged as she took me deep. It was slow and perfect, just like her hand cupping my sac. Even as great as this was, it was nothing compared to being inside of her.

"Take off your clothes," I told her.

She stopped, and her eyes latched onto mine. "I want to be inside of you. Like now."

Her shirt and bra went first, followed by her pants and panties. My pants, boxers, and shirt disappeared in a flash.

"On your knees." I didn't give her much time to get situated before I slid all the way inside her drenched core. "Oh, God, you're amazing."

Her moans were the sexiest things I'd ever heard. Every time I slid back in, she let one out and it drove me to the brink of orgasm. I wrapped an arm around her waist and bent over her as I continued to pump into her.

"Ah, yes."

"Damn, that's hot."

I reached between her thighs to set her off, and it didn't take, but a few strokes with my finger before her inner muscles clenched down on me in a series of spasms. That was enough for me to get my own. I poured myself into her until she milked me dry. We both panted as I hugged her to my stomach. Rolling to my back, and taking her with me, I said, "That was epic."

"Mmm. Yes, it was."

Turning her over to face me, I tugged her in for a quick kiss. "You are the sexiest woman. I adore the sounds you make."

"Yeah?"

"They're a total turn on."

"I thought it was just me." Her finger circled my nipple and sent shivers all over me.

"What do you mean?"

"You make this groan that totally sets me off. I thought I was the only one to react like that."

"It's mutual. And if you keep playing with my nipple like that, we're going to go in for round two."

"Is that a threat or a promise?" She put her mouth on my nipple and proceeded to suck and bite it.

"It's both." I threw her on her back, pushed her legs up to her chest and asked, "Are you ready?"

"Do you even have to ask?"

I crawled down and my mouth went straight between her

thighs. She sighed softly at first, until my tongue picked up speed and my fingers found their way inside her.

"Oh, yes, please."

I met her demands until she moaned out another orgasm. My dick must've heard her, because it roared back to life. Kneeling between her thighs, I entered her, and she let out a squeal of surprise. Then we got down to business.

"I didn't think you could ..."

"Neither did I but you made it happen."

"Harder."

I was happy to find she liked it a little rough. I stared at this beauty as she lay there, legs spread wide, taking the length of me eagerly, and wondered where she'd been all my life. We banged another one out, and when we finished, we both lay there gasping.

My hand reached for hers and I said, "I was wrong. You don't need to run. You'll get your cardio in the bedroom with me."

She moved my hand to her chest. "Feel that? I believe I do need cardio. I'm totally out of shape."

"No worries, babe. I'll have you there in no time." I pulled her over, so she was lying across me.

"I hate to even bring this up but ..."

"You don't have to. It's late and I need to sleep too." I kissed her, long and slow. Then I got up.

As I was leaving, I said, "I can't wait for the day we can sleep in each other's arms all night." I didn't give her a chance to respond before I softly closed the door behind me. If I had stayed to listen to anything she said, I would've crawled back in the bed, held her against me, and refused to leave her side. We couldn't take the chance of Montana finding us because if any kind of misbehavior between us came out, it would not look good for her. I wanted to ensure her reputation as a mother was as pristine as possible.

Sleeping alone wasn't the worst thing I could endure. I'd

already been through that. Those demons still visited me at night, but when they did, I brought my arsenal of weapons to the surface—thoughts of Rose and Montana. It didn't push the desire for drugs completely away, but as long as I had their beautiful faces to conjure up, I felt anything was possible.

Chapter Thirty-Five

ROSE

THE DELICIOUS SORENESS BETWEEN MY LEGS REMINDED ME OF what Pearson and I had shared the night before. It brought a huge grin to my face as I showered and got ready for work. Seeing him in the kitchen that morning, looking utterly sexy and edible after his morning run, made me want to crawl on his lap and kiss him all over. Montana was chatting away at the table so that wasn't remotely possible.

Axel was waiting on me and Petey was there for Montana when I walked out, ready to go. The trial was next week so tonight, Pearson and Miles were going to review everything with Montana for the first time. Miles would be coming for dinner and afterward, we would sit down and discuss it with her.

Sylvie popped into my office to see how things were going right before lunch. "I just wanted to check in. You already know I'm testifying so I'm going to be talking to Pearson and Miles before the trial."

I suggested we go to lunch to discuss what's been happening.

"I'm super nervous over everything," I told her.

"Where's your medallion diffuser?"

"I know, I keep forgetting it."

"Don't forget that and you also have the best attorney representing you."

"Sylvie, you don't know Greg."

"Hello, it's me. I'm the one who's been by your side this entire time. Of course I know that jack ass. I saw him attack you. Why do you think I'm a character witness?"

"Okay. You're right. You get it. But I'm still nervous. Just knowing he's going to be in the same room with Montana and me, freaks me out."

"Listen. You'll be safe. Pearson would never put either of you in danger."

I grabbed her hand. "It's not Pearson. Greg is manipulative. I don't trust whatever it is he has up his sleeve. If he loses, which Pearson is certain he will, all bets are off. I'm so scared for Montana. We have bodyguards—"

She squeezed my hand, painfully, and said, "Wait. What did you say?"

"I'm fearful for—"

Sylvie waved a hand like she was swatting at gnats. "No, not that. The part about bodyguards."

"I thought I told you."

"No, you did not."

"Pearson hired bodyguards right before Greg was released. He wanted to make sure we were safe."

Her knowing grin told me what she was thinking. "Aw, you two. I knew you'd make the perfect couple."

"Stop," I said, my face heating.

"Don't be embarrassed. You deserve the best and there's none better than his family. So, how's he doing since his release?"

"Pretty good. He'd mentioned getting a place of his own, so he could test himself on living without me. He wants to ensure he doesn't need a crutch and I encouraged it. Only now he wants to wait until after the trial and I do too. I'm too scared to be alone right now."

Sylvie nodded. "That's completely understandable and the two of you don't need the added stress.

Frowning, I said, "Marrying Greg was a huge mistake, but if I hadn't, I wouldn't have Montana who is my greatest joy. By the way, she adores Pearson. She's so funny with him too." I told her how she refuses to stop calling him Mister.

"Even after all this time?"

"It's become kind of special between them now."

Her hands covered her chest. "That's too sweet. Never thought of Pearson as the sweet kind of guy, but then again he hadn't met the right woman either."

I know I'm blushing furiously. My face feels like I stuck it in a kiln.

"What aren't you telling your closest friend, Rose?"

"Nothing."

"Come on. I'm not stupid and not only that, the color of your face is a dead giveaway. You're hiding something. You're a terrible liar, you know."

"I'm not lying."

"Okay, but you're also keeping something from me and it's about my cousin. You guys are pretty serious, aren't you?"

"Maybe," I mumbled.

"What?"

"Oh, all right. Yeah, we are. We're exclusive and we're serious. But he doesn't want to commit until he's a year out in his sobriety and I agree. It's not only me in this relationship. I have Montana and I don't want her hurt in any way."

"I love the way you two are going about this. And after you're both comfortable and your ex is serving a sentence for domestic abuse, Pearson can get his own place to prove to you both that he's capable of living on his own. You guys are awesome, but I knew that before you two were together." She's practically jumping up and down in her chair.

"Calm down."

"One other thing. I want to be maid of honor in your wedding."

"Oh my God. You really need to calm down. And do me a huge favor. Do not share any of this with anybody. No one knows."

"You have to be joking. Looking at the two of you paints the picture. I've never seen you so happy as when you talk about him."

Sylvie was right. Pearson made me extremely happy. Happier than I'd ever been. "I am very happy with him, but I have a huge obstacle to get over next week. Afterward, I can relax a bit and I'll really relax when or if he goes to prison."

"There's no if on that."

I shook my head. "He's a slimy bastard. If anyone can get out of it, he can. I don't put anything past him." I didn't add that I had a really bad feeling about it all. Even though I trusted Pearson to win custody, there was something foreboding about it all. Montana's safety would still be a concern. If Greg didn't go to prison, I knew there would always be a chance he'd try to abduct her, and I would never rest knowing that risk existed.

Chapter Thirty-Six

PEARSON

THE TRIAL WENT AS I EXPECTED. GREG WALKED INTO THE courtroom cocky as hell, with Tom as his attorney. That surprised me. I didn't anticipate Tom to dirty his hands with someone who'd served jail time for domestic abuse or aggravated assault. When he saw me sitting with Miles as Rose's attorney, his eyes bulged. He hadn't banked on me being there either. I suppressed a laugh when his surprise turned to smugness. There wasn't a doubt in my mind he figured he had this one in the bag. I couldn't wait to see his expression when the judge named Rose as the sole custodial parent.

Miles called Rose to the stand to give her testimony. We prepared her for the kinds of questions Greg's attorney would ask her. Knowing Tom as I did, I knew he would play dirty. I slipped her a note before she went up to apprise her of this.

He's going to use every trick in the book. Use your expertise, as you would with a drug addict.

She nodded her understanding. I was so proud of her as she walked up to the stand, head held high.

Miles approached Rose after she was sworn in and asked her to chronicle the domestic abuse. It took a while, but she did. Then Miles submitted his proof to the judge. There were X-Rays and hospital documentation from her many visits. Greg squirmed in his seat as Tom's face grew more crimson by the second. For a moment I didn't think he'd be able to hold his temper.

Then Miles asked, "What made you stay?"

Rose shrugged. "I was scared he'd find me and do something even worse. He threatened it all the time. And then there was Montana's safety I was concerned about." She dabbed the tears that spilled down her cheeks.

"And now?" Miles asked.

"I'm frightened to death, especially for my daughter's safety since he's been released from jail. He's told me he'll stop at nothing until she's back with him."

"When did he do this?"

"Last week on the phone," Rose said, her hands trembling as she still wiped her tears.

"Thank you, Ms. Wilson."

He looked at the judge and said, Your Honor, I would like to submit evidence to support the witness' statements. There are audio recordings of Ms. Rose Wilson being threatened by Mr. Greg Wilson on several occasions.

"I object," Tom said. "We knew nothing of this."

"Counsel, approach the bench."

Miles and Tom were whispering feverishly to the judge, and I surmised what was being said. Tom was arguing that the evidence was inadmissible since Greg hadn't known about it, and Miles was arguing that if he had, he wouldn't have said it. This went on for several minutes until they both returned to their seats. Miles was smiling.

"This court will allow the evidence. Court will recess for forty-five minutes," the judge announced.

Rose asked, "What does this mean?"

"It's good. Really good. The judge is going to listen to the recordings. Come on, let's go get some coffee and see Montana."

We left the courtroom and Montana was with Petey. She was teaching him how to dance. God love him for his patience. When she saw us walk into the room, she ran and hugged us. "Is it over?"

"No, we're taking a break," I told her.

"Already?" Petey asked.

"Yep. How's it going?" I asked.

"Not good. Petey needs dance lessons. He's not getting any better. Maybe he can come with me." Montana stuck her lower lip out. Petey grinned.

We drank our coffee and went back to the courtroom after thirty-five minutes with a promise to Montana that it would be over soon.

Court resumed with Rose back on the stand. Miles asked her why she was afraid for Montana's safety.

"My daughter says she's not allowed to leave her room. She's frightened and her father won't respond to her. She has to stay there with the exception of meals."

"And you believe your daughter?

"Of course. She wouldn't lie to me. For a while, she wouldn't tell me anything about what went on at her dad's house. She was afraid to. She says they're always fighting and yelling."

"Who's they?"

"Greg and his wife," Rose answered.

"Do you think that could be scaring her?"

"Possibly, but she wasn't eating much when she used to come to my home. She wouldn't laugh and she was anxious all the time. As a psychologist, I know what to look for in terms of child abuse. I believe Montana was suffering from it. When I was awarded custody, I began taking her to counseling and her psychologist evaluated her. She believes the same thing."

"Thank you, Ms. Wilson. No further questions, Your Honor."

The judge looked at Tom. "Mr. Dawkins?"

Tom approached Rose like a panther approaches his prey. Now came the intimidation. He was going to do his best to rattle her during his cross-examination. I knew she was nervous, but it didn't show. She was brilliant.

"Ms. Wilson, if you are such a stellar mother, why were you absent so much when you were married and why were you not awarded custody in your divorce?" Tom asked.

She smiled. "First, my ex-husband had an excellent attorney and mine was horrible. But the real truth was I was in school getting my degree, which my ex failed to mention. By the time he told me he'd filed for divorce, he had stripped all of our bank accounts, leaving me penniless. I couldn't afford a decent attorney. I was only trying to do what was best for our family and that was getting an education, Mr. Dawkins."

"So, by abandoning your daughter for hours at a time, you thought that was helping your family?"

"Mr. Dawkins, I have a master's degree in psychology. You will not coerce me into agreeing with that question. Many mothers work outside the home and are not considered to be abandoning their children. I was only doing the same, except I was taking classes. Had I been working a job instead, it would've spent the same amount of time away from home."

She stumped him. His mouth opened and closed several times. Finally, the judge asked, "Is there anything else?"

"Uh, yes. Ms. Wilson, you said your husband allegedly hit you."

"There is no allegedly about it. He hit me quite often. The last time he did it I fell and broke my wrist. My attorney witnessed it and he has the hospital records to prove it."

"Are you sure you weren't clumsy?"

Rose laughed. "I've been accused of many things, but not

clumsiness." We anticipated this and she was prepared for her response. "Mr. Dawkins, I'm sure you know what yoga is."

"I do."

"I have a license to teach advanced yoga and am able to do the most difficult poses."

His smug expression returned. "Care to demonstrate?"

"Here? In court?" Her tone indicated he was crazy. But he'd find out soon she was going to make him look like a fool.

"Why not. If you're so sure of yourself."

"You actually want me to do yoga poses for you?"

"Yes, I would like a demonstration, please."

Rose shrugged, stepped down, and moved to where the judge could see her. She did a pose where she stood on one foot, held the other with one hand and extended her arm out in front of her. She didn't even wobble. "This is a balance pose."

"That doesn't look so difficult," Tom said.

"Would you care to try it?"

"Ms. Wilson, I'm not the one demonstrating my balance, you are."

"Then how about this?" She stood with her legs spread wide apart. Then she dropped one hand by her right foot and lifted the right leg. Her body bent over that leg and her left arm bent over her body, grabbing her right foot from over her head. The only things on the floor was a foot and a hand. It looked like a pretzel pose to me.

"Fine, you're flexible."

After she stood, she said, "Flexibility is one thing, but to hold the pose and balance is another. I am not clumsy, Mr. Dawkins."

The judge said, "I think Ms. Wilson has made her point, counsel. Ms. Wilson, you may be seated."

Rose sat back down in the witness stand.

"Counsel, continue," the judge said.

"Ms. Wilson, you said your child is in counseling. When you chose a psychologist, did you tell that particular one you suspected child abuse?"

"No, I did not. I wanted an unbiased opinion."

"And you believed everything your daughter told you and that it was not a part of an overactive imagination?"

"Mr. Dawkins, my daughter wouldn't make anything like that up."

"Are you so sure?"

"Yes," Rose said.

"Did you know she has not one but two imaginary friends?"

Rose didn't skip a beat. "I do. Children, especially ones who don't have playmates are known to make up imaginary friends. It's not uncommon."

"You believe this overactive imagination of hers couldn't possibly have made up the part where she is forced to stay in her room all the time?"

"No, I don't believe so and neither does her therapist."

"Ms. Wilson, you should study up on this more. It's been shown that children with overactive imaginations are quite capable of making up lots of different things. No more questions, Your Honor.

Then he asked, "Mr. Sinclair, do you have any more witnesses?"

"Yes, your honor. We'd like to call Sylvie West to the stand."

Sylvie came up and testified. Hers was brief, telling the court how Rose was an exemplary employee but had been having issues with Greg. Miles asked her to explain and she told about how unreasonable he was and how Sylvie had to get one of her neighbors to pick up Montana one day because he couldn't wait an extra hour for Rose to show up, which was their scheduled and agreed upon time. She made him sound like an ass. She also told about when he showed up at the center and assaulted her and they had to call the police. Tom scowled and declined to question her.

"Mr. Sinclair, any more to question?"

"Yes, Your Honor. At this time, we'd like to call Montana Wilson to the stand. Your Honor, given the circumstances, we've also invited Montana's bodyguard and her psychologist to be in the courtroom with her."

One of our representatives went to get Montana and Petey. Montana's therapist was already present.

Miles met Petey and Montana and ushered them both in. Petey took a seat up front so Montana could see him while the bailiff swore her in. She looked damned adorable.

"Do you swear to tell the truth, the whole, and nothing but the truth so help you God."

"I promise cuz I don't never lie," she said with her hand on the Bible. The corner of the judge's mouth turned up.

Miles said, "Montana, you know who I am?"

"Uh huh. You're Mister's friend."

"Can you point to Mister?"

She aimed her pointer finger at me and said, "He's right there sitting next to Mommy. Hi Mommy. Hi Petey." She waved. There was a collective chuckle in the room.

Miles came back to the table and I handed him the stuffed animals. "Montana, can you show me, using these, what it was like for you to stay at your daddy's?"

"Uh huh." She took the toys and said, "This one's me and this one's my daddy. He says in a mean voice, 'You can't leave your room.' I cry and cry, but no one comes." She looks around and when doesn't seem to find anything she flattens her hand and puts the toy underneath it. "I hide under my bed because I'm scared of the big monsters in the woods."

"What big monsters?" Miles asked.

"The ones that live back there that will come and get me. I stay there all night till the light comes. I hate it there. I'm all alone and sometimes they don't get me for supper."

"Can you tell me more about that?"

"Yeah, I'm hungry a lot. They don't call me to eat. I don't hear it when they do and then I don't get nothing." Her brow was creased as she told her version of life with Daddy.

"What do you mean?"

She shrugged. "Daddy yells at me when I don't hear him. But I can't leave my room cuz the door is locked and then I get in trouble."

"Let me see if I understand. If you don't go when he calls, you get in trouble, but you can't go because your door is locked?"

"Uh huh."

"And then you don't get dinner?"

"Yeah. And Miss Caroline cries a lot."

"Miss Caroline?"

"Daddy's person."

"You mean his wife?"

"Uh huh. That's her. She doesn't like me."

"What makes you say that?"

"She won't let me play anywhere but my room and yells at me when she's not sleeping."

Rose was rocking back and forth as this was upsetting her. It couldn't be helped, and we had warned her. But to see this beautiful child having to tell this story was emotional as hell. I grabbed her slender hand and stroked it with my thumb, doing my best to offer her comfort.

"And how has it been since you've gone back to your mommy's?"

A smile that sent beams of sunshine into the room lit up her face. "I like it at Mommy's! I have new friends at my school. Miss Cathie is my teacher and she's nice. I'm taking clicky shoe dancing and I'm real good. Wanna see?"

"Not right now maybe later, but can you tell me more about being at your mommy's?"

"Yeah, we eat pizza and sometimes she makes me homemade cookies. And we go see the monkeys at the zoo. Do you like monkeys? They're my favorite. And we play bunny rabbit in the backyard. Daddy would never let me hippity-hop around, but I can do it all the time at Mommy's. Do you like to hippity-hop?"

"I'm not sure. Maybe you can show me."

She jumped out of her seat before Miles could stop her and did her bunny rabbit hop. "Now you try." Miles looked at the judge.

He said, "Well, Mr. Sinclair, what are you waiting for?" I knew we had the judge then.

Miles mimicked Montana in her hop. Then she turned to the judge and said, "Mr. Honor, do you want to try?"

"Young lady, I think I'll pass, but you do a marvelous hippity-hop."

"Thank you. Mommy always told me I'm to thank people when they complex me."

The room broke out into another chuckle.

"Your Honor, no more questions."

The judge asked Tom if he cared to cross-examine.

"Yes, Your Honor."

"Mr. Dawkins, I'm going to warn you. No shenanigans here. Am I clear?"

"Yes, Your Honor."

"Montana, my name is Tom. I'm a friend of your daddy's." He stuck out his hand for her to shake, but she only stared at it. No one had ever done this to her.

"Mr. Dawkins, she's four-years-old. I doubt she's familiar with shaking hands."

"Mr. Honor, I'm four and a half. My birthday's next month and Mommy said I could get an ice cream cake."

"Well, isn't that something?" the judge said as Montana nodded vigorously.

"Carry on, Mr. Dawkins."

"Montana, were you really scared at your daddy's that monsters were coming?"

"Yes. They were in the forest. Daddy said so. He said if I wasn't good the monsters were coming."

"From the forest?"

"The one behind the house. There are all kinds of monsters living back there. I hear them."

"You do?" Tom asked. "What do they say?"

"They tell me they're going to take me away and I'll never see my mommy again." Poor thing's eyes were almost jumping out of her head.

"Move on, counselor," the judge said.

"Montana, is it really true your daddy didn't let you eat?"

Her head bobbed up and down, curls flying everywhere. "I was always hungry. I cried for Mommy every night."

"No more questions, Your Honor." It was clear that her testimony was damaging his case even further.

Petey escorted her out of the room and she stopped to hug Rose on the way. "Bye Mommy."

When the door closed behind her, the judge asked, "Any more to testify, Mr. Sinclair?"

"I'd like to call Dr. Cheryl Somers."

Montana's psychologist walked up to the stand and was sworn in. She verified everything Rose said and told us she believed Montana had been abused and neglected. "She is a different child now than when I first started seeing her."

"How so?" Miles asked.

"When she first came in, she practically cowered from everything. Every question I asked she hesitated to answer. I had to use your toy method to learn anything from her. She, I believe, was removed from her father's home before irreparable damage occurred."

"Irreparable damage?"

Dr. Somers said, "Childhood psychological trauma can be permanent, much like PTSD. She was suffering from that and exhibiting signs of it. Once I broke through her barriers, and she began talking, she began to get better. She was so afraid of her father coming back into her life. She still will not be in a room with a closed door, but I imagine, that will end one day."

"No further questions, your honor," Miles said.

The judge asked, "Mr. Dawkins?"

"Yes, your honor." He asked about her education and credentials. Then he asked, "How long have you known Rose Wilson?"

"Ever since her daughter became one of my patients."

"No further questions, your honor."

Tom realized he was fucked.

"Court is recessed for one hour."

We left and went to see Montana. It was nearly lunchtime, so I had one of our assistants run out to grab us all a quick bite. We could eat something more substantial later. I had a really great feeling we'd be celebrating tonight.

"Mister, did I do good?" Muffin asked.

"You did great! Get over here."

She ran into my arms and I lifted her high above my head as she squealed with delight. Then I kissed the tip of her nose. "The best part was how you made Miles do the hippity-hop."

"Mr. Miles, you havta work on it some. You weren't very good."

"I promise I will," Miles said.

Rose watched us with a cheerful expression. It was a relief to see her so happy. Petey was standing there so I said, "Hey Petey, wanna give us a demo of your dancing skills?"

He said with a laugh, "Nah, I'll pass."

When's your birthday?" I asked him.

"August. Why?"

"Hmm. Only four months away. I know what you're getting." I grinned wickedly.

"You wouldn't?"

"Wouldn't what?" I asked innocently.

"Never mind. I don't want to give you ideas."

Our food arrived and we sat down to nibble on it. Montana wolfed hers down. She must've been starved.

I checked the time when we were finished and the hour was about up. We left Montana with Petey and headed back to the courtroom.

The judge entered and said, "I've read through my notes, the documentation, listened to the audio, and looked over the testimonies. On account of you, Mr. Wilson, and your tendency for violence, I must agree with Ms. Wilson that you are not fit to be the custodial parent. At this time, I am awarding full custody to Ms. Wilson. Mr. Wilson, you may have one two-hour supervised visit every other Saturday or Sunday, whichever suits Ms. Wilson. After your domestic violence and aggravated assault trial, if you are found guilty, this may be amended to no visitation at all. You need to seek counseling for anger management. If in the future it is deemed safe for your daughter to spend time with you, it will only be after intense therapy *and* after a home study. The fact that you locked your daughter in her room and did not feed her is appalling. If I had my choice, you would never get any type of custody again. Violence of any kind is taken very seriously in this state. Ms. Wilson has an order of protection against you. You have a problem that needs to be addressed. I am recommending you take care of it as soon as possible.

"Court is adjourned."

Chapter Thirty-Seven

ROSE

IMMENSE RELIEF FLOODED ME, AND I SAGGED IN MY SEAT UPON hearing the judge's words. I wanted to jump for joy, but my legs were too shaky to stand. Pearson and Miles did, and when they didn't see me, they both turned to find me slumped in the chair.

"Rose, are you okay?" Pearson asked.

"Yes, I'm fine, but I can't seem to move right now. I'm relieved after all this time. My body's turned into a noodle."

He eyed me for a second. "You're decompressing. Come on, let's go tell the Pop Tart." He helped me to my feet and while doing so, my eyes accidentally landed on Greg's. I didn't intend for them to, it simply happened. And what a mistake that was. He didn't shoot daggers at me, he annihilated me with laser beams of hatred. I literally shrank from the intensity of his glare.

Pearson felt it and asked, "What is it?"

"Just get me out of this room. Now."

He turned to see what I had seen and saw Greg glaring at

me. But now Pearson and Greg locked onto each other's. Then Greg sneered. I'm not sure why, but chills ran up my spine and I shivered. "Please, Pearson, let's go." I tugged on his arm. He turned back to me and nodded.

Montana ran to us when we walked in, yelling, "Did you get me?"

"We got you!" Pearson told her.

She jumped into his arms and hugged him until he passed her off to me. Then she kissed me and asked, "I never have to go back there, right Mommy?"

"Right, Pop Tart." Her arms went around my neck and squeezed me as hard as I'd ever felt.

"Can we go see the monkeys at the zoo?"

Before I could answer, Pearson said, "I don't see why not. Let's go home and change clothes."

"Yay." I put her down and she hippity-hopped around the room until she grabbed Petey's hand. "Can you go too, Petey?"

"I sure can," he said.

After thanking Miles profusely, and inviting him to join us for dinner on Friday, I grabbed Pearson's hand and we followed Petey and Montana out to our cars. They made quite a pair, she the tiny thing next to the giant of a man.

"She really loves him. I wonder what she'll do when we no longer have to use his services," I said.

"That's not going to happen until Greg is locked away for years. I don't trust him," Pearson said.

Those shivers returned and I couldn't get rid of that awful feeling. "Did you see that look he gave me?"

"You weren't the only one he gave it to. He's definitely pissed, which is why you two will keep the bodyguards. I don't trust him at all. Even with this win, he's still unstable as hell. Until he receives treatment, which is highly unlikely, he's a definite threat to you both."

"I wish that weren't true, but you're right. As long as he

controlled me through Montana, he was fine, but now, he's a loose cannon for sure."

"And I don't want that thing firing off in either of your two's direction. I have a mind to increase your protection." We slid into his car and he didn't say anything.

"How would you increase it? We already have coverage to and from work, and at home. Petey stays at school with Montana."

"I'm wondering if you should be accompanied at all times. Montana is and I think you should be too."

I didn't say anything because it would make me feel a ton better to have someone like Petey or Axel around me all the time.

"How do you feel about that?" he asked.

"To be honest, it would make me feel better. At first, I didn't think it was necessary, but after today, he totally unnerved me."

Pearson picked up his phone and made a call. "This is Pearson West. I'd like to have the coverage increased on Rose Wilson. She needs to have someone with her at all times now."

He paused, which I assumed the other person on the line was speaking.

"Yes, that's correct. A driver and he's to remain with her one hundred percent of the time, even at work. He can stand outside of her office when she's in session."

Pause.

"To begin immediately."

Another pause.

"We're headed to her home right now and then to the zoo, but Petey will drive us all."

Pause.

"Excellent, we'll be home by six thirty. And thank you."

He turned to me and said, "A team will be at the house around six forty-five to meet you. After tonight, you'll have someone twenty-four/seven."

"Thanks. I do feel better about this."

"So do I." He pushed the ignition button and we drove home.

As soon as we got to the zoo, Montana grabbed Pearson's and my hand and asked to go see the monkeys.

"I'm going to call you my monkey girl from now on," Pearson said.

"But I thought I was Muffin."

"I like monkey girl too," he said.

"Then I'm gonna call you tiger-r-r-r," she said with a growl.

"Good. I like tigers. Can we go see them after the monkeys?"

"Mommy?"

"Of course."

"Yay. Come on, Mister. Let's run." She ran holding Pearson's hand, leaving Petey and me to follow. When we got there, Pearson was showing her how to make monkey faces. Montana was doing her best to imitate him, and she looked hilarious. Taking out my phone, I snapped a bunch of photos of the two of them.

When she saw me, she called out, "Mommy, come and make monkey faces. Mister can teach you. Petey, you do it too." The four of us looked like goofballs making faces at the poor monkeys. Eventually, they wandered off and didn't pay us any attention.

"Why did they go away?" Montana asked.

"I suppose they think we look goofy," I said.

"But I like looking like a monkey."

"Maybe we can practice more when we get home," I suggested.

"Okay, let's go see the tigers now so Mister can see how big they are." She growled but sounded more like a hungry kitten.

We got to the tigers and Montana went up to the glass that separated us from them, and she growled. One tiger was there, and he walked closer and tilted his head. Montana did the same and growled again. The tiger flicked his tail and ears and crouched while we all watched in fascination. What happened

next was unexpected. He leaped at the window in attack mode
going after Montana. She was safe, of course, but screamed
nevertheless, as did I. I picked her up and jumped back, almost
falling, but was saved by Petey's humongous arms.

Pearson was by my side instantly, as Montana shook in my
arms. He took her from me, asking if she was okay.

"That tiger was gonna eat me, Mister. He was real mean."

"I believe he saw you as prey."

"I wasn't praying I was growling."

"No, he thought you were food."

"But I don't look like a pizza."

"No, you don't, but tigers don't eat pizzas. They eat smaller
animals and sometimes they even eat large animals," Pearson
said.

"I'm not an animal. I'm a girl." She stuck her hip out and put
her hand on it, exactly like I did sometimes. It was the first time
I'd seen her do this and look like me.

Pearson explained, "To the tiger, you were an animal. And
they eat animals to survive in the wild."

"But, Mister, that's silly. They're in the zoo."

"Yes, they are, but they don't really know that."

"How come? Didn't the zoo people tell them?"

Petey and I were suppressing our laughter. Pearson, sighed.
"Maybe they just didn't listen when they arrived. I'm not sure,
my little monkey."

"Monkeys are nicer than tigers. I don't like tigers. Can we go
see the bunnies now? The ones with long ears?"

"I think that's a good idea."

Pearson still carried her while we walked and she peppered
him with questions. "Mister, how come those tigers don't eat
pizza? Don't they like it?"

"I'm sure they would, but it's not good for them."

"Why?"

"I don't really know, but I think it has something to do with
the cheese."

"They don't like cheese?"

"Nope."

"Why?"

"It hurts their tummies." He seemed satisfied with his answer.

Until she asked, "Why?"

"Um, I'm not sure but do you know what bunny rabbits eat?"

"Yeah, everyone knows that."

"Tell me," he said.

"Carrots."

"What else?"

"Easter eggs, purple, pink, blue, and yellow ones. And they like jelly beans too."

"They do, huh?"

"Yep."

"How did you get so smart?" he asked.

She did an exaggerated shrug. "I don't know but I get all the answers right in school and Miss Cathie says very good to me a lot. Plus I get star stickers. Did you get star stickers in school?"

"Sometimes, but I bet you get wayyyyy more than I ever did."

"Probly."

We entered the barn where the rabbits lived, and Pearson set Montana down. She ran ahead of us directly to where her favorite rabbits were kept. Each time we visited here, she begged me to buy her one. The answer was always the same—no. Maybe one day we'd get a cat or a dog, but a rabbit was totally out of the question.

"Look, Mister, here's my favorite bunny rabbit." It wasn't the same one, I was sure, but the same breed … a lop eared and she adored them.

The cages were low enough so someone her age could pet them and there were signs on the ones that could be held.

"Mommy, can we pick this one up?"

"I think we can."

Her arms extended as her hands opened and closed in excitement. Pearson bent over and picked the thing up. "Boy is he ever soft. I've never held one of these."

"Feel his ears, Mister."

I watched Pearson pet him and it was a joy to see. Obviously, the man enjoyed animals. He'd grown up with them and his brother was a veterinarian. He was gentle with the thing as he passed it to Montana. "Now careful with him. Don't drop him."

"I know how. I love these bunnies," she said. Then she plopped down on the straw covered floor with the rabbit in her arms and played with it. His nose twitched as she stroked its soft fur.

"Mommy, you have to hold him. He's so soft. Can we take him home? Pleeeaaase?"

"Not today, honey."

"But Mommy, he's the bestest bunny ever."

"Maybe so, but we can't have a bunny, Montana. Remember what I said? One day we'll get a cat or a dog, but not a bunny."

"But I don't want a cat or dog. I want a bunny like him. We can call him Ears."

Pearson started talking. "Monkey, maybe — "

I cut him off. He tended to spoil her and there was no way we were bringing a bunny into my home. Or our home or whatever. "Montana," I used my warning tone. "I said no. You can play with the bunny here, but no means, no. Understand?"

"Yes, Mommy."

Then I glanced at Pearson and his brows were raised. I mouthed — no bunny ever.

He mouthed back — why?

I pulled him aside and whispered, "They're super messy and a pain. No arguing, please."

"You got it." He kissed my cheek. I would have to talk to him again about overindulging her. Montana was a great kid, but that didn't mean she could get her way whenever she wanted.

When we were finished visiting all of Montana's favorite

animals, we left and went to get something to eat. Since it was late, we decided on carry-out at a Chinese restaurant.

Once home, we all took a seat at the table and Petey and Pearson tried to teach Montana how to eat with chopsticks. It was funny until she didn't bother to eat. That's when I had to put my foot down.

"Okay everyone, you two men included. Put down the chopsticks and pick up the forks. Eat your dinner or no dessert for the three of you. The food is getting cold."

"But Mommy ..."

"No, but Mommy. You're having more fun with those toys and before I know it, you won't want to eat. Now eat your lo mien and eggroll, which is what you begged me to order."

"Yes, Mommy."

I had cut the noodles up for her so it was easier to eat. She still made somewhat of a mess, but she ate it, along with half of her eggroll. The men wolfed down theirs and the boxes were soon emptied.

Pearson, in his sassy voice, asked, "Were we good, Mommy?" He smirked and I couldn't help but laugh.

"Nope. Not nearly good enough."

"But our plates are clean."

"You haven't done the dishes yet." He hopped up and proceeded to clean everything up. I offered him a fortune cookie when he was done.

"Is this my dessert?" he asked.

"No, but you have to read it first."

He cracked the thing open and read, "You will experience difficulty, but your mate will come to your rescue."

We laughed and I said, "We should've had that a few months back."

"True. Read yours."

"Be on the lookout for coming events... they cast shadows beforehand."

I asked Petey, "What about yours?"

He read, "Fortune favors the brave."

"Those were interesting," Pearson said. "It was almost like the Chinese were trying to tell us something.

"Yeah, I like the funny ones better," I said. Then I asked who wanted ice cream to which everyone responded yes. After I scooped out four bowls, we all ate it in silence. I'm not sure if it was because the ice cream was delicious or because we were thinking about those silly fortunes. I couldn't get them out of my mind. Were they a prophecy of what was to come or just a coincidence? I hoped it was the latter. I wasn't superstitious by nature but lately, everything freaked me out.

I was putting the bowls in the dishwasher when the doorbell rang, Montana yelled, "I'll get it."

"Stop!" I shouted. She did and I added, "You are never to answer the door, young lady."

Her round eyes told me I'd frightened her. "Petey, can you explain this to her?"

He took her into her room and Pearson went to the door. I joined him in the living room a few moments later. He'd let the team in. There were five men, all of them large and intimidating. I felt exactly the way I did when I'd met Axel and Petey. I was sure I'd warm up to them too. We all sat down and introduced ourselves.

Pearson started off by explaining what was going on in my life and why I needed protection. When he was finished, he told the men exactly what he wanted and asked them their thoughts.

The team leader whose name was Mack, said, "I agree with everything you've said. A driver for everything, even a quick trip to the store and you should be accompanied at all times. When you go to work, you should have protection inside too. Is there a window in your office?"

"No, it's pretty small," I answered.

"Good. Like Mr. West said, during your sessions, he can stand outside, but when you go to lunch, he's to be with you, or at any other times. Is that reasonable?"

"Yes, I agree," I said.

"It'll work exactly like your daughter's bodyguard," Mack said. "Sometimes he will have to rotate due to scheduling changes, but for the most part, you'll have the same person every day."

"Won't I have Axel anymore?"

"I'm afraid not. Axel will still be on your case, but he'll be on watch. In other words, he'll be on the outside. He's familiar with your surroundings, so we'd like to keep him there. From now on you'll have Rex here."

Rex was very dangerous looking. Tall, maybe six and a half feet, looked like a boxer or fighter, he was that muscular, with dark skin and hair, he currently scared me. But when he smiled and held out his hand, I relaxed. "Ms. Wilson, I'll do my very best to keep you safe."

"Thank you, Rex. I appreciate that."

Our discussion lasted about an hour and they left.

"So, what do you think?"

"If I was scared of Rex, I'm pretty damn sure any assailant would be too."

Pearson laughed. "You have a solid point there." Then he hugged me. I hoped this was an overreaction and we wouldn't need Rex or Petey, or Axel, or anybody else. Time would tell and it was nerve-racking thinking about the waiting.

Chapter Thirty-Eight

PEARSON

A MONTH HAD PASSED SINCE THE TRIAL AND NOTHING. NO
threats from Greg, no calls, not a word. That was good in a
sense, but it made me more concerned about when he would
strike. That he would, I had no doubts. He wanted Montana to
get to Rose. That was clear. I just wasn't positive if he'd go
directly for Rose or Montana. If he went for Rose, I wasn't sure
if he'd try to kill her or not. It put a knot in my gut the size of
Texas to think about it.

I met with Reese before one of my meetings and explained
what was going on.

"Shit, man, you've had a lot on your plate. I'm doubly proud
of you for maintaining your sobriety. That's so awesome,"
he said.

"I've had urges, but nothing I couldn't handle. I wanted to
get that apartment, but with this going on, I need to be there
with Rose for safety reasons."

"Yeah, I don't blame you. Can I ask, have you hired a PI to

check up on him? Maybe that would clue you in to what he's up to."

"We had one, but he didn't turn up anything, so we let him go. But now that you mention it, maybe he was just outsmarting him. He's a wily SOB."

"I know a guy who is excellent. Let me know if you change your mind."

"Thanks, I will. Let me talk to Rose about it first."

We went to the meeting and afterward, talked again. "I can't tell you how amazed I am at your progress. Would you consider coming into Manhattan and speaking to my group?"

"Sure, if you think I could do some good."

"I need people who are four to five months out to motivate my people. Some of them think they'll never get there. You're a fantastic example."

"Then yeah, I'd love to. Just throw out a date when you want me to be there. I've been doing a lot of work with Miles, so I'd need advanced notice."

"Not a problem. I'll let you know and give me a call about the PI. I promise you won't be sorry. If anyone can find something, he can."

We shook hands and went our own ways. When I got home that evening, I told Rose about the private investigator.

"You mean to follow Greg?" she asked.

"Exactly. To keep tabs on what he's up to. I thought for sure he'd have a court date by now, but Tom or whoever is handling his case is probably trying to get it pushed back."

We talked it over and decided it was a good idea. I called Reese and he gave me the PI's number. I made a note to call him in the morning.

In the morning, after we did our usual routines at home, I left for the office and the first thing on the agenda was to call the PI. He wasn't in yet, so I left a message and approximately thirty minutes later, he returned the call.

"Mr. West, this is Case Jordan. What can I do for you?"

After I told him who referred me and what I was interested in, he took down all the information and said he would start assessing everything that day. "I'll get back to you first thing tomorrow with what I have. It sounds like you have a real issue on your hands."

"You can say that again." I also informed him of the bodyguards I had on Rose and Montana.

"I was going to recommend that so I'm glad to hear you've already gone that route. Are they there twenty-four hours a day?"

"Yes, and they accompany them everywhere. Rose even has one at work, and of course Montana has hers at school all day too."

"Excellent. Let me get started on what I can find and I'll get back to you in the morning on my recommendations."

"Thank you."

He chuckled. "You won't be thanking me when you get the bill."

"Money's not an issue. The only thing I'm concerned about is Rose's and Montana's safety."

"I hear you loud and clear."

Miles and I were working on a case similar to Rose's. The ex was a real douche and we were trying to get total custody. It was currently fifty-fifty, but he rarely showed up, and when he did, he was usually drunk. The mother was afraid to allow him to take the boy, and he'd end up getting violent with her. This had been going on for six months. The local women's shelter had called us because she had gone there to hide out from him. We were doing the case pro bono.

"Hey Pearson, check this out," Miles called out. "This dude is in arrears for child support."

"How long since he paid?"

"By the looks of it at least a year."

"He's going to be one pissed off daddy by the time we're

through." I didn't get why they had kids and then refused to pay for them.

"You can count on it. Maybe even jail time for him on this."

"Is Mariana still at the shelter?"

"Yeah, and I'm suggesting she stay there until this is resolved. The guy is unstable, particularly when he drinks," Miles said.

"Has he been served yet?"

"No, and that's why she needs to stay there. When he is, that's when the shit will hit the fan."

"Oh yeah. Doesn't it always. How is she?"

Miles shook his head. "Not good. She's talking about going home, but we keep telling her not to."

"Hey, how about I get Rose to talk to her?"

Miles looked pointedly at me. "You know that's an excellent idea. I can bring her and her son over. Would that be okay? It might work better to see Rose and how happy she is in her own environment."

"Let me call her, but I'm sure she'll agree, not to mention we have the added bonus of her being a psychologist."

Miles snapped his fingers. "That's right! I hadn't even thought of that."

I made a quick call to Rose and luckily, I caught her between patients. She was more than happy to do it and suggested that evening, if Mariana was available. I passed the news on to Miles who said he'd give her a call.

At seven, Miles brought Mariana and her son Charlie over. Montana latched onto him, even though he was seven, and after we all ate a dinner of pizza and chocolate chip cookies, she tugged him into Rose's bedroom to watch some movies. I was worried she would try to make him dance, but Petey was there to chaperone and get things back to the movie if she did.

Rose brought the conversation around to Mariana's ex. "I understand you and I have a great deal in common, Mariana."

"That's what Miles said. I wish I were as brave as you."

Rose tapped her arm. "You have it all wrong. I'm not brave at all. If it weren't for those two men, I'd still be stuck, not seeing my daughter. My ex had sole custody and it was a mess. He made our lives miserable."

Mariana stared at Rose. "I thought I had it bad. Jeremy is very abusive."

"Mine was extremely abusive too. I was a regular at the ER while we were married and even afterward. If I can impart one piece of wisdom to you, it is to let Pearson and Miles do their jobs and listen to what they say. You won't regret it and, in the end, you'll have your son."

"I'm so afraid of what Jeremy will do."

"That's why you're staying at the women's shelter. He can't hurt you there," Rose reminded her.

"Yes, I know, but there's always that nagging feeling in the back of my mind."

"I know that feeling well. Just put your trust in them and they'll make it work for you. And if you ever need to talk or just want to come over and hang out, the door is always open."

She threw her arms around Rose and hugged her. Miles took her and her son home about thirty minutes later.

"Thanks for doing that," I said to Rose.

"It's not necessary. I wish I'd had someone to talk to when I was going through it."

I frowned. "You had me."

She leaned into me and kissed me. "Yes, I did. But it's different having another woman who experienced the same thing. Don't think I didn't appreciate you though. I totally did."

I kissed her back. "I know and I appreciate you too. Let's go tuck in the little one."

We went to her room and Petey was reading her a bedtime story. They looked perfectly content together.

"Hey, monkey, did you have a good time with Charlie?" I asked.

"Yeah, but he only likes to throw balls. He's not a dancer."

"That's okay. I'll teach you how to throw balls one day."

She scrunched up her mouth. "Is that cool?"

"What do you mean?"

"I only want to do cool things."

"Where is this coming from?" Rose asked.

"Sallie in school. She says she only does cool things."

"Is that so?"

"Uh huh."

"I think throwing balls is real cool," Petey said.

"You do?" Montana asked.

"Yeah," he said back.

"So do I," I chimed in.

"Me too," Rose said.

"Then it's unanimous," I announced.

"What's you namus?" Montana asked.

Rose answered, "It means we all agree. But now it's lights out."

"But Mommy, Petey's almost done."

"Okay, but as soon as he's finished, lights out. Kiss me goodnight, Pop Tart."

She gave us both a good night kiss and we watched them from the doorway. When Petey finished, he kissed her cheek, tucked her in, and turned off the light. As he was leaving, she called out, "Love you, Petey."

"Love you too, squirt."

My heart clenched. I was happy she found Petey to be her great friend, but I was also jealous of their bond. Childish? Of course, but I couldn't help but want her love for myself. Would I get over it? Yes, because I wanted the best for that little girl, no matter what.

Chapter Thirty-Nine

ROSE

TODAY WAS MONTANA'S BIRTHDAY, SO WE WERE GOING TO Pearson's parents' house. I had suggested a restaurant, but Paige insisted on having the party there. Pearson explained there would be no changing her mind, so I accepted her kind offer under the condition that I'd bring the cake. Since it was a Saturday, Hudson and his family would be able to come out too.

Rick would be grilling hot dogs and burgers for everyone and it would be a fun day for the kiddos. I got her favorite ice cream cake, but the best surprise would be waiting for us when we got there. We were arriving at two, but everyone else, along with the surprise, would get there at one thirty.

"Do you think I need my clicky shoes?"

"Bring them just in case," I said as we were leaving. We piled into the car and left.

When we got to Paige and Rick's everyone's car was already there, along with the surprise.

"What's that?" Montana asked, pointing to a truck with a

trailer behind it. It was a good thing she couldn't read everything yet.

"You'll see," Pearson said.

We went in through the front door and I stuck the cake in the freezer. Then we headed out to the back yard where everyone waited. It was decorated with balloons and they all yelled, "Happy Birthday, Montana," when we walked out.

Then Montana's eyes landed on the pony that was saddled up and waiting to take her for a ride.

"Mommy, Mister, look. A pony!" She ran straight toward it and the man helped her up as he walked her all around the yard. It was a tan Shetland pony and cute as could be. I was snapping photos like crazy. The other kids waited patiently for their turns and when Montana got off, she ran to thank me.

"Pop Tart, you need to thank Mister. This is his present to you."

She ran up to him and he picked her up, swinging her high in the air. The pony turned out to be a huge hit. It ended up being the best babysitter ever, leaving us girls available to hang out.

"Rose, how are the dance lessons going?" Milly asked.

I groaned. "I'm sure Marin can tell you more than me."

"That bad, huh?"

"Oh, God. She's awful."

Milly laughed. "Wiley's afraid of Kinsley because she made him dance too much."

"Unfortunately, my daughter loves it."

Marin came up to us and said, "Are you discussing clicky shoes?"

"Yes," I said. "But let's change the subject." Then I laughed.

"So how is Pearson?" Marin asked.

"He's great. He has been my lifesaver in getting full custody of Montana. And he's doing really well in NA. I couldn't be more proud of him."

"We're so happy to hear that."

Rick called out that the food was ready so we had to prepare plates for the kids. After lunch, I served up the birthday cake. Montana had good luck blowing out all the candles.

The kids got to ride the pony again for a little while before the man left. It was around six o'clock so everyone started heading home.

"Paige, let me help you clean up," I said.

She batted a hand. "There's nothing to clean. That's why I used paper plates today," she said with a smile. "I'm just so happy you let me do this here."

"You? I'm so thankful you offered." I hugged her. "Thank you for the hospitality."

"Anytime."

We loaded up the car with the presents Montana received and headed on home. The little tyke was exhausted and didn't make it to seven thirty that night.

Sunday flew by and I dreaded Monday because it was going to be a busy week ahead.

ON MONDAY, PEARSON LEFT TO GO RUNNING AT SIX A.M. AND I started my yoga workout. When I was finished, I took a shower and got ready for work. I checked the other bathroom because by this time he was usually finished with his shower and getting dressed, but he wasn't home yet. That was strange, but I didn't think much about it. I poured a cup of coffee and started Montana's breakfast. Then I woke her and got her clothes ready.

"I don't want to get up, Mommy."

"But it's a school day and Petey will be here soon to eat breakfast with you."

"Can he just come and sleep with me instead?"

"Not today, honey. Up and at 'em"

She groaned but crawled out of bed. "Do I gotta wash my face today?"

"Yep."

"And brush my teeth too?"

"Of course. You don't want stinky breath, do you?"

That brought a giggle out of her. She plodded to the bathroom and took care of things. By the time she came back, she was a bit more chipper. I'd laid an outfit out for her, but she asked, "Mommy, can I wear my cow outfit?"

"I don't see why not." She had a top with black cow spots on it and pants to match. Running to her closet, she located it and pulled it off the hangers. Then she pulled the shirt on, followed by the pants. It was adorable. "Aw, you look so cute in it. Let me fix your hair."

"Can I have pigtails?"

"Now why would you want pigtails when you have on a cow outfit."

She frowned for a second until she understood my little joke, then her giggling started. "That's funny, Mommy. Maybe I should have cow tails instead."

"That's a great idea." I gave her braided pigtails. "How's that?"

"Good. Can I eat now?"

We went to get breakfast and she asked, "Where's Mister?"

"I don't know. He hasn't come back from his run yet."

"Oh."

Petey knocked on the back door and I let him in. After I filled Montana's bowl with cereal and milk, I went into the bedroom and called Petey back there. Then I told him about Pearson not showing up.

"Do you know where he went running?"

"No, but he likes to run on those trails near Benson Park."

"I know the ones. Let's give him some more time. Have you called Miles?"

"Not yet."

Petey said, "If he's not back by the time I leave, call Miles and then let Axel know. He can call someone to drive by there. Maybe he fell and got injured."

"Oh, hell." I grabbed my phone and called Pearson. He always ran with music so he'd have his phone with him. But it went straight to voicemail.

"No answer?"

"No. It went straight to voicemail. That's really odd. He'd answer if he had his phone with him."

"The battery must be dead," Petey said.

"No, he charges it every night."

"Maybe he forgot."

"Yeah, maybe," I said, but still not convinced. It was bothering me, but I had to get Montana off, and Axel would be here any minute. My patience ran out and I called Miles.

"Hello."

"Miles, it's Rose. Have you talked to Pearson this morning?"

"No, why?"

"He never came home from his run."

"Hmm. Maybe he sprained an ankle or something. Let me call the emergency rooms in the area. If he's hurt, he may have gone straight there."

"Good point. I tried his phone, but it went straight to voicemail."

"That's not like him, but maybe it's dead."

"Yeah, that's what Petey said. Let me know if you find out anything."

"I will and you do the same."

Axel arrived and Petey left with Montana. I explained the situation to Axel, and he said he'd call in to have someone run by the park just to check.

I arrived at work, anxious as hell. I'm not sure why, but I had a terrible feeling that something awful had happened to Pearson. My bodyguard, Rex, was with me and asked if I needed anything.

"Yes, find Pearson."

"We're on it, Ma'am."

"I know." I didn't stop at my office but went directly to

Sylvie's. One look at me and she instantly knew something wasn't right.

"What is it?"

"Pearson went for a run this morning and never came back."

"Maybe he twisted his ankle or something."

"That's what everybody keeps saying, but why didn't he call?"

"Okay, don't panic yet."

"I am panicking. This is not like him at all. His phone goes directly to voicemail. He hasn't done this ever. Miles hasn't heard from him either."

She tapped a pen on her desk and said, "I'm going to call Grey. Maybe he knows something." I watched and listened. I didn't like what I heard. When she ended the call, she made the next one to Hudson. That one didn't go well either. "Neither of them have heard from him. Grey is going to call the local ERs to see if he's there."

"That's what Miles was going to do but Grey may have more leverage. The company that provides our bodyguards is sending out someone to check the area where he runs. Oh, Sylvie, what if something happened to him?"

"You don't know my cousin very well. He can probably kick anyone's ass. Have you seen him? I mean really seen him?"

I flashed her one of those *are you serious* looks. "You're really asking me that?"

"Right." She let out an awkward laugh. "I wasn't thinking."

"Just because he's built like a brick wall doesn't mean a thing when someone holds a gun to his head."

"What's that supposed to mean?" she asked.

"You remember that crazy fool I was once married to? I wouldn't put a thing past him."

Sylvie stood and came around her desk to hold my hand. "Rose, I don't think Greg would do anything as foolish as that."

"Then you don't know him at all. He's a wild card and capable of anything."

She pulled me over to the chairs and made me sit. "The best thing right now is for both of us to remain calm until we find something out."

We sat there, silently, but my mind churned with all kinds of horrible things. If something happened to him because of me, I'd never forgive myself.

Sylvie finally asked, "When's your first client?"

"Shit!" I checked the time and blew out a breath. "Not for another twenty minutes."

"Perhaps you should cancel. You're not in any condition to counsel anyone right now."

She had a point. "True."

"Let me handle this." She started to leave, and I asked where she was going. "I'm getting the director to reschedule your patients today."

"Thank you," I said, relieved.

As she was almost out the door, her phone rang. It was Grey. After the call, she told me, "Pearson isn't in any of the ERs so he hasn't injured himself."

I got up and let Rex know so he could pass it on. Then I called Miles and told him the same. Miles asked, "Any other news?"

"Nothing. I'm hoping to hear something soon. I'll let you know when I do."

"Rose, Pearson was talking to that PI. Maybe you should call him. His card is on Pearson's desk."

"Can you text me his number?"

"Sure."

"Thanks. And I'll be in touch."

About an hour later, Axel came into my office. Sylvie and I were there with Rex. One glance at his face and I knew it wasn't good.

"Rose, we found his car in the parking lot of Benson park. We sent several of the team out to comb all the trails and unfortunately, we found no trace of him. His car was unlocked, the door ajar, and his phone was smashed underneath it."

I sucked in a breath and all my thoughts vanished into thin air. I couldn't think clearly. All I knew was Pearson was either in extreme danger or possibly dead.

"Rose? Rose, talk to me." Sylvie grabbed my hands that were shaking uncontrollably.

"D d do y-you think h-h-he's alive?"

Axel knelt down in front of me, as I was sitting and said, "We have no way of knowing, but there was no blood at the scene, if that's what you're asking. In my opinion, I think he was taken and probably by your ex."

I pulled my hands away from Sylvie, gripped the chair, and let out a blood-curdling scream. "I'm going to find that fucker and when I do, I'm going to kill him."

Axel grabbed my arm and said firmly, his tone cutting through the room, "No! That's exactly what he wants. He's probably tried to go for you or Montana and couldn't because of us. So, he went for Pearson instead, knowing you'd come running. Let us and the police handle it."

"He's right, Rose. If you charge over there, he'll kill you for what you did to him in court," Sylvie said.

"If he so much as touches one hair on Pearson's head, I'll kill him. He won't have an opportunity to kill me because he'll be dead."

"And you'll spend the rest of your life in prison," Axel said.

"I don't care," I screamed.

"Think about your daughter. Where will she end up? In foster care. Do you want that?"

That shut me up fast.

"Rose," Axel said softly, "let us handle it."

"Right. I'm also going to call the private investigator that Pearson called."

"Fine, and we can work together, but promise me you'll stay away from your ex." His eyes dug into mine and I nodded.

"Good." Axel stood and went to Rex. They spoke in hushed tones as I picked up the phone to contact the PI.

I checked my texts and found his number.

"Case Jordan."

"Case, my name is Rose Wilson and I understand Pearson West contacted you yesterday. The reason for my call is he went out for a run this morning and never came back. I need to enlist your services to help find him."

"Tell me where you are Ms. Wilson and I'm on the way."

Chapter Forty

PEARSON

THE JACKHAMMER IN MY HEAD WAS RELENTLESS. IT MADE MY stomach nearly heave. What the hell was going on? My thoughts were scrambled and any attempts to clear my head were fruitless. Maybe I'd been sick because I had a case of severe chills. When I tried to roll onto my side, I couldn't. Everything was jumbled into one huge ball of confusion. Opening my eyes wasn't an option because of the throbbing in my head and I knew it would make my nausea even worse. I willed myself to go back to sleep in the hopes when I woke up again, I'd feel better.

It didn't work out quite that way. In fact, I woke up to a complete fucking nightmare. This time, I braved it and opened my eyes to figure out why I couldn't move. It was because my wrists were handcuffed to an iron bed. When I looked at my legs, my ankles were zip tied to the bed too. I was in a dark room with one small window at the top of the wall, indicating it was maybe a basement. Finally, putting the pieces together, I remembered finishing up my run, going back to the car, opening it, but that's it. Whatever happened, happened then. Something happened at that point, and I had a good idea of what it was. I'd been so diligent on guarding Rose and Montana, I hadn't given a thought to myself. I'd made a monumental error.

As I lay there, I wondered what his bargaining chip would be. How would he go about this? He didn't know me very well if he thought I'd give them up. My biggest regret was how worried Rose must be. I hated that. She was so kind and caring, I knew she would be out of her mind by now.

Handcuffs were nearly impossible to get out of unless you knew how to pick a lock, which I did not. I wondered how sturdy the bed was though. I tugged on it and it seemed fairly solid. Having my feet loose would help, but it wouldn't help me free my hands. As I conjured up ideas, the door opened and in he walked.

"I see you're awake." His smug expression grated on my nerves, so I decided to match it.

"Yes, and thank you for the comfortable bed."

His smugness disappeared and was immediately replaced by anger. "You won't be thanking me soon. You'll be begging me."

"For what?"

He pulled a packet of white powder out of his pocket and dangled it in front of my face. "This."

Oh, fuck no. He was going to shoot me up. "What exactly do you want?" I tried to stay calm, but my heart was racing. I could *not* let him do this. If he did, he'd either get me addicted again or overdose me.

"You really have to ask me that, Mister Attorney?"

"Yes, because we can work something out."

"You must really take me for an idiot if you think I'm going to fall for your games."

"You're you married, aren't you Greg?"

He stopped what he was doing and turned to stare at me. "Are you kidding?"

"Why would I be kidding?"

"That piece of shit I call a wife?"

"Why do you call her that?"

"She's nothing but a heroin addict. Oh yeah, you'd know all about that, wouldn't you?" he sneered. His words surprised me, but I didn't let it show.

Calmly, I said, "I can help her if you'll let me."

He roared with laughter. "You'd like that, wouldn't you?"

"Yes, I would."

"Forget it. I don't want *her*. Never did. I want Rose and Montana. Rose, with her naivete. And my daughter with her innocence. And you, you bastard, took them both away."

"No, I didn't. You lost them long before I entered the picture."

"No! I had them exactly where I wanted them. And now I'm going to have you exactly where I want you."

He went to a small table in the room I hadn't noticed earlier and began the process of melting down the heroin. Then he drew it up into a syringe. He came to the bed and tied a latex tourniquet around my arm in order to locate a vein.

"Please don't do this. I swear I can help you. It's not as hard as you think. I can get Rose to bring Montana here and I can help with your wife."

"Honestly, you must think I was born without a brain. If I let you go, you'll end up at the police and I'll go directly to prison."

"No. I won't say a word. Just don't push that into my vein."

He laughed and stuck the needle in. Seconds later I was floating on that familiar cloud I wanted to hate, the one I had worked so hard to free myself from. There was no doubt he would have me addicted again in no time or kill me. My life as it had become was over and I never had a chance to tell Rose how much I loved her or Montana either. I heard him through the haze, laughing crazily.

"Cry, Mr. Tough Guy. Cry. You put this on yourself." He left the room and I lay there in silence.

HE CAME BACK, AGAIN AND AGAIN, TO GIVE ME MORE HEROIN. He was kind enough to give me water. I guess he wanted to keep me alive for a certain amount of time. I was lucid for short periods, but didn't recognize the passage of time. Was it hours? Days? Maybe even weeks. At this point, I didn't care anymore. All I cared about was when my next hit was coming. He was sporadic so I'd beg him for it when he walked through the door. And beg him I did. I'd say anything he wanted. When the beautiful rush hit me, I'd sigh and float. But they weren't lasting long enough, and I'd beg him not to leave or to come back sooner and sooner. I wasn't even sure what he was saying anymore. All I knew was the drug. Until he didn't come one day and withdrawal struck. I thought I was dying. Perhaps I was. He finally came and gave me some after he punched me in the face. He told me to beg for that too. I didn't care as long I got my drug.

My time turned into this. Drug … withdrawal … beating … drug … withdrawal … beating and so on. I lost all awareness but this. I was beyond sick and prayed he would overdose me. But that didn't happen. Something else did.

As I lay there one day, waiting and praying for my next hit, the door crashed in, though I was barely conscious, and the room swarmed with people. But she was there. Brushing the hair off my forehead and telling me how sorry she was. I remembered how soft and warm her hand was and that she never let it go. And then I must've died because all the lights went out.

Chapter Forty-One

ROSE

WE FINALLY FOUND HIM, OR I SHOULD SAY CASE DID. HIS team of PI's didn't let up and his connections with the police helped too. It took almost three weeks and when they got a hit on where he was, a team of police, along with Case, Axel, Rex, Grey, Hudson, and me rode along. Rex wouldn't let me go in. I jumped out of the car when we arrived at a run-down shack of a house. The paint was flaking off and the windows looked like someone had broken into the place several times. The screen door was hanging off its hinges and it gave me the creeps. Case and his team found it because it was rented under the name of Caro Bluffton. That was Greg's wife's maiden name. I suppose he thought he was being clever.

I tried to run to the front door, but Rex's huge arms circled me and held me back.

"Rose, let them do their job. It's dangerous in there. We don't want you getting hurt."

"I don't care about me."

"We do," Rex said. "Remember your promise to Case?"

I nodded. Case said I could come along if I swore to remain in the car. Grey and Hudson had gotten out but came over to where we were.

"Rose, calm down," Grey said. "They're going in and getting him."

"What if he's ..." I couldn't finish. I broke down again. It had been too much for me. Rex held me as I cried.

Through the glaze of my tears, I watched as the men disappeared inside. It was the longest passage of time I'd ever endured. Two of them finally emerged with Greg in handcuffs. He was smiling as if he'd won the lottery. What was up with that?

I ran up to him, balled up my fist and slugged him in the jaw. His maniacal laugh sent pinpricks of ice all over me.

"Your man awaits you." And he spat out blood and laughed some more as they continued walking him toward a police car, where they shoved him inside.

I ran up to one of the officers asking, "Can I go inside?"

"Ms. Wilson, it's best if you wait."

"Is he okay?"

"Ma'am, he needs medical attention."

Grey took off, followed by Hudson. Grey yelled, "I'm a doctor." Hudson echoed, "So am I."

By this time, Rex had me back in his grip. "I need to go. I have to see him."

"It's your call ma'am, but he's in pretty bad shape," one of the officers said.

"Rex, let me go." My tone gave Rex no choice and I took off. When I got inside, there were people standing around, taking in hushed tones. "Where is he?" I asked.

"In the basement. Over there." One of them pointed me in the right direction. When I got down to the dank space, there was a door to my right where people were spilling out of.

I shoved my way through and the first thing I saw was a

small table. What I saw on it made my blood chill. "That son of a bitch," I muttered. I kept moving until I laid eyes on him. And when I did, I almost threw up. My beautiful Pearson had been reduced to a quivering mass of skin and bones. Greg had brought him back into his drug addicted world again. That fucking bastard.

Case took my arm and said, "An ambulance is almost here."

"Do you know how much he's had?"

"The best we can tell is he's been getting it ever since he was taken. Wilson wouldn't tell us much more, but I aim to find out during his interrogation."

"Did Pearson recognize anyone? Did he know Grey or Hudson?"

"No. But he will when he comes to in the hospital. One of the officers gave him Narcan just in case that jerk tried to overdose him so he'll be in rapid withdrawal."

"All of his hard work, down the drain. I could kill that asshole." Anger drove through me, washing away any sadness or concern I'd had.

"Hey, he has you and his network at NA. He can get through this. But he'll need a lot of reassurance over the next few days."

"Case, it's my fault this happened to him."

"You can't blame yourself, Rose. It's not your fault. It's your ex-husband's. He's a sick man."

I went over to Pearson and put my hand on his head. He was clammy and shaking. The withdrawal had already begun. He needed methadone, but no one here had any. I'm not even sure if they carried it on the ambulance.

"Pearson, can you hear me?"

He opened his eyes and looked directly at me.

"We're going to get through this. Do you understand me?" I took his hand giving it a firm squeeze. "I'll be with you every step of the way. I won't leave your side. I hope you hear and understand me." I bent down and kissed his cheek. That was when I saw the tears running down it. I wiped them gently away. "I'll always be here. I promise."

The paramedics came in and transferred him to the gurney. His wrists and ankles were terribly bruised and cut from whatever Greg had used to bind him. It pissed me off all over again and I wished I'd kicked his balls in instead of punching him in the jaw.

When he was covered and strapped on, they carried him out, as I followed. "I want to ride with him."

"Are you family?"

"Yes."

Grey smiled at that. He and Hudson said they'd meet me at the hospital. I held Pearson's hand the whole way. When we got to the ER, I told them he needed methadone, stat, that he was a recovering heroin addict, but had been held captive and given the drug again. They asked me a lot of questions and dosed him with the appropriate medications. I told them I was an addiction counselor, which helped.

By that time, Grey and Hudson had arrived. Grey talked to the physician and nurses, giving them more information. I placed an urgent call to Dr. Martinelli, and she came over as quickly as she could.

With Pearson dosed up, he was now resting comfortably. I asked if I could bathe him, because he was a filthy mess.

The doctor wanted to give him a few hours before we did anything to him. Each time I looked at him, my heart shattered. I thought of how he did his best to protect Montana and me, but he was the one who'd been in danger. I slumped in the chair and my attempt to hold the tears back failed. They shoved their way past my lids, and that's all it took for the storm to break loose. Hudson was on one side and Grey on the other. But I didn't want them. I wanted Pearson to get out of that bed and hold me, tell me he was okay, and walk out of the hospital. But that wasn't going to happen. It would be rehab all over again. Only this time would be worse. I knew how it worked. The patient had more difficulty in believing in themselves the second time around.

Dr. Martinelli crouched in front of me and took my hands in hers. "We know he can do it, Rose. He's strong and willful. He has you on his side and all the elements necessary to succeed."

"I understand that, but he'll also feel more vulnerable."

"Yes, he will, and you and I will talk him through those weak moments. We'll get Reese to help and his other sponsor at the local NA group here. He'll go back to rehab and do everything necessary to make it happen. But there's one thing he needs most of all and that's for *you* to believe. You have to have faith that he can do it. If you show even the tiniest hint of weakness, he'll see that and then he'll begin to have doubts. Do you understand?"

I nodded. "Yes, you're right."

"I need you to talk to Reese too. He fell off the wagon. And Case."

"Case?"

Dr. Martinelli smiled. "You didn't know?"

"Know?"

"Case is Reese's sponsor."

"Really?"

"Reese should share his story with you, as it's not my place, but yes. I'm sure he shared it with Pearson. He'll talk with him, and so will Case. Rose, I promise, that man in there has what it takes to get through this. With you by his side, showing your strength and encouragement, he'll do it."

I gripped her hands. Dr. Martinelli knew what she was talking about and I believed her. "Yes, you're right. I know that. Pearson is strong and has a lot of faith." I turned to his brothers. "His family is also supportive, and I'll rely on your help too."

Grey spoke first. "You know you can always count on us."

"I second that," Hudson said. "Anything you need, you let us know."

"Rose!"

I glance up to see Sylvie running down the hall. I stood and went to her where she hugged me so hard, I could barely breathe.

"Oh, God. How is he?"

"He'll have to go through rehab again."

"Oh, no. What happened?"

After I explained the whole story, Sylvie's face was as pale as a ghost. Before she could say a word, Pearson's parents showed up. After we all shared a hug, Grey explained what happened. My emotions tore into me and I apologized.

"I am so sorry for all of this. It's my fault."

"How in the world is this your fault?" Paige asked.

"He was protecting me from my ex. He's the one who did this to Pearson. And Pearson was in danger the entire time."

Paige put her arm around my shoulders and said, "Oh, honey, you can't blame yourself. Pearson would've done it anyway. He cares deeply for you and wanted to help. That man was dangerous. How could you have known this would've happened? It's not your fault and you must stop thinking this. The only thing we need to concern ourselves with now is getting Pearson back on track and with your help, I believe it can be done. You're the best thing that's ever happened to him."

"I am?"

"Of course you are. I've never seen him look at a woman the way he looks at you. You only have to take care of him the way you've been doing and with his hardheadedness, I believe he'll beat this."

"Thank you, Paige. I needed to hear those words."

Rick asked, "Can we see him?"

Grey said, "Yeah, but he's sleeping. If you want to peek in there, it's fine. A word of caution, he looks awful because he's lost a lot of weight and hasn't had a bath in a while."

Rick waved his hand. "I don't care about that. He's my son and I love him. I only care that he's safe."

He opened the door and he and Paige took a quick look inside. Once satisfied, they came back out.

Paige grinned. "Needs a bath is an understatement."

"Mom," Hudson admonished. "He was held captive."

"I know, but he does smell awful."

Rick shook his head and said, "Leave it to your mother to notice that."

It was sort of comical, but I wasn't in the mood for funny, so I let it pass.

Dr. Martinelli left and promised to come back by that afternoon.

A couple of hours later, two nurses came by and to give Pearson a bath. He was still asleep, and I asked if it was okay for them to wake him.

"The doctor gave his approval since his withdrawal is well controlled by now," one of them answered. "We'll call you in when we're finished. Then we're going to put him on clear liquids for a day to see how he handles that."

"Thank you," I said. Grey explained that was normal as far as his diet would go. Pearson probably wouldn't develop an appetite right away, but it would return little by little. There was no telling how much he'd eaten in the last couple of weeks. The doctor said he was dangerously dehydrated, so they were pushing IV fluids in like crazy.

Each time I checked on him, his color had gotten better and better. Thirty minutes had passed when the nurses said it was okay for us to go in. Paige was especially happy that he was cleaned up.

"Hey there." I went to him and kissed him on the lips. "How are you feeling?"

"Like a drug addict." His voice was gruff.

"We're going to change that," I said. "I'm so sorry you have to go through this again."

"Not any more than I am."

I took his hand and said, "You won't be alone in this. I promise."

He dropped his head, staring at his lap. The room was filled with people, so I asked if we could have a private moment. Everyone filed out.

"Pearson, I have to tell you a few things." I sat on the side of his bed and didn't let go of his hand. "When you didn't come home that morning, I … I started thinking about where you could be. A car accident? Did you get hurt running? I thought of all possibilities and called in the posse. Case was the one who figured out where you were. Thank God. I never would've guessed, and I know you didn't either, that Greg would go for you. It was all my fault you got tangled up in this and I'm so very sorry. It's because of me you're having to go through this again. But even if it weren't, I would be by your side every step of the way. There's a reason for this. When you were gone, I realized something. I figured out that I didn't want a life without you in it. I'll take you any way I can. I know you have the strength and power to do this again. I'll help you any way possible. I'll stand by you, be with you, support you, help you, do whatever it takes for you to succeed. With the two of us, side by side, I don't think there is anything in the world we can't do. I love you, Pearson. And love means going the distance. I'm here with you and I'm going the distance with you. Do you get this?"

He finally half smiled, but I'd take it. "It's not going to be easy, Rose."

"Don't you think I know that? I'm an addiction counselor."

"Oh, yeah."

"I have a little bit of knowledge in this area."

"Yeah, that's right."

"Can I please kiss you? I've missed the hell out of you."

"Wait. I have a few things to tell you too. When I was hand-cuffed to that bed, the only things that kept me going were thoughts of you and Montana. I'd think of all the great times we had and figured I'd never get out of there alive. I thought he'd overdose me on purpose. Every time he came to hit me up, I filled my mind with images of your beautiful face and went to my happy place, because I figure if I died then, it would be knowing I died with the most beautiful woman on my mind."

"Oh, God." Tears rolled freely down my cheeks. "I promised myself I wouldn't cry and now look at me."

"I'm sorry, babe, but it's the truth. I love you too and you were the one who kept me alive. If not for you I would've given up hope. But I figured you'd suspect him and someone would find where he was keeping me."

"Case is amazing. Did you know he was Reese's sponsor?"

"Actually, no. But I'm sure I'll find out all about it. I wish you could lay down with me."

"Me too. But your family is anxious to see you and so is one precocious little girl. She's missed her Mister."

"I'd better see her while I'm on methadone because when they take that away, it'll be ugly."

"True. Now can I kiss you?"

"Yeah. Come here, babe."

I bent over him and touched my lips to his. I was gentle because the dehydration had done a number on him. I didn't want to hurt him any more than he already was.

"I love you so much, Rose."

"I love you too, Pearson." I hugged him and almost cried because he'd lost so much weight in those three weeks. "Let me get your family. I don't want them to murder me."

When I motioned them in, it was a loud reunion. I stood to the side and observed. This was a family who loved and loved hard. I'd never experienced that before, and it was special to see. I never knew anything like this before.

"Come over here, babe." I went to his side where he had me sit down next to him. "Everyone, I may as well let you in on something. I'm going to marry this woman someday. I was going to ask her before all this happened, but now it'll have to wait until I get sober again. And that is if she'll have me." He looked up at me as the corners of his mouth curved up.

"After what I just told you, you have to ask?"

"Of course he has to ask," Paige said.

"See, Mom would kill me if I didn't."

"And that wasn't a proper proposal anyway," Paige said.

"I'm saving the proper proposal for the right moment," Pearson said. "I'm a romantic at heart."

"Since when?" Hudson asked.

"Since I met my beautiful Rose."

Chapter Forty-Two

PEARSON

THE SCREAMS OF TERROR WOKE ME, AND ROSE WAS THERE calling my name. "Pearson, it's a dream. You're safe. You're in the hospital and I'm here." Her hands brushed through my hair and she lowered her cheek next to mine, murmuring words of comfort. My arms wrapped around her, holding her tightly. The terror still held me in its grip, not knowing if I would live or die. I was soaked in my own sweat, and the walls were crashing in on me.

"Fuck, fuck, fuck. I was back there, and he was coming for me." I couldn't stop shaking. It was the most helpless I'd felt in my life, feeling that weak.

"He's not. He's going to prison this time."

"Jesus, I'm so fucking weak and so out of it."

"It's okay," she said.

"No! It is anything but okay! I'm a fucking addict, Rose. Don't you see?" I shouted the words at her.

"Calm down, Pearson."

"How the fuck can I calm down? Do you realize what I'm facing? Again? It was bad enough the first time, but to have to go through it again." If I could've ripped my hair out, I would have.

She didn't react to my yelling at her. She only kept her hands on me, smoothing my hair back and touching me everywhere.

"For the life of me, I don't know how you can stand to be near me."

In a soft tone, she said, "There's a simple explanation for that. I love you, Pearson. Love means standing by that person, going the distance, no matter what. You may not remember, but when they found you, I made a promise to you that I was going to be with you every step of the way. I know it will be God awful hard on you … the hardest thing you've ever done. I wish with every part of me that I could take it away. But I can't. The only thing I can do is promise to help you and to try to make it as easy as possible. I know that's not much, but it's the best I can do. We're in this together, you and me. We are partners, a team."

I couldn't tear my gaze off of her. The last time I did this, I had the support of my family, but I didn't have the best woman in the world at my side. I had to believe in us to make it through and I had to believe in myself too. "I'll get there, Rose. I'm sorry, but I'm still so out of it. And really pissed and upset. After all my hard work … it's all down the drain."

"I know, but it still brought you to me and for that, I'll always be grateful." She bent down and pressed her lips to mine.

"You've been on methadone ever since they brought you in. They're going to start lowering your dose in a few days or so. It's important for you to get your appetite back."

I sighed. "I can't remember the last time I ate anything."

"That's why you have to start eating."

"I agree. But I'm glad I'm away from there." I rubbed my wrist. "When I realized how thin I'd gotten, I tried to get free, but I wasn't clear-headed enough."

She took my hand and lightly touched the bruises on my wrist. "It looks so painful."

"It's fine. Not as bad as getting drug free will be. I begged him not to do it. He was maniacal. I'm so glad you left him, Rose. He probably would've killed you if you hadn't."

I felt her shiver. "Let's not talk about him anymore. He's taken up too much of our lives already."

"But the strange thing is if it weren't for him, we probably wouldn't be together."

She looked at me oddly. "That or the drug recovery. Isn't it strange how something so terrible can bring two people together?"

"I'm glad it was you."

"So am I," she said.

<hr />

WITHDRAWAL THE SECOND TIME AROUND WASN'T ANY WORSE than the first, but it seemed to linger longer. The psychological aspects of it sunk its claws into my brain and didn't want to let loose. It was a real mind fuck this time around. I didn't want to be away from Rose. I didn't want to stay in the sterile environment of the inpatient hospital, but I knew it was a must. I went to the city, back to where first my treatment began. Dr. Martinelli and I had our daily sessions, but the good thing about it was we weren't starting from scratch. We knew each other well and my relapse wasn't because of anything I had done. But in many ways, it was worse, because my anger was always lurking, simmering below the surface. This time around, I couldn't accept responsibility for something that wasn't my fault. It was most difficult to come to grips with that and accept it.

"Pearson, you have to let it go. There's nothing you can do about it anymore," Gabby said. After all this time, Dr. Martinelli had asked me to call her by her first name, since we'd been seeing each other so much. I looked at her as more of a friend than my psychiatrist.

"That's easy for you to say."

"True, but in order for you to get on with your recovery, part of it is letting go of that anger. I understand why you're angry and I'm not saying you don't have a right to be, but that's out of your control. Remember what we've discussed?" She leaned forward as she spoke.

"I do, but every time I think about why I'm here, I become enraged. He's taken everything away from me."

"Don't you see you're letting him win? And what exactly has he taken? Yes, he forced you into addiction again, but you have the strength to combat that. You still have Rose. You have a career waiting for you. Montana is eager to see her Mister. Your family is waiting with open arms. I'm not sure what he's taken from you."

"My dignity," I said through clenched teeth.

"Only because you're allowing him to. You're choosing to give him this power over you, Pearson. Remember what we talked about the other day? This is exactly what he wanted to accomplish. When you helped Rose gain custody of Montana, you stripped him of his power over her. This is what he's doing to you now. Stop letting him. You have the power to. You have that choice. Move on, choose to *really* go into recovery, let everything that Greg Wilson is go, and become the real Pearson West again. Stop allowing him to hold you back."

She was right and I felt it all the way down to my marrow. I needed to release his hold over me. "How do I do this?"

"You know how."

I was terrified because I didn't. Ever since I'd woken up in that basement and begged him not to shoot me up, I knew he had complete control over me. It wasn't the drugs this time, it was him. And even though I was in rehab, he was still pulling the strings.

"Gabby, I ..."

"What?"

"I'm petrified I won't beat it this time."

"Why is that?"

"It's more than just heroin. It's him. He had the control. He basically owned me." Jesus, I was trembling with *fear*.

"Pearson, I'm here. I'm not going to let you fail. Let's take this step by step, okay?"

I nodded.

"You fear the control he had, is that right?"

I let out a long breath. "Yeah."

"He's in jail without bail. He can't get near either you, Rose, or Montana. There's no way he can leverage control over any of you anymore."

"Cognitively, I get that. But when it comes down to it, I get freaked out like some pussy."

"Don't ever say that. Someone who's been through what you have has every right to feel the way you do." Her tone was fierce and made me stiffen my spine.

"I'm ashamed that I begged him not to inject me."

"Why?" she snapped. "You went through recovery and knew what hell it was. Why in the hell would you be ashamed of that?"

I could only shrug.

Her tone softened when she said, "Pearson, when people fear for their lives, they'll stop at nothing to save themselves. You not only feared for yours, you also feared for Rose's and Montana's. Besides that, you feared becoming an addict again. Had I been in your shoes, I would've begged, bargained, done anything I could have. Greg Wilson is a very sick man. You're lucky he didn't kill you. This is what you have to come to grips with."

"Doc, how do I get there?"

"First, patience. Second, let him go. Expunge him from your life. I know, easier said than done. You used meditation at one time. It would be of great benefit to you now. You're regaining your strength but aren't quite there yet to work out. Maybe take walks with Reese when he's here. I'll write a note so you can do that. Let's begin there and see what happens in a week. I'm also going to reduce your methadone dose again. I'd like you off that completely by next week. One other thing, and I doubt you'll like this very much. You went to Flower Power last time for thirty days. I'm recommending you go somewhere else this time."

My heart sank at her words.

"I understand why you'd want to go back there, and you had great success there. However, Rose and you are extremely close now. The whole point of committing to an inpatient rehab center is to be away from all family and friends and I believe it would serve you better to go someplace else. I'm going to recommend The Summit. It's here in Manhattan. Both Reese and Case can tell you more about it if you'd like, but I'm very impressed with their capabilities and therapists. I work very closely with them too."

"Does Rose know?"

"No. It's your responsibility to tell her. I doubt she'll be surprised though. Lastly, this time with all the issues you're facing, I'm really going to push you to go on an antidepressant. I'd like you to try it for at least six months. They can take up to six weeks to work at the proper dosage, but Pearson, you're a different man facing different circumstances this go around. Antidepressants work on neurotransmitters in the brain and yours have been really messed with by what you've been through. Please heed my advice. I promise they'll help. And if one doesn't, we'll find another that will. After six months, when you're past this huge obstacle you're facing, we can talk about slowly tapering you off."

"I think you're right. I haven't felt myself at all lately and it's not fair to Rose either."

Gabby smiled. "Excellent decision. You won't be sorry." She scribbled something down in her notes and asked if I wanted to discuss anything else.

"How long do you recommend for my next step?"

"You mean The Summit?"

"Yeah."

"Minimum sixty days and I'll reassess."

I frowned. The thought was depressing.

"It's not what you want to hear, I know, but it's for your livelihood. You know I wouldn't do this if I didn't think you needed it. Your brain has been dealt two major blows. It needs time to heal."

"Yeah, I know."

She stood and patted my shoulder. "I have great faith in you. If you need me, and I don't care what time of day, you call. Understood?"

"Sure, Gabby, and thanks."

———

AFTER MY THIRTY DAYS WERE UP, I MOVED TO THE SUMMIT. While it was every bit as nice as Flower Power, but not as hippie-ish, I missed seeing Rose and Sylvie. They offered meditation and had a nice workout center. I'd begun doing that, but I was in bad shape, so I had a ways to go on that account.

My counselor's name was Thomas. He was in his early fifties and a good fit because he had relapsed five times before he finally remained sober. He'd been clean now for ten years. It was nice to be able to bounce my problems off someone who could relate. In many ways, he was much better than Rose (no, I did not tell her that) because he could understand how complex it was dealing with the urges. He still had them after all this time.

When I first got there, my story was made up. In other words, I didn't want anyone to know the real truth about how I'd been abducted and made an addict again. It made me feel super weak and I couldn't bring those memories to the surface. But after the first month, I owned up to it and the real truth came out. Compassion flowed from my fellow inpatients. Telling my story was pure catharsis.

"I was barely conscious when they found me and honestly, I

don't really remember it. I do remember waking up in the hospital, my girlfriend and family there. If it hadn't been for my girlfriend and a persistent PI, most likely I would've died." I broke down into sobs, something I hadn't really done. Everyone surrounded me and that's when I was able to cut Greg out of my life. The shame left and the healing began.

THREE MONTHS LATER

ROSE PULLED UP IN THE HALF CIRCLE DRIVE AS I WAITED FOR her, my bags packed. I'd been at The Summit for ninety days. After the initial sixty, I wasn't quite there yet, so we decided another month would be best. I'd been allowed to have visitors on weekends, but I'd asked not to see Montana until I was as good as I could be. I wanted to be a better man for her.

My family decided to let Rose pick me up and then we'd go to my parents for dinner the next day, Sunday. I watched her put the car in park and leap out. She didn't walk to the door, she ran. The smile on her face was brighter than the sun. I didn't wait for her to get inside. I'd already signed all the release papers, so I was through the door and picked her up as soon as we met. Our lips were on each other's before we even said hello. It had been a week since I'd seen her, but I hadn't kissed her like this in months. God, she tasted like heaven.

She pulled back with a giggle and asked, "Where are your bags?"

"Right inside the door. I couldn't wait to see you."

"Same here. I've missed you so much."

"Not nearly as much as I've missed you." I kissed her again, dying for another taste of her sweet lips.

"Let's get your things and get out of here. Someone at home is bouncing off the walls to see you."

"Can we stop somewhere on the way to … you know?" I asked.

"Hmm, I don't know."

"Pleeeease," I begged.

"Where did you have in mind?"

"Don't worry about that. Just come on."

I grabbed my bags and loaded them. And we got on the road. It wasn't a long drive, but when we got off the highway, I pulled off the main road onto a dirt side road. It was one we used to drive down when we were home from college and wanted to hang out and drink some beers with the guys.

"Where are we?" Rose asked.

"Nowhere. Just somewhere private. When we were out of sight, I parked the car and said, "Get over here, babe."

She crawled over and straddled my hips. We started making out like teenagers. I thought about how I did this in high school and how the windows would get steamed up. It was late August and the air conditioner was running so no chance of that.

My hands drifted under her shirt to her bra where I found her hardened nipples. She sucked in her breath when I tugged and twisted them. I pulled her bra down and lifted her shirt so they were available to my mouth. When I sucked them, she moaned. Her hand moved to my zipper and she tugged it down until my stiff cock sprang free. We were both panting so I unzipped her jeans and when she lifted her ass, I pulled them down in order to slide a finger between her folds. She was slick and wet. I plunged a finger inside her and she tried to ride it. Fuck that, it was time for the real thing. She cried out when I took my finger away.

"Don't worry, babe. You'll like this even better." I positioned us so she could ride my cock. With her hands on my shoulders, we discovered a rhythm until we both chased and found our own climaxes.

"Thank God that was quick. We have to get home before Montana starts calling and wondering where we are."

"Rose, we've been without each other for four months. Did you think we'd last very long?"

"Uh, not really. I've never had car sex before."

We pulled our clothes back on and I asked, "Well? How'd you like it?"

"It was sort of fun, but I banged my head on the ceiling a time or two." She laughed.

"When you have a comfortable bed to do it in, the car loses its appeal."

"True, but the shower doesn't," she said.

"Shut up. You'll make me want you again."

When we pulled into the driveway, Montana ran out of the house yelling, "Mister, Mister, you're home!"

I jumped out of the car and she was in my arms in the blink of an eye. "I missed you, monkey. So much."

"I missed you too. Don't go away no more. I didn't like it. Not at all." She hugged me but didn't let me go as usual.

"Never again, monkey."

"My daddy isn't gonna get you no more, is he?" She was crying.

I didn't realize they'd told her about Greg. My eyes met Rose's. She shook her head.

"Hey, hey. Don't you cry about that. And no, he's not ever going to get any of us. You don't have to worry about that. Do you understand?"

She looked at me with her big innocent eyes and asked, "How do you know? Did God tell you?"

"No, God didn't tell me. But your daddy is going to jail and he's going to stay there a mighty long time. What he did was bad and bad people have to go to jail to pay."

"My daddy is a very bad man. But you're not. You're a good man. I love you, Mister."

"I love you too, monkey. You're my sweet little girl. Now give me another hug because I missed you a ton."

We hugged each other and I carried her into the house with Rose following us.

Once inside, Montana said, "Guess what?"

"What?"

"I got something to show you." She ran out of the room.

That's when Rose said, "I didn't plan to tell her. She heard it on TV, so I had to explain everything."

"I guess she would've found out eventually."

Montana ran back into the room and said, "I learnt a new clicky shoe dance. Watch." She turned on her clicky shoe music and proceeded to dance. It was awful. Her legs still did those twisted movements while her arms stuck stiffly by her side. I'm not sure how she did it, but she managed to look like a half pretzel on the go. When she was finished, I applauded as loud as possible because she was my little monkey girl and I adored her, no matter what she did. She flew into my lap and kissed my cheek.

"That was the best clicky dance I've ever seen." Montana glowed and my heart swelled. This child was precious beyond words and I couldn't possibly say how much she meant to me. My eyes were damp from emotion.

"Mommy, let's show him our surprise."

"Okay, you go get it."

She slid off my lap and clicked her way down the hall. Moments later she was back, carrying what appeared to be a … "Is that a painting?" My eyes pinged back and forth between the two of them. Montana's grin was a big as I'd ever seen it and Rose's wasn't far behind.

"Yeah, look, Mister." She flipped it around and it was a painting of the three of us. It looked like it had been done from one of the snapshots of us, and it was spectacular.

"Oh, God. That's beautiful." I was holding Montana and Rose was on my side. Our smiles captured our emotions. "You two, this is the best gift I've ever received. Thank you."

"Mister, why're you crying?"

"Because I'm so happy. I love this present. Come here," I said to Rose. "This calls for one big cluster hug." We all hugged, and I told the two of them that I loved them both. "You two are the most important people in the world to me. You're my girls and I love you."

"Are you gonna make a kissy face with Mommy?"

"Do you want me to?"

"Yeah!" Montana clapped her hands.

I put my lips on Rose's and made a loud smacking noise. Montana let out a loud laugh.

That night when we tucked the little one into bed, she said her prayers first.

"Dear God, thank you for bringing Mister home and making him my new daddy. I love him bestest of all, besides my mommy. Amen."

Then she looked at me and asked, "Can I call you Daddy?" I almost fell back on the floor. I didn't know how to respond. "You know, Wiley calls Milly his MillyMom and Kinsley called Marin her MarnieMom for a while. Maybe you can call me your MisterDad?"

"Yeah, I like that."

"And then after your mommy marries me, maybe, and only if you want, you can call me Daddy."

"Yay!"

Rose stared at me and put a hand over her heart. I was fairly positive when I proposed, she'd say yes. We tucked in the mighty mite and went to the living room.

"Well? Will you be my Mrs.?"

Her arms came around me and she answered, "I thought you'd never ask."

"I haven't had a chance to pick out a ring, so I thought we could do it together."

"No. I want you to do it. I want it to be a surprise."

"You sure?"

"Positive."

"You've made me the happiest man, Rose."

"You've made me happy too, Pearson."

"Pass the potatoes, please," Grey said.

"Only if you share that gravy that you've been hogging," I said.

We switched off bowls and filled our plates. I hadn't been to Sunday dinner here in a while and couldn't wait to dig in. Mom made her famous chicken, which I was going to gobble down like a starving man.

We talked about mundane things during dinner and afterward, everyone teased me about the number of chicken bones on my plate.

"Hey, I've been in rehab for four months and haven't eaten this well since then. The food at The Summit wasn't nearly as good as at Flower Power. I deserved it."

"Yeah, but look at that," Hudson said. "Are you working out?" He was pointing at my biceps.

"You bet. Lifting weights and running every morning."

"You're not running at that park, are you?" Mom asked.

"Not yet, Mom. I just got out, but when I do, I'll have protection in the form of Petey."

"Petey?"

Montana piped up and explained who Petey was. "He's my best friend and body man."

We had to explain Petey further, but it satisfied Mom. After all this went down, the bodyguard team was let go, but Petey still came around to hang out with us and then took up running. He agreed to run with me when I left rehab. If I failed to mention it, Petey carried when he ran.

"Since we're all together, I'd like to make an announcement. Rose has kindly agreed to become my wife. And before you ask all kinds of questions like when, we haven't set a date and I haven't gotten her ring yet."

"Oh, that's wonderful. I can help with the wedding plans," Mom said.

"When we decide what we want, we'll let you know, Mom."

Montana and Kinsley got up, whispered together and then Kinsley announced, "We have a special surprised for you. Can you all please move to the living room?"

"But we haven't had dessert yet," Mom said.

"We can have it afterward," Kinsley said, in a bossy tone.

There was no use arguing with them, so we assembled in the living room and the girls disappeared. They came back out with their clicky shoes on and treated us to a recital. They were terrible. Grey and Marin cringed more than once. Hudson laughed with Dad, Mom, and Milly as they hid their laughter behind their hands. Wiley flatly refused to come in the room. For the record, Kinsley scared him. Rose and I gaped because we thought for sure Kinsley would've gotten better by now. When they finally finished, we clapped as hard as we could and went back for our dessert.

Hudson said, "I think I may have indigestion now."

Grey added, "I definitely do. Will this torture ever end?"

"I doubt it," I said.

The girls came back with smiles on their faces and Dad said, "Girls, that was magnificent. Now, who wants cake?"

Thank God for cake. Lots and lots of cake.

Chapter Forty-Three

ROSE

WE BOTH DECIDED A NOVEMBER DESTINATION WEDDING WAS what we wanted. We picked the Caribbean. At first, Pearson mentioned Italy, but I had always wanted to visit the islands and never had. We finally decided on St. Lucia.

It was a small affair with only family and a few close friends invited. Unbeknownst to Pearson's parents, we also invited Rick's brother's family. We kept it a secret so they wouldn't be angry. I wanted Sylvie there and we couldn't invite her without inviting the rest of the family. Besides, it was time for the family feud to end.

Everyone flew in on Thursday, with a pre-wedding beach party on Friday night, and then the wedding on Saturday. We would stay for the following week for our honeymoon.

When Paige and Rick saw his brother, John and his wife, they were stunned into silence. But I broke the ice by hugging Sylvie. Then Sylvie introduced me to her sisters, Piper and

Reynolds, and after that, everything was great. Piper and Reynolds were younger than Sylvie and they idolized her, but it was hilarious as the three of them were always finishing each other's sentences. The little girls hovered around them and hung on them like ivy and the older ones loved it.

Miles and his wife were there, and of course Petey. Pearson invited Evan, and another friend of his, Davis, from law school.

The day of the wedding dawned, and Montana and I went to get our hair done, along with Sylvie, who was to be my maid of honor.

My hair was done in a fancy updo with a gazillion bobby pins. The stylist explained how to set the wreath of flowers on so it would stay. Sylvie left hers down and Montana wanted hers done like mine, so the stylist did a modified version. She looked precious.

When it was time to get dressed, Montana wanted to put her own dress on. I watched her slip in on. It was fashioned after mine—very simple, but instead of hers being a halter, it was sleeveless. Neither of us were wearing shoes. That was Montana's idea since she loved to go barefoot.

She "helped" me put my dress on. It was a silk halter, with no embellishments. I wasn't the fancy sort, so this dress suited me fine. Then I put the wreath on my head. It was woven with tropical flowers and it was gorgeous. Montana had one to match.

"Mommy, do we look like twins?"

"I think we do. Here's your bouquet." Again, it was a smaller version of mine, all tropical flowers that matched the ones in our head wreaths.

There was a knock on the door, and it was Sylvie. "You ready?"

"As ever."

"Hudson is waiting." He was going to escort me down the aisle and Grey was the best man.

We were getting married at sunset on the beach. The guys wore casual outfits—linen shirts and dark pants.

Hudson was waiting in a golf cart where we would be driving down to the water.

He stood up when he saw me. "Sister, you look beautiful." He kissed my cheek.

"What about me?" my mini-me asked.

"And you, my dear, look gorgeous."

Montana giggled because he said it in a very exaggerated way.

"A crowd awaits so we should be off." We all piled in and the driver took us away. Montana loved it.

He stopped where the gathering couldn't see us and then the music started playing. I said to Montana as the wedding planner handed her a basket of flower petals, "Now you remember what to do?"

"Yes, Mommy. Throw them down."

"Good girl."

She was off and she threw them all right. Everywhere she could, even at the people. Good Lord! When she saw Petey, she almost abandoned her task and ran to him. Thank God, Marin stopped her. She finally made it to the end, but it was definitely a Montana show.

Sylvie made it down and then Hudson said, "You sure you want to marry that brother of mine. He's a scoundrel and a troublemaker."

I smacked his arm. "I think you're the troublemaker. Marin told me how you sent her dick pics." He gaped and then hurried me down the aisle as I grinned from ear to ear.

When he passed me off to Pearson, he said, "Good luck with this one, bro. You're gonna need it."

I snickered.

"What was that all about?" he whispered.

"I'll tell you later."

The minister said the vows and we said the "I wills" and we were pronounced Mr. and Mrs. Pearson West. It was one of the proudest moments of my life. Montana stood up and yelled, her voice carrying through the crowd, "Mister Dad is my daddy now."

She stole the show.

PEARSON'S ARM HELD ME CLOSE AS WE DANCED. "HOW IS Mrs. West doing tonight?"

"Mrs. West is doing great. What about Mr. West?"

"He is feeling extremely horny. Ever since he saw his lovely Rose walking down the aisle, all he could think about was what she wore under that gorgeous dress she had on."

"Hmm, Mr. West is going to have to wait and see." I ran a finger down his cheek.

"By the way, what did Hudson mean by that comment when he handed you off to me?"

"Ha! He tried to tell me you were a troublemaker, but I called him on it."

Pearson leaned back and gave me one of his curious looks. "And how did you manage that?"

"Oh, I used a tidbit of gossip that Marin had shared with me." I couldn't keep the proud smirk off my face.

"You're not going to share?"

"Okay. So, apparently…" and I whispered what happened. He threw back his head and let out an enormous laugh. All heads turned our way.

"Oh God. I'm so glad I have that to hold over his head."

"It's a good one, isn't it?" I asked.

"The best." Then he kissed me. "How about we head to our bridal suite? I haven't been with you in days and I've missed you."

"Good idea."

Montana was staying with Grey and Marin. Paige and Rick had offered, but Kinsley had begged for her to stay with them.

She would fly home with the family and spend the week with them. We made sure it was fine, and the girls were excited about their spending the next week together.

After we received a send-off with everyone blowing bubbles at us, we were driven in a golf cart decorated with "Just Married." It was super cute. Waiting in our room was a bottle of alcohol-free champagne, fruit, and an array of cheeses, and desserts.

We didn't bother with any of it. Pearson wasted no time in unzipping me and ogling what I had on underneath, which was only the tiniest thong. It was white with tiny satin bows that tied on the sides. He pulled the little satin strings and the scrap of material fell to my feet. I was hoisted into his arms and carried to the massive bed.

He took his time teasing me and kissing every inch of my body. By the time his mouth reached the juncture of my thighs, I was writhing. My fingers threaded into his hair and I jerked him closer to me as his tongue worked my clit and his fingers pumped inside of me. Over and over he teased until I begged him to let me come. He finally did as all the sensations came crashing into me. I fell into an earth-shattering climax, calling out his name. Before I could pull myself together, he was pushing himself inside of me, stretching and filling me.

"Missed this so much, babe. I love your tight pussy. Now it's officially mine."

I moaned at his words. "Missed this too. It's always been yours, but I'm glad I'm now Mrs. West."

His mouth crashed onto mine and he kissed me. The rocking of his hips took me to a new height of arousal as he thrust inside me. I was getting close to another climax when he pulled my hand up over my head and linked our fingers. His mouth latched onto one nipple and sucked hard, then moved to the next as he continued to drive into me. God, he was amazing. All I could think of were the myriad of sensations my body was experiencing. When he slid his hand between us and his finger rubbed my clit, I was almost delirious. "Give it to me, babe. I want it all from you."

Hearing those words pushed me off the edge. My orgasm hit, and when it did, his came too. He groaned loud and deep as he poured himself into me.

As he began to pull out, I said, "Don't. I like you there."

He rolled us so we faced each other on our sides. "I like it there too." I wrapped a leg over his hip. His fingers sunk into the flesh of my ass as he pressed us closer together.

We ended up making out like a couple of teenagers. My face was scraped raw from his beard, but I didn't mind. He ran the back of his fingers over my chin.

"You're a little red there."

"Chafed from kissing. But it was worth it."

"Can I tell you something?" he asked.

"Anything. Anything at all." He linked our hands together again.

"My life wasn't worth a damn. This includes before I started using. It was empty without your love, but I had no idea exactly how empty it was. All that time I spent chasing women and lying to myself about how I didn't want to be in a relationship was because I hadn't met the right person ... I hadn't met *you*. Then I started using and things turned to shit. Everything went up in smoke ... my career, my dreams, everything I'd built. Until you walked into my life and changed everything. You lit a fire in my soul, Rose, and you boosted me up, made me believe in myself. But more than that, you helped me to understand the true meaning of love. Love isn't seeing what's perfect about the other person. It's accepting all the flaws and loving them in spite of those flaws. You did that with me and helped me realize that's what it's all about. You lit a flame in me and as long as there is breath in my body and yours, that flame will keep burning."

Tears of joy filled my eyes and my heart was filled with such happiness I was speechless. When the words finally came, all I said was, "I adore you, Pearson West. Thank you for letting me turn your life from smoke to flames and my flame will *always* be lit for you."

Epilogue

SYLVIE

GROANING, I ROLLED OVER, OR TRIED TO ANYWAY. MY HEAD
clanged like the Liberty Bell—that is if it could still actually
clang—and my mouth felt like a hundred possums had died in it.
What the hell had happened? "Ugh, water. I need water."

"Hang on a sec, sweets. I'll get you some," a deep, sexy
voice said.

Wait a second. I had my own room. Who the hell was that? I
opened one eye and saw a man's naked ass climbing out of bed
and walking to the small fridge. I might add, said ass was
perfectly formed and sculpted with those hot indentations on the
sides that flawless muscular men had. He bent down, grabbed
two waters, and turned back toward the bed.

Oh, fuck no. Please to God tell me I didn't sleep with Evan Thomas.

I lifted the covers ever so slightly and yep, I was bare-assed
naked too.

Ahh, double fuck. I was so screwed.

Mr. Hot and Sexy Muscular Ass and Perfect Face and Body,

Evan, slid back into bed and handed me a water, after he opened the bottle. "Here ya go, sweets. How ya feeling?"

"Uh, er, not too good."

"Yeah, I kept telling you last night to take it easy on the Reposado, but you kept telling me it was fine."

"I did?" I mumbled into the sheets.

"Uh huh. Your exact words were, 'I'm a tequila expert, slick. Pass me that bottle.'"

"I did?" I actually squeaked that time.

"Yep, and that was after you kicked off your shoes dancing on the table. Then we could never find them. You jumped on my back, begging for a piggyback ride, slapping my ass the whole time, yelling, 'Yeehaw. Giddyup.'"

"Oh, God." I buried my face in the pillow.

"You were adorable. Pearson never told me how much fun his cousin was."

Suddenly, the pillow I was hiding behind vanished, and he was hovering over me. "Sylvie, you can't hide from me." Then his mouth dipped to kiss me.

"No!"

He backed away and asked, "What's wrong, sweets?"

"You can't kiss me!"

"Why not. After what we did last night, I wouldn't think you'd be opposed to a little kiss."

Oh, God, what the hell did we do last night?

"My breath smells," I yelled, "like a bunch of dead possums."

He stared at me a second, then said, "I love dead possums," right before he kissed me. This was no casual peck on the lips. This was the real deal—he even gave me tongue. Jesus, I needed to get him the hell out of here. Wait. What if I was in *his* room? Fuck, fuckery, fuck. How did I let myself end up in this situation? Oh, right. I was drunk off my ass.

"Hey, sweets. Let's get dressed and go eat. I'm starved. But I'd love a little shower action first." He took my hand and pulled.

"W-wait. You have to fill in the blanks."

"Huh?"

"I'm sorry, but my memory is a bit fuzzy." I finally made that confession to him.

Why, oh why did I do that? It was the worst thing I could've done. Instead of insulting him, he treated me to his woman-killer smile. It always had melted me. This time, my heart nearly combusted. Perfect teeth, lips, and a face to match, he was every woman's dream. Dark hair, all tousled from a night's sleep—or maybe rough sex—bright green eyes and that damn sexy body, made my vagina clench.

"Sweets, you were *crazy wild* in bed." He winked. "I'm talking my kind of woman."

What the hell did I do? I always considered myself tame between the sheets.

"Um, would you care to explain?"

His cheeks turned positively pink! Oh shit. That spelled trouble.

"Yeah, well, first you jumped on the bed like a five-year-old. Then you stripped and jumped on the bed, and sweets, it was fabulous. Then you undressed me and made me jump on the bed, but you got worried my head would hit the ceiling, even though I tried to tell you it wouldn't. And then ..." he rubbed his face and looked very sheepish. What could I possibly have done?

"What? Tell me!"

"Yeah, you went down on me like a Dyson, and asked me if I owned a butt plug."

"I what?" I choked on the words.

"Uh huh. And you wanted to know if I had any handcuffs to which I said no. Then you asked if I would spank you, which I did. Your ass was a lovely shade of pink. You wanted to know how good of a flogger I was. I admitted not good at all seeing as I'd never flogged anyone."

"Flogger?"

"Yep. Said you'd always wanted your clit flogged."

"Oh, my God. Stop. I don't want to know anymore." I

wanted to crawl into a hole and die. Clit flogging? Where the hell did that come from?

"Out of curiosity, is that a real thing? Clit flogging?"

"How would I know? I've never heard of it until now."

"Weird. Ever since you mentioned it, it's made me wonder."

My hand unconsciously reached for said clit. "Wouldn't that hurt?" I asked.

"No clue, seeing as I don't have one. A clit that is."

"I have to go." I tried to get up.

"Sweets, we need to shower first. All that sex we had last night, we sort of reek."

Sniff sniff. The entire room smelled of sex now that he mentioned it. "Whose room is this?"

"It's yours."

Thank fuck. "Evan, what time is it?"

"Nine thirty, why?"

"Oh, shit. Oh fuck. Evan, I'm happy we had a great time last night and all, but I have an eleven o'clock plane to catch so I need you to leave. Now."

"Wow. I've never had to do the walk of shame before."

"Sorry, but I have to hurry. So, if you can get dressed and go, I'd really appreciate it."

"No problem. But Sylvie, one thing first. This thing between us. It's far from over." He dropped another kiss on my lips, flashed me a sexy grin and got out of bed. Damn, the guy was one sexy dude.

But he was completely wrong. This thing between us was dead and buried. I would never show my face to him again, under any circumstances.

He dressed and left. After he was gone, I wondered a lot of things. Did he use a condom? Was he clean? How many times did we do it? From the feel of things between my thighs, it was a lot. Damn, why did I get myself into this mess?

The End

Find out what happens to Sylvie and Evan in ***One Indecent Night*** ... A West Sisters Novel ... Coming late Spring 2019!

If you haven't read the other West Brothers Novels, you can do so right now!

From Ashes To Flames

From Ice To Flames

If you would like to read about Reese Christianson, you can do so in Secret Nights, my surprise release available now!

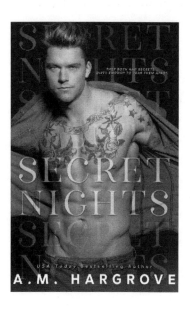

They both had secrets dirty enough to tear them apart ...

It started the night a mysterious stranger saved me from a horrific fate.

Not only was he elusive, he was also the most beautiful man I'd ever seen.

Endless blue eyes, muscles stacked upon muscle, and a mouth that ... well you get the idea.

But he was hiding something.

His gorgeous body was covered in scars he wouldn't acknowledge.

Shadows hid pieces of him I was desperate to see.

He was my magnet ... I couldn't stay away.

Every night, my body and soul screamed for more.

I'd return to him and share things I'd never shared with any other man.

I knew I should avoid him.

No, not should. Must.

I was keeping secrets of my own.

If he ever discovered the truth, I would be shot out of his life faster than a speeding bullet.

My shame forced me into silence, knowing my fairy tale couldn't last forever.

Until that tragic day arrived, but foolishness had lured me into a false sense of hope.

Little does he know that I'm a survivor and a fighter and giving up has never been an option for me.

*Please note: This book was previously published as Dirty Nights: The Novel. The title and cover have been changed and the novel itself has undergone updating and editing.

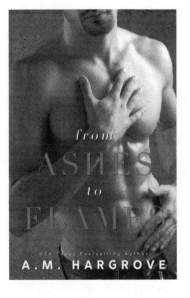

FROM ASHES TO FLAMES (A West Brothers Novel)

She was the nanny. He was the boss. Most of the time he thought he worked for *her*.

Dr. Greydon West had it all … or at least that's what everyone said.

The broody, single father of two was nothing like I'd imagined.

He was my boss … I was the nanny.

Hot-tempered and regimented, with spreadsheets for everything, he had me wondering why he'd ever had kids in the first place.

The word *fun* did not exist in his vocabulary.

And then one day I stumbled upon his secrets… the mystery behind his brusque behavior.

I began to soften towards him and notice things I hadn't before.

That was when those sexy dreams started waking me up at night.

The lust that exploded within me was impossible to ignore.

And that kiss ... I definitely should *not* have let that happen.

Nothing good could result from that.

If I wasn't careful, everything, including my heart, would go up in flames.

Also available in Audible.

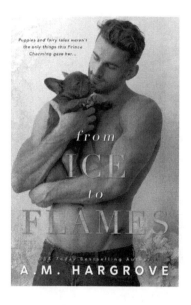

FROM ICE TO FLAMES (A West Brothers Novel)

One Rule: No More Men.

Two years ago I walked away from a marriage I thought would last forever and all I got from it was Dick ...

And I don't mean the one between my stupid ex's legs.

I'm talking about the one hundred fifty pound furry dog said ex dropped off at my doorstep.

But I'd take Dick over any man, any day.

So why did I resemble my dog, panting and drooling, whenever I ran into Hudson West, my sexy new neighbor?

True, the gorgeous veterinarian was hotter than sin.

And my new roommate only made it impossible for me to avoid conversation with a man I didn't need.

Until tragedy struck and some jerk decided to run Dick down.

It was *hotter than sin* Hudson who came to his rescue.

Then it became impossible to ignore him.

It was only supposed to be a fling, a quickie, a one and done.

We both had reasons to keep it that way ... my one rule and his five-year-old son.

Except things didn't quite work out that way.

One turned into two, then three, annnnd you get the picture.

Before we knew it, he gave me a lot more than puppies and fairy tales.

And that stupid rule?

I should've stuck to it because now more than my heart was at risk.

Also available in Audible.

Acknowledgements

IT TAKES A TEAM AND A MIGHTY ONE TO CREATE A NOVEL, AND that includes all the readers who take a chance on me. So first off I'd like to thank every reader, including all you wonderful bloggers out there, who's ever done that, whether you've been with me from the start, or if you're a first timer. Thank you for taking a chance on me. It means the world to me. You are truly my inspiration to do this every day.

Thank you to my book world besties, Terri E. Laine (my book wifey too) and Amy Jennings, who I chat with almost on a daily basis. You guys are my people and I love you ladies to pieces!

Thank you to Harloe Rae for your continued patience and help. You have so much info and are willing to share, I can't tell you how blessed I am to have you in my life.

Thank you to my beta team. You guys are the greatest and I sincerely mean it! I would be a floundering fool without you.

Thank you to Nasha Lama for several things—for being an awesome PA and web designer. You're always there, taking care of the details I don't know how to handle. And you make the most beautiful teasers ever. I'd be lost without you. For realz.

Diane Plourde—you are an amazing assistant. I have no idea what I would do without you. Thank you for coming to my rescue.

Thank you to my editing team of Ellie McLove and Petra Gleason. You two are definitely a great duo and I appreciate you soooo much!

Thank you Give Me Books for promoting this release. I love working with you ladies! You make everything soooo easy.

Thank you to all the members of Hargrove's Hangout. You guys are my people and I adore you!

Letitia Hasser—what can I say? You have created a cover that's ON FIRE this time. I drool when I look at it. Thank you!

Follow Me

If you would like to hear more about what's going on in my world, please subscribe to my mailing list on my website at
http://bit.ly/AMNLWP
You can also join my private group—Hargrove's Hangout— on Facebook if you're up to some crazy shenanigans!
Please stalk me. I'll love you forever if you do. Seriously.

www.amhargrove.com
Twitter @amhargrove1
www.facebook.com/amhargroveauthor

https://www.facebook.com/anne.m.hargrove

www.goodreads.com/amhargrove1
Instagram: amhargroveauthor
Pinterest: amhargrove1
annie@amhargrove.com

For Other Books by A.M. Hargrove visit www.amhargrove.com

The West Sisters Novels:
One Indecent Night (Spring 2019)
One Shameless Night (TBD)
One Blissful Night (TBD)

The West Brothers Novels:
From Ashes to Flames
From Ice to Flames
From Smoke to Flames

Stand Alones
Secret Nights
For The Love of English
For The Love of My Sexy Geek (The Vault)
I'll Be Waiting (The Vault)

The Men of Crestview:
A Special Obsession
Chasing Vivi
Craving Midnight

Cruel & Beautiful:
Cruel and Beautiful
A Mess of a Man
One Wrong Choice

A Beautiful Sin

The Wilde Players Dirty Romance Series:
Sidelined
Fastball
Hooked

Worth Every Risk

The Edge Series:
Edge of Disaster
Shattered Edge
Kissing Fire

The Tragic Duet:
Tragically Flawed, Tragic 1
Tragic Desires, Tragic 2

The Hart Brothers Series:
Freeing Her, Book 1
Freeing Him, Book 2
Kestrel, Book 3
The Fall and Rise of Kade Hart

Sabin, A Seven Novel

The Guardians of Vesturon Series

About The Author

ONE DAY, ON HER WAY HOME FROM WORK AS A SALES manager, USA Today bestselling author, A. M. Hargrove, realized her life was on fast forward and if she didn't do something soon, it would be too late to write that work of fiction she had been dreaming of her whole life. So she made a quick decision to quit her job and reinvented herself as a Naughty and Nice Romance Author.

Annie fancies herself all of the following: Reader, Writer, Dark Chocolate Lover, Ice Cream Worshipper, Coffee Drinker (swears the coffee, chocolate, and ice cream should be added as part of the USDA food groups), Lover of Grey Goose (and an extra dirty martini), #WalterThePuppy Lover, and if you're ever around her for more than five minutes, you'll find out she's a non-stop talker. Other than loving writing about romance, she loves hanging out with her family and binge watching TV with her husband. You can find out more about her books www.amhargrove.com.

To keep up to date with my new releases subscribe to my newsletter here: http://bit.ly/AMNLWP

Made in the USA
Middletown, DE
18 July 2023

35389300R00203